INTER SECTIONS

INTERSECTIONS

THE SYCAMORE HILL ANTHOLOGY

EDITED BY
JOHN KESSEL,
MARK L. VAN NAME,
AND RICHARD BUTNER

A TOM DOHERTY ASSOCIATES BOOK
NEW YORK

TOR®

INTERSECTIONS: THE SYCAMORE HILL ANTHOLOGY

Copyright © 1996 by John Kessel, Mark L. Van Name, and Richard Butner

This book is printed on acid-free paper.

A Tor Book
Published by Tom Doherty Associates, Inc.
175 Fifth Avenue
New York, NY 10010

Tor Books on the World-Wide Web:
http://www.tor.com

Tor® is a registered trademark of Tom Doherty Associates, Inc.

Library of Congress Cataloging-in-Publication Data

Intersections: the Sycamore Hill anthology / John Kessel, Mark L. Van Name, and Richard Butner, editors.
    p.   cm.
  "A Tom Doherty Associates book."
  ISBN 0-312-86090-0
  1. Science fiction, American. I. Kessel, John. II. Van Name, Mark L. III. Butner, Richard.
PS648.S3I58   1996
813'.0876208—dc20   95-41237
                                CIP

First edition: January 1996

Printed in the United States of America

0 9 8 7 6 5 4 3 2 1

COPYRIGHT ACKNOWLEDGMENTS

CONTENTS

ACKNOWLEDGMENTS

We'd like to thank the following people for help both with Sycamore Hill over the years and with putting together this anthology:

Rana Van Name, Sue Hall, Allyn Vogel, Jacquelyn Paris, Jan Fesperman and the staff of the Governor Morehead School, Beverly Jones Williams and the staff of the North Carolina State University Department of Housing, John Bassett, Carmine Prioli, Thomas Lisk and the NCSU Department of English, Lew Shiner, Ralph Vicinanza and Chris Lotts, and Beth Meacham.

INTERSECTIONS

INTRODUCTION
Fun in the Burn Ward

JOHN KESSEL, MARK L. VAN NAME,
AND RICHARD BUTNER

WHAT YOU HOLD in your hands is a collection of stories written for the seventh Sycamore Hill Writers' Conference, which took place from July 31 to August 8, 1994, in a dormitory on the campus of North Carolina State University in Raleigh.

It's also an attempt to document a social phenomenon peculiar to the science fiction world. SF writers do something that other sorts of writers, once they are established professionals, don't do as much, or as intimately. They gather in circles and submit manuscripts, hot off the printer, for criticism. Putting their egos on the line, they talk honestly about each other's work.

At Breadloaf or Sewanee, student writers may submit their work for the consideration of established authors, but as far as we know there are no mainstream workshops that take the all-Indians, no-chiefs approach common in SF workshops that follow the Milford tradition. Folklore has it this tradition started, as did so many things that characterize modern SF, with Damon Knight. When Knight lived in Milford, Pennsylvania, in the 1950s, he would invite a stellar cast of East Coast SF writers (among them C. M. Kornbluth, Frederik Pohl, Kate Wilhelm, Algis Budrys, Carol Emshwiller, and Theodore Sturgeon) to his house for mutual story critiques. Stories from early Milford gatherings decorated the science fiction magazines of the late fifties and early sixties, and gossip from them is still being purveyed at SF conventions today.

In an essay in the *SFWA Bulletin* a few years ago, James Patrick Kelly described the Milford method:

> The Milford model works best with between five and seventeen members. Too few and the workshop loses its necessary diversity, too many and the critique of each story drags on to excruciating lengths. The group usually gathers together in one place for some length of time . . . five days to a week for a national workshop like the old Milford. . . . Only writers with manuscripts in the workshop take part in the critique; no audience is allowed. While the furnishings of the workshop room is a matter of circumstance or taste, the optimal arrangement is for the group to sit around a large table or otherwise gather the wagons into a circle. The stories are read beforehand; the more conscientious critics read more than once. Each critic holds forth in turn, most referring to notes they've taken. The custom is to pass these notes [and the manuscripts—Ed.] to the writer at the end of the session. During critiques the writer may not respond to comments unless asked a direct yes-or-no question. No one is supposed to interrupt another's critique, although there's often some—usually trifling—cross-talk. Repetition is inevitable, although wistful sighs and vacant stares can sometimes prod repeaters to pass when they have nothing new to add. After everyone else has spoken, the writer gets the opportunity to give thanks, explain, rebut, or say nothing. A free-form discussion occasionally ensues; otherwise it's on to the next story.

Milford followed Knight through several transcontinental moves into the 1970s. In the late seventies, Knight passed the name and method to Ed Bryant, who ran several Milfords in Colorado. In 1980, Ed invited John Kessel, a newly published writer, to a Milford workshop in Glenwood Springs, Colorado. There John met Connie Willis, Dan Simmons, George R. R. Martin, and other writers, received useful criticism, and for the first time felt part of a community of writers.

John enjoyed Milford so much that when Bryant didn't run one for a couple of years, and Greg Frost suggested that Mark L. Van Name's then-new house would make a good place for a workshop, John and Mark decided to try a local version of the Colorado Milfords. They invited writers within a one-state drive from Raleigh (Virginia, Georgia, the Carolinas) plus a couple of old friends like Scott Russell Sanders from Indiana and Steve Carper from New York.

The conference worked. The next year, they decided to emerge from the Stone Age and invite women. Rebecca Ore, Shariann Lewitt, Susan Palwick, Karen Joy Fowler, Connie Willis, and Nancy Kress all attended. They also moved the workshop out of Mark's home and into a mirrorless house on the campus of the Governor Morehead School for the Blind. The next three Sycamore Hills took place in a larger building on the Governor Morehead campus.

For the 1994 SycHill, our critique room was the Merry Monk Lounge, a large room on the sixth floor of North Hall, a dorm on the NCSU campus. North Hall was once a motel that the university subsequently took over, its top-floor lounge originally a restaurant and bar. You must imagine the critiques described in the afterwords to these stories taking place in an enormous, dimly-lit room showing shabby signs of lost motel-quality elegance. Picture faux-Gothic room dividers, bench seats along long windows, many round tables, armchairs, and a large nonfunctioning vacant mirror-backed bar. Several North Carolina thunderstorms pouring through the leaky ceiling added to the gothic ambience.

Calling the workshop the "Burn Ward" makes it sound like a macho experience. In practice the sessions range from hilarious good fellowship to barely repressed antagonism to complete snoozaramas. Yes, it has been tough at times, but we didn't start SycHill as a test of manhood. We don't mean to imply that writers who are comfortable in workshops are somehow better than those who aren't. Nor has SycHill been an attempt to grab hold of SF and bend the field to any particular direction.

Instead, we saw Sycamore Hill as a chance for writers to get together and reduce their alienation, talk across the divide of ideology. This process doesn't occur only in the critique circle. There are late-night conversations and early-morning workouts, basketball games, impromptu singing and dancing, excursions to local restaurants, experimental cooking in the dormitory kitchens. John's wife Sue Hall and Mark's wife Rana, and other local friends, contribute in too many ways to mention, especially by throwing the traditional Wednesday- and Saturday-night parties. Attendees bring books and magazines for the brag table. Friendships are kindled and rekindled.

Adequate Science Fiction

Near the end of the first SycHill, Jim Kelly remarked that the stories we'd brought would make a perfectly adequate issue of an SF magazine. Immediately our slogan was born: Adequate Science Fiction. It summed up something to us. We aimed to write better, but we could not claim to be the best. But we also thought that much published SF was inadequate. The ensuing years of SycHill have been a continuing attempt to define just what "adequate" means with regard to SF under changing literary, scientific, and social circumstances.

It happened that the first Sycamore Hill, in 1984, occurred at a particularly interesting time, when science fiction was undergoing one of its periodic eras of ferment, controversy, and the advent of new writers. Or rather, writers who had entered the field during the late seventies to early eighties were finding their voices and beginning to be noticed.

Some of these writers weren't just finding voices, they were making noise. The cyberpunks questioned the basis of SF (and at times the common sense of their contemporaries). The descendants of the new wave brought high literary ambition to SF. Magic realism was having its influence. The field had expanded commercially. Hard science fiction had found a new audience even as much of it was drifting rightward politically. Tolkienesque fantasy rivaled SF and often dominated it on the paperback racks. Media science fiction sold more copies than ever before. An inflated field was splitting into subfields. In such conditions it was not easy to talk about "science fiction" with any expectation that everybody meant the same thing by the term.

It would be unnatural if a workshop taking place in 1984 did not reflect any of these trends. Even the first workshop contained Scott Sanders, a college professor who came to SF from the academy; Tim Sullivan, who was soon to move off to the wilds of Hollywood; Orson Scott Card, who had started his career writing plays and was rapidly becoming one of SF's biggest names, courting controversy with his opinions on the role of "Li-Fi" versus popular fiction; Jim Kelly, who was beginning his dalliance with cyberpunk and brought two cutting-edge stories, one of which was the seed for his novel *Wildlife,* and the other of which, written in Mark's basement over the weekend, ended up in *The Norton Book of Science Fiction.*

The next Sycamore Hill brought strong feminist voices in Karen Fowler, a poet-turned-SF-writer and recent winner of the Writers of the Future Contest, and Connie Willis, who combined literary acumen with pop-lit sensibility. Bruce Sterling showed up, the Chairman himself, ready to rip the lungs out of SF or die trying.

Was there a program? We confess that we had a prejudice for what we thought of as "ambitious" writers, writers who were out for more than popular success and major book contracts, though it's probable that no one ever sat at the Sycamore Hill critique table who didn't hope for big sales and advances. And we did seek different points of view. But SycHill has always tended to the "literary" end of the SF specturm.

This Year's Model

After the 1994 workshop we sent everyone home with a pile of critiques and a schedule. Each writer was to produce a rewrite and an afterword reacting to the criticism, commenting on the workshop method, and discussing any other issue relevant to the story or this year's workshop. If you read through some of these afterwords you should get some of the flavor of a critique session—minus a lot of the jokes.

Although we talk about SycHill as a science fiction workshop, and the writers we invite are invariably associated with SF and fantasy, we don't require people to write SF. In our invitation letter this year, in which we proposed this anthology, we said, "We don't want to dictate what kind of story you must write. People generally bring SF or fantasy to SycHill, but there's no rule about it. Think of this as an opportunity to try whatever you would like. Push the outside of your personal envelope. We'd rather see you write well than write to genre expectations." Nineteen ninety-four was fairly typical in that we saw some stories that walked the very edges of the genre, like Karen Fowler's "The Marianas Islands," as well as a chapter from Carol Emshwiller's forthcoming novel, *Ledoyt*, a western. (Though from what we've seen, *Ledoyt* is likely to resemble *Wuthering Heights* more than it does *The Virginian*.)

We also have state-of-the-art SF in Bruce Sterling's "Bicycle Repairman," allegorical SF in Jonathan Lethem's "The Hardened Criminals," and near-future social SF in Nancy Kress's "Sex Education." Michaela Roessner's "The Escape Artist" and Gregory Frost's "That Blissful Height" present different takes on the human costs of nineteenth century attempts to contact the dead. You can make an anything-but-sentimental return to the sixties in James Patrick Kelly's "The First Law of Thermodynamics," or take an allusive look at pop-star self-destruction in Richard Butner's neo-cyberpunk "Horses Blow Up Dog City." Remember to bring your bass lures to Mark L. Van Name's SF romantic comedy "Missing Connections." Greek mythology meets hardboiled detective story in Alex Jablokov's "The Fury at Colonus," while hard-boiled detective story meets altered Hollywood in John Kessel's "The Miracle of Ivar Avenue." Maureen McHugh's dancer of the future explores life outside the insulated world of her art in "Homesick," and Bob Frazier takes us on a paranoid biotech road trip in "Body & Soul."

Martian Concentration Camps and Other Hazards

At the end of this anthology you'll find "The Turkey City Lexicon," compiled by one of the stronger regional workshops, Turkey City in Austin, Texas. Over the years, Turkey City members have included Joe Pumilla, Lewis Shiner, Bruce Sterling, Lawrence Person, Leigh Kennedy, Howard Waldrop, and Stephen Utley. The lexicon contains terms developed over many workshops, some of them associated with particular writers or editors, to describe habitual problems SF stories encounter. Some of these problems are common to all fiction; others speak to the particular difficulties of SF. In reading these terms you'll hear the echoes of debates that once must have raged around critique circles.

Far from being a drawback, the controversies that arise over what is and is not acceptable in an SF story can be one of the virtues of a workshop. Even if you're not a participant in the debate, such disagreements often make you see your work in new ways. At SycHill '94, Bruce Sterling's comments on Jonathan Lethem's story sparked a running discussion for the week, clarified further by something similar Bruce said in reaction to Jim Kelly's story.

Bruce said that the hardened criminals in Jonathan's story were a violation of taste, an attempt to draw emotion using an unreal situation. His objection was that inventing an imaginary world and characters, then using that invented situation to evoke emotions from the reader, is almost necessarily bathetic. It's as if we invented a concentration camp on Mars and filled it with starving green aliens, whose tortures evoke our pity and terror. In a world of real concentration camps, how can we justify imaginary ones? Is the metaphorical story always guilty of bathos? What is the function of taste? Are there rules we can rely on?

John suggested that Bruce's objection to fictional tragedy would apply to non-SF. Should Shakespeare be ashamed to make us cry over the fate of an imaginary king in *King Lear*? Is Kafka's "Metamorphosis" suspect because it asks us to care for Gregor Samsa's plight, although in the real world nobody turns into a gigantic insect?

As Bruce pointed out, none of us is Shakespeare, and too much SF and fantasy does suck emotions from us by pushing our buttons. In addition, the SF story that uses the rocket as a metaphor instead of a technological artifact runs the risk of trivializing the rocket, violating what we know about real science to make a point that has nothing to do with science. He asked whether

Kelly's metaphorical use of the first law of thermodynamics was merely a move to get a mainstream story into *Asimov's*.

By the end of the week some of us had pursued the argument far enough to propose a rule something along these lines: The unreal situation must have some real counterpart, the science must be functional. The unreality must do something you could not do in a realistic story, something more than eliciting an emotional response. It must have an intellectual reason for being.

In the end the point of this isn't to determine who's right, or to establish the Absolute Rules of Science Fiction, or to add a new term to the lexicon, but to use such debates to sharpen our awareness of what we're doing, and to improve our fiction. Discussions like these show that it's possible for writers to talk to each other across the gulf of their idiosyncrasies and ideologies. That's one of the main values of a workshop like Sycamore Hill. Often we think that differences of opinion imply hostility. They don't have to.

The SycHill Mafia

Sycamore Hill is by no means the only descendant of Milford. Others include Evergreen, Philford, Cambridge, Clarion, and Turkey City. Like those workshops, SycHill surfaces from time to time as the topic of SF rumor and gossip: Did you hear what X said to Y at Sycamore Hill? Did you hear that Z made the Nebula ballot because of block voting by the SycHill Mafia?

The SycHill Mafia? Well, no SycHill story had ever won a major award until, as we were writing the first draft of this introduction, Connie Willis's "Death on the Nile," which she brought to the 1992 Sycamore Hill, won the Hugo Award. But because this is her ninth major award, and none of the others were SycHill stories (Willis had been to three previous SycHills), we can conclude that the SycHill Mafia is singularly ineffective, or that Willis didn't think it was worth it to bring her best stuff to the workshop, or that the effect of the workshop on her stories was to turn award winners into also-rans.

To inoculate yourself against this insidious influence, a complete list of all SycHill attendees as of 1994 is available in the appendix.

Validation, Community, Influence, and Controversy

SycHill has caused some of the worst moments in our lives in the last ten years, but it has also produced more of the best. We have experienced emotions ranging from the immense feeling of validation because some of the best writers in the genre treated us as equals, to the embarrassment we've all known when we realized the pieces we had on the table were full of obvious flaws.

Writers spend a lot of time alone in their rooms, in their heads. A workshop offers them a chance to spend some time with their peers. But balance is all. At a workshop like Sycamore Hill, lots of psychological forces are at play, both at the critique table and away from it. Getting the most out of it demands a delicate balance between pigheaded insistence that you know what you want in your writing, and sensitivity to what other people have to say about it. The fact that these other people are bright, articulate, experienced professionals who have passions, programs, and prejudices of their own, complicates the whole process. If you're not strong-willed, you can get swept away on a tide of advice. On the other hand, if your nerves are set too close beneath your placid surface, you may be unwilling to hear things that might make your work grow and strengthen.

To write well is a hard thing, a psychological balancing act. There are a hundred ways to go wrong and many fewer ways to go right. We reveal ourselves, often in ways we are not aware of, through our writing. This is, in our opinion, a good thing. It's what gives fiction force and conviction. But it's also scary, and it takes considerable maturity to face what you sometimes find reflected in others' eyes when they look at your work. It's a maturity we have at times had difficulty mustering. But after playing the workshop game for quite a few years now, this is what we value the most: A good workshop offers you the chance to grow as a person as well as a writer.

John Kessel
Mark L. Van Name
Richard Butner

Bicycle Repairman

BRUCE STERLING

REPEATED TINNY BANGING woke Lyle in his hammock. Lyle groaned, sat up, and slid free into the tool-crowded aisle of his bike shop.

Lyle hitched up the black elastic of his skintight shorts and plucked yesterday's grease-stained sleeveless off the workbench. He glanced blearily at his chronometer as he picked his way toward the door. It was 10:04.38 in the morning, June 27, 2037.

Lyle hopped over a stray can of primer and the floor boomed gently beneath his feet. With all the press of work, he'd collapsed into sleep without properly cleaning the shop. Doing custom enameling paid okay, but it ate up time like crazy. Working and living alone was wearing him out.

Lyle opened the shop door, revealing a long sheer drop to dusty tiling far below. Pigeons darted beneath the hull of his shop through a soot-stained hole in the broken atrium glass, and wheeled off to their rookery somewhere in the darkened guts of the high-rise.

More banging. Far below, a uniformed delivery kid stood by his cargo tricycle, yanking rhythmically at the long dangling string of Lyle's spot-welded doorknocker.

Lyle waved, yawning. From his vantage point below the huge

girders of the cavernous atrium, Lyle had a fine overview of three burnt-out interior levels of the old Tsatanuga Archiplat. Once-elegant handrails and battered pedestrian overlooks fronted on the great airy cavity of the atrium. Behind the handrails was a three-floor wilderness of jury-rigged lights, chicken coops, water tanks, and squatters' flags. The fire-damaged floors, walls, and ceilings were riddled with handmade descent-chutes, long coiling staircases, and rickety ladders.

Lyle took note of a crew of Chattanooga demolition workers in their yellow detox suits. The repair crew was deploying vacuum scrubbers and a high-pressure hose-off by the vandal-proofed western elevators of Floor 34. Two or three days a week, the city crew meandered into the damage zone to pretend to work, with a great hypocritical show of sawhorses and barrier tape. The lazy sons of bitches were all on the take.

Lyle thumbed the brake switches in their big metal box by the flywheel. The bike shop slithered, with a subtle hiss of cable-clamps, down three stories, to dock with a grating crunch onto four concrete-filled metal drums.

The delivery kid looked real familiar. He was in and out of the zone pretty often. Lyle had once done some custom work on the kid's cargo trike, new shocks and some granny-gearing as he recalled, but he couldn't remember the kid's name. Lyle was terrible with names. "What's up, zude?"

"Hard night, Lyle?"

"Just real busy."

The kid's nose wrinkled at the stench from the shop. "Doin' a lot of paint work, huh?" He glanced at his palmtop notepad. "You still taking deliveries for Edward Dertouzas?"

"Yeah. I guess so." Lyle rubbed the gear tattoo on one stubbled cheek. "If I have to."

The kid offered a stylus, reaching up. "Can you sign for him?"

Lyle folded his bare arms warily. "Naw, man, I can't sign for Deep Eddy. Eddy's in Europe somewhere. Eddy left months ago. Haven't seen Eddy in ages."

The delivery kid scratched his sweating head below his billed fabric cap. He turned to check for any possible sneak-ups by snatch-and-grab artists out of the squatter warrens. The government simply refused to do postal delivery on the Thirty-second, Thirty-third, and Thirty-fourth floors. You never saw many cops inside the zone, either. Except for the city demolition crew, about the only official functionaries who ever showed up in the zone were a few psychotically empathetic NAFTA social workers.

"I'll get a bonus if you sign for this thing." The kid gazed up in squint-eyed appeal. "It's gotta be worth something, Lyle. It's a really weird kind of routing, they paid a lot of money to send it just that way."

Lyle crouched down in the open doorway. "Let's have a look at it."

The package was a heavy shockproof rectangle in heat-sealed plastic shrink-wrap, with a plethora of intra-European routing stickers. To judge by all the overlays, the package had been passed from postal system to postal system at least eight times before officially arriving in the legal custody of any human being. The return address, if there had ever been one, was completely obscured. Someplace in France, maybe.

Lyle held the box up two-handed to his ear and shook it. Hardware.

"You gonna sign, or not?"

"Yeah." Lyle scratched illegibly at the little signature panel, then looked at the delivery trike. "You oughta get that front wheel trued."

The kid shrugged. "Got anything to send out today?"

"Naw," Lyle grumbled, "I'm not doing mail-order repair work anymore; it's too complicated and I get ripped off too much."

"Suit yourself." The kid clambered into the recumbent seat of his trike and pedaled off across the heat-cracked ceramic tiles of the atrium plaza.

Lyle hung his hand-lettered OPEN FOR BUSINESS sign outside the door. He walked to his left, stamped up the pedaled lid of a jumbo garbage can, and dropped the package in with the rest of Dertouzas's stuff.

The can's lid wouldn't close. Deep Eddy's junk had finally reached critical mass. Deep Eddy never got much mail at the shop from other people, but he was always sending mail to himself.

Big packets of encrypted diskettes were always arriving from Eddy's road jaunts in Toulouse, Marseilles, Valencia, and Nice. And especially Barcelona. Eddy had sent enough gigabyte-age out of Barcelona to outfit a pirate data-haven.

Eddy used Lyle's bike shop as his safety-deposit box. This arrangement was okay by Lyle. He owed Eddy; Eddy had installed the phones and virching in the bike shop, and had also wangled the shop's electrical hookup. A thick elastic curly-cable snaked out the access-crawlspace of Floor 35, right through the ceiling of Floor 34, and directly through a ragged punch-hole in the aluminum roof of Lyle's cable-mounted mobile home. Some unknown contact of Eddy's was paying the real bills on that electrical feed. Lyle cheerfully covered the expenses by paying cash into an anonymous post-office box. The setup was a rare and valuable contact with the world of organized authority.

During his stays in the shop, Eddy had spent much of his time buried in marathon long-distance virtuality sessions, swaddled head to foot in lumpy strap-on gear. Eddy had been painfully involved with some older woman in Germany. A virtual romance in its full-scale thumping, heaving, grappling progress, was an embarrassment to witness. Under the circumstances, Lyle wasn't too surprised that Eddy had left his parents' condo to set up in a squat.

Eddy had lived in the bicycle repair shop, off and on, for almost a year. It had been a good deal for Lyle, because Deep Eddy had enjoyed a certain clout and prestige with the local squatters. Eddy had been a major organizer of the legendary Chattanooga Wende of December '35, a monster street-party that had climaxed in a spectacular looting-and-arson rampage that had torched the three floors of the Archiplat.

Lyle had gone to school with Eddy and had known him for years; they'd grown up together in the Archiplat. Eddy Dertouzas was a deep zude for a kid his age, with political contacts and heavy-duty network connections. The squat had been a good deal for both of them, until Eddy had finally coaxed the German woman into coming through for him in real life. Then Eddy had jumped the next plane to Europe.

Since they'd parted friends, Eddy was welcome to mail his European data-junk to the bike shop. After all, the disks were heavily encrypted, so it wasn't as if anybody in authority was ever gonna be able to read them. Storing a few thousand disks was a minor challenge, compared to Eddy's complex, machine-assisted love life.

After Eddy's sudden departure, Lyle had sold Eddy's possessions, and wired the money to Eddy in Spain. Lyle had kept the screen TV, Eddy's mediator, and the cheaper virching helmet. The way Lyle figured it—the way he remembered the deal—any stray hardware of Eddy's in the shop was rightfully his, for disposal at his own discretion. By now it was pretty clear that Deep Eddy Dertouzas was never coming back to Tennessee. And Lyle had certain debts.

Lyle snicked the blade from a roadkit multitool and cut open Eddy's package. It contained, of all things, a television cable settop box. A laughable infobahn antique. You'd never see a cablebox like that in NAFTA; this was the sort of primeval junk one might find in the home of a semiliterate Basque grandmother, or maybe in the armed bunker of some backward Albanian.

Lyle tossed the archaic cablebox onto the beanbag in front of the wallscreen. No time now for irrelevant media toys; he had to get on with real life. Lyle ducked into the tiny curtained privy and urinated at length into a crockery jar. He scraped his teeth with a flossing spudger and misted some fresh water onto his face and hands. He wiped clean with a towelette, then smeared his armpits, crotch, and feet with deodorant.

Back when he'd lived with his mom up on Floor 41, Lyle had used old-fashioned antiseptic deodorants. Lyle had wised up about a lot of things once he'd escaped his mom's condo. Nowadays, Lyle used a gel roll-on of skin-friendly bacteria that greedily devoured human sweat and exuded as their metabolic by-product a pleasantly harmless reek rather like ripe bananas. Life was a lot easier when you came to proper terms with your microscopic flora.

Back at his workbench, Lyle plugged in the hot plate and boiled some Thai noodles with flaked sardines. He packed down breakfast with 400 cc's of Dr. Breasaire's Bioactive Bowel Putty. Then he checked last night's enamel job on the clamped frame in the workstand. The frame looked good. At three in the morning, Lyle was able to get into painted detail work with just the right kind of hallucinatory clarity.

Enameling paid well, and he needed the money bad. But this wasn't real bike work. It lacked authenticity. Enameling was all about the owner's ego—that was what really stank about enameling. There were a few rich kids up in the penthouse levels who were way into "street aesthetic," and would pay good money to have some treadhead decorate their machine. But flash art didn't help the bike. What helped the bike was frame alignment and sound cable-housings and proper tension in the derailleurs.

Lyle fitted the chain of his stationary bike to the shop's flywheel, straddled up, strapped on his gloves and virching helmet, and did half an hour on the 2033 Tour de France. He stayed back in the pack for the uphill grind, and then, for three glorious minutes, he broke free from the domestiques in the peloton and came right up at the shoulder of Aldo Cipollini. The champion was a monster, posthuman. Calves like cinderblocks. Even in a cheap simulation with no full-impact bodysuit, Lyle knew better than to try to take Cipollini.

Lyle devirched, checked his heart-rate record on the chronometer, then dismounted from his stationary trainer and drained a half-liter squeezebottle of antioxidant carbo refresher. Life had been easier when he'd had a partner in crime. The shop's flywheel was slowly losing its storage of inertia power these days, with just one zude pumping it.

Lyle's disastrous second roommate had come from the biking crowd. She was a criterium racer from Kentucky named Brigitte Rohannon. Lyle himself had been a wannabe criterium racer for a while, before he'd blown out a kidney on steroids. He hadn't expected any trouble from Brigitte, because Brigitte knew about bikes, and she needed his technical help for her racer, and she wouldn't mind pumping the flywheel, and besides, Brigitte was lesbian. In the training gym and out at racing events, Brigitte came across as a quiet and disciplined little politicized treadhead person.

Life inside the zone, though, massively fertilized Brigitte's eccentricities. First, she started breaking training. Then she stopped eating right. Pretty soon the shop was creaking and rocking with all-night girl-on-girl hot-oil sessions, which degenerated into hooting pill-orgies with heavily tattooed zone chyx who played klaxonized bongo music and beat each other up, and stole Lyle's tools. It had been a big relief when Brigitte finally left the zone to shack up with some well-to-do admirer on Floor 37. The debacle had left Lyle's tenuous finances in ruin.

Lyle laid down a new tracery of scarlet enamel on the bike's chainstay, seat post and stem. He had to wait for the work to cure, so he left the workbench, picked up Eddy's settopper and popped the shell with a hexkey. Lyle was no electrician, but the insides looked harmless enough: lots of bit-eating caterpillars and cheap Algerian silicon.

He flicked on Eddy's mediator, to boot the wallscreen. Before he could try anything with the cablebox, his mother's mook pounced upon the screen. On Eddy's giant wallscreen, the mook's waxy, computer-generated face looked like a plump satin pillowcase. Its bowtie was as big as a racing shoe.

"Please hold for an incoming vidcall from Andrea Schweik of Carnac Instruments," the mook uttered unctuously.

Lyle cordially despised all low-down, phone-tagging, artificially intelligent mooks. For a while, in his teenage years, Lyle himself had owned a mook, an off-the-shelf shareware job that he'd installed in the condo's phone. Like most mooks, Lyle's mook had one primary role: dealing with unsolicited phone calls from other people's mooks. In Lyle's case these were the creepy mooks of career counselors, school psychiatrists, truancy cops, and other official hindrances. When Lyle's mook launched and ran, it appeared online as a sly warty dwarf that drooled green ichor and talked in a basso grumble.

But Lyle hadn't given his mook the properly meticulous care and debugging that such fragile little constructs demanded, and eventually his cheap mook had collapsed into artificial insanity.

Once Lyle had escaped his mom's place to the squat, he had gone for the low-tech gambit and simply left his phone unplugged most of the time. But that was no real solution. He couldn't hide from his mother's capable and well-financed corporate mook, which watched with sleepless mechanical patience for the least flicker of video dialtone off Lyle's number.

Lyle sighed and wiped the dust from the video nozzle on Eddy's mediator.

"Your mother is coming online right away," the mook assured him.

"Yeah, sure," Lyle muttered, smearing his hair into some semblance of order.

"She specifically instructed me to page her remotely at any time for an immediate response. She really wants to chat with you, Lyle."

"That's just great." Lyle couldn't remember what his mother's mook called itself. "Mr. Billy," or "Mr. Ripley," or something else really stupid. . . .

"Did you know that Marco Cengialta has just won the Liege Summer Classic?"

Lyle blinked and sat up in the beanbag. "Yeah?"

"Mr. Cengialta used a three-spoked ceramic wheel with internal liquid weighting and buckyball hubshocks." The mook paused, politely awaiting a possible conversational response. "He wore breathe-thru kevlar microlock cleatshoes," it added.

Lyle hated the way a mook cataloged your personal interests and then generated relevant conversation. The machine-made intercourse was completely unhuman and yet perversely interesting, like being grabbed and buttonholed by a glossy magazine ad. It had probably taken his mother's mook all of three seconds to snag and download every conceivable statistic about the summer race in Liege.

His mother came on. She'd caught him during lunch in her office. "Lyle?"

"Hi, Mom." Lyle sternly reminded himself that this was the one person in the world who might conceivably put up bail for him. "What's on your mind?"

"Oh, nothing much, just the usual." Lyle's mother shoved aside her platter of sprouts and tilapia. "I was idly wondering if you were still alive."

"Mom, it's a lot less dangerous in a squat than landlords and cops would have you believe. I'm perfectly fine. You can see that for yourself."

His mother lifted a pair of secretarial half-spex on a neckchain, and gave Lyle the computer-assisted once-over.

Lyle pointed the mediator's lens at the shop's aluminum door. "See over there, Mom? I got myself a shock-baton in here. If I get any trouble from anybody, I'll just yank that club off the doormount and give the guy fifteen thousand volts!"

"Is that legal, Lyle?"

"Sure. The voltage won't kill you or anything, it just knocks you out a good long time. I traded a good bike for that shock-baton, it's got a lot of useful defensive features."

"That sounds really dreadful."

"The baton's harmless, Mom. You should see what the cops carry nowadays."

"Are you still taking those injections, Lyle?"

"Which injections?"

She frowned. "You know which ones."

Lyle shrugged. "The treatments are perfectly safe. They're a lot safer than a lifestyle of cruising for dates, that's for sure."

"Especially dates with the kind of girls who live down there in the riot zone, I suppose." His mother winced. "I had some hopes when you took up with that nice bike-racer girl. Brigitte, wasn't it? Whatever happened to her?"

Lyle shook his head. "Someone with your gender and background oughta understand how important the treatments are, Mom. It's a basic reproductive-freedom issue. Antilibidinals give you real freedom, freedom from the urge to reproduce. You should be glad I'm not sexually involved."

"I don't mind that you're not involved, Lyle, it's just that it seems like a real cheat that you're not even *interested.*"

"But, Mom, nobody's interested in me, either. Nobody. No woman is banging at my door to have sex with a self-employed fanatical dropout bike mechanic who lives in a slum. If that ever happens, you'll be the first to know."

Lyle grinned cheerfully into the lens. "I had girlfriends back when I was in racing. I've been there, Mom. I've done that. Unless you're coked to the gills with hormones, sex is a major waste of your time and attention. Sexual Deliberation is the greatest civil-liberties movement of modern times."

"That's really weird, Lyle. It's just not natural."

"Mom, forgive me, but you're not the one to talk about natural, okay? You grew me from a zygote when you were fifty-five." He shrugged. "I'm too busy for romance now. I just want to learn about bikes."

"You were working with bikes when you lived here with me. You had a real job and a safe home where you could take regular showers."

"Sure, I was working, but I never said I wanted a *job,* Mom. I said I wanted to *learn about bikes.* There's a big difference! I can't be a loser wage-slave for some lousy bike franchise."

His mother said nothing.

"Mom, I'm not asking you for any favors. I don't need any bosses, or any teachers, or any landlords, or any cops. It's just me and my bike work down here. I know that people in authority can't stand it that a twenty-four-year-old man lives an independent life and does exactly what he wants, but I'm being very quiet and discreet about it, so nobody needs to bother about me."

His mother sighed, defeated. "Are you eating properly, Lyle? You look peaked."

Lyle lifted his calf muscle into camera range. "Look at this leg! Does that look like the gastrocnemius of a weak and sickly person?"

"Could you come up to the condo and have a decent meal with me sometime?"

Lyle blinked. "When?"

"Wednesday, maybe? We could have pork chops."

"Maybe, Mom. Probably. I'll have to check. I'll get back to you, okay? Bye." Lyle hung up.

Hooking the mediator's cable to the primitive settop box was a problem, but Lyle was not one to be stymied by a merely mechanical challenge. The enamel job had to wait as he resorted to miniclamps and a cable cutter. It was a handy thing that working with modern brake cabling had taught him how to splice fiber optics.

When the settop box finally came online, its array of services was a joke. Any decent modern mediator could navigate through vast information spaces, but the settop box offered nothing but "channels." Lyle had forgotten that you could even obtain old-fashioned "channels" from the city fiber-feed in Chattanooga. But these channels were government-sponsored media, and the government was always quite a ways behind the curve in network development. Chattanooga's huge fiber-bandwidth still carried the ancient government-mandated "public access channels," spooling away in their technically fossilized obscurity, far below the usual gaudy carnival of popular virching, infobahnage, demo-splintered comboards, public-service rants, mudtrufflage, remsnorkeling, and commercials.

The little settop box accessed nothing but political channels.

Three of them: Legislative, Judicial, and Executive. And that was the sum total, apparently. A settop box that offered nothing but NAFTA political coverage. On the Legislative Channel there was some kind of parliamentary debate on proper land use in Manitoba. On the Judicial Channel, a lawyer was haranguing judges about the stock market for air-pollution rights. On the Executive Channel, a big crowd of hicks were idly standing around on windblown tarmac somewhere in Louisiana waiting for something to happen.

The box didn't offer any glimpse of politics in Europe or the Sphere or the South. There were no hotspots or pips or index tagging. You couldn't look stuff up or annotate it—you just had to passively watch whatever the channel's masters chose to show you, whenever they chose to show it. This media setup was so insultingly lame and halt and primitive that it was almost perversely interesting. Kind of like peering through keyholes.

Lyle left the box on the Executive Channel, because it looked conceivable that something might actually happen there. It had swiftly become clear to him that the intolerably monotonous fodder on the other two channels was about as exciting as those channels ever got. Lyle retreated to his workbench and got back to enamel work.

At length, the President of NAFTA arrived and decamped from his helicopter on the tarmac in Louisiana. A swarm of presidential bodyguards materialized out of the expectant crowd, looking simultaneously extremely busy and icily unperturbable.

Suddenly a line of text flickered up at the bottom of the screen. The text was set in a very old-fashioned computer font, chalk-white letters with little visible jagged pixel-edges. *"Look at him hunting for that camera mark,"* the subtitle read as it scrolled across the screen. *"Why wasn't he briefed properly? He looks like a stray dog!"*

The President meandered amiably across the sun-blistered tarmac, gazing from side to side, and then stopped briefly to shake the eager outstretched hand of a local politician. *"That must have hurt,"* commented the text. *"That Cajun dolt is poison in the polls."* The President chatted amiably with the local politician and an elderly harridan in a purple dress who seemed to be the man's wife. *"Get him away from those losers!"* raged the subtitle. *"Get the Man up to the podium, for the love of Mike! Where's the Chief of Staff? Doped up on so-called smart drugs as usual? Get with your jobs, people!"*

The President looked well. Lyle had noticed that the President of NAFTA always looked well, it seemed to be a professional requirement. The big political cheeses in Europe always looked somber and intellectual, and the Sphere people always looked humble and dedicated, and the South people always looked angry and fanatical, but the NAFTA prez always looked like he'd just done a few laps in a pool and had a brisk rubdown. His large, glossy, bluffly cheerful face was discreetly stenciled with tattoos: both cheeks, a chorus line of tats on his forehead above both eyebrows, plus a few extra logos on his rocklike chin. A President's face was the ultimate billboard for major backers and interest groups.

"Does he think we have all day?" the text demanded. *"What's with this dead air time? Can't anyone properly arrange a media event these days? You call this public access? You call this informing the electorate? If we'd known the infobahn would come to this, we'd have never built the thing!"*

The President meandered amiably to a podium covered with ceremonial microphones. Lyle had noticed that politicians always used a big healthy cluster of traditional big fat microphones, even though nowadays you could build working microphones the size of a grain of rice.

"Hey, how y'all?" asked the President, grinning.

The crowd chorused back at him, with ragged enthusiasm.

"Let these fine folks up a bit closer," the President ordered suddenly, waving airily at his phalanx of bodyguards. "Y'all come on up closer, everybody! Sit right on the ground, we're all just folks here today." The President smiled benignly as the sweating, straw-hatted summer crowd hustled up to join him, scarcely believing their luck.

"Marietta and I just had a heck of a fine lunch down in Opelousas," commented the President, patting his flat, muscular belly. He deserted the fiction of his official podium to energetically press the Louisianan flesh. As he moved from hand to grasping hand, his every word was picked up infallibly by an invisible mike, probably implanted in one of his molars. "We had dirty rice, red beans—were they hot!—and crawdads big enough to body-slam a Maine lobster!" He chuckled. "What a sight them mudbugs were! Can y'all believe that?"

The President's guards were unobtrusively but methodically working the crowd with portable detectors and sophisticated spex equipment. They didn't look very concerned by the President's supposed change in routine.

"I see he's gonna run with the usual genetics malarkey," commented the subtitle.

"Y'all have got a perfect right to be mighty proud of the agriculture in this state," intoned the President. "Y'all's agro-science know-how is second to none! Sure, I know there's a few pointy-headed Luddites up in the snowbelt, who say they prefer their crawdads dinky."

Everyone laughed.

"Folks, I got nothin' against that attitude. If some jasper wants to spend his hard-earned money buyin' and peelin' and shuckin' those little dinky ones, that's all right by me and Marietta. Ain't that right, honey?"

The First Lady smiled and waved one power-gloved hand.

"But folks, you and I both know that those whiners who waste our time complaining about 'natural food' have never sucked a mudbug head in their lives! 'Natural,' my left elbow! Who are they tryin' to kid? Just 'cause you're country, don't mean you can't hack DNA!"

"He's been working really hard on the regional accents," commented the text. *"Not bad for a guy from Minnesota. But look at that sloppy, incompetent camera work! Doesn't anybody care anymore? What on earth is happening to our standards?"*

By lunchtime, Lyle had the final coat down on the enameling job. He ate a bowl of triticale mush and chewed up a mineral-rich handful of iodized sponge.

Then he settled down in front of the wallscreen to work on the inertia brake. Lyle knew there was big money in the inertia brake—for somebody, somewhere, sometime. The device smelled like the future.

Lyle tucked a jeweler's loupe in one eye and toyed methodically with the brake. He loved the way the piezoplastic clamp and rim transmuted braking energy into electrical battery storage. At last, a way to capture the energy you lost in braking and put it to solid use. It was almost, but not quite, magical.

The way Lyle figured it, there was gonna be a big market someday for an inertia brake that captured energy and then fed it back through the chaindrive in a way that just felt like human pedaling energy, in a direct and intuitive and muscular way, not chunky and buzzy like some loser battery-powered moped. If the system worked out right, it would make the rider feel completely natural and yet subtly superhuman at the same time. And it had to be simple, the kind of system a shop guy could fix with hand tools. It wouldn't work if it was too brittle and fancy, it just wouldn't feel like an authentic bike.

Lyle had a lot of ideas about the design. He was pretty sure he could get a real grip on the problem, if only he weren't being worked to death just keeping the shop going. If he could get enough capital together to assemble the prototypes and do some serious field tests.

It would have to be chip-driven, of course, but true to the biking spirit at the same time. A lot of bikes had chips in them nowadays, in the shocks or the braking or in reactive hubs, but bicycles simply weren't like computers. Computers were black boxes inside, no big visible working parts. People, by contrast, got sentimental about their bike gear. People were strangely reticent and traditional about bikes. That's why the bike market had never really gone for recumbents, even though the recumbent design had a big mechanical advantage. People didn't like their bikes too complicated. They didn't want bicycles to bitch and complain and whine for attention and constant upgrading the way that computers did. Bikes were too personal. People wanted their bikes to wear.

Someone banged at the shop door.

Lyle opened it. Down on the tiling by the barrels stood a tall brunette woman in stretch shorts, with a short-sleeve blue pullover and a ponytail. She had a bike under one arm, an old lacquer-and-paper-framed Taiwanese job. "Are you Edward Dertouzas?" she said, gazing up at him.

"No," Lyle said patiently. "Eddy's in Europe."

She thought this over. "I'm new in the zone," she confessed. "Can you fix this bike for me? I just bought it secondhand and I think it kinda needs some work."

"Sure," Lyle said. "You came to the right guy for that job,

ma'am, because Eddy Dertouzas couldn't fix a bike for hell. Eddy just used to live here. I'm the guy who actually owns this shop. Hand the bike up."

Lyle crouched down, got a grip on the handlebar stem and hauled the bike into the shop. The woman gazed up at him respectfully. "What's your name?"

"Lyle Schweik."

"I'm Kitty Casaday." She hesitated. "Could I come up inside there?"

Lyle reached down, gripped her muscular wrist, and hauled her up into the shop. She wasn't all that good looking, but she was in really good shape—like a mountain biker or triathlon runner. She looked about thirty-five. It was hard to tell, exactly. Once people got into cosmetic surgery and serious bio-maintenance, it got pretty hard to judge their age. Unless you got a good, close medical exam of their eyelids and cuticles and internal membranes and such.

She looked around the shop with great interest, brown ponytail twitching. "Where you hail from?" Lyle asked her. He had already forgotten her name.

"Well, I'm originally from Juneau, Alaska."

"Canadian, huh? Great. Welcome to Tennessee."

"Actually, Alaska used to be part of the United States."

"You're kidding," Lyle said. "Hey, I'm no historian, but I've seen Alaska on a map before."

"You've got a whole working shop and everything built inside this old place! That's really something, Mr. Schweik. What's behind that curtain?"

"The spare room," Lyle said. "That's where my roommate used to stay."

She glanced up. "Dertouzas?"

"Yeah, him."

"Who's in there now?"

"Nobody," Lyle said sadly. "I got some storage stuff in there."

She nodded slowly, and kept looking around, apparently galvanized with curiosity. "What are you running on that screen?"

"Hard to say, really," Lyle said. He crossed the room, bent down and switched off the settop box. "Some kind of weird political crap."

He began examining her bike. All its serial numbers had been removed. Typical zone bike.

"The first thing we got to do," he said briskly, "is fit it to you properly: set the saddle height, pedal stroke, and handlebars. Then I'll adjust the tension, true the wheels, check the brakepads and suspension valves, tune the shifting, and lubricate the drivetrain. The usual. You're gonna need a better saddle than this—this saddle's for a male pelvis." He looked up. "You got a charge card?"

She nodded, then frowned. "But I don't have much credit left."

"No problem." He flipped open a dog-eared catalog. "This is what you need. Any halfway decent gel-saddle. Pick one you like, and we can have it shipped in by tomorrow morning. And then"—he flipped pages—"order me one of these."

She stepped closer and examined the page. "The 'cotterless crank-bolt ceramic wrench set,' is that it?"

"That's right. I fix your bike, you give me those tools, and we're even."

"Okay. Sure. That's cheap!" She smiled at him. "I like the way you do business, Lyle."

"You'll get used to barter, if you stay in the zone long enough."

"I've never lived in a squat before," she said thoughtfully. "I like the attitude here, but people say that squats are pretty dangerous."

"I dunno about the squats in other towns, but Chattanooga squats aren't dangerous, unless you think anarchists are dangerous, and anarchists aren't dangerous unless they're really drunk." Lyle shrugged. "People will steal your stuff all the time, that's about the worst part. There's a couple of tough guys around here who claim they have handguns. I never saw anybody actually use a handgun. Old guns aren't hard to find, but it takes a real chemist to make working ammo nowadays." He smiled back at her. "Anyway, you look to me like you can take care of yourself."

"I take dance classes."

Lyle nodded. He opened a drawer and pulled a tape measure.

"I saw all those cables and pulleys you have on top of this place. You can pull the whole building right up off the ground, huh? Kind of hang it right off the ceiling up there."

"That's right, it saves a lot of trouble with people breaking and entering." Lyle glanced at his shock-baton, in its mounting at the door. She followed his gaze to the weapon and then looked at him, impressed.

Lyle measured her arms, torso length, then knelt and measured her inseam from crotch to floor. He took notes. "Okay," he said. "Come by tomorrow afternoon."

"Lyle?"

"Yeah?" He stood up.

"Do you rent this place out? I really need a safe place to stay in the zone."

"I'm sorry," Lyle said politely, "but I hate landlords and I'd never be one. What I need is a roommate who can really get behind the whole concept of my shop. Someone who's qualified, you know, to develop my infrastructure or do bicycle work. Anyway, if I took your cash or charged you for rent, then the tax people would just have another excuse to harass me."

"Sure, okay, but . . ." She paused, then looked at him under lowered eyelids. "I've gotta be a lot better than having this place go empty."

Lyle stared at her, astonished.

"I'm a pretty useful woman to have around, Lyle. Nobody's ever complained before."

"Really?"

"That's right." She stared at him boldly.

"I'll think about your offer," Lyle said. "What did you say your name was?"

"I'm Kitty. Kitty Casaday."

"Kitty, I got a whole lot of work to do today, but I'll see you tomorrow, okay?"

"Okay, Lyle." She smiled. "You think about me, all right?"

Lyle helped her down out of the shop. He watched her stride away across the atrium until she vanished through the crowded doorway of the Crowbar, a squat coffeeshop. Then he called his mother.

"Did you forget something?" his mother said, looking up from her workscreen.

"Mom, I know this is really hard to believe, but a strange woman just banged on my door and offered to have sex with me."

"You're kidding, right?"

"In exchange for room and board, I think. Anyway, I said you'd be the first to know if it happened."

"Lyle—" His mother hesitated. "Lyle, I think you better come right home. Let's make that dinner date for tonight, okay? We'll have a little talk about this situation."

"Yeah, okay. I got an enameling job I gotta deliver to Floor 41, anyway."

"I don't have a positive feeling about this development, Lyle."

"That's okay, Mom. I'll see you tonight."

Lyle reassembled the newly enameled bike. Then he set the flywheel onto remote, and stepped outside the shop. He mounted the bike, and touched a password into the remote control. The shop faithfully reeled itself far out of reach and hung there in space below the fire-blackened ceiling, swaying gently.

Lyle pedaled away, back toward the elevators, back toward the neighborhood where he'd grown up.

He delivered the bike to the delighted young idiot who'd commissioned it, stuffed the cash in his shoes, and then went down to his mother's. He took a shower, shaved, and shampooed thoroughly. They had pork chops and grits and got drunk together. His mother complained about the breakup with her third husband and wept bitterly, but not as much as usual when this topic came up. Lyle got the strong impression she was thoroughly on the mend and would be angling for number four in pretty short order.

Around midnight, Lyle refused his mother's ritual offers of new clothes and fresh leftovers, and headed back down to the zone. He was still a little clubfooted from his mother's sherry, and he stood breathing beside the broken glass of the atrium wall, gazing out at the city-smeared summer stars. The cavernous darkness inside the zone at night was one of his favorite things about the place. The queasy 24-hour security lighting in the rest of the Archiplat had never been rebuilt inside the zone.

The zone always got livelier at night when all the normal people started sneaking in to cruise the zone's unlicensed dives and nightspots, but all that activity took place behind discreetly closed doors. Enticing squiggles of red and blue chemglow here and there only enhanced the blessed unnatural gloom.

Lyle pulled his remote control and ordered the shop back down.

The door of the shop had been broken open.

Lyle's latest bike-repair client lay sprawled on the floor of the shop, unconscious. She was wearing black military fatigues, a knit cap, and rappelling gear.

She had begun her break-in at Lyle's establishment by pulling his shock-baton out of its glowing security socket beside the doorframe. The booby-trapped baton had immediately put fifteen thousand volts through her, and sprayed her face with a potent mix of dye and street-legal incapacitants.

Lyle turned the baton off with the remote control, and then placed it carefully back in its socket. His surprise guest was still breathing, but was clearly in real metabolic distress. He tried clearing her nose and mouth with a tissue. The guys who'd sold him the baton hadn't been kidding about the "indelible" part. Her face and throat were drenched with green and her chest looked like a spin-painting.

Her elaborate combat spex had partially shielded her eyes. With the spex off she looked like a viridian-green raccoon.

Lyle tried stripping her gear off in conventional fashion, realized this wasn't going to work, and got a pair of metal-shears from the shop. He snipped his way through the eerily writhing power-gloves and the kevlar laces of the pneumoreactive combat boots. Her black turtleneck had an abrasive surface and a cuirass over chest and back that looked like it could stop small-arms fire.

The trousers had nineteen separate pockets and they were loaded with all kinds of eerie little items: a matte-black electrode stun-weapon, flash capsules, fingerprint dust, a utility pocket-knife, drug adhesives, plastic handcuffs, some pocket change, worry beads, a comb, and a makeup case.

Close inspection revealed a pair of tiny microphone amplifiers inserted in her ear canals. Lyle fetched the tiny devices out with needlenose pliers. Lyle was getting pretty seriously concerned by this point. He shackled her arms and legs with bike security cable, in case she regained consciousness and attempted something superhuman.

Around four in the morning she had a coughing fit and began shivering violently. Summer nights could get pretty cold in the shop. Lyle thought over the design problem for some time, and then fetched a big heat-reflective blanket out of the empty room. He cut a neat poncho-hole in the center of it, and slipped her head through it. He got the bike cables off her—she could probably slip the cables anyway—and sewed all four edges of the blanket shut from the outside, with sturdy monofilament thread from his saddle-stitcher. He sewed the poncho edges to a tough fabric belt, cinched the belt snugly around her neck, and padlocked it. When he was done, he'd made a snug bag that contained her entire body, except for her head, which had begun to drool and snore.

A fat blob of superglue on the bottom of the bag kept her anchored to the shop's floor. The blanket was cheap but tough upholstery fabric. If she could rip her way through blanket fabric with her fingernails alone, then he was probably a goner anyway. By now, Lyle was tired and stone sober. He had a squeezebottle of glucose rehydrator, three aspirins, and a canned chocolate pudding. Then he climbed in his hammock and went to sleep.

Lyle woke up around ten. His captive was sitting up inside the bag, her green face stony, eyes red-rimmed and brown hair caked with dye. Lyle got up, dressed, ate breakfast, and fixed the broken door-lock. He said nothing, partly because he thought that silence would shake her up, but mostly because he couldn't remember her name. He was almost sure it wasn't her real name anyway.

When he'd finished fixing the door, he reeled up the string of the doorknocker so that it was far out of reach. He figured the two of them needed the privacy.

Then Lyle deliberately fired up the wallscreen and turned on the settop box. As soon as the peculiar subtitles started showing up again, she grew agitated.

"Who are you really?" she demanded at last.

"Ma'am, I'm a bicycle repairman."

She snorted.

"I guess I don't need to know your name," he said, "but I need to know who your people are, and why they sent you here, and what I've got to do to get out of this situation."

"You're not off to a good start, mister."

"No," he said, "maybe not, but you're the one who's blown

it. I'm just a twenty-four-year-old bicycle repairman from Tennessee. But you, you've got enough specialized gear on you to buy my whole place five times over."

He flipped open the little mirror in her makeup case and showed her her own face. Her scowl grew a little stiffer below the spattering of green.

"I want you to tell me what's going on here," he said.

"Forget it."

"If you're waiting for your backup to come rescue you, I don't think they're coming," Lyle said. "I searched you very thoroughly and I've opened up every single little gadget you had, and I took all the batteries out. I'm not even sure what some of those things are or how they work, but hey, I know what a battery is. It's been hours now. So I don't think your backup people even know where you are."

She said nothing.

"See," he said, "you've really blown it bad. You got caught by a total amateur, and now you're in a hostage situation that could go on indefinitely. I got enough water and noodles and sardines to live up here for days. I dunno, maybe you can make a cellular phone-call to God off some gizmo implanted in your thighbone, but it looks to me like you've got serious problems."

She shuffled around a bit inside the bag and looked away.

"It's got something to do with the cablebox over there, right?"

She said nothing.

"For what it's worth, I don't think that box has anything to do with me or Eddy Dertouzas," Lyle said. "I think it was probably meant for Eddy, but I don't think he asked anybody for it. Somebody just wanted him to have it, probably one of his weird European contacts. Eddy used to be in this political group called CAPCLUG, ever heard of them?"

It looked pretty obvious that she'd heard of them.

"I never liked 'em much either," Lyle told her. "They kind of snagged me at first with their big talk about freedom and civil liberties, but then you'd go to a CAPCLUG meeting up in the penthouse levels, and there were all these potbellied zudes in spex yapping off stuff like, 'We must follow the technological imperatives or be jettisoned into the history dump-file.' They're a bunch of useless blowhards who can't tie their own shoes."

"They're dangerous radicals subverting national sovereignty."

Lyle blinked cautiously. "Whose national sovereignty would that be?"

"Yours, mine, Mr. Schweik. I'm from NAFTA, I'm a federal agent."

"You're a fed? How come you're breaking into people's houses, then? Isn't that against the Fourth Amendment or something?"

"If you mean the Fourth Amendment to the Constitution of the United States, that document was superseded years ago."

"Yeah . . . okay, I guess you're right." Lyle shrugged. "I missed a lot of civics classes. . . . No skin off my back anyway. I'm sorry, but what did you say your name was?"

"I said my name was Kitty Casaday."

"Right. Kitty. Okay, Kitty, just you and me, person to person. We obviously have a mutual problem here. What do you think I ought to do in this situation? I mean, speaking practically."

Kitty thought it over, surprised. "Mr. Schweik, you should release me immediately, get me my gear, and give me the box and any related data, recordings, or diskettes. Then you should escort me from the Archiplat in some confidential fashion so I won't be stopped by police and questioned about the dye-stains. A new set of clothes would be very useful."

"Like that, huh?"

"That's your wisest course of action." Her eyes narrowed. "I can't make any promises, but it might affect your future treatment very favorably."

"You're not gonna tell me who you are, or where you came from, or who sent you, or what this is all about?"

"No. Under no circumstances. I'm not allowed to reveal that. You don't need to know. You're not supposed to know. And anyway, if you're really what you say you are, what should you care?"

"Plenty. I care plenty. I can't wander around the rest of my life wondering when you're going to jump me out of a dark corner."

"If I'd wanted to hurt you, I'd have hurt you when we first met, Mr. Schweik. There was no one here but you and me, and I could have easily incapacitated you and taken anything I wanted. Just give me the box and the data and stop trying to interrogate me."

"Suppose you found me breaking into your house, Kitty? What would you do to me?"

She said nothing.

"What you're telling me isn't gonna work. If you don't tell me what's really going on here," Lyle said heavily, "I'm gonna have to get tough."

Her lips thinned in contempt.

"Okay, you asked for this." Lyle opened the mediator and made a quick voice call. "Pete?"

"Nah, this is Pete's mook," the phone replied. "Can I do something for you?"

"Could you tell Pete that Lyle Schweik has some big trouble, and I need him to come over to my bike shop immediately? And bring some heavy muscle from the Spiders."

"What kind of big trouble, Lyle?"

"Authority trouble. A lot of it. I can't say any more. I think this line may be tapped."

"Right-o. I'll make that happen. Hoo-ah, zude." The mook hung up.

Lyle left the beanbag and went back to the workbench. He took Kitty's cheap bike out of the repair stand and angrily threw it aside. "You know what really bugs me?" he said at last. "You couldn't even bother to charm your way in here, set yourself up as my roommate, and then steal the damn box. You didn't even respect me that much. Heck, you didn't even have to steal anything, Kitty. You could have just smiled and asked nicely and I'd have given you the box to play with. I don't watch media, I hate all that crap."

"It was an emergency. There was no time for more extensive investigation or reconnaissance. I think you should call your gangster friends immediately and tell them you've made a mistake. Tell them not to come here."

"You're ready to talk seriously?"

"No, I won't be talking."

"Okay, we'll see."

After twenty minutes, Lyle's phone rang. He answered it cautiously, keeping the video off. It was Pete from the City Spiders. "Zude, where is your doorknocker?"

"Oh, sorry, I pulled it up, didn't want to be disturbed. I'll bring the shop right down." Lyle thumbed the brake switches.

Lyle opened the door and Pete broad-jumped into the shop. Pete was a big man but he had the skeletal, wiry build of a climber, bare dark arms and shins and big sticky-toed jumping shoes. He had a sleeveless leather bodysuit full of clips and snaps, and he carried a big fabric shoulderbag. There were six vivid tattoos on the dark skin of his left cheek, under the black stubble.

Pete looked at Kitty, lifted his spex with wiry callused fingers, looked at her again bare-eyed, and put the spex back in place. "Wow, Lyle."

"Yeah."

"I never thought you were into anything this sick and twisted."

"It's a serious matter, Pete."

Pete turned to the door, crouched down, and hauled a second person into the shop. She wore a beat-up air-conditioned jacket and long slacks and zipsided boots and wire-rimmed spex. She had short ratty hair under a green cloche hat. "Hi," she said, sticking out a hand. "I'm Mabel. We haven't met."

"I'm Lyle." Lyle gestured. "This is Kitty here in the bag."

"You said you needed somebody heavy, so I brought Mabel along," said Pete. "Mabel's a social worker."

"Looks like you pretty much got things under control here," said Mabel liltingly, scratching her neck and looking about the place. "What happened? She break into your shop?"

"Yeah."

"And," Pete said, "she grabbed the shock-baton first thing and blasted herself but good?"

"Exactly."

"I told you that thieves always go for the weaponry first," Pete said, grinning and scratching his armpit. "Didn't I tell you that? Leave a weapon in plain sight, man, a thief can't stand it, it's the very first thing they gotta grab." He laughed. "Works every time."

"Pete's from the City Spiders," Lyle told Kitty. "His people built this shop for me. One dark night, they hauled this mobile home right up thirty-four stories in total darkness, straight up the side of the Archiplat without anybody seeing, and they cut a big hole through the side of the building without making any noise, and they hauled the whole shop through it. Then they sank explosive bolts through the girders and hung it up here for me in midair. The City Spiders are into sport-climbing the way I'm into bicycles, only, like, they are very *seriously* into climbing and there are *lots* of them. They were some of the very first people to squat the zone, and they've lived here ever since, and they are pretty good friends of mine."

Pete sank to one knee and looked Kitty in the eye. "I love breaking into places, don't you? There's no thrill like some quick and perfectly executed break-in." He reached casually into his shoulderbag. "The thing is"—he pulled out a camera—"to be sporting, you can't steal anything. You just take trophy pictures to prove you were there." He snapped her picture several times, grinning as she flinched.

"Lady," he breathed at her, "once you've turned into a little wicked greedhead, and mixed all that evil cupidity and possessiveness into the beauty of the direct action, then you've prostituted our way of life. You've gone and spoiled our sport." Pete stood up. "We City Spiders don't like common thieves. And we especially don't like thieves who break into the places of clients of ours, like Lyle here. And we thoroughly, especially, don't like thieves who are so brickhead dumb that they get caught red-handed on the premises of friends of ours."

Pete's hairy brows knotted in thought. "What I'd like to do here, Lyle ol' buddy," he announced, "is wrap up your little friend head to foot in nice tight cabling, smuggle her out of here down to Golden Gate Archiplat—you know, the big one downtown over by MLK and Highway Twenty-seven?—and hang her head-down in the center of the cupola."

"That's not very nice," Mabel told him seriously.

Pete looked wounded. "I'm not gonna charge him for it or anything! Just imagine her, spinning up there beautifully with all those chandeliers and those hundreds of mirrors."

Mabel knelt and looked into Kitty's face. "Has she had any

water since she was knocked unconscious?"

"No."

"Well, for heaven's sake, give the poor woman something to drink, Lyle."

Lyle handed Mabel a bike-tote squeezebottle of electrolyte refresher. "You zudes don't grasp the situation yet," he said. "Look at all this stuff I took off her." He showed them the spex, and the boots, and the stun-gun, and the gloves, and the carbon-nitride climbing plectra, and the rappelling gear.

"Wow," Pete said at last, dabbing at buttons on his spex to study the finer detail, "this is no ordinary burglar! She's gotta be, like, a street samurai from the Mahogany Warbirds or something!"

"She says she's a federal agent."

Mabel stood up suddenly, angrily yanking the squeezebottle from Kitty's lips. "You're kidding, right?"

"Ask her."

"I'm a grade-five social counselor with the Department of Urban Redevelopment," Mabel said. She presented Kitty with an official ID. "And who are you with?"

"I'm not prepared to divulge that information at this time."

"I can't believe this," Mabel marveled, tucking her dog-eared hologram ID back in her hat. "You've caught somebody from one of those nutty reactionary secret black-bag units. I mean, that's gotta be what's just happened here." She shook her head slowly. "Y'know, if you work in government, you always hear horror stories about these right-wing paramilitary wackos, but I've never actually seen one before."

"It's a very dangerous world out there, Miss Social Counselor."

"Oh, tell me about it," Mabel scoffed. "I've worked suicide hotlines! I've been a hostage negotiator! I'm a career social worker, girlfriend! I've seen more horror and suffering than you *ever* will. While you were doing push-ups in some comfy cracker training-camp, I've been out here in the real world!" Mabel absently unscrewed the top from the bike bottle and had a long glug. "What on earth are you doing trying to raid the squat of a bicycle repairman?"

Kitty's stony silence lengthened. "It's got something to do

with that settop box," Lyle offered. "It showed up here in delivery yesterday, and then she showed up just a few hours later. Started flirting with me, and said she wanted to live in here. Of course I got suspicious right away."

"Naturally," Pete said. "Real bad move, Kitty. Lyle's on antilibidinals."

Kitty stared at Lyle bitterly. "I see," she said at last. "So that's what you get, when you drain all the sex out of one of them. . . . You get a strange malodorous creature that spends all its time working in the garage."

Mabel flushed. "Did you hear that?" She gave Kitty's bag a sharp angry yank. "What conceivable right do you have to question this citizen's sexual orientation? Especially after cruelly trying to sexually manipulate him to abet your illegal purposes? Have you lost all sense of decency? You . . . you should be sued."

"Do your worst," Kitty muttered.

"Maybe I will," Mabel said grimly. "Sunlight is the best disinfectant."

"Yeah, let's string her up somewhere real sunny and public and call a bunch of news crews," Pete said. "I'm way hot for this deep ninja gear! Me and the Spiders got real mojo uses for these telescopic ears, and the tracer dust, and the epoxy bugging devices. And the press-on climbing-claws. And the carbon-fiber rope. Everything, really! Everything except these big-ass military shoes of hers, which really suck."

"Hey, all that stuff's mine," Lyle said sternly. "I saw it first."

"Yeah, I guess so, but. . . . Okay, Lyle, you make us a deal on the gear, we'll forget everything you still owe us for doing the shop."

"Come on, those combat spex are worth more than this place all by themselves."

"I'm real interested in that settop box," Mabel said cruelly. "It doesn't look too fancy or complicated. Let's take it over to those dirty circuit zudes who hang out at the Blue Parrot, and see if they can't reverse-engineer it. We'll post all the schematics up on twenty or thirty progressive activist networks, and see what falls out of cyberspace."

Kitty glared at her. "The terrible consequences from that stupid and irresponsible action would be entirely on your head."

"I'll risk it," Mabel said airily, patting her cloche hat. "It might bump my soft little liberal head a bit, but I'm pretty sure it would crack your nasty little fascist head like a coconut."

Suddenly Kitty began thrashing and kicking her way furiously inside the bag. They watched with interest as she ripped, tore and lashed out with powerful side and front kicks. Nothing much happened.

"All right," she said at last, panting in exhaustion. "I've come from Senator Creighton's office."

"Who?" Lyle said.

"Creighton! Senator James P. Creighton, the man who's been your Senator from Tennessee for the past thirty years!"

"Oh," Lyle said. "I hadn't noticed."

"We're anarchists," Pete told her.

"I've sure heard of the nasty old geezer," Mabel said, "but I'm from British Columbia, where we change senators the way you'd change a pair of socks. If you ever changed your socks, that is. What about him?"

"Well, Senator Creighton has deep clout and seniority! He was a United States Senator even before the first NAFTA Senate was convened! He has a very large, and powerful, and very well seasoned personal staff of twenty thousand hardworking people, with a lot of pull in the Agriculture, Banking, and Telecommunications Committees!"

"Yeah? So?"

"So," Kitty said miserably, "there are twenty thousand of us on his staff. We've been in place for decades now, and naturally we've accumulated lots of power and importance. Senator Creighton's staff is basically running some quite large sections of the NAFTA government, and if the Senator loses his office, there will be a great deal of . . . of unnecessary political turbulence." She looked up. "You might not think that a senator's staff is all that important politically. But if people like you bothered to learn anything about the real-life way that your government functions, then you'd know that Senate staffers can be really crucial."

Mabel scratched her head. "You're telling me that even a lousy senator has his own private black-bag unit?"

Kitty looked insulted. "He's an excellent senator! You can't have a working organization of twenty thousand staffers without taking security very seriously! Anyway, the Executive wing has had black-bag units for years! It's only right that there should be a balance of powers."

"Wow," Mabel said. "The old guy's a hundred and twelve or something, isn't he?"

"A hundred and seventeen."

"Even with government health care, there can't be a lot left of him."

"He's already gone," Kitty muttered. "His frontal lobes are burned out.... He can still sit up, and if he's stoked on stimulants he can repeat whatever's whispered to him. So he's got two permanent implanted hearing aids, and basically . . . well . . . he's being run by remote control by his mook."

"His mook, huh?" Pete repeated thoughtfully.

"It's a very good mook," Kitty said. "The coding's old, but it's been very well looked-after. It has firm moral values and excellent policies. The mook is really very much like the Senator was. It's just that . . . well, it's old. It still prefers a really old-fashioned media environment. It spends almost all its time watching old-fashioned public political coverage, and lately it's gotten cranky and started broadcasting commentary."

"Man, never trust a mook," Lyle said. "I hate those things."

"So do I," Pete offered, "but even a mook comes off pretty good compared to a politician."

"I don't really see the problem," Mabel said, puzzled. "Senator Hirschheimer from Arizona has had a direct neural link to his mook for years, and he has an excellent progressive voting record. Same goes for Senator Marmalejo from Tamaulipas; she's kind of absentminded, and everybody knows she's on life support, but she's a real scrapper on women's issues."

Kitty looked up. "You don't think it's terrible?"

Mabel shook her head. "I'm not one to be judgmental about the intimacy of one's relationship to one's own digital alter-ego. As far as I can see it, that's a basic privacy issue."

"They told me in briefing that it was a very terrible business, and that everyone would panic if they learned that a high government official was basically a front for a rogue artificial intelligence."

Mabel, Pete, and Lyle exchanged glances. "Are you guys surprised by that news?" Mabel said.

"Heck no," said Pete. "Big deal," Lyle added.

Something seemed to snap inside Kitty then. Her head sank. "Disaffected émigrés in Europe have been spreading boxes that can decipher the Senator's commentary. I mean, the Senator's mook's commentary. . . . The mook speaks just like the Senator did, or the way the Senator used to speak, when he was in private and off the record. The way he spoke in his diaries. As far as we can tell, the mook *was* his diary. . . . It used to be his personal laptop computer. But he just kept transferring the files, and upgrading the software, and teaching it new tricks like voice recognition and speechwriting, and giving it power of attorney and such. . . . And then, one day the mook made a break for it. We think that the mook sincerely believes that it's the Senator."

"Just tell the stupid thing to shut up for a while, then."

"We can't do that. We're not even sure where the mook is, physically. Or how it's been encoding those sarcastic comments into the video-feed. The Senator had a lot of friends in the telecom industry back in the old days. There are a lot of ways and places to hide a piece of distributed software."

"So that's all?" Lyle said. "That's it, that's your big secret? Why didn't you just come to me and ask me for the box? You didn't have to dress up in combat gear and kick my door in. That's a pretty good story, I'd have probably just given you the thing."

"I couldn't do that, Mr. Schweik."

"Why not?"

"Because," Pete said, "her people are important government functionaries, and you're a loser techie wacko who lives in a slum."

"I was told this is a very dangerous area," Kitty muttered.

"It's not dangerous," Mabel told her.

"No?"

"No. They're all too broke to be dangerous. This is just a kind of social breathing space. The whole urban infrastructure's dreadfully overplanned here in Chattanooga. There's been too much money here too long. There's been no room for spontaneity. It was choking the life out of the city. That's why everyone was secretly overjoyed when the rioters set fire to these three floors."

Mabel shrugged. "The insurance took care of the damage. First the looters came in. Then there were a few hideouts for kids and crooks and illegal aliens. Then the permanent squats got set up. Then the artist's studios, and the semilegal workshops and redlight places. Then the quaint little coffeehouses, then the bakeries. Pretty soon the offices of professionals will be filtering in, and they'll restore the water and the wiring. Once that happens, the real-estate prices will kick in big-time, and the whole zone will transmute right back into gentryville. It happens all the time."

Mabel waved her arm at the door. "If you knew anything about modern urban geography, you'd see this kind of, uh, spontaneous urban renewal happening all over the place. As long as you've got naive young people with plenty of energy who can be suckered into living inside rotten, hazardous dumps for nothing, in exchange for imagining that they're free from oversight, then it all works out just great in the long run."

"Oh."

"Yeah, zones like this turn out to be extremely handy for all concerned. For some brief span of time, a few people can think mildly unusual thoughts and behave in mildly unusual ways. All kinds of weird little vermin show up, and if they make any money then they go legal, and if they don't then they drop dead in a place really quiet where it's all their own fault. Nothing dangerous about it." Mabel laughed, then sobered. "Lyle, let this poor dumb cracker out of the bag."

"She's naked under there."

"Okay," she said impatiently, "cut a slit in the bag and throw some clothes in it. Get going, Lyle."

Lyle threw in some biking pants and a sweatshirt.

"What about my gear?" Kitty demanded, wriggling her way into the clothes by feel.

"I tell you what," said Mabel thoughtfully. "Pete here will give your gear back to you in a week or so, after his friends have photographed all the circuitry. You'll just have to let him keep all those knickknacks for a while, as his reward for our not immediately telling everybody who you are and what you're doing here."

"Great idea," Pete announced, "terrific, pragmatic solution!" He began feverishly snatching up gadgets and stuffing them into his shoulderbag. "See, Lyle? One phone-call to good ol' Spider Pete, and your problem is history, zude! Me and Mabel-the-Fed have crisis negotiation skills that are second to none! Another potentially lethal confrontation resolved without any bloodshed or loss of life." Pete zipped the bag shut. "That's about it, right, everybody? Problem over! Write if you get work, Lyle buddy. Hang by your thumbs." Pete leapt out the door and bounded off at top speed on the springy soles of his reactive boots.

"Thanks a lot for placing my equipment into the hands of sociopathic criminals," Kitty said. She reached out of the slit in the bag, grabbed a multitool off the corner of the workbench, and began swiftly slashing her way free.

"This will help the sluggish, corrupt, and underpaid Chattanooga police to take life a little more seriously," Mabel said, her pale eyes gleaming. "Besides, it's profoundly undemocratic to restrict specialized technical knowledge to the coercive hands of secret military elites."

Kitty thoughtfully thumbed the edge of the multitool's ceramic blade and stood up to her full height, her eyes slitted. "I'm ashamed to work for the same government as you."

Mabel smiled serenely. "Darling, your tradition of deep dark government paranoia is far behind the times! This is the postmodern era! We're now in the grip of a government with severe schizoid multiple-personality disorder."

"You're truly vile. I despise you more than I can say." Kitty jerked her thumb at Lyle. "Even this nut-case eunuch anarchist kid looks pretty good, compared to you. At least he's self-sufficient and market-driven."

"I thought he looked good the moment I met him," Mabel replied sunnily. "He's cute, he's got great muscle tone, and he doesn't make passes. Plus he can fix small appliances and he's got a spare apartment. I think you ought to move in with him, sweetheart."

"What's that supposed to mean? You don't think I could manage life here in the zone like you do, is that it? You think you have some kind of copyright on living outside the law?"

"No, I just mean you'd better stay indoors with your boyfriend here until that paint falls off your face. You look like a poisoned raccoon." Mabel turned on her heel. "Try to get a life, and stay out of my way." She leapt outside, unlocked her bicycle and methodically pedaled off.

Kitty wiped her lips and spat out the door. "Christ, that baton packs a wallop." She snorted. "Don't you ever ventilate this place, kid? Those paint fumes are gonna kill you before you're thirty."

"I don't have time to clean or ventilate it. I'm real busy."

"Okay, then I'll clean it. I'll ventilate it. I gotta stay here a while, understand? Maybe quite a while."

Lyle blinked. "How long, exactly?"

Kitty stared at him. "You're not taking me seriously, are you? I don't much like it when people don't take me seriously."

"No, no," Lyle assured her hastily. "You're very serious."

"You ever heard of a small-business grant, kid? How about venture capital, did you ever hear of that? Ever heard of federal research-and-development subsidies, Mr. Schweik?" Kitty looked at him sharply, weighing her words. "Yeah, I thought maybe you'd heard of that one, Mr. Techie Wacko. Federal R and D backing is the kind of thing that only happens to other people, right? But Lyle, when you make good friends with a senator, you *become* 'other people.' Get my drift, pal?"

"I guess I do," Lyle said slowly.

"We'll have ourselves some nice talks about that subject, Lyle. You wouldn't mind that, would you?"

"No. I don't mind it now that you're talking."

"There's some stuff going on down here in the zone that I didn't understand at first, but it's important." Kitty paused, then rubbed dried dye from her hair in a cascade of green dandruff. "How much did you pay those Spider gangsters to string up this place for you?"

"It was kind of a barter situation," Lyle told her.

"Think they'd do it again if I paid 'em real cash? Yeah? I thought so." She nodded thoughtfully. "They look like a heavy outfit, the City Spiders. I gotta pry 'em loose from that leftist gorgon before she finishes indoctrinating them in socialist revolution." Kitty wiped her mouth on her sleeve. "This is the Senator's own constituency! It was stupid of us to duck an ideological battle, just because this is a worthless area inhabited by reckless sociopaths who don't vote. Hell, that's exactly why it's important. This could be a vital territory in the culture war. I'm gonna call the office right away, start making arrangements. There's no way we're gonna leave this place in the hands of the self-styled Queen of Peace and Justice over there."

She snorted, then stretched a kink out of her back. "With a little self-control and discipline, I can save those Spiders from themselves and turn them into an asset to law and order! I'll get 'em to string up a couple of trailers here in the zone. We could start a dojo."

Eddy called, two weeks later. He was in a beachside cabana somewhere in Catalunya, wearing a silk floral-print shirt and a new and very pricey looking set of spex. "How's life, Lyle?"

"It's okay, Eddy."

"Making out all right?" Eddy had two new tattoos on his cheekbone.

"Yeah. I got a new paying roommate. She's a martial artist."

"Girl roommate working out okay this time?"

"Yeah, she's good at pumping the flywheel and she lets me get on with my bike work. Bike business has been picking up a lot lately. Looks like I might get a legal electrical feed and some more floorspace, maybe even some genuine mail delivery. My new roomie's got a lot of useful contacts."

"Boy, the ladies sure love you, Lyle! Can't beat 'em off with a stick, can you, poor guy? That's a heck of a note."

Eddy leaned forward a little, shoving aside a silver tray full of dead gold-tipped zigarettes. "You been getting the packages?"

"Yeah. Pretty regular."

"Good deal," he said briskly, "but you can wipe 'em all now. I don't need those backups anymore. Just wipe the data and trash the disks, or sell 'em. I'm into some, well, pretty hairy opportunities right now, and I don't need all that old clutter. It's kid stuff anyway."

"Okay, man. If that's the way you want it."

Eddy leaned forward. "D'you happen to get a package lately? Some hardware? Kind of a settop box?"

"Yeah, I got the thing."

"That's great, Lyle. I want you to open the box up, and break all the chips with pliers."

"Yeah?

"Then throw all the pieces away. Separately. It's trouble, Lyle, okay? The kind of trouble I don't need right now."

"Consider it done, man."

"Thanks! Anyway, you won't be bothered by mailouts from now on." He paused. "Not that I don't appreciate your former effort and goodwill, and all."

Lyle blinked. "How's your love life, Eddy?"

Eddy sighed. "Frederika! What a handful! I dunno, Lyle, it was okay for a while, but we couldn't stick it together. I don't know why I ever thought that private cops were sexy. I musta been totally out of my mind. . . . Anyway, I got a new girlfriend now."

"Yeah?"

"She's a politician, Lyle. She's a radical member of the Spanish Parliament. Can you believe that? I'm sleeping with an elected official of a European local government." He laughed. "Politicians are *sexy*, Lyle. Politicians are *hot*! They have charisma. They're glamorous. They're powerful. They can really make things happen! Politicians get around. They know things on the inside track. I'm having more fun with Violeta than I knew there was in the world."

"That's pleasant to hear, zude."

"More pleasant than you know, my man."

"Not a problem," Lyle said indulgently. "We all gotta make our own lives, Eddy."

"Ain't it the truth."

Lyle nodded. "I'm in business, zude!"

"You gonna perfect that inertial whatsit?" Eddy said.

"Maybe. It could happen. I get to work on it a lot now. I'm getting closer, really getting a grip on the concept. It feels really good. It's a good hack, man. It makes up for all the rest of it. It really does."

Eddy sipped his mimosa. "Lyle."

"What?"

"You didn't hook up that settop box and look at it, did you?"

"You know me, Eddy," Lyle said. "Just another kid with a wrench."

Workshop Comments

Robert Frazier: "The sweet, sweet triumph of the self-made neuter—a straight-on bullet to the heart of the *Analog* story."

Maureen McHugh: "It's not profound, but it's funny, clever and chock-full of nifty ideas. I like government-is-stupid stories a lot better than I like the lethal, well-oiled-ninjas-of-the-supersecret-agency-who-can-do-almost-anything worldview, and I really like this story."

Carol Emshwiller: "Too much story might spoil this kind of comedy. Talking heads that talk so well are okay to me."

Richard Butner: "Gonzo verbiage and precision detailwork only make the dull stuff look duller. You need to machine the edges of the always-clever extrapolations so they fit together to form a synergistic whole."

Nancy Kress: "An overly sweet story with too little attention to characters and to the seriousness of the ideas, so that the whole thing ends up more lightweight than it should be, even for a comedy. Take some chances here, Bruce. Let something *matter*."

Alexander Jablokov: "A complex, glittering mechanism with a discharged battery. Crank up the conflicts, and it will go. A blast, still, of course. Just get the flywheel moving."

John Kessel: "Title sucks rocks. First twenty pages are steam-grommet factory mode. Story doesn't start properly until Kitty shows up. I love Mabel."

James Patrick Kelly: "The last half of the story is static and talky but there is no dialogue here. Lyle defeats Kitty but a zone needs a city to exist in the same way that a city needs a zone for creativity and vitality. Give them something to offer each other. If it's not a love story then make the politics sexy; both sides must be attractive."

Mark Van Name: "Blow off the love story, ignore the obvious Freudian reading, ignore the less obvious but still real objective-correlative reading,* and focus more strongly on the social extrapolation and the tale of cultural power-shifts."

(*Van Name's objective-correlative reading for "Bicycle Repairman":
  Lyle Schweik = Bruce Sterling
  Deep Eddy = William Gibson
  bike shop = Bruce Sterling's office
  Kitty = fiction publishing companies, like Bantam, Ace, and Millennium
  City Spiders = Sterling's nonfiction clients, like *Wired, Mondo,* and *Boing-Boing*
  Mom = Sterling's family, the home and hearth
  Mabel = Sterling's political commitments)

Karen Joy Fowler: "Bruce—I have only a series of small, whiny complaints. Your ending lines are weak. Your mook should be funnier while maintaining its essential banality. I don't like your hyphenated adjectives. But really you seduce me through the story with the simple technique of being continually hilarious. I liked in particular your hardened social worker exposing the coddled life of the ninja warrior. And the mom was an elegant touch, perfectly executed. I was still amused long after I put the story away. I'm *still* amused and an entire night has passed."

Jonathan Lethem: "Genuine grown-up extrapolation like our field barely ever sees—inextricably wedded to teenage wish-fulfillment like our field is straining to outgrow—you've indulged it here to such an extent that it's almost a satire. Super penis is detachable and never soft and explodes with such force that females are knocked unconscious and indelibly marked. . . . Well, you get my drift."

Michaela Roessner: "I love stories where the 'average Joe' (regardless of gender) is smarter than 'the dark forces' pitted against them, especially when done with some humor. However, I'm sorry you made the dark forces a proto-stupid right-wing cabal in this story. It works, but it turns the tale into a utopic cartoon. I'd like to see it changed just a little, where Kitty really is a smart, savvy intelligence agent instead of this ranting, raving mouthpiece. I think such a scenario is workable, because relatively well trained, intelligent agents of the über-death are being caught up short all the time. And yes, of course once she is co-opted she would start up a dojo."

Gregory Frost: "The Monty Python–inspired title supports the 'everyman as superman' reading of this story. This is a social takedown of useless, blowhard political rants, both left and right. Lyndon LaRouche and Ollie North have a pissing contest. But the story is not yet able to stand on its own because the characters, in making the points you want to make, violate themselves—Kitty in particular."

Afterword to "Bicycle Repairman"

Neither this story nor its predecessor, "Deep Eddy," would have existed without Sycamore Hill. My colleagues politely demanded that I write some kind of story and bring it with me before they'd let me in the workshop door. It is not exactly true that I attend Sycamore Hill just because Mark Van Name always takes me out to eat the barbecue at Bullock's in Durham, but, hell, why hide it. That North Carolina stuff is fine, and I say that as a Texan who knows barbecue!

As for the story, it's okay I guess. It's better now in the rewrite than when I showed it around at SycHill. I should write a lot more stories like these. They're good for me, they seem to scrub my brain a lot better than those pesky F&SF Science columns where I'm pretending to be a real journalist. Thanks to Jim Kelly for adjusting the ending, to Alex Jablokov for pointing out that ceramic is weak under tension, to Greg Frost for bicycle minutiae, to Nancy Kress for scaldingly scolding me as a sentimental saccharine sissy, and to Karen Fowler for publicly admiring a cyberpunk character cool enough to have a mom and survive it.

Bruce Sterling

The Marianas Islands

KAREN JOY FOWLER

A map of the world that does not include Utopia is not worth even glancing at, for it leaves out the one country at which Humanity is always landing. —Oscar Wilde

ONCE WHEN I was four or five I asked my grandmother to tell me a secret, some secret thing only grown-ups knew. She thought a moment, then leaned down close to me and whispered. "There are no grown-ups," she said.

According to my father, my grandmother was one of those remarkable women who completely reinvented themselves during the seventies. He remembers her as a sort of Betty Crocker figure. She wore lipstick, pumps, and aprons. She put up fruits. One day she metamorphosed into Betty Friedan. She phoned over to him in his dorm room at college. "Mom," he said. "I've been trying to get you. I need a shirt mended and I need it by Friday. Can I drop it by?"

"My sewing basket is in the laundry room," she said. "Pick a spool that matches the color of the shirt. Knot one end of the thread and put the other end into the needle. Use the smallest needle you can manage. I'm in jail. This is my one phone call. We've agreed to refuse bail. You can get the needle and thread when you go by to feed Angel. It's her night for the Tuna Platter."

Grams had joined the San Francisco Fairmont sit-in to protest racist hiring policies. She appeared on the news that night, being dragged into the police van; my dad's entire dormitory watched it. Her form, my father always said, was perfect. It was the first of many such phone calls. There was the Vietnam War. There were the nuclear tests. She chained herself to a fence in Nevada. The last wild-water rivers needed to be saved. By the time I was born, my grandmother had an arrest record the size of a Michener novel. One of my earliest memories is of my father, hanging up the phone and reaching for his coat to go and feed Angel, who was by this time an ancient Siamese with a sensitive stomach. "She won't eat if I feed her. You should see the look she gives me." My father shook his head. " 'Methinks the lady doth protest too much.' "

Her husband, my grandfather, died before my father's first birthday, shot down in the Pacific, in the battle off Samar. The angriest I ever saw my grandmother was one time when my father suggested that if her husband had been alive, she might not have been quite so unrestrained. "Your father gave his life to make the world a better place," she said. "So don't you think for one minute he would have minded making his own supper in the same cause."

I, myself, at five was deeply in love with my grandmother. At sixteen, when I liked no one else, I still made an exception for her. If Grams had ruled the world, the people at my high school would have known how to treat me. You could go to her with problems; her advice was always good. She had the best possible combination of imagination and pragmatism, and she never told you you didn't have a problem when you thought you did.

I was not the only troubled person who found her serenity and sympathy irresistible. She drew a parade of eccentrics into her parlor, where they played bridge and she played straight man. When I was sixteen and had my wisdom teeth out, I was allowed to recuperate on her couch. I lay under the overhang of her enormous split-leaf philodendron, with Angel$_2$ rumbling against my legs and a knitted afghan made in Grams' Betty Crocker days wrapped around my shoulders. Out the window the sparrows dipped and shook in the birdbath.

The bridge table that day included a British-Indian woman named Dot, who, for reasons of faith, ate nothing but oatmeal and black tea, and a psychic named Sam. Grams' partner was a man whose name no one knew, but who called himself the Great Unknown. Doped to the gills, I floated in and out of their conversation.

"Do you think you hear the bullet that gets you?" the Great Unknown asks as I drift away. "I mean in a battle with all the other noise. Do you think you hear the one that's yours?" He takes a trick, gathering in the cards.

When I wake up next, Dot is dealing. This is worth waking up for. She ruffles and riffles; the cards fall in a solid sheet from one hand to the other, click satisfyingly onto the table. "But what does normal mean?" the Great Unknown asks, collecting and arranging his hand. "We use the word as if it means something."

Grams opens with one heart.

"I don't know anyone normal," says the Great Unknown. "Do you?"

"I know people who can pass," says Sam. "I pass."

"Three clubs," says the Great Unknown. "So our polity is based really on deception and hypocrisy. The dishonest dissemblers triumphing over the honestly deranged."

"So normal is abnormal," Dot says. "So everyone you know is normal. It's a sort of koan. Pass."

"Why in the world would you jump to three clubs?" Grams asks the Great Unknown.

"I know why," says Sam.

"Well, of course you do," Grams says to Sam. "If only you'd use your powers for good instead of evil."

A little later I am aware of Grams shuffling. "I don't care if they want to hang suspended by their feet in gas masks and scuba gear," she says. "In fact, I admire their imagination. I just don't see why they insist on calling it sex."

I wake up next in tears. The air has the early tint of evening. Angel is gone, and my mouth is full of blood. Up until now, the extractions have been good fun—sleep, and dreams, and narcotics. But the anesthetic is wearing off. There is a *pop, pop, pop* of pain pulsing in my jaw and my mouth tastes of the ocean.

"Do you think you could eat something?" Grams asks, giving me a large pill and a glass of warmish water to chase it down.

"No." I am really crying now. "This is awful." My speech is muffled. I realize I have layers of gauze shoved into the back of my mouth. I pull them out and they are soaked red and smell of sickness.

Dot and Sam and the Great Unknown crowd around my couch. It's the final scene in *The Wizard of Oz*. "Don't cry," says Dot. "We can't bear it." She strokes my hand open, traces along the lines with a fingernail. "Very good," she assures me. "Very deep, distinct lines. Very little confusion in your life."

"I suppose that's good," the Great Unknown says doubtfully. "Do you really believe in palmistry?" The Great Unknown prides himself on hardheaded skepticism.

"I trained in India," says Dot.

While Dot is reading my palm, Sam is reading my mind. "Mind over matter," he suggests, and then recoils, presumably from what I think of his suggestion.

I am in such pain, it makes me want to be rude. "I don't believe in palmistry or ESP. I'm so sorry." I am, of course, no such thing and Sam knows it.

"If I was Tinkerbell, you'd be sorry," says Sam. "Real sorry." He clears his throat two or three times. "I sense that I'm developing a cough."

"Here's what I don't believe in," says the Great Unknown. He ticks them off on his fingers for me. "I don't believe in astrology, numerology, pyramid power. I don't believe in the tooth fairy, sad for you, because you stand to make out well today. I don't believe in God, although I accord Him the capital *G*, as a courtesy to those who do." He pauses here to nod to Grams who has always been a churchgoer, then picks right up. "I don't believe in phlogiston, extraterrestrials who abduct you and probe Uranus, the orgone box, Silva Mind Control, Scientology"—he has come to the end of his fingers and starts with the first again— "or witchcraft."

"Abracadabra," says Grams, and pulls a red bandanna out of her sleeve for me. I wipe my eyes and blow my nose. The bandanna smells of Grams and her Estee Lauder cologne.

"I think that our inept government could never keep a secret as big as a CIA-slash-Mafia-slash-Cuban conspiracy to kill JFK," says the Great Unknown. "Or fake the Moon Landing, although I could be wrong about that one—that one might not be too hard.

"What I do believe in is the desperate fight against the perils of routine living that they all represent. I believe in each man's need to feel that he has somehow been chosen. It's not everyone who has a submarine." He fixes Grams with a stern look. "The rest of us must simply make do with Elvis sightings.

"Life is a series of evasive maneuvers," he observes in conclusion. "You have to envy anyone with the means to make a clean escape."

"But I could never do that," says Grams. "I could never leave the rest of you behind."

Perhaps it is a little late to be bringing up the submarine. Not quite cricket, not exactly Chekhovian of me. There is no doubt that the submarine looms very large in my family lore. It was designed and built by my great-grandfather—not my grandmother's father, but her husband's. In my defense, let me just add that it's really a very small submarine, very unimposing, a one-person affair, no more than fourteen feet long.

And it's not as if the submarine were on the mantelpiece. No, sadly, the submarine lies sunk in the furry scum of Lake Emily. Lake Emily is a small body of water, a pond really, with an oily surface and no fish more interesting than perch. It occupies the northwest corner of the Gutierrez property about fifty miles north of my grandmother's house.

For the longest time the submarine was in my grandmother's garage. I've been inside it often, and it's not all that thrilling. It had a stale, metallic smell. Here is my objection to submarines and space travel: not enough windows. What difference does it make if you're in outer space, or underwater, or wherever, if you can't feel, or hear, or see, or smell it? You might as well be locked in a closet. But my grandmother tells me it's too dark to see under the ocean anyway. "The fall is the lovely part," she says. "The water goes from blue to gray to black, as if you're out in space, falling through the stars."

Maria Gutierrez and the Great Unknown took the sub out one day to see how hard she would be to handle, and, having forgotten to tighten two screws in the bottom, filled her up immediately with water and ran her aground. They learned a lot in the process, however, and the Great Unknown was all for hoisting her up, drying her out, and taking her straight to Scotland. Grams was not opposed to this project, but she had been working with the World Hunger people, and cranes and divers would have to be organized and she hadn't gotten around to it. Besides she wanted the Great Unknown to work out for a while first. She was not sure he was physically fit enough. Like her, he was in his sixties. We thought. The submarine was built for a younger man.

Although my great-grandfather spent the latter half of his life convinced he was being stalked by Fenians, it was a point of honor in my family to consider him a genius. The party line was that he was one of those nineteenth-century men who were masters of many fields, sort of like the explorer Richard Burton. Genius and madness have a particular affinity for each other, my father says, which doesn't mean that there's not a whole lot of madness and only modest amounts of genius in the world. My great-grandfather had little formal education, but a wonderfully prehensile mind. He was a tolerable musician, a decent artist in the pen-drawing school, and spectacularly good with gadgets. One day, no one remembers why, he played the violin for eight straight hours. In doing this, he strained a nerve in his left hand from which it took him some weeks to recover. This lack of music brought about a period of frustration and general twitchiness that just about drove his wife crazy. "Go take a walk," she told him. "Learn to ride a bicycle."

The bicycle is a wonderfully designed machine. My great-grandfather had been enchanted with them from the very start. Riding them was a different matter. He came back with a sprained ankle and had to be put to bed. The situation reached crisis proportions.

But one morning, when his wife took him his breakfast, she found him calm and clear-eyed, scribbling away on the inside covers of several books. "Are you aware that most of the world is underwater?" he asked her. "What mountains we have never climbed. What caves we have never explored. What jungles!" The year was 1910. My great-grandfather had suddenly noticed that women were about to get the vote. When that happened, he believed, they would embark on a devastating national shopping spree. In anticipation, he was looking to get out of paying his taxes. The first tax-time after women got the vote he planned to spend safely underwater.

The big surprise was that he actually built her. He started

with a thirty-inch model he could maneuver through the rain barrel. It was propelled by a spring and the insides of a pocket watch. The fourteen-foot version used a bicycle chain and pedals. Pitch and direction were controlled by levers in the nose. These were adjusted by hand. To propel the boat took all four limbs. It took strength and coordination. It took practice. She was merely a prototype. My great-grandfather was a family man; the final submarine was supposed to be large enough to hold his wife and son. This early model he called *The New Day*, in honor of Day, the tragic inventor of an early sub.

Day's version was much like an ordinary boat, only it had an airtight chamber inside. Day occupied the chamber and then his associates sank the boat by piling more than thirty tons of stones on it. It worked like a dream. But the same associates were less zealous in raising the craft. Day was sealed tight in his chamber and could only be brought up by removing the stones, which were now under several yards of water. This required divers and continuous effort. Somehow, there was a miscommunication between the associates. Each thought the other was organizing the ascent, each had private and pressing business elsewhere. Day never was recovered. It was a story and a name that made my great-grandmother very nervous.

Great-grandfather worked with *The New Day* every weekend in the Passaic River. He grounded her three times before he made the crossing. The locals began to plan picnics with roast corn and sack races around his field trials. He would emerge from the craft to cheers and toasts. It was, undoubtedly, a happy time for him. But at the end of the last trial run, he told his wife he had seen a man watching him with binoculars from behind a tree. He came home upset, agitated. A week later, *The New Day* disappeared. "So the Fenians have her at last," he said calmly. "And a very bad day indeed to the man who tries her out."

Another week passed and then he disappeared himself. Because of the timing, his family believed that his talk of losing the submarine had been a ruse, and that he had finally taken *The New Day* down. "Those underwater mountains," Grams told me her mother-in-law said to her once, years later. "You'd have to climb them downwards." It was the sort of thing you might say if you'd given it a whole lot of thought. She waited a long time for him to surface.

I'll tell you what I think. A submarine can't have been cheap and he had a fiddler's salary. Where did he get the money to build *The New Day*? No one in the family knows, but it's my belief that the paranoid delusions which began to haunt him were neither paranoid nor delusionary. "Went over the edge," was the way the family finally chose to explain it, but "sleeps with the fishes" is the phrase that comes to my mind.

Years later, after he was declared dead, and his wife had also died, and also his son, my grandmother received a letter from an attorney. His client was a man in upstate New York, one James Fortis, who had known my great-grandfather. One night my great-grandfather had come to him and asked that he hide *The New Day* in his barn, to prevent her, he said, from falling into the wrong hands. He made Mr. Fortis swear never to speak of it, since those who wanted the boat were cunning, relentless, and well connected. He would be back for her soon, my great-grandfather had said, and had gone in a hurry, looking right and left.

Out of friendship, Mr. Fortis had agreed, and had kept the secret, although the years dragged on and the space taken up by the submarine, according to the letter, could have held four additional cows. But now Mr. Fortis was an elderly man with medical expenses. He was selling the farm and he wished to be rid of the submarine. His attorney had determined that the sub belonged to Grams. Included in the letter was a bill for thirty-five years of storage. In addition, the sub had to be shipped all the way across the country. It took a chunk of change.

Grams moved her car out of the garage and the submarine in. "A person with a submarine will never lack for friends," she was fond of telling me, and, of course, someday the submarine was to be mine.

I wonder sometimes about my grandmother as a young woman and when I think it through, the Betty Crocker stuff seems just as remarkable as the Betty Freidan. She was a war widow with a young child. That Betty Crocker my father remembers, she must have been made with guilt, smoke, and mirrors. Grams never remarried although even in her sixties there were opportunities. I see now that my grandmother must have spent her whole life desperately in love with a dead man.

One of the times I asked about my grandfather, Grams

showed me a map. It was made of nylon, mostly white, but printed with a grid and a number of curving red arrows. Along the base of the grid were the words *Map of the Marianas Islands.* And if you looked closely, you might actually be able to find the islands, green flea specks in the enormous expanse of white ocean.

So it was, in fact, a map of air and water. It had been commissioned by the War Department, which gave it to pilots during the war in the Pacific. The arrows showed the currents and wind patterns. The theory was that if a pilot was shot down he could calculate his last known position, catch the nearest current, and float to land. The War Department, having the same map, would know where to look for him. It gave me a sense of vertigo, trying to imagine what it would be like, falling into that featureless landscape with nothing to secure you but that featureless map.

At the time of my extractions, while I lay on her couch and wrapped myself in her afghan, and a phantom bird pecked rhythmically into the sorest part of my jaw, Grams was already suffering from the first signs of Alzheimer's. I don't know if she knew this; certainly she was far too cunning to be caught at it. Three years later it was unmistakable. She got lost on the way to the corner market and she couldn't remember my mother's name. "Eleanor," Dad reminded her. "Ellie. Why did you always tell people Ellie was much too good for me?" Growing up as he did, with only the two of them, many things were tangled between them. He was hastily trying to settle what he could in those lucid moments before she disappeared.

"I was being charmingly modest," she said.

I was off at college by now and paying little attention. She moved in with my parents for a while and then Dad called to tell me Grams had gone into a home. Not only did this move break her heart, it also emptied her bank accounts. Her house would have to be sold. Angel was staying on with my father and mother and was no happier about it than Grams. It was a short phone call with a number of silences.

The next time I talked to my father he seemed better. "They've prescribed a pill for paranoia," he told me. "But she's too suspicious to take it." The nurses were in an uproar. My father was obviously charmed.

By the time I got to see her it was Christmas break. I'd come home and Dad and I had gone over together. By now she was taking her medications. "She's being a good girl today," the nurse told us. "She's being an angel."

Grams was wearing a robe printed with little yellow flowers although she had never been a little-yellow-flower kind of person. Her hair stuck out around her ears as if no one had brushed it. I gave her a box of chocolate turtles to which she was indifferent. She didn't seem to know I was there. Perhaps I was not the person she loved best in all the world, after all. I was content at this time to give up the honor to my father. "How are you?" Grams asked him.

"I'm good."

"And how are your father and mother?"

"My father's fine," said Dad. "But we're a little worried about Mom."

The whole time we were there, we could hear another woman down the hall. "Help me, please. Help me, please," she sobbed in a continuous rhythmical plea.

"That goes on all the time," my dad told me. "Like she was frozen in some moment of torment." His eyes were cracked with red, and glassy. "At least that's not Mom." When we got in the car to drive home, he mentioned the sobbing woman again. "I just keep thinking, what if it's something simple? What if she just needs her socks pulled up or a glass of water or something. What if it was something we could fix, but she's forgotten how to say it?"

My father had joined the Food Not Bombs people. When we went back to the house, there were stacks of pamphlets in the living room. Angel lay in the sunshine on top of one and raised her head crossly at the disturbance. "Now we see the real danger of this three-strikes nonsense," my father said. "Now that they want to make it a felony to feed people." He pitched his voice to match that of the Wicked Witch of the West. "What a world, what a world," he said.

The Great Unknown had also gone to the nursing home to visit with my grandmother, and afterward he dropped by the house to see me as well. He was calling himself Carroll Leary now. "Where's the submarine?" he asked me, almost immediately, so I was cautious when I answered; it occurred to me that Leary was an Irish name and that Carroll had always been extremely interested in *The New Day*. It would be so like Grams to play bridge with the IRA. I just said she was in storage, and that she was mine now.

In fact, she was right where he left her, back in the mud on the floor of Lake Emily. Grams was able to keep her, because she was a hidden asset, and she's mine, all right, any time I can raise the money to raise her. "I hope you handle it as gracefully as your grandmother always did. She didn't choose it, you know. She married into it," said Carroll. He gave me a look. Don't ask me what kind of look. I could never read him. "It's an enormous responsibility, owning a submarine," he said.

My father joined us. "It's an enormous lack of responsibility," he argued. "When you have a boat, you don't need a plan"—but I know what my grandmother would want. Someday I'll hoist her up, take her down, join Greenpeace. When I get older, say around menopause, I'll become a pirate, harry the shipping lanes along the coast. When I'm really old I'll settle in the Marianas Islands.

That night I slept again in my old bedroom in my parents' house. I hadn't been there for a while and I woke once during the night, completely disoriented. It was so dark, even though I'd been sleeping, even though my night vision was fully engaged, I couldn't see. The first thing you need to know is where you are. I had to imagine shapes around me; I had to make up a context. I closed my eyes and I went on imagining. I made myself hear voices around me, hushed so as not to wake me, and hands stroking my hair, straightening my blankets. The bed began to rock, like a boat, like a cradle. Then I got lucky; I was home. I fell asleep again and it was a slow, sweet descent.

Workshop Comments

Richard Butner: "Asking for changes to this story is like asking for wings on a greyhound. Don't change it."

James Patrick Kelly: "I love this story; it is practically perfect. I was uneasy about the narrator's age, sex, and position in time, but these mild qualms come only after waves of pleasure and *envy*."

Carol Emshwiller: "I just love this. That's all I have to say. I love this! I think you ought to have a big grant, and one that would keep 'life' out of your way, too—at least a little bit."

Michaela Roessner: "An exquisitely painful and subtle rendering of the losing but necessary battle against loss."

Greg Frost: "Karen Fowler stands between Thurber and Blaylock, with benign lunacy in a cross-generational tale, both funny and quietly sad and respectful. Page 62's tense shift doesn't work and is in effect violated later as it turns out not to be the most 'present' of all sections. The line summing it all up for me is on page 64: 'What I do believe in is the desperate fight against the perils of routine living that they all represent.' The Great Unknown is *always* visiting, isn't it?"

Maureen McHugh: "It is an elliptical and evasive story. The ending, where the narrator claims the sunken submarine, makes it clear that the story is the narrator's but most of the rest of the story is not. Except for the scene where the narrator lies on the couch recovering from dental surgery, she exists in the story only as the sensibility that orders the story. But still, for me, it works. It is seamless.

"I resist critique. 'We murder to dissect' —Wordsworth."

Bruce Sterling: "The godlike genius of Karen Fowler defies the critical calipers."

Bob Frazier: "To me this story is a Saki game. I got a totally spin-dizzy take on this. A characterless character tells us all about her eccentric family—most of it lies. Lies because she believes in nothing romantic, is trapped into a pragmatic rut, and must invent utopia to escape a seeming 'Hell of the Benign.' I think to make this Saki game work on the reader, the last paragraph needs to be in present tense, a structural signal to send us back to the key on page 64 that unlocks the story—the sentence 'You have to envy anyone with the means to make a clean escape.' "

Alexander Jablokov: "In stating a critique of this story, I feel like someone critiquing a magician demonstrating a woman floating in midair. I look for wires—there are no wires. I look for a crane—no crane. Eventually the woman floats out over the audience and out a window, leaving me openmouthed, calipers and flashlight in hand, standing alone onstage. A superb story, pain under family eccentricities, and I am very impressed.

"That said, I have a few nits and one reluctant suggestion. I feel like there is one emotional confrontation missing. Grams' Alzheimer's is gentle, which is all right. But she fades gently and politely out of the story. I think Leary is there to take Grams away on page 69. I don't want to push the tragedy too far into the foreground, but I want a sense of reading that is sharper than what is there. So, in this scene they *take* her to the home, rather than having her already be there."

Nancy Kress: "I actually have no idea how to critique this. I have modest nits . . . but they are just nits. Otherwise, the formless shape, superb language, and deft emotional note escape criticism. I loved it. This doesn't seem much help to have traveled three thousand miles for, but there it is."

Jonathan Lethem: "I know how useless this is, but it's simply the only thing I can say—this piece is pure pleasure for me and I don't think you need to change more than a word or two. I can't say what you've accomplished, but it's magic."

Mark Van Name: "I absolutely loved this funny yet dark story. To me, it is a gem: no matter how you hold it to the light, it glows richly and interestingly."

John Kessel: "Beautiful. A quiet, funny, terrifying story about irrevocable loss, how people we love disappear without a trace. Ending with a foreboding of our own eventual loss.

"I'm amazed, as always, at the way seemingly casual details turn out to be absolutely essential, how actual becomes metaphorical without ever giving up its heartbreaking actuality. This author loves life."

Afterword to "The Marianas Islands"

For a few days every couple of summers, I am allowed to live in an alternate universe where books and reading are important. Naturally it feels very unreal. I look forward to Sycamore Hill as my own private Brigadoon, an effect Nancy Kress and I attempt to heighten through the week with our own unique stylings of Broadway show tunes. By the time my work comes up for critique, I believe it is, by virtue of contrast, a bit of a relief.

Others have referred to the workshop as a summer camp for writers, or a week in Biosphere 2. I come to North Carolina from California, at the parched end of summer, and there's always a thunderstorm, something straight out of Brontë, and if I'm really lucky it happens sometime during the week itself, and not when I'm in the air. I sleep very little and drink enormous quantities of Coca-Cola so I have a nice edge for the critique table. I lose track of the date, and of major political movements and sporting events.

The actual setting has often been otherworldly. We used to meet at the School for the Blind and live without mirrors for a week. This year our critiques took place in the abandoned Merry Monk bar, as if we were the last correspondents out of Vietnam. I missed the announcement concerning the demise of the answering machine and believed, blissfully, all week that my family was doing fine without me. The only outside news important enough to break through the cone of silence was Michael Jackson's marriage to Lisa Marie Presley. Our source was Nancy Sterling. I wouldn't have believed it had it come from anyone else. The announcement made the actual fiction seem sadly unimaginative.

The day you get critiqued is awkward. People avoid you at lunch; conversations seem to stop abruptly when you approach. We sit in a circle and critique from the writer's left on around, so if you are looking for bad signs, you watch to see how much trouble people are having choosing a seat. I have been in many workshops, and in this particular workshop every year except for the infamous first year when no girls were allowed and it was really fun. So I've heard many of these same people critique some sixty stories and yet I never have a clue what they're going to say about mine until they've said it. Even then it's sometimes hard to believe.

I won the unofficial award this year for hardest story to critique, but I got a lot out of my session. More than I realized at the time, which is nice. So often—as you must know if you've been in workshops yourself—so often it works the other way around. I am always surprised that, for someone who passes as educated, I can make so many mistakes. My colleagues made corrections that were botanical and historical, medical and literary, as well as pointing out that I had named a character Carroll O'Connor, which was surely a misstep.

To read through the official responses, you would think hardly a critical word was spoken. In fact, my colleagues wondered about the narrator's ghostliness, but had more difficulty with the tardy specificity of the word *menopause.* They questioned the plausibility of a Betty Crocker–like war widow and they discussed my inexplicable tense changes.

The name Thurber came up quickly. I was actually aiming for Thurber—having just reread *My Life and Hard Times,* but one doesn't want to be *transparent* about it. The other name invoked was Blaylock. I was told that I had written science fiction in the Blaylockian, "is that a dinosaur I see in the shadows?" mode.

In the rewrite, I have added some bits about Grams' life as a single mother, toughened up the Alzheimer's, and erased some of my more riotous tense changes. Others I left. I can give you a plausible, if unpersuasive excuse for the tense shifts that remain, but the truth is that they just felt right and I was unhappy when I removed them. Magical and masterful, or annoying and artsy-fartsy? You be the judge!

I have spent a great deal of time fussing with the final paragraph, more time than I spent dealing with anything else. I was told it suffered from excessive poetic compression. I wondered how much of the effect hinged on the single but critical word *sweet.* I tried removing it. I put it back. I took it out. I rearranged some sentences as suggested by Sterling. I put the word *sweet* back in.

The final and most intriguing issue was my use of SF tropes—the mad inventor, the submarine. Was it a problem that I took the fun stuff of science fiction, the zip, the doo-dah, and twisted them to my own private purposes until they represented madness and death? Was it fair to the field? Didn't I do this a lot?

What if everyone did it?

I am still working out the answer.

Karen Joy Fowler

Sex Education

NANCY KRESS

WHEN THE PEOPLE came, Mollie was playing in the backyard with Emily Gowan. They'd made an excellent fort out of the picnic table turned on its side and backed up to the wooden fence. From behind the table they could throw Kooshballs, which were too soft and floppy to hurt, at Brandy. He wagged his tail and peered around in this funny way that sent Mollie and Emily into giggles. Mariah Carey played on Emily's boom box. Mollie threw another Kooshball, orange and yellow. She didn't realize then that these weren't actually the first people; that there had been others.

"Mollie, dear, turn off the music and say hello to some friends of mine," Mommy said. She balanced on the grass in high heels, which sank into the dirt a half-inch. It was weird that Mommy was dressed in her receptionist clothes in the middle of a Saturday morning. Usually she just wore jeans. Mollie came out from her fort.

"Hi."

"Hello, there," the man said heartily. He wasn't dressed up like Mommy, but he wore a big ring on his right hand. "I'm Mr. Berringer, and this is Mrs. Berringer."

"Call me Susie," the woman said to Mollie. She had long fluffy blonde hair and lines on her neck. Mollie wasn't supposed to call adults by their first names, which she thought was a stupid rule. She smiled at Mommy: *See?*

"Hi, Susie."

"My, you're a pretty little thing. Look at those eyes, Tom. And those gorgeous curls! Her hair is almost exactly the same color as mine!"

"Yeah," Mr. Berringer said. "Mollie, I'd like to ask you some questions, and I want you to answer truthfully, like a good girl. Mrs. Carter, I'd rather talk to Mollie alone, please."

Mollie looked at Mommy. Why should she have to answer this man's questions? But Mommy just nodded and went back into the house, her heels making a line of little holes in the grass. Brandy bounced up with a Kooshball in his mouth.

"This is Brandy," Mollie said. "And my friend Emily Gowan."

The Berringers didn't say hi to Emily. Susie said, "Tom, don't let that dog drool on my dress!"

"Chill, Sue. Your damn dress is fine. Now, Mollie, are you ever sick?"

"Sick?" Mollie said. "You mean, like with a cold?"

"With anything."

"I had the chicken pox when I was little." She glanced at Emily. What business was it of his if she was ever sick? Emily looked down at her Reeboks. Brandy thrust the drippy Kooshball into Mollie's hand.

"Did you miss any school last year because you got sick?" Mr. Berringer asked.

"No."

"The year before that?"

"No."

"Do you have a lot of friends?"

"Yes." Mollie scanned the house. Mommy stood in the kitchen window, watching.

"Who are your best friends?"

"Emily. Jennifer Sawicki. Sarah Romano."

"Do you ever get mad at your friends?"

Mollie glanced sideways at Emily. "Sometimes."

"Really, really mad? Enough to hit them?"

"No."

"Do you ever get really, really mad at your parents?"

"No."

"Not *ever*?"

"*No*," Mollie said. She looked again to make sure Mommy was still in the window.

"Are you strong? Can you run fast?"

"I won the Third Grade Field Day race at school."

"Did you!" Mr. Berringer said. "Hear that, Suze?"

"I hear it." Susie smiled at Mollie, who didn't smile back. Mr. Berringer said, "Do you like school?"

"Yes," Mollie said.

"Who was your teacher last year? Did you like her?"

"Mrs. Stallman. She was okay."

"What's your favorite subject?"

"Science." Mollie threw the Kooshball for Brandy. He bounded after it.

"Tell me one thing you learned last year in science."

Mollie wanted to say *"Why?"* but she wasn't supposed to be rude to adults. Even when *they* were. She said, "We learned about the sun. We learned it stays hot because atoms smash together so hard they get joined up, and you get a new kind of atom and a lot of heat and light. It's called fusion." Brandy brought her back the Kooshball, wetter than ever.

"Good!" Mr. Berringer said. "Fine! What was the lowest mark on your last report card, Mollie?"

"I got a B in social studies. All the rest were A's."

The Berringers went on smiling at her. Mollie threw the ball again so she wouldn't have to look at them.

"Well, it's been good meeting you, Mollie," Mr. Berringer said. "Come on, Sue."

"Such incredibly blue eyes," Susie murmured.

When they'd gone, Emily said, "Who *were* those creepy people?"

"I don't know. Friends of my mother's, I guess. Let's go play Nintendo." She wanted to go inside and close the door of her room.

Emily said, "Did you see his diamond ring? They must be really rich."

Mollie didn't answer. Mommy wasn't in the kitchen; she'd

walked the Berringers to their car. On the table lay all Mollie's
report cards, along with a bunch of other papers. The third-grade
report lay open on the top of the pile. Her B in social studies was
printed clearly in Mrs. Stallman's purple ink.

Just after Christmas, when Mollie was halfway through the
fourth grade, her mother knocked on Mollie's bedroom door.
Mommy looked serious. Had she found out about the paint that
Mollie and Emily had spilled in the garage? They'd cleaned it all
up with some stuff from Emily's basement. Almost all up.

"Mollie, there are some people coming this afternoon to talk
to you. To ask you some questions," Mommy said. She had a
piece of paper in her hand.

"People? What for?"

"It doesn't matter. Just answer all their questions politely.
And wear your blue dress. But that's not what I want to talk to
you about. I got a letter from your school."

So it wasn't the paint. Mollie tried to think what had happened at school before Christmas vacation. She couldn't remember anything bad. Mommy sat on the bed and patted the bedspread beside her. Mollie sat down.

"Mollie—" Mommy started, then stopped. She breathed
deep and looked around the room, like she didn't know what to
say next. Scared now, Mollie looked around, too. Her bedroom
was pretty, with a new canopy bed and a white dresser with a big
mirror and her own CD player. The whole house had been
redecorated at the end of last summer, the same time Daddy
bought the big new car.

"Mollie, this letter says your class will start sex education
next semester. And before you do, I want to explain to you myself how babies get born. It's my responsibility to explain to you,
not the school's."

Mollie clasped her hands in her lap and studied her fingers.
She already knew about sex. Alexandra McCandless, who was in
the fifth grade, told her and Emily and Jennifer Sawicki, in Jennifer's tree house. But not Sarah Romano. Alexandra made them
all say "Fuck the holy ghost" before she'd tell them anything,
and Sarah wouldn't say it, so she had to leave. But Mollie wasn't
going to tell any of that to Mommy.

"When a man and a woman are married," Mommy said, "they lie in bed very close together and the man puts his penis in the woman's vagina. Little seeds go from him into her, and sometimes one of his seeds joins up with a little egg that's already in her body."

"Oh," Mollie said, because Mommy seemed to expect her to say something. "Like fusion."

"Like what?"

"Fusion. You know, in the sun. Two atoms smash together into each other, and they make a new kind of atom and a lot of energy."

Mommy smiled. "Well, I don't know if a sperm and egg 'smash together' exactly, but I guess it's sort of the same."

"Can I go now?"

"In a minute. The egg grows inside the woman until the baby's ready to be born."

Mollie blurted, "Does it hurt?"

"Does sex hurt?"

"No," Mollie said. She already knew that sex hurt, but only the first time. Alexandra McCandless said so. There was blood and crying and burning like you were on fire. After that it felt better than anything in the world and you would do anything to have it every night. "Does the baby getting born hurt?"

Mommy hesitated, which meant yes. "No, not really. There's some discomfort, but it's all worth it when you see your perfect little baby."

"Okay. Now can I go?"

"Mollie, don't be so impatient! I'm trying to explain something important here!"

"You explained it already."

"Well, there's more." Mommy pushed her hair back from her face and looked at her fingernails. "Sometimes a woman's egg and a man's sperm can't seem to join by themselves, for different reasons. So scientists help. They join a sperm from the father to an egg from the mother in a test tube, and when they're sure the two are really joined, they put the egg back in the mother."

"Oh," Mollie said. Alexandra hadn't said anything about this. How did they put the egg back in? Did they have to cut the woman open? Suddenly Mollie didn't want to know. "Is that all? Emily's waiting for me."

"If you'd just sit still and listen for even five minutes—"

So there was more. Mollie said, "I'm sorry, Mommy. But Emily's *waiting.*"

"Oh, Mollie, why do you make it so hard lately for me to talk to you?"

"I don't!"

"Yes, you do. And this is important. Your daddy and I have been saving money for your college education, you know we want you to be able to go—"

"Yes, yes," Mollie said, because she didn't want to hear yet again about how Mommy and Daddy couldn't go to college but Mollie must and so it was her responsibility to work hard at school. And make something of her life. And be the best Mollie she could be.

"It's so *complicated,*" Mommy said. "We do the best we can."

"I know you do," Mollie said. If *she'd* used that tone, Mommy would have called it whining.

Mommy looked at her helplessly, and Mollie smiled, kissed her mother, and escaped.

She'd have to get Jennifer to ask Alexandra McCandless back to the tree house. But Jennifer didn't like Alexandra since they had a fight over Luke Perry, so maybe Jennifer wouldn't do it.

Maybe Mollie wouldn't have to know any more just yet.

In February she turned ten. In March she got a new bike, a ten-speed, and an A on her project on the solar system. In April Alexandra's period started and she demonstrated to Mollie and Jennifer and Emily how to put in a tampon; Mollie thought the whole thing was gross. In May, a truck pulled up beside Mollie when she and Emily were walking home from the library, and two people jumped out.

"There she is! Hey, Mollie, look this way!"

A camera flashed. A man in a suit shoved a microphone at her while a woman wearing jeans and carrying a camcorder walked backward in front of Mollie and Emily.

"Mollie, have you heard about the lawsuit the Berringers have filed about your embryonic clone?"

Mollie stared. What was an embryonic clone? She remembered the Berringers, from last summer. Susie said Mollie's hair was the same color as hers. Beside her, Emily clutched Mollie's hand.

The man said, "Clones were made of your embryo, Mollie. Before you were born. Twelve of them. Five have been sold and implanted so far—"

"Roger," the woman with the camcorder said, "maybe we shouldn't . . . You're scaring her."

"I'm not scared!" Mollie said, although she was. She squeezed Emily's hand.

"Good girl," the man said. "The babies born are just like you, Mollie, they're made of your genes. Didn't your parents tell you this? No? Except, the last baby was born with something wrong with it—Kelly, keep filming!"

"No," the woman said. "I didn't expect . . . Mollie, you go on home, honey."

"Damn it, Kelly, keep filming! We can edit it to her reaction!"

"*Look* at her! Mollie, go on home!"

Mollie bolted, dragging Emily with her. More people with microphones and cameras waited outside the house. "There she is!"

Mollie let go of Emily's hand. "Run, Emily!" Emily rushed to her own house. Then Mollie's father was there, lifting Mollie in his arms like she was still a little girl. He fought his way through the people, who shouted at him.

"Mr. Carter, what legal liability do you think you have for—"

"Is the rumor that something went wrong at Veritech going to affect your defense in—"

"Is Mollie aware of—"

Daddy carried Mollie through the front door and slammed it. "Irresponsible assholes! They should all be shot!"

Mollie wriggled free. "What's going on? Why are these people here!"

"Mollie, sweetheart—"

"Why, Mommy? What's an embryonic clone? Tell me!"

Her mother knelt on the floor beside Mollie. "I *tried* to tell you, Mollie. More than once. Remember, we had the first talk in your bedroom, and you didn't want—"

"This isn't your responsibility, Mollie," her father broke in. "And not ours, either. We just wanted to give you the best life we could. And the Berringers couldn't have a baby of their own, so we were helping them to have one just as perfect as you are. And for that good deed they're blaming *us*!"

"You're upsetting her, Paul."

"The *situation* is upsetting her! Those jackals outside, those assholes—"

"But what's an embryonic clone?" Mollie cried.

Her mother said, "It's when a sperm and an egg are joined in a scientist's laboratory, like I told you. Only instead of putting the embryo in the mommy right away, the scientists make it divide first, to get more just like it. Like . . . like making Xerox copies. Do you understand, Mollie?"

Mollie nodded. She felt calmer now, listening. This made sense.

Mommy stayed kneeling next to her. "Your extra embryos helped other people have babies just as wonderful as you. Only with the Berringers' baby, something went wrong while it was growing inside Mrs. Berringer. We never realized . . . never dreamed . . ."

Mollie said, "I see." Outside, more cars pulled up. "Only—"

"Only what, honey?" Mommy stood up, pushing her dark hair off her face.

"Only how will we get out with all those cars in the driveway?"

"Get out? Get out where?"

"Out of the garage!" Mollie said.

Daddy looked puzzled. "Why would we want to get out of the garage?"

"To go get the baby. The one the Berringers don't want."

Mommy and Daddy stared at her.

"The baby that's me," Mollie said.

They went on staring at her.

"Oh," Mollie said. "*Oh . . .*"

"Mollie. Honey . . ."

Mollie ran to her room and locked the door.

"You come back here!" Daddy called.

Her curtains were closed, but she could hear the reporters out on the sidewalk, talking and shouting questions. Mommy knocked but didn't try to force the door open.

Later, when Brandy scratched at her door, Mollie let him in. She sat on the bed hugging him hard, her ear pressed against his soft red fur.

Mommy and Daddy kept trying to talk to her about it. They kept explaining how they weren't responsible. Mollie had to listen, but she didn't have to say anything back, and she didn't.

After a few weeks, Mommy said they were taking Mollie to a therapist.

The reporters had gone away from the house. Mollie didn't go to school. She played with Brandy, and with Emily and Jennifer after school. Mollie could see they didn't want to talk about all this weird stuff, so she didn't. They just played Nintendo and Barbies and *Where in the World is Carmen Sandiego?* on Emily's father's computer.

Mollie traded her Barbie, which had black hair and green eyes, for Jennifer's, which was blonde with blue eyes.

Mollie wasn't allowed to watch TV except when Mommy was in the living room. The newspaper stopped coming. When Mommy talked on the phone she always used the phone in her bedroom, and she locked the door. Mollie lifted the receiver in the kitchen very carefully, so Mommy wouldn't know she was there.

"—filed this morning," her father's voice said. "Both our countersuits. The one against Veritech claims negligence as the cause of the birth defect. Bad refrigeration or deficient procedure, or something."

"Do you think that happened?" her mother asked.

"God, Libby, you can't express doubt now! You'll probably have to testify!"

"I know. Go on."

"Rizetti says Veritech will undoubtedly claim an implied risk in the procedure, even beyond what our contract specified, with neither fraud nor guarantee applicable. They'll ask for the case to be dismissed. Our countersuit against the Berringers includes asking for them to pay our court costs. After all, the baby is their problem, not ours, and they shouldn't saddle us with any negative consequences arising from it when we honored the contract completely. How's Mollie? Does she go to that therapist this afternoon?"

"At three. I'm so worried about her, Paul."

"Me, too."

"I tried to explain again to her that the cloned embryos are no different than delayed twinning, but she won't even listen to me. She stands there, but she's not really listening."

"Poor kid. It's those fucking irresponsible reporters!"

"I know."

"Call me after the appointment."

Mollie carefully set down the phone. By the time Mommy came to look for her, she was reading *Boxcar Children* in the living room.

The therapist was an old woman in a big, high-ceilinged room with rows of bookshelves. Her face was kind. She and Mollie sat facing each other in blue armchairs.

"A lot has happened to you in the last few weeks, Mollie."

"I guess," Mollie said.

"Some of it sounds a little bit scary."

Mollie didn't answer. She studied her hands lying in her lap. She'd painted the tips of the fingernails gold with polish borrowed from Emily's big sister. The nails looked like small faces with short blonde hair.

"Are you feeling a little bit scared by everything that's happened?" the therapist said.

"I don't know."

"I think *I'd* be a little frightened."

"I guess."

"Do you miss going to school?"

"I don't know."

"You can return to school if you want to, Mollie. You have the right to make that decision for yourself."

Again Mollie didn't answer. She studied the tiny faces on her fingers. Ten of them.

"Mollie," the therapist said gently, "do you believe your parents love you?"

Mollie looked at the rows of books. Many of them had the same color backs, like they were part of a set. "Yes. They love me."

"And how does that—"

"They think I'm perfect."

"And how—"

"I want to go home now," Mollie said. She stood, leaving the therapist sitting by herself in the blue chair.

At home she closed her bedroom door and dragged her desk chair in front of it. Leaning toward her dresser mirror, she studied herself, in her sleeveless Esprit tee. Blue eyes, blonde curls, white even teeth. She knew she was pretty. And strong, and smart. And now there were five other baby Mollies someplace who were also pretty and strong and smart. Except for the one that wasn't.

And it wasn't anybody's fault, they all said. It wasn't Mommy and Daddy's fault because they were just helping the Berringers to have a baby like Mollie. It wasn't the scientists' fault because they were just helping, too. It wasn't the Berringers' fault because they didn't ask to have a baby that wasn't perfect. It wasn't the court's fault because somebody else had to pay the court money. No one was responsible.

But the clone baby, made out of Mollie's egg, wasn't pretty and strong and smart, and all the while Mollie knew whose responsibility that really was.

It was hers.

She waited until Daddy had left for work and Mommy was in the shower. She dressed in jeans and a sweater, pushed her hair up under a Buffalo Bills cap, and put on sunglasses. Although she didn't exactly look like a kid who had a good reason for not being in school, she didn't look like a dork, either, which she would have in her blue dress. She put some things in her backpack, took thirty dollars from her mother's purse, and locked Brandy in the garage so he wouldn't follow her.

The address had been in the newspapers at Emily's house. PROTOTYPE EMBRYOS ON TRIAL, one paper said. And HOW MUCH IS THAT BABY IN THE WINDOW? And, in a paper with very big lettering and lots of pictures, SHELLPORT SHIRLEY TEMPLE FLOPS IN RERUN.

Mollie had never taken the bus from Shellport to the city, but she'd seen it leave from in front of the park. She stood close to a woman in a flowered dress, and put the same amount of money in the slot that the woman had. No one noticed her.

The bus took forty minutes to get to the downtown terminal, which was just outside a mall. A lot more people pushed and shoved, but there were also more kids by themselves. Mollie went up to a woman in a pretty red suit carrying a briefcase.

"What bus do I take to get to Gerard Street?"

The woman smiled at her. "I'm not sure. You can ask inside." She pointed.

There was no line at the bus window. Heart hammering, Mollie asked her question.

"Bus Twenty. Leaves from slot six. You want to buy tokens?"

She hesitated. "Yes, please. Two."

Outside, she found slot 6. There was a long bench to wait on, but one end was occupied by three loud teenage boys. She stood by slot 5.

The bus was full of kids carrying book bags that said SISTERS OF MERCY JUNIOR HIGH. Some of them weren't any bigger than Mollie. "So he laid this bitch at Christmas vacation and now she's knocked up," a boy said. "And my friend said—"

Mollie turned away, watching street signs.

Gerard Street was long. It changed from stores to rows of small houses to regular houses like Mollie's to very big places with fancy flower beds. At the end, only a few women in maids' uniforms were left on the bus with Mollie.

There were no reporters at the Berringers' house. Mollie moved across the wide lawn from tree to tree, staying hidden. In the front was a big screened porch. She peered through the wire mesh; nobody there.

The back door wasn't locked.

Mollie wiped her hands on her jeans. They were sweaty, but cold. Her eyes burned. It was wrong to go into somebody's house. But not as wrong as everything else.

She left the back door open, and listened. No sounds. And then, somewhere to her left, a baby fussing.

The baby wasn't in a real nursery, like Jennifer's baby brother had. Instead there was a portacrib in the kitchen; maybe Susie had been cooking while she watched the baby. But the kitchen was empty. Through a window Mollie saw a woman in a side garden, picking daffodils. The woman wore a white uniform. She wasn't Susie.

Mollie walked slowly to the crib. She felt funny, light and cold at the same time. What if the baby had two heads, or no arms, or half a head? How much bad genes had Mollie given it?

She stumbled toward the crib.

The baby looked normal. It had blue eyes, and blonde fuzz, and was impossibly tiny. It was fussing a little, but not much.

The refrigerator turned on with a sudden clank, and the baby jumped and screwed up its face.

Mollie picked her up in her blankets. She knew to support the baby's head, because of Jennifer's baby brother. The baby stopped fussing. Mollie ran back through the house and out the door. The baby, held up against her shoulder, felt light. On the street, she started back toward the bus stop. This time, nobody else waited for the bus.

A man in a green track suit jogged toward her. Mollie gathered herself up to run, but the man smiled and said, "Out for a walk with your dolly?" and kept on going.

When the bus came, Mollie tried to hold the baby like a doll. The baby was getting heavier.

Halfway to the city, the baby began to wail. A few people glanced at her. Mollie kept her sunglasses on and jiggled the baby against her shoulder. It still cried. At the downtown stop, the bus driver started to say something to her, but Mollie hurried down the steps and ran into the mall.

In here nobody looked at her, even though the baby cried loudly. She went into a Rite Aid and bought some bottles with formula already in them, plus a package of Huggies. In the mall she sat on a bench and fed the bottle to the baby. A few women smiled at her, but nobody spoke until a black girl also carrying a baby sat down next to her.

"You be stuck with your brother, too?"

Mollie hesitated. "Sister."

The girl sighed. "Your mama working?"

"Yes."

"Better than not working."

Mollie didn't answer. The other girl made her nervous. She was glad when after a few minutes the girl picked up her brother, who was old enough to hold a rattle, and drifted away.

Afterward, Mollie wished she'd talked to her longer.

The baby finished the bottle and fell asleep. Mollie laid her on the bench and broke open the box of Huggies. She stuffed as many as would fit into her backpack and left the rest in the box. Maybe the black girl would come back and take them.

She found a number 18 bus and rode home.

On her block, she crept through the backyards with the sleeping baby, moving from bushes to garages to fences. Kids were still in school, even the high-schoolers. Adults were at work. But her father's car was in the driveway, which meant her mother had called him to come home.

She crept to the cellar window, which she'd left unlatched. She laid the baby on the grass and slipped through the window onto Daddy's workbench. Then she pulled the baby through the window and carried her to the box behind the furnace, lined with a bedspread from the linen closet. Nobody went here since Mommy got the new washer and dryer in the new laundry room off the kitchen.

She changed the baby again and laid her in the box. Mollie still couldn't see anything wrong with the baby. She had all her toes and everything. While Mollie changed her, the baby woke up and regarded Mollie from big blue eyes the same shape as Mollie's own.

"Jessica," Mollie said. But that wasn't right. The baby didn't look like a Jessica. Ashley? Brittany? Nicole?

The baby regarded her solemnly. What was aortic stenosis?

"Don't cry," Mollie whispered. "Don't cry, Mollie."

She hid the diaper under an old sofa and snuck upstairs to her own room.

"One more time," her father said. He'd stopped shouting, but his face was still red. "Where were you for three hours?"

"In my room," Mollie said. Her throat hurt and her eyes burned.

"No, you weren't! Jesus Christ, Mollie, don't we have enough problems without you worrying everybody sick? It's your responsibility to tell your mother when you go out. Can't you act your age, for chrissakes?"

"Paul, calm down," Mollie's mother said. "Please."

"I was in my room," Mollie said. She wouldn't cry. She wouldn't.

"Mollie, you've never lied to us before," her mother said. *She* was crying. Mollie tried not to look at her. The door rang.

"Don't answer it, Paul," her mother said. "I don't want to see anybody just now."

Her father glanced at the window. "Christ, it's the cops."

Mollie looked at the dark window, but from this angle, all she could see was her own reflection. She looked instead at the floor. This part of the house wasn't over the furnace; only the fruit cellar was underneath her feet.

"Paul Carter? We'd like to ask you a few questions, please."

Mollie started to hum, so she wouldn't hear.

". . . disappeared this morning . . . whereabouts of both you and your wife . . . search the premises . . ."

She beamed the humming through the floor, down to the baby.

"Not without a warrant," her father said. "What the hell is this, anyway? Why would *I* have her? We're fighting a lawsuit to avoid having to raise her!"

—*in the treetop, when the wind blows*—

"What are you really after?" her father shouted. "We have a lawsuit pending against these people! You're not coming in without a search warrant!"

—*the cradle will rock*—

"You just do that!" her father said. The door closed.

—*when the bough breaks*—

"Not possible," her mother whispered, and even through her humming, Mollie heard her. She looked up. Mommy and Daddy both stared at her. She hated them.

"Mollie," her mother whispered, "where were you this morning?"

"I was in my room," Mollie said.

She sprawled across her bed and pretended to sleep. Her mother opened the door. Light slanted across the pretty carpet, the expensive canopy bed. AVERAGE COST OF TEST-TUBE BABY TOPS $80K, Emily's newspaper said. Mommy closed the door softly. A few minutes later Mollie went down to the basement.

The baby was crying. It was three hours since Mollie had fed her. Did babies always need to eat so soon? Mollie gave her another bottle and changed her diaper again. This time the diaper was poopy. Mollie got some on her hands. She breathed deep to keep from puking, and washed her hands in the old laundry tub.

But the baby was still crying. Mollie put her on her shoulder and walked, jouncing the baby with each step, the way she'd seen Jennifer's mother do. She hummed softly and patted the baby on the back. The baby stopped crying, but every time Mollie stopped walking, she started again.

"Please, sweet baby, please sweet baby . . ." Mollie crooned. Pretty soon it was a prayer, and then Mollie was crying, and the baby wouldn't stop crying, and Mollie's legs hurt but she had to keep going because nobody wanted this baby with the broken thing in her heart, nobody would accept the responsibility, and the baby was hers, was her, please sweet baby please sweet baby—

She was sobbing and walking and patting, and the baby was wailing, when feet clattered down the steps and her mother said, "Oh my God." The policeman holding a piece of paper didn't say anything, and Mollie couldn't see him clearly anyway because her eyes were burning, but even through the burning she suddenly saw the revolving light beyond the cellar window, red and blue and red again, mirrored in the metal side of the cold furnace.

"I don't care!" Mollie screamed. "You want her to die!"

"Nobody wants the baby to die, Mollie," her father said. His face was all smoothed out and his eyes were wide open, like he was very surprised by something. Brandy crouched beside him, his furry face on the floor. "You don't understand."

"I understand nobody wants her! She's made out of me, and nobody wants her!"

"She's not made out of you. She's . . ."

"Nobody loves her because she's not perfect! I'm the only one who will take care of her!"

"Mollie, the baby will be placed in a foster—"

"I hate you!" Mollie screamed.

Her father reached for her. Her mother, on the phone with the therapist, fumbled with the receiver and dropped it. Outside, the trucks and cars and vans of the reporters clogged the street. Mollie shoved her father away and ran upstairs. Brandy raced after her.

"Mollie, you come back here!" her father shouted.

She didn't. She ran past her own room and into her parents' bedroom. Her eyes burned. There was the bed they did it on, with the gold trim and the green bedspread. They made babies here, her father putting his penis into her mother . . . *fucking.* And then the people had come, all the people she'd answered questions for and looked pretty for . . . been perfect for . . . She grabbed her mother's nail scissors off the dresser and started hacking at her curls. Her father rushed into the room and started toward her.

She threw the nail scissors at him.

He stopped, gasping, even though the scissors had bounced off his arm.

"I hate you!" Mollie screamed. "You make babies out of me and don't love them when they're not . . . I'm not . . ."

Her father started toward her again. She grabbed a metal bookend and threw it at him. Then she grabbed the other one and threw it at the mirror, which shattered.

Her father gripped his arm. Her mother stood in the doorway with her fist in her mouth. Mollie flung everything around the room: clothes and drawers and books and pillows.

"I hate you!"

"Mollie! Stop it!" Her father, his arm bleeding, caught her and pinned her arms to her side. Another piece of the mirror fell out of the frame, into a silvery pile. Mollie could hear the baby cry even though the baby wasn't here anymore, the policeman had taken her away.

"Stop it! You hear me! Stop it!"

Crying and crying—

"Stop it! Mollie!"

She bit him hard.

He dropped her. Mollie backed away from him, suddenly calm. Downstairs, the baby cried.

Then the crying stopped.

In the abrupt silence, Mollie and her parents looked at each other. Her mother, dead white, said in a quavery voice, "Mollie, look at this room, you're . . . you're responsible for this mess . . ."

"No," Mollie said. "I'm not." And then, "Nobody is."

Brandy tried to lick her hand, but Mollie pushed the dog away. She walked to her own room and shut the door.

Workshop Comments

John Kessel: "This story works effectively, but comes perilously close to propaganda for me. The adults are all so greedy, irresponsible, insensitive, inhumane. The story is powerful, but too schematic for my tastes. Everything too tidily contributes to your message."

Karen Joy Fowler: "This is one of my favorite kinds of stories, in that it continues in my mind past the last page. Now the family has a child, just like the Berringers', who is not perfect, and they will have to learn to love her (or not) anyway.

"Because the real story takes place in the intimate family setting, I would cut the kidnapping, which seems unnecessary and melodramatic."

Robert Frazier: "I ate through this like mild salsa only to bite down hard on the last searing-hot mouthful. Don't condense this. I do think you can attenuate the emotional zinger here, though—which for me is the devastating effects of conditional love, of shattered love."

James Patrick Kelly: "This is a deft portrayal of life from a child's point of view, but the lines of good and evil are too clearly drawn. The violent outburst by Mollie at the end is way out of proportion to her situation and needs to be foreshadowed by darker behavior earlier on."

Richard Butner: "You've got to sell the central idea (embryonic clone sales) and all the attendant extrapolation, and right now I have too many questions about that idea. The narration by Mollie makes her seem alternately dumb and precious. Is Mollie falling apart psychologically? That's one possibility to look at."

Maureen McHugh: "I didn't initially see Bob and Karen's reading of this story, as a story about conditional love, but I had credibility problems with the abduction and with the relationship between Mollie and her parents. But this is a pretty demanding level of criticism. As it stands, the story is already strong, well-written, professional."

Bruce Sterling: "This story evokes such painful wretchedness and humiliation and furtive shame that it brilliantly conceals its somewhat pat and manipulative underpinnings. Reading it really hurts, in at least five different ways. Two or three of these may be good for us. The others just plain hurt."

Carol Emshwiller: "I go along with Bob and Karen's interpretation, but I think the first section could have more mystery and tension, be more tantalizing. The characters, too, are too cut to fit your story. They should be more quirky, and more sympathetic. Sympathetic people *can* do terrible things."

Mark Van Name: "This story is quite powerful, and the issues it explores are fascinating and worthwhile. However, it often feels overly manipulative. Let the Berringers use the money from selling off the embryos for Mollie, or let them give the embryos to friends. You also push the fusion metaphor too hard and too long. Finally, the story of the relationship between Mollie and her parents, not the action outside the home, should dominate."

Jonathan Lethem: "At first I wanted more—more glimpses of the larger reality, more result: What happens to the other five families after Mollie becomes a nightmare? Now, however, I'm quite convinced by Karen and Bob's viewpoint: Home in on the dark heart. . . . Your prose is incredibly clean, lean and tight. The quality of the handling excites me more than the ideas in this story."

Alex Jablokov: "I'm completely manipulated, but I didn't mind too much, although I was less happy on the reread. Greedy, over-dressed parents, overdressed adopters, improbably 1950s Mollie, sick baby, cute dog . . . if I have any buttons unpushed, I'm not sure what they are. And I have problems with some of the legal and biological issues. However, I don't think you should change this story very much. It does its job, and does it well."

Greg Frost: "I think Bruce eloquently expressed what gets under my skin in this story. The SF tropes are unnecessarily drenching the heart of the story."

Michaela Roessner: "This is a strong, brave, painful story told in exactly the right voice. But I was confused about where the baby is at the end—in the basement or with the police? I agree with Bruce that you need to tone down the stabbing at the end—have her just throw the scissors."

Afterword to "Sex Education"

Sometimes, an author doesn't know what his or her story is about until members of a workshop thoroughly discuss it. The ostensible plot may be clear, but not the thematic or emotional implications. Other times, a story is clear to the author *until* a workshop discusses it. Then the contradictory criticism and pas-sionate suggestions hopelessly loosen whatever grip the writer thought he had on his own material.

This year at Sycamore Hill, I was lucky. The critiques of "Sex Education" were certainly contradictory, but also enormously helpful. And until Bob Frazier and Karen Fowler articulated that this story is about conditional love, I didn't realize that myself. I'd thought it was about that perennial SF staple, the unexpected personal fallout of impersonal technological advances. Which of course it *is*, but in a secondary way. The story's primary meaning is exactly what Bob and Karen described: a child's deep and pain-ful discovery that she is only loved if everything goes well and she remains exactly what her parents wish her to be.

After my critique session, I let the story sit for a week or so, and then began wading through 356 pages of marked-up manuscript and written notes. (26 story pages times 13 critics, plus miscellaneous extra offerings.) As with any critique, I took what made sense to me and discarded the rest. Mollie's parents, whom I had drawn as ogres, became more human, better motivated, more concerned for their child. The technological and legal concerns were clarified. I tried to better ground the story in a larger world of headlines, kids' products, and comprehensible bus lines. One scene was cut, another lengthened, a third toned down. The emphasis was shifted to Mollie's struggle with adult evasions of the responsibility that must accompany genuine love.

The result is a story subtly, although not markedly, different from the one I showed up with on Sunday night. I think it's a better story. More important than the work to this particular story, however, are the larger ideas about writing discussed at Sycamore Hill. Should SF be producing stories about child abuse, concentration camps, helpless people forced into desperate situations that closely parallel those in the real world? When we write such stories, are we illuminating suffering—or exploiting it? How far can a story stray from its central idea, in the interest of replicating life's messy non-patterning, before it becomes too diffuse, obscure, or boring? Is a tightly woven story, one in which the authorial purpose of every line is very clear, too mechanical?

All of us who write fiction struggle with these questions. Usually that struggle is solitary. To grapple in a group—a disparate, noisy, argumentative group—feels wonderful. For me, that's Sycamore Hill—a group grapple.

I'm very glad I went.

Nancy Kress

The Hardened Criminals

Jonathan Lethem

THE DAY WE went to paint our names on the prison built of hardened criminals was the first time I had ever been there. I'd seen pictures, mostly video footage shot from a helicopter. The huge building was still as a mountain, but the camera was always in motion, as though a single angle were insufficient to convey the truth about the prison.

The overhead footage created two contradictory impressions. The prison was an accomplishment, a monument to human ingenuity, like a dam, or an aircraft carrier. At the same time the prison was a disaster, something imposed by nature on the helpless city, a pit gouged by a meteorite, or a forest-fire scar.

Footage from inside the prison, of the wall, was rare.

Carl Hemphill was my best friend in junior high school. In three years we had graduated together from video games to petty thievery, graffiti, and pot smoking. It was summer now, and we were headed for two different high schools. Knowledge that we would be drawn into separate worlds lurked indefinably in our silences.

Carl involved me in the expedition to the prison wall. He was the gadfly, moving easily between the rebel cliques that rarely attended class, instead spending the school day in the park outside, and those still timid and obedient, like myself. Our group that day included four other boys, two of them older, dropouts from our junior high who were spending their high-school years in the park. For them, I imagined, this was a visit to one of their own possible futures. They must have felt that it was possible they would be inside someday. I was sure that for me it was not that but something else, a glimpse of a repressed past. My father was a part of the prison.

It was secret not only from the rest of our impromptu party, but from Carl, from the entire school. If asked, I said my father had died when I was six, and that I couldn't remember him, didn't know him except in snapshots, anecdotes. The last part of the lie was true. I knew of my father, but I couldn't remember him.

To reach the devastated section that had been the center of the city we first had to cross or skirt the vast Chinese ghetto, whose edge was normally an absolute limit to our wanderings. In fact, there was a short buffer zone where on warehouse doors our graffiti overlapped with the calligraphs painted by the Chinese gangs. Courage was measured in how deep into this zone your tag still appeared, how often it obliterated the Chinese writing. Carl and one of the older boys were already rattling their spray cans. We would extend our courage today.

The trip was uneventful at first. Our nervous pack moved down side streets and alleys, through the mists of steaming sewers, favoring the commercial zone where we could retreat into some Chinese merchant's shop, and not be isolated in a lot or alley. The older Chinese ignored us, or at most shook their heads. We might as well have been stray dogs. When we came to a block of warehouses or boarded shops we found a suitable door or wall and tagged up, reproducing with spray paint those signature icons we'd laboriously perfected with ballpoint on textbook covers and desktops. Only two or three of us would tag up at a given stop before we panicked and hurried away, spray cans thrust back under our coats. We were hushed, respectful, even as we defaced the territory.

We were at a freeway overpass, through the gang zone, we thought, when they found us. Nine Chinese boys, every one of them verging on manhood the way only two in our party were.

Had they been roaming in such a large pack and found us by luck? Or had one or another of them (or even an older Chinese, a shopkeeper perhaps) sighted us earlier and sounded a call to arms? We couldn't know. They closed around us like a noose in the shadow of the overpass, and instantly there was no question of fighting or running. We would wait, petrified. They would deliver a verdict.

It was Carl who stepped forward and told them that we were going to the prison. One of them pushed him back into our group, but the information triggered a fast-paced squabble in Chinese. We listened hard, though we couldn't understand a word.

Finally a question was posed, in English. "Why you going there?"

The oldest in our group, a dropout named Richard, surprised us by answering. "My brother's inside," he said. None of us had known.

He'd volunteered his secret, in the cause of obtaining our passage. I should chime in now with mine. But my father wasn't a living prisoner inside, he was a part of the wall. I didn't speak.

The Chinese gang began moving us along the empty street, nudging us forward with small pushes and scoffing commands. Soon enough, though, these spurs fell away. The older boys became our silent escort, our bodyguards. In that manner we moved out of the ghetto, the zone of warehouses and cobblestone, to the edge of the old downtown.

The office blocks here had been home to squatters before being completely abandoned, and many windows still showed some temporary decoration, ragged curtains, cardboard shutters, an arrangement of broken dolls or toys on the sill. Other windows were knocked out, the frames tarnished by fire.

The Chinese boys slackened around us as the prison tower came into view. One of them pointed at it, and pushed Carl, as though to say, *If that's what you came for, go.* We hurried up, out of the noose of the gang, towards the prison. None of us dared look back to question the gift of our release. Anyway, we were hypnotized by the tower.

The surrounding buildings had been razed so that the prison stood alone on a blasted heath of concrete and earth five blocks wide, scattered with broken glass and twisted tendrils of orange steel. Venturing into this huge clearing out of the narrow streets seemed dangerously stupid, as though we were prey coming from the forest to drink at an exposed water hole. We might not have done it without the gang somewhere at our back. As it was, our steps faltered.

The tower was only ten or eleven stories tall then, but in that cleared space it already seemed tremendous. It stood unfenced, nearly a block wide, and consummately dark and malignant, the uneven surfaces absorbing the glaring winter light. We moved towards it across the concrete. I understand now that it was intended that we be able to approach it, that striking fear in young hearts was the point of the tower, but at the time I marveled that there was nothing between us and the wall of criminals, that no guards or dogs or Klaxons screamed a warning to us to move away.

They'd been broken before being hardened. That was the first shock. I'd envisioned some clever fit, a weaving of limbs, as in an Escher print. It wasn't quite that pretty. Their legs and shoulders had been crushed into the corners of a block, like compacted garbage, and the fit was the simple, inhuman one of right angle flush against right angle. The wall bulged with crumpled limbs, squeezed so tightly together that they resembled a frieze carved in stone, and it was impossible to picture them unfolded, restored. Their heads were tucked inside the prison, so the outer wall was made of backs, buttocks, folded swollen legs, feet back against buttocks, and squared shoulders.

My father had been sentenced to the wall when it was already at least eight stories high, I knew. He wasn't down here, this couldn't be him we defaced. I didn't have to think of him, I told myself. This visit had nothing to do with him.

Almost as one, and still in perfect silence, we reached out to touch the prison. It was as hard as rock but slightly warm. Scars, imperfections in the skin, all had been sealed into an impenetrable surface. We knew the bricks couldn't feel anything, yet it seemed obscene to touch them, to do more than poke once or twice to satisfy our curiosity.

Finally, we required some embarrassment to break the silence. One of the older boys said, "Get your hand off his butt, you faggot."

We laughed, and jostled one another, as the Chinese gang had jostled us, to show that we didn't care. Then the boys with spray cans drew them out.

The prison wall was already thick with graffiti from the ground to a spot perhaps six feet up, where it trailed off. There were just a few patches of flesh or tattoo visible between the trails of paint. A few uncanny tags even floated above reach, where the canvas of petrified flesh was clearer. I suppose some ambitious taggers had stood on others' shoulders, or dragged some kind of makeshift ladder across the wastes.

We weren't going to manage anything like that. But our paint would be the newest, the outermost layer, at least for a while. One by one we tagged up, offering the wall the largest and most elaborated versions of our glyphs. After my turn I stepped up close to watch the paint set, the juicy electric gleam slowly fading to matte on the minutely knobby surface of hardened flesh.

Then I stepped back. From a distance of ten feet our work was already nearly invisible. I squinted into the bright sky and tried to count the floors, thinking of my father. At that height the bricks were indistinguishable. Not that I'd recognize the shape of my father's back or buttocks even up close, or undistorted by the compacting. I couldn't even be sure I'd have recognized his face.

A wind rose. We crossed the plain of concrete, hands in our pockets, into the shelter of the narrow streets, the high ruined offices. We were silent again, our newfound jauntiness expelled with the paint.

They were on us at the same overpass, the moment we came under its shadow. The deferred ambush was delivered now. They knocked us to the ground, displayed knives, took away our paint and money. They took Carl's watch. Each time we stood up they knocked us down again. When they let us go it was one at a time, sent running down the street, back into the Chinese commercial street alone, a display for the shopkeepers and deliverymen, who this time jeered and snickered.

I think we were grateful to them, ultimately. The humiliation justified our never boasting about the trip to the prison wall, our hardly speaking of it back at school or in the park. At the same time, the beating served as an easy repository for the shame we felt, shame that otherwise would attach to our own acts, at the wall.

In fact, we six never congregated again, as though doing so would bring the moment dangerously close. I only once ever again saw the older dropout, the one whose brother was in the prison. It was during a game of touch football in the park, and he went out of his way to bully me.

Carl and I drifted apart soon after entering separate schools. I expected to know him again later. As it happened I missed my chance.

"Stickney," the guard called, and the man on my right stepped forward.

By the time I entered the prison it was thirty-two stories high. I was nineteen and a fool. I'd finished high school, barely, and I was living at home, telling myself I'd apply to the state college, but not doing it. I'd been up all night drinking with the worst of the high-school crowd when I was invited along as an after-thought to what became my downfall, my chance to be a by-stander at my own crime. I drove a stolen car as a getaway in a bungled armored-car robbery, and my distinction was that I drove it into the door of a black-and-white, spilling a lieutenant's morning coffee and crushing his left forearm. The trial was suf-fused with a vague air of embarrassment. The judge didn't men-tion my father.

"Martell."

I'd arrived in a group of six, driven in an otherwise empty bus through underground passages to the basement of the prison, and ushered from there to a holding area. None of us were there to be hardened and built into the prison. We were all first-time offend-ers, meant to live inside and be frightened, warned, onto the path of goodness by the plight of the bricks.

"Pierce."

We stood together, our bodies tense with fear, our thoughts desperately narrowed. The fecal odor of the prison alone over-whelmed us. The cries that echoed down, reduced to whispers. The anticipation of the faces in the wall. We turned from each other in shame of letting it show, and we prayed as they pro-cessed us and led us away that we would be assigned different cells, different floors, never have to see one another. We would rather face the sure cruelties of the experienced convicts than have our green terror mirrored.

"Deeds, Minkowitz."

I was alone. The man at the desk flicked the papers before him, but he wasn't looking at them. When he said my name it was a question, though by elimination it was the one of which he could have been certain. "Nick Marra?"

"Yes," I said.

"Put him in the hole," he said to the guards who remained.

I must have aged ten years by the time they released me from that dark nightmare, though it only lasted a week. But when the door first slammed I actually felt it was a relief that I was hidden away and alone, after preparing or failing to prepare for cell-mates, initiations, territorial conflicts. I cowered down at the middle of the floor, holding my knees to my chest, feeling myself pound like one huge heart. I tried closing my eyes but they insisted on staying open, on trying to make out a hint of form in the swirling blackness. Then I heard the voices.

"Bad son of a bitch. That's all."

"—crazy angles on it, always need to play the crazy angles, that's what Lucky says—"

"C'mere. Closer. Right here, c'mon."

"Don't let him tell you what—"

"Motherfuck."

"—live like a pig in a house you can't ever go in without wanting to kill her I didn't think like that I wasn't a killer in my own mind—"

"Wanna get laid? Wanna get some?"

"Gotta get out of here, talk to missing persons, *man.* They got the answers."

"Henry?"

"Don't listen to him—"

They'd fallen silent for a moment as the guards tossed me into the hole, been stunned into silence perhaps by the rare glimpse of light, but they were never silent again. That was all the bricks were anymore, voices and ears and eyes; the chips that had been jammed into their petrified brains preserved those capacities and nothing more. So they watched and talked, and the ones in the hole just talked. I learned to plug my ears with shreds from my clothing soon enough, but it wasn't sufficient to block out the murmur. Sleeping through the talk was the first skill to master in the prison built from criminals, and I mastered it alone in the dark.

Now I went to the wall and felt the criminals. Their fronts formed a glossy, encrusted whole, hands covering genitals, knees crushed into corners that were flush against blocked shoulders. I flashed on the memory of that long-ago day at the wall. Then my finger slipped into a mouth.

I yelped and pulled it out. I'd felt the teeth grind, hard, and it was only luck that I hadn't really been bitten. The insensate lips hadn't been aware of my finger, of course. The mouth was horribly dry and rough inside, not like living flesh, but it lived in its way, grinding out words without needing to pause for breath. I reached out again, felt the eyes. Useless here in the hole, but they blinked and rolled, as though searching, like mine. The mouth I'd touched went on—"never want to be in Tijuana with nothing to do, be fascinating for about three days and then you'd start to go crazy"—the voice plodding, exhausted.

I'd later see how few of the hardened spoke at all, how many had retreated into themselves, eyes and mouths squeezed shut. There were dead ones, too, here and everywhere in the wall. Living prisoners had killed the most annoying bricks by carving into the stony foreheads and smashing the chips that kept the brain alive. Others had malfunctioned and died on their own. But in the dark the handful of voices seemed hundreds, more than the wall of one room could possibly hold.

"C'mere, I'm over here. Christ."

I found the one that called out.

"What you do, kid?"

"Robbery," I said.

"What you do to get thrown in *here*? Shiv a hack?"

"What?"

"You knife a guard, son?"

I didn't speak. Other voices rattled and groaned around me.

"My name's Jimmy Shand," said the confiding voice. I thought of a man who'd sit on a crate in front of a gas station. "I've been in a few knife situations, I'm not ashamed of that. Why'd you get thrown in the bucket, Peewee?"

"I didn't do anything."

"You're here."

"I didn't do anything. I just got here, on the bus. They put me in here."

"Liar."

"They checked my name and threw me in here."

"Lying motherfucker. Show some respect for your *fucking* elders." He began making a sound with his mummified throat, a staccato crackling noise, as if he wanted to spit at me. I backed away to the middle of the floor and his voice blended into the horrible, chattering mix.

I picked the corner opposite the door and away from the wall for my toilet, and slept huddled against the door. I was woken the next morning by a cold metal tray pressing against the back of my neck as it was shoved through a slot on the door. Light flashed through the gap, blindingly bright to my deprived eyes, then disappeared. The tray slid to the floor, its contents mixing. I ate the meal without knowing what it was.

"Gimme some of that, I hear you eating, you son of a bitch."

"Leave him alone, you constipated turd."

They fed me twice a day, and those incidental shards of light were my hope, my grail. I lived huddled and waiting, quietly masturbating or gnawing my cuticles, sucking precious memories dry by overuse. I quickly stopped answering the voices, and prayed that the bricks in the walls of the ordinary cells were not so malicious and insane. Of course, by the time I was sprung I was a little insane myself.

They dragged me out through a corridor I couldn't see for the ruthless light, and into a concrete shower, where they washed me like I was a dog. Only then was I human enough to be spoken to. "Put these on, Marra." I took the clothes and dressed.

The man waiting in the office they led me to next didn't introduce himself. He didn't have the grey deadness in his features that I already associated with prison staff.

"Sit down."

I sat.

"Your father is Floyd Marra?"

"Why?" I meant to ask why I'd been put in isolation. My voice, stilled for days, came out a croak.

"Leave the questions to us," said the man at the desk, not unkindly. "Your father is Floyd Marra?"

"Yes."

"You need a glass of water? Get him a glass of water, Graham." One of the guards went into the next room and came back with a paper cone filled with water and handed it to me. The man at the desk pursed his lips and watched me intently as I drank.

"You're a smart guy, a high-school graduate," he said.

I nodded and put the paper cone on the desk between us. He reached over and crumpled it into a ball and tossed it under the desk.

"You're going to work for us."

"What?" I still meant to ask *Why*, but he had me confused. A part of me was still in the hole. Maybe some part would be always.

"You want a cigarette?" he said. The guard called Graham was smoking. I did want one, so I nodded. "Give him a cigarette, Graham. There you go."

I smoked, and trembled, and watched the man smile.

"We're putting you in with him. You're going to be our ears, Nick. There's stuff we need to know."

I haven't seen my father since I was six years old, I wanted to say. *I can't remember him.* "What stuff?" I said.

"You don't need to know that now. Just get acquainted, get going on the heart-to-hearts. We'll be in touch. Graham here runs your block. He'll be your regular contact. He'll let me know when you're getting somewhere."

I looked at Graham. Just a guard, a prison heavy. Unlike the man at the desk.

"Your father's near the ceiling, left-hand, beside the upper bunk. You won't have anyone in the cell with you."

"Everybody's going to think you're hot shit, a real killer," said Graham, his first words. The other guard nodded.

"Yes, well," said the man at the desk. "So there shouldn't be any problem. And Nick?"

"Yes?" I'd already covered my new clothes with sweat, though it wasn't hot.

"Don't blow this for us. I trust you understand your options. Here, stub out the coffin nail. You're not looking so good."

I lay in the lower bunk trying not to look at the wall, trying not to make out differences in the double layer of voices, those from inside my cell, from the wall, and those of the other living prisoners that echoed in the corridor beyond. Only when the lights on the block went out did I open my eyes—I was willing myself back into the claustrophobic safety of the hole. But I couldn't sleep.

I crawled into the upper bunk.

"Floyd?" I said.

In the scant light from the corridor I could see the eyes of the wall turn to me. The bodies could have been sculpture, varnished stone, but the shifting eyes and twitching mouths were live, more live than I wanted them to be. The surface was layered with defacements and graffiti, not the massive spray-paint boasts of the exterior, but scratched-in messages, complex ingravings. And then there were the smearings, shit or food, I didn't want to know.

"—horseshoe crab, that's a hell of a thing—"

"—the hardest nut in the case—"

"—ran the table, I couldn't miss, man. Guy says John's gonna beat that nigger and I say—"

The ones that cared to have an audience piped up. There were four talkers in the upper part of the wall of my cell. I'd soon get to know them all. Billy Lancing was a black man who talked about his career as a pool hustler, lucid monologues reflecting on his own cleverness and puzzling bitterly over his downfall. Ivan Detbar, who plotted breaks and worried prison hierarchies as though he were not an immobile irrelevant presence on the wall. And John Jones—that was Billy's name for him—who was insane.

The one I noticed now was the one who said, "I'm Floyd."

A muscle in my chest punched upward against my windpipe like a fist. Would meeting him trigger the buried memories? I felt a surge of powerful emotion, but it was virtual emotion. I didn't know this man. I should want to.

I was trembling all over.

My father was missing an eye. From the crushed rim of the socket it looked like it had been pried out of the hardened flesh of the wall, not lost before. And his arms, crossed over his stomach, were scored with tiny marks, as though someone had used him to count their time in the cell. But his one eye lived, examined mine, blinked sadly. "I'm Floyd," he said again.

"My name is Nick," I said, wondering if he'd recognize it and perhaps ask my last name. He couldn't possibly recognize me. After my week in the hole I looked as far from my six-year-old self as I ever would.

"Ever see a horseshit crap, Nick?" said John Jones.

"Shut up, Jones," said Billy Lancing.

"How'd you know my name?" said my father.

"I'm Nick Marra," I said.

"How'd you know my name?" he said again.

"You're a famous fuck," said Ivan Detbar. "Word is going around. 'Floyd is the man around here.' All the young guys want to see if they can take you."

"Horseshoe crab, horseradish fish," said John Jones. "That's a hell of a thing. You ever see—"

"Shut up."

"You're Floyd Marra," I said.

"I'm Floyd."

I turned away, momentarily overcome. My father's plight overwhelmed mine. The starkness of this punishment suddenly was real to me, in a way it hadn't been in the hole. This view out over the bunk and through the bars, into the corridor, was the only view my father had seen since his hardening.

"I'm Nick Marra," I said. "Your son."

"I don't have a son."

I tried to establish our relationship. He agreed that he'd known a woman named Doris Thayer. That was my mother's name. His pocked mouth tightened and he said, "Tell me about Doris. Remind me of that."

I told him about Doris. He listened intently—or I thought that I could tell he was listening intently. Whenever I paused he asked a question to keep me on the subject. At the end he said only, "I remember the woman you mean." I waited, then he added, "I remember a few different women, you know. Some more trouble than they're worth. Doris I wouldn't mind seeing again."

Awkwardly I said, "Do you remember a boy?"

"Cheesedog crab," said Jones. "That's a good one. They'll nip at you from under the surf—"

"You fucking loony."

"A boy?"

"Yes."

"Yes, there was a boy—" All at once my father began a rambling whispered reminiscence, about *his* father, and about himself as a boy in the Italian ghetto. I leaned back on the bunk and looked away from the wall, towards the bars and the trickle of light from the hallway as he told me of merciless beatings, mysterious nighttime uprootings from one home to another, and abandonment.

Around us the other voices from the wall babbled on, as constant as televisions. I was already learning to tune them out like some natural background—crickets, or surf pounding. I fell asleep to the sound of my father's voice.

The next morning I joined the prison community. The two-tiered cafeteria called Mess Nine was a churning, teeming place, impossible not to see as a hive. Like the offices, it was on the interior, away from the living wall. I escaped notice until I took my full tray out towards the tables.

"Hey, lonely boy."

"He's not lonely, he's a psycho. Aren't you, man?"

"They're afraid of this skinny little guy, he's got to be psycho."

"Who you kill?"

I went and set my tray on an empty corner of a table and sat down, but it didn't stop. The inmate who'd latched on first ("lonely boy") followed and sat behind me.

"He needs his privacy, can't you see?" said someone else. "Let him eat and go back to his psycho cell."

"He can't socialize."

"I'll socialize him."

"He wants to fuck the wall."

"He was up late fucking the wall last night for sure. Little hung over, lonely boy?"

"Fuck the wall," I came to know, was an all-purpose phrase, in constant use either as insult or as an expression of rebellion, of yearning, of ironic futility. The standing assumption was that the dry, corroded mouths would gnaw a man's penis to bloody shreds in a minute. Stories circulated of those who'd tried, of the gangs who'd forced it on a despised victim, of the willing brick

somewhere in the wall who encouraged it, got it round the clock and asked for more.

I survived the meal in silence. Better for the moment to truck on my reputation as a dangerous enigma, however slight, than expose it with feeble protests. The fact of my unfair treatment wouldn't inspire any more sympathy from the softer criminals than it had from Jimmy Shand, in the wall of the hole. I shrugged away comments, thrown bits of rolled-up bread, and a hand on my knee, and did more or less as they predicted by retreating to my cell. The television room, the gym, the other common spaces, were challenges to be met some other day.

"Shoecat cheese!" said John Jones. "Beefshoe crab!"

"Quiet, you goddamn nut!"

"If you'd seen it you wouldn't laugh," said Jones ominously.

They were expecting me in the upper bunk. My father had been listening to Billy Lancing tell an extended story about a hustle gone bad in western Kansas, while they both fended off Jones.

"Nick Marra," said my father.

I was pleased, thinking he recognized me now. But he only said, "How'd you get sent up, Marra?" It occurred to me that he didn't remember his own last name.

"Robbery," I said. I still responded automatically with the minimum. My crime didn't get more impressive with the addition of details.

"You're in a rush?" said Floyd.

"What?"

"You haven't got all day? You're going somewhere? Tell your story, kid."

We talked. He drew the tale of my crime and arrest out of me. He and Billy Lancing laughed when I got to the collision, and Floyd said, "Fucking cop was probably jerking off with the other hand."

"He'll be telling it that way from now on," said Billy. "Won't you, Nick?"

"What?"

"Too good not to tell it like that," agreed Floyd.

And then he began to talk about his own crimes, and his punishments, before he was hardened. "—hadn't been sent upstairs to get the money he forgot I woulda been killed in that crossfire like he was. 'Course, my reward for living was the judge gave me all the years they wanted to give him—"

"Shit, you weren't more than a boy," said Billy.

"That's right," said Floyd. "Like this one."

"They all look like boys to me. Tell him how you used to work for the prison godfather, man."

"Jesus, that's a long time ago," said Floyd, like he didn't want to get into it. But he was just warming up.

The stories carried me out of myself, though I felt that I'd been warned that embellishments were not only possible, but likely. Floyd and Billy showed me that prison stories were myths, told in individual voices. What mattered were the universals, the telling.

I'd been using my story to show a connection between myself and Floyd, but the bricks were no longer interested in connections. Billy and Floyd might have been accomplices in the job that got them sent up or they might never have met; either way they were now lodged catty-corner to one another forever, and the stories they told wouldn't change it, wouldn't change anything. The stories could only entertain, and get them attention from the living prisoners. Or fail to.

So I let go of trying to make Floyd admit that he was my father, for the moment. It was enough to try to understand it myself, anyway.

On the way back from dinner Lonely Boy and two others followed me back to my cell. The hall was eerily empty, every adjoining cell abandoned. I learned later that such moments were no accident, but well orchestrated. The three men twisted my arms back, pushed me into the toilet stall, out of sight of the wall, and stripped down my pants.

I will not describe them or give them names.

What they did to me took a long time.

Lonely Boy stroked the nape of my neck all through the ordeal. What they did was seldom tender, but he never stopped stroking the small hairs of my neck and talking to me. His words were all contradictions, and I soon stopped listening to them. The sound was the point anyway, a kind of cooing interspersed with jagged accusations. Rhythm and counterpoint; Lonely Boy was teaching me about my loss, my helplessness, and the music of his words was a hook to help me remember. "Little special boy, special one. Why are you the special one? What did they choose you for? They pick you out for me? They send me a lonely one? You supposed to be a spy here, you want to in-fil-trate? How are you gonna spend your lonely days? You gonna think of me? I know I been thinking of you. This whole place is thinking of you. They'll kill you if I don't watch out for you. I'm your pro-tec-tor now—"

When I finally was alone I crawled into the lower bed and turned away from the wall. But I heard Ivan Detbar's voice from above. He was making sure to be heard.

"You don't have to go looking to find the top dog on the floor. The top dog finds you, that's what makes him what he is. He finds you and he's not afraid."

"Shit," said Billy Lancing.

"That's who you've got to take," said Detbar. "You've got to get on him like *thunder.* There is no other way."

"Shit," said Billy again. "First thing I learned in the joint is a virgin asshole's nothing to die for. It doesn't make the list."

Floyd wasn't talking.

Graham and another guard took me into an office the next day, an airless room on the interior.

"Okay," he said.

"Okay what?"

"Are you doing what we told you?"

"Talking? You didn't tell me anything more than that."

"Don't be smart. Your father trusts you?"

"Everything's great," I said. "So why don't you tell me what this is all about?" I didn't bother to tell him that Floyd didn't agree that he was my father, that we hadn't even established that after almost three days of talk.

I was feeling oddly jaunty, having grasped the depths of my situation. And I wasn't all that impressed with Graham on his own. There wasn't anything he could take away from me.

I wanted more information, and I suspected I could get it.

"There's time for that," said Graham.

"I don't think so. All this weird attention is going to get me killed. They think I'm a spy for you, or they don't know what to think. I'm not going to be alive long enough for you to use me."

I wasn't interested in telling him about the previous night. I knew enough to know that it wouldn't improve anything for me. The problem was mine alone. I didn't know whether I was ever going to confront Lonely Boy, but if I did it would be on prison terms. My priority now was to understand what they wanted from me and my father.

"You're exaggerating the situation," said Graham.

"I'm not. Tell me what this is about or I'll ask Floyd."

Graham considered me. I imagine I looked different than when they first dragged me out of the hole. I felt different.

He made a decision. "You'll be brought back here. Don't do anything you'll regret."

The other guard took me back to my cell.

It was a few hours later that I was standing in front of the man who didn't introduce himself the first time. He didn't again. He just told me to sit down. Graham stood to one side.

"Do you know the name Carl Allen Hemphill?" asked the man.

"Carl," I said, surprised.

"Very good. Have you been speaking with your father about him?"

"What? No."

"Did you know he was a prisoner here?"

"No." I'd heard he'd been a prisoner. But I didn't know he'd been a prisoner in the prison built of human bricks. "He's here now?" Somehow I was stupid enough to yearn for an old friend inside the prison, to imagine they were offering a reunion.

"He's dead."

I received it as a small, blunt impact somewhere in my stomach. It was muffled by the distance of years since I'd seen him, and by my situation, my despair. Sure he was dead, I thought. Around here everything is dead. But why tell me?

"So?" I said.

"Listen carefully, Nick. Do you remember the unsuccessful attempt on the President's life?"

"Sure."

"The assassin, the man that was killed—that was your friend."

"Bottmore," I said, confused. "Wasn't his name Richard

Bottmore, or Bottomore, something like that—"

"That wasn't his real name. His real name was Carl Allen Hemphill."

"That's crazy." I'd barely begun to struggle with the notion of Carl's having been here, his death. The assassination was too much, like being suddenly asked to consider the plight of the inhabitants of the moon. The point of this conversation, the answers I was seeking, seemed to whirl further and further out of my reach. "Why would he want to do that?"

"We'd very much like the answer to that question, Nick." He smiled at me as though he'd said enough, and thought I could take it from there. For a blind, hot second I wanted to kill him. Then he spoke again.

"He did his time quietly. Library type, loner. Nothing that was any indication. He was released five months before the attempt."

"And?"

"He had your cell."

"That's what this is about?" It seemed upside down. Was he saying that my real connection with Floyd didn't interest them, wasn't the point?

"Floyd hasn't said anything?"

"I told you no."

This time it was the man at the desk who lit a cigarette, and he didn't offer me one. I waited while he finished lighting it and arranging it in his mouth.

When he spoke again his expression was oddly distanced. It was the first time I felt I might not have his full attention. "Hemphill left some papers behind. Very little of any value to the investigation so far. But he mentioned your father. It's one of the only interesting leads we have. . . .

"The people I work with believe Hemphill didn't act alone. The more we dig up on his background, the more we glimpse the outlines of a conspiracy. You understand, I can't tell you any more than that or I'll be putting you in danger."

His self-congratulatory reluctance to "put me in danger" put a bad taste in my mouth. "You're crazy," I said. "Floyd doesn't know anything about that."

"Don't try to tell me my job," said the man behind the desk.

"Hemphill left a list of targets. This is not a small matter. It was your father's name in his book. Not some other name. Floyd Marra."

I felt an odd stirring of jealousy. Carl and my father, my father who wouldn't admit he was. "Why don't you talk to Floyd yourself?"

"We tried. He played dumb."

What if he is dumb? I wanted to say. I was trying to square these bizarre revelations with the face in the wall, the brick I'd conversed with for the past three days. Trying to picture them questioning Floyd and coming away with the impression that he was holding something vital back.

"Can't bug the wall, either," said Graham. "Fuckers warn each other. Whisper messages."

"The wall doesn't like us, Nick. It doesn't cooperate. Floyd isn't stupid. He knows who he's talking to. That's why we need you."

He doesn't know who he's talking to when he's talking to me, I wanted to say.

"I'll ask him about Carl for you," I said. I knew I would, for my own reasons.

"Crabshit fish," interrupted Jones. "That's a hell of a thing."

It nearly expressed the way I felt. "He almost started a war," I said to Floyd, trying harder to make my point.

"He was a good kid," said Floyd. "Like you."

"Scared like you, too," said Ivan Detbar.

I had to remind myself that the bricks didn't see television or read newspapers, that Floyd hadn't lived in the world for over thirteen years. The President didn't mean anything to him. Not that he did to me.

"How'd you know him?" said Floyd. "Cellmates?"

It was an uncharacteristic question. It acknowledged human connections, or at least it seemed that way to me. Something knotted in my stomach. "We were in school together, junior high," I said. "He was my best friend."

"Best friend," Floyd echoed.

"After you were put here," I said, as though the framework were understood. "Otherwise you would have known him. He was around the house all the time. Mom—Doris—used to—"

"Get this cell rat," said Floyd. "Talking about the past. His mom."

"Hey," said Billy Lancing.

"That's a lot like that other one," said Ivan Detbar. "What's his name, Hemphill. He was a little soft."

"No wonder they were best friends," said Floyd. "Mom. Hey Billy, how's your *mom*?"

"Don't know," said Billy. "Been a while."

Now I hated him, though in fact he'd finally restored me to some family feeling. He'd caused me to miss Doris. She knew who I was, would remember me, and remember Carl as I wanted him remembered, as a boy. And besides, I knew her. I didn't remember my father and I was sick of pretending.

What's more, in hating him I recalled trying to share in Doris' hatred of him, because I'd envied her the strength of the emotion. She'd known Floyd, she had a person to love or hate. I had nothing, I had no father. There was the void of my memories and there was this scarred brick, and between them somewhere a real man had existed, but that real man was forever inaccessible to me. I wanted to go back to Doris, I wanted the chance to tell her that I hated him now, too. I felt that somehow I'd failed her in that.

I was crying, and the bricks ignored me, I thought.

"Hemphill sure got screwed, didn't he?" said Billy.

"The kid couldn't take this place," said Ivan Detbar.

"But he was a good kid," said Floyd.

"Wasn't his fault, something tripped him up bad," said Billy. "Something went down."

Through my haze of emotions—jealousy, bitterness, desolation—I realized they were offering me warnings, and perhaps some sort of apology.

And the talk of Carl made me remember my assignment.

"You guys talked a lot?" I said.

"I guess," said Floyd.

"Nothing else to do," said Billy. " 'Less I'm missing something. Floyd, you been holding out on me?"

"Heh," said Floyd.

"There wasn't any talk about what he was going to do when he got out?" I asked. My task might only be an absurd joke, but at the moment it was all I had.

"I don't hear you talking about what you're going to do when you get out, and you're only doing a three-year stretch," said my father.

"What?"

"That's the last thing you want to think about now, isn't it? Maybe when you get a little closer."

"I don't understand."

"That poor kid was here at the start of ten years," said Floyd. "Hey, Billy. You ever meet a guy at the start of a long stretch wants to talk about what he's gonna do when he *finishes*?"

"Not unless he's planning a break, like Detbar here. Hah."

"I'll do it, too," said Detbar. "And I ain't taking you with me, you motherfucker."

"But he got out," I said, confused. "Hemphill, I mean."

"Yeah, but all of a sudden," said Floyd. "He *thought* he was doing ten years."

"Why all of a sudden?" I said. "What happened?"

"Somebody gave him a deal. They had a job for him. Let him out if he did it."

"Yeah, but that just made him sorrier," said Billy. "He was one screwed-up cat."

"He was okay," said Floyd. "He just had to tough it out. Like Marra here."

It was as disconcerting to hear him use the last name as though it had nothing to do with him as it was to be linked again and again with Carl. The dead grown-up would-be assassin, and the lost child friend. It drew me out of my little investigation, and back to my own concerns.

I couldn't keep from trying again. "Floyd?" What I wanted was so absurdly simple.

"Uh?"

"I want to talk to you about Doris Thayer," I said. I wasn't going to use the word *mom* again soon.

"Tell me about her again."

"She was my mother, Floyd."

"I felt that way about her too," said Floyd. "Like a mother. She really was something." He wasn't being funny this time. His tone was introspective. It meant something to him, just not what I wanted it to mean.

"She was really my mother, Floyd. And you're my father."

"I'm nobody's father, Marra. What do I look like?"

That wasn't a question I wanted to answer. I'd learned that I didn't even want to watch his one eye blink, his lips work to form words. I always turned slightly away. If I concentrated on his voice he seemed more human, more real.

"Come on, Marra, tell me what you see," said Floyd.

I realized the face of the brick was creeping into my patched-together scraps of memory. For years I'd tried to imagine him in the house, to play back some buried images of him visiting, or with Doris. Now when I tried I saw the empty socket, the flattened skull, the hideous naked stone.

I swallowed hard, gathering my nerve, and pressed on. "How long ago did you come here?"

"Been a million years."

"Million years ago the dogshit bird ruled the earth," said John Jones. "Crawled outta the water, all over the place. It's *evolutionary*."

"Like another life to me," said Floyd, ignoring him. His voice contained an element of yearning. I told myself I was getting somewhere.

"Okay," I said. "But in that other life, could you have been somebody's father?"

A shadow fell across the floor of my cell. I looked up. Lonely Boy was leaning against the bars, hanging there with his arms up, his big fingers inside and in the light, the rest of him in darkness.

"Looking for daddy?" he said.

The next day I told Graham I wanted another meeting. The man who never introduced himself was ready later that afternoon. I was getting the feeling he had a lot of time on his hands.

His expression was boredom concealing disquiet, or else the reverse. "Talk," he said.

"Floyd doesn't really know anything. He's never even heard of the assassination attempt. I can't even get him to focus on that."

"That's hard to believe, under the circumstances."

"Well, start believing. You have to understand, Floyd doesn't think about things that aren't right in front of him anymore. His world is—small. Immediate." Suddenly I felt that I was betraying my father, describing him like an autistic child, when what I meant was, *He's been built into a wall and he doesn't even know who I am.*

It didn't seem right that I should have to explain it to the men responsible. But the man behind the desk still inspired in me a queasy mixture of defiance and servility. All I said was, "I think I might have something for you anyway."

"Ah," he said. "Please."

I was going to tell him that he was right, there had been a conspiracy, and that Carl had been recruited from inside. An insipid fantasy ran in my mind, that he would jump up and clap me on my back, tell me I'd cracked the case, deputize me, free me. But as I opened my mouth to speak the man across the desk leaned forward, somehow too pleased already, and I stopped. I thought involuntarily: *What I'm about to tell him, he knows.* And I didn't speak.

I have often wondered if I saved my own life in that moment. The irony is that I nearly threw it away in the next. Or rather, caused it to be thrown.

"Yes?" he said. "You were going to say?"

"Floyd remembered Carl talking about some—group," I said, inventing. "Some kind of underground organization."

He raised his eyebrows at this. It was not what he was expecting. It seemed to take him a moment to find his voice. "Tell me about this—organization."

"They're called the Horseshoe Crabs," I said. "I don't really know more than that. Floyd just isn't interested in politics, I guess. But anyway, that should be enough to get you started."

"The Horseshoe Crabs."

"Yes."

"An *in-prison* underground?"

"No," I said quickly. "Something from before." I was a miserable liar.

I must have been looking at the floor. I didn't even see him leave his seat and come around the desk, let alone spot the fury accumulating in his voice or expression. He was just suddenly on me, my collar in his hand, his face an inch from mine. "You're fucking with me, Nick," he said.

"No."

"I can tell. You think I can't tell when I'm being fucked by an *amateur*?" He shoved me to the floor. I knocked over a trash basket as I fell. I looked at Graham. He just stood impassively watching, a foot away but clearly beyond appeal.

"What are the Horseshoe Crabs?" said the man. "Is Floyd a Horseshoe Crab?"

"He just said the name, that Carl used it. That's all I know."

"Stand up."

I got to my feet, but my knees were trembling. Rightly, since he immediately knocked me to the floor again.

Then Graham spoke. "Not here."

"Fine," said the man, through gritted teeth. "Upstairs."

They took me in an elevator up to the top floor, hustling me ahead of them roughly, making a point now. As they ran me through corridors, Graham pushing ahead and opening gates, living inmates jeered maliciously from their cells. They made a kind of wall themselves, fixed in place and useless to me as I went by. Graham unlocked the last door and we went up a stairway to the roof and burst out into the astonishing light of the sky. It was white, grey really, but absolutely blank and endless. It was the first sky I'd seen in two weeks. I thought of how Floyd hadn't seen it in thirteen years, but I was too scared to be outraged for him.

"Grab him," the man said to Graham. "Don't let him do it himself."

The roof was a worksite; they were always adding another level, stacking newly hardened bricks to form another floor. The workers were the first-timers, the still-soft. But there was nobody here now, just the disarray of discontinued work. A heap of thin steel dowels, waiting to be run through the stilled bodies, plastic barrels of solvent for fusing their side surfaces together into a wall. In the middle of the roof was a pallet of new human bricks, maybe twenty-five or thirty of them, under a battened-down tarp. In the roar of the wind I could still just make out the sound of their keening.

Graham and the man from behind the desk took me by my arms and walked me to the nearest edge. Crossing that open distance made me know again how huge the prison was. I kept my head down, protecting my ears from the cold whistle of the wind and my eyes from the empty sky.

The new story was two bricks high at the edge we reached. The glossy top side of the bricks had been grooved and torn with metal rasps, so the solvent would take. Graham held me by my arms and bent me over the short wall, just as Lonely Boy and the others had bent me over the toilet.

"Take a look," said the man.

"Looks like rain to me," said one of the nearby bricks chattily.

My view was split by a false horizon: the dark mass of the sheer face of the prison receding earthward below the dividing line, the empty acres of concrete and broken glass above. From the thirty-two-story height the ground sparkled like the sea viewed from an airplane.

Graham jammed me harder against the rough top of the bricks, and tilted me further towards the edge. I grunted, and watched a glob of my own drool tumble into the void.

"I hate to be fucked with," said the man. "I don't have time for that."

I made a sound that wasn't a word.

"Maybe we'll chop your father out of the wall and throw you both off," said the man. "See which hits the ground first."

I managed to think how odd it was to threaten a man in prison with the open air, the ultimate freedom. It was the reverse of the hole, all space and light. But it served their purposes just as well. Something I reflected on later was that just about anything could be turned to serve purposes like these.

"What are the Horseshoe Crabs?" he said.

I'd already forgotten how this all resulted from my idiotic gambit. "There are no Horseshoe Crabs," I gasped.

"You're lying to me."

"No."

"Throw him over, Graham."

Graham pressed me disastrous inches closer. My shirt and some of the skin underneath caught on the shredded upper surface of the wall.

"You're not telling me why I should spare you," said the man.

"What?" I said, gulping at the cold wind.

"You're not telling me why I should spare you."

"I'll tell you everything you want to know," I said.

Graham pulled me back.

"Are you lying to me again?" said the man.

"No. Let me talk to Floyd. I'll find out whatever you want."

"I want to know about the Horseshoe Crabs."

"Yes."

"I want to know anything he knows. You're my listening device, direct from him to me. I don't want any more noise in the signal. Do you understand?"

I nodded.

"Take him back, Graham. I'm going to have a cigarette."

Graham took me to my cell. I climbed into the top bunk and lay still until my trembling faded.

"The kid's getting ready to make his move," said Ivan Detbar.

"You think so?" said Floyd.

It was dinner hour. Inmates were shambling through the corridor towards Mess Nine.

My thoughts were black, but I had a small idea.

It seemed to me that one of my problems might solve the other. The way Graham had said "not here" to the man behind the desk made me think that the man's influence might not extend very far within the prison, however extensive and malignant it was in the world at large. I had never seen him command anyone besides Graham. Graham was in charge of my block, but the trip upstairs had made me remember the immensity of the prison.

My idea was simple, but it required physical bravery, not my specialty to this point. The cafeteria was the right place for it. With so many others at hand I might survive.

"Floyd," I said.

"Yeah?"

"What if you weren't going to see me anymore? Would that change anything?"

"What are you getting at?"

"Anything you'd want to say?"

"Take care, nice knowing ya," he said.

"How about 'Don't do anything I wouldn't do'?" said Billy Lancing.

Floyd and Billy laughed at that. I let them laugh. When they were done I said, "One last question, Floyd."

"Shoot."

I'd thought I was losing interest, growing numb. I guess in the longer term I was. But I was still pressing him. "Did you know your father?"

"You're asking me—what? My old man?" Floyd's eye rolled, like he thought his father had appeared somewhere in the cell.

"You knew him?"

"If I could get my hands around the neck of that son of a bitch—"

"You talk big, Floyd," said Ivan. "What about when you had your chance?"

"Fuck you," said Floyd. "I was a kid. I barely knew that motherfucker."

"The Motherfuck Dog," said John Jones. "He lives under the house—"

The tears were on my face again, and without choosing to do it I was beating my fist against the wall, against Floyd's petrified body. Once, twice, then it was too painful to go on. And I don't think he noticed.

I got down from the bunk. I had another place for the fury to go, a place where it might have a use. I only had to get myself to that place before I thought twice.

Dinner was meatballs and mashed potatoes covered with steaming greyish gravy. I took two cups of black coffee aboard my tray as well. I turned out of the food line and located Lonely Boy, sitting with his seconds at a table on the far side of the crowded room. Before I could think again, I headed for them.

"Hey, lonely boy, you want to sit?"

I flung the tray so it spilled on all three of them. I was counting on that to slow the other two; all my attention would be on Lonely Boy. I knew I'd lose any fight that was a contest of strategy or guile, lose it badly, that my only chance was blind, instantaneous rage. So I went in with my hands instead of picking up a fork or some other weapon. For my plan to work, Lonely Boy had to live. With what I knew was in me to unleash, his life seemed as much at risk as mine.

They pulled us apart before very long, but I'd already gotten my hands around his throat and begun hitting his head against the table, rhythmic revenge. One of his seconds had taken a tray and lashed open my scalp with it, and my blood was running into my opponent's eyes, and my own, and mixing with the coffee on the table. The voices around us roared.

Back in the hole for the night that followed, I screamed, bled, shat. I shoved the morning tray back out as it was coming through the slot. I attacked the men that came for me. How much was pretense I can't really say. Maybe none. When they got me into the shower I calmed down somewhat. I didn't feel human, though. I felt mercenary and cold, like frozen acid.

They put six stitches in my scalp in the prison hospital and led me to another, larger office, with more file cabinets and chairs, more ashtrays. Graham was there, with two other men. One of the others did the talking.

Those others were my margin, I knew. My glint of light.

The one who spoke asked me about the fight.

"If I'm put back in the block with him one of us will have to die," I said simply.

I could see a look of satisfaction on the face of the other of the men, not Graham. I assumed Lonely Boy had been trouble to this man before. I assumed, too, that I'd done damage. I smiled back at this man, and I smiled at Graham.

Graham kept his face impassive.

The man who was talking explained to me that Lonely Boy was an established presence on Block Nine, that he had more support than might have been apparent—did I understand that?

"Move me upstairs," I said. "As far away as possible. If I see him again I'll have to kill him."

The one who was talking told me that I'd likely find men like Lonely Boy wherever I went in the prison.

Nobody said the word *rape*.

"I'll never be in this position again," I said. "I can promise you that. Nobody will ever be permitted to make the mistake he made."

The man raised his eyebrows. The other one, the smiling one, smiled. Graham sat.

"Just move me," I said.

"We don't let prisoners make our decisions for us, Mr. Marra," said Graham.

"Your unusual handling put me at a disadvantage in the situation, Mr. Graham. If you keep me on Block Nine I intend to be treated like the other prisoners."

The man who had been talking turned and looked at Graham, and in that moment I knew I would be transferred.

"Unusual handling?" said the man who'd smiled. He'd directed the question at me, but it was Graham who spoke.

"He presents unique difficulties," he said. "His father is in the prison. In the wall. I thought it was better to address it directly."

I took a leaf from Floyd's book. It was pure improvisation, but my skills at lying were improving rapidly. "He isn't my father."

The smiling man made an inquiring face.

"He knew my mother, I guess. But she told me later he wasn't my father. He's just some guy. Just another brick to me."

The smiling man smiled at Graham. "This doesn't seem to me to require special treatment."

"I had the impression—" Graham began.

The smiling man laughed. "Apparently mistaken, Graham."

Graham laughed along.

Graham never spoke to me again, though I lived in fear of some reprisal. I would see him moving through the corridors with the men in charge of my block or other blocks and think he was about to point a finger at me and say, *"Marra, come with me,"* but he never did. I don't think he cared enormously. It might have been some relief to him to be able to say to the man behind the desk that I'd slipped away. Graham was a man with a difficult job and dealing with the man behind the desk was clearly not an easy part of it.

I never saw the man behind the desk again.

He was a sadist and an idiot. The two were not mutually exclusive, I understood, after that day on the roof. The agency or service he worked for had assigned him the task of tracing a conspiracy he was a member of himself. Sending me in to question my father was just ritual activity. He might have been curious to know whether Hemphill had been talking about what was happening to him, but he wasn't worried. He hadn't even bothered to wire the cell, or he'd have known how I came up with "horseshoe crabs." Until I'd panicked him, triggered his paranoia with that bluff, he was just making a show of activity by torturing me. And keeping himself entertained, I suppose, killing time on an absurd assignment.

The only deeper explanation was that I'd become a kind of stand-in for Carl, the other young prisoner they'd had in their grasp. He'd been theirs, for a time, and then he twisted loose, became history. I don't know if what he did was a disastrous perversion of their plans, or whether it served them, but I sensed that either way they experienced a loss. The mechanism of control was more precious than any outcome. I'd become the new instrument, the new site where control was enacted. Until I broke the spell.

From then on, I became another prisoner in a cell, living out my hours, protecting my back. I spent days in the weight room, years in the television room. I told lies to make the time pass. The rest of my story was no different from anyone else's, so in the telling I made it as different as I could. I learned to use the phrase "fuck the wall," though like a million other cowards, I never tried it.

My thoughts rarely turned to Carl. I hadn't learned much about the tortured prisoner and would-be assassin, and I didn't have any interest in trying to learn more. The image of my thirteen-year-old friend had been obliterated without anything taking its place. I didn't object. He was just a ghost now, and there were plenty of more substantial ghosts available, in the wall.

I didn't see my father again until a week before I left the prison, when I was granted a minute in my old cell.

Billy Lancing was still the same. He looked me over when I came in and said, "Marra?"

"Yeah."

"I remember you. Where'd you go?"

"Upstairs."

"Well, I remember you."

I climbed up into the top bunk.

Ivan Detbar was dead, his eyes stilled. I recognized it instantly by now. John Jones was still raving, but more quietly, not looking for an audience anymore.

My father was still alive, if that's the word for it, but someone had pried out his other eye, splintering the stony bridge of his nose in the process.

His mouth was moving, but nothing was coming out.

"Floyd's not good," said Billy.

I went over and put my hand on him. He couldn't feel it, of course. I was touching my father, but it didn't matter to either of us.

I wondered if it had been Graham or the man behind the desk who'd removed the eye, in some offhand act of revenge. It could as easily have been a living prisoner, someone in that top bunk who'd taken offense at too much attention, or a joke.

Floyd, like Billy, had listened fairly well. That was the only real difference between him and the hundreds of other bricks I'd met by that time. What had happened between him and Carl was absurdly simple, but the man behind the desk was puzzled, because it wasn't supposed to happen to an assassin-in-training, or to a human brick. They'd become friends. Floyd had expressed his dim, blundering sympathy, and Carl had listened, and been drawn out of his fear.

Which was more or less all Floyd had done with me.

Had he been pretending not to know me, pretending not to make the connection between my stories, my family history, and his? I'd stopped wondering pretty quickly. I had more immediate problems, which was part of his point, I think, if he was making one.

Bricks only face one direction.

I let my hand slip from the wall, and left the cell.

Afterword to "The Hardened Criminals"

The draft shown at Sycamore Hill stinted on the emotional material, and Nancy Kress, Karen Joy Fowler, Maureen McHugh, and Mark Van Name called me on it directly. Others responded to this shortage by bearing down hard on what *was* on the page, and exposing extrapolative flaws or plot implausibilities. Robert Frazier said it needed a "trope fix." Richard Butner thought the assassin stuff was a huge mistake. Others lingered over the biological reality of the hardened criminals. I tend to think a "tour de force" approach is best when cursed, as I am, with an implausible imagination. In my rewrite I tried to cook the emotional ingredients and hoped the resulting steam and stink would cloud the senses of naysayers.

I got some suggestions that I couldn't begin to use. Alexander Jablokov revised my prison into pure allegory: the walls extend an infinite distance into the sky and below the ground, and being released from imprisonment inside turns out to mean being hardened into a brick and added to the wall. James Patrick Kelly and Robert Frazier seemed ready to collaborate on a story of escaping bricks, chopped out of the wall, and trying to make a life on the outside. The stories remain theirs to write. I'd like to read them.

                                                        Jonathan Lethem

The Escape Artist

MICHAELA ROESSNER

HARRY HOUDINI AND his wife drove out and away from the town of San Jose through the sweet warm smell of orange blossoms. Harry held Bess's hand throughout the long drive until the hired carriage dropped him at the back door of the Victorian mansion, as Harry had requested. Even here, on the grounds' circling drive, the sounds of construction deep within the house could be heard: the hollow deep sounds of hammering, the ghostly wasp-whine breath of saws.

The driver looked at him curiously as if to wonder why an elegant and expensively dressed man like Harry chose to present himself at the servants' entrance.

Harry smiled. His success, recent and hard-won, depended on thorough and painstaking research into everything he attempted, like his research into this estate. Two years before, Theodore Roosevelt had been refused entrance after that great man and his retinue had presented themselves at the front door.

Harry kissed Bess's cheek. "I'll see you back at the hotel," he said as he stepped down. "Have a lovely lunch with the Ladies' Auxiliary."

A seasoned performer, Bess liked as much as he did to take advantage of every opportunity for favorable publicity. She'd agreed to give a luncheon presentation on their recent travels and exploits in Europe. After Bess's groundwork Harry knew their three performances in San Jose would sell out. The audiences would include everyone considered elite and cultured in this area. With the exception of the reclusive owner of this mansion.

Harry waved to Bess until he could no longer see her merry dark eyes or lopsided smile. The carriage became a cart, a toy, a dot, as it diminished from the estate's outbuildings and vast fields.

He turned and faced the mansion and whistled as he tried to take it all in. It loomed, crept, and sprawled. Bank after bank of windows stared with a blind introspection. Whole wings turned and tucked into each other in incestuous lovers' knots. A dainty disorganized army of minarets peered down, casting Harry into shadow. They themselves were eclipsed by the somber seven-story observation tower. The sound of hammering grew louder.

Harry walked up the tunnel-like entrance until he found the back door. He knocked. A maid in a long pinafore and starched apron opened the door. Harry handed her his calling card. "I have an appointment with Mrs. Winchester," he said. The maid ushered him in. "Please follow me," she said.

She drew him through a maze of hallways. They passed a kitchen busy as a hive. White-jacketed cooks worked in their nest of gleaming copper, yellow tiles, and oak butcher block. The maid took him around a corner. They made a left turn and passed another kitchen, this one lined with blue and white porcelain, equally filled with chefs.

Staircases led off and away. One climbed steeply for three stories, then wound around in a listless short promenade only to descend again. Another set of steps led straight up into a ceiling. Hand-carved columns had been installed upside down. Windows were set into floors.

The mansion housed incredible treasures. Six safes, in fact, full of delectables such as a solid gold dining service. The mansion had never been breached by thieves. Yet it boasted no greater security measures than its isolation in the country, a six-foot cypress hedge, and the presence of numerous loyal servants.

No thief would enter a structure from which he couldn't make an easy escape, let alone one he might wander lost in for days. Such matters were Harry's stock-in-trade, although he was no thief. Every lock known to man was a maze Harry had already traversed and solved. To him, the mansion was like an enormous puzzle that he had the luxury of physically traveling within as he solved it. Hansel-like he dropped mental pebbles at each landmark as he passed it.

Then he chided himself. He wasn't here to indulge in his art. The only escape he intended to accomplish this day was that of the mansion's owner: her escape from the needless guilt that this bizarre mansion was an expression of.

And to that end he noticed that so far he had seen no grand weapons-display common to the homes of the rich; not a single racked and mounted rifle, though rifles were the source of all this eccentric display of wealth.

The maid brought him to a small study on the third floor. A woman rose from behind a rosewood ebony- and silver-inlaid desk and extended her hand to him.

"I'm Frances Merriman," the woman said as he took her hand and pressed it. "Welcome to Llanda Villa. I'll take you to Aunt Sarah."

Of course. The niece who acted as Sarah Winchester's secretary and sole companion.

Miss Merriman dismissed the maid and guided Harry back down through the house, by yet another route than the one taken up. She took him past rooms of mahogany cabinets spilling over with bolts of cloth, sitting rooms furnished with chinoiserie, bathrooms graced with spiderweb leaded casements. The sounds of construction intensified. Harry heard the tearing and wrenching of walls being torn apart.

Sawhorses with planks thrown across them served carpenters as temporary worktables. The air itched with sawdust and the smell of raw wood. Harry looked around uneasily. He was sure he'd passed through that very hall when he'd entered the mansion, yet had seen no evidence of all this activity so close by.

Frances Merriman coughed politely. Harry turned. A burly man wearing a leather work apron and carpenter's tool belt bent over spread-out plans, his attention drawn to where an ivory finger pointed. The finger belonged to a small figure swathed in black watered satin and dense lace.

"Aunt Sarah," Frances Merriman said in formal tones, "may I present Mr. Harry Houdini. Mr. Houdini, this is my aunt, Mrs. William Wirt Winchester."

The tiny dark figure looked up. Harry saw the gleam of eyes behind the heavy veil. Her extended hand was as small and fragile as a porcelain doll's. He pressed it carefully.

"Mr. Houdini, you are gratifyingly prompt." Sarah Winchester's voice was clear and bright in spite of the muffling fabric. She hesitated a moment and seemed to be staring past Harry to where he himself had been gazing just seconds before, to the way he'd come in.

"Please forgive me, Mr. Houdini. Do you mind a slight delay while I go over some last-minute changes with my foreman?"

"Of course not." Harry drew himself together in a short European bow of acquiescence.

"Thank you." She turned to her niece. "Frances, please inform the kitchen that I'd like brunch served shortly in . . ." She thought a moment. "The north conservatory."

"Very good," Frances said, and left.

While he waited, Harry entertained himself by watching Mrs. Winchester practice her highly peculiar brand of architecture. She and the foreman worked off several large sheets of paper that in no way resembled blueprints. Little sketches drawn on scraps of anything handy fluttered on the walls nearby like pinned butterflies.

Mrs. Winchester took a grease pencil and slashed bold marks through her earlier drawing. "Then move this here, here, and here, and divert around to there," she said. The foreman scratched his head, looking only mildly puzzled. Then he nodded. This was clearly a scene that had been repeated a hundred times or more. The foreman called down a hallway and six workers laboring under sheets of European pressboard struggled into the room.

"Mr. Houdini, shall we?" Mrs. Winchester proffered her arm. Harry tucked it into his own as she gestured them out the door. "I hope you have an appetite."

Harry could barely hear her over the pounding of nails. He knew that this went on day and night, month after month, year after year, without stopping for Easter, Christmas, or Thanksgiving.

"A ride through good country air always makes me hungry." Harry had to shout the words. He glanced back.

The corridor behind him was being boarded over, turning the hallway into a narrow, claustrophobic room. A dead end.

As he walked with Sarah Winchester deeper into the house Harry felt chilled: a response he would feel if an escape route were cut off, or a lock clicked inexplicably into place behind him.

Those were the reactions he elicited from his audiences—sensing a trap and fearing it. It was one of the factors that made him such a success. He shrugged off the feeling.

Such emotions had nothing to do with the pure mechanical logic that allowed him to effect his escapes. In fact, such feelings were antithetical to the process. It was just such sentiments that had led Mrs. Winchester to be snared in this extravagant trap of her own making. If he were to feel anything at all at this moment it should be pity.

Mrs. Winchester walked gingerly and very slowly. She suffered from severe arthritis. Her arm resting on his communicated brief, unconscious twinges of habitual pain.

"I'd suggest we take an elevator up, but the closest one is being worked on, and the other two are on the other side of this wing." They moved together up a ramp that coiled around a short set of steps surmounted by a free-standing door.

"This is the farmhouse," Mrs. Winchester said.

"The farmhouse?"

"This is what is left of the property's original farmhouse. Llanda Villa eventually overwhelmed it. These were the back porch steps and door."

"Like Jonah," Harry said.

"Jonah?"

"Jonah swallowed alive by the whale."

"Ah, yes." Harry sensed a smile behind the veil. "I like that. Llanda Villa is nothing if not leviathan. I'll call these my Jonah steps from now on."

The next set of stairs reminded Harry of hiking with Bess in the Bavarian Alps. The stairway consisted of a number of switchbacks, and the steps themselves were only an inch or two high. A lengthy way to ascend a floor, but surely kinder on Mrs. Winchester's swollen and aching joints.

Mrs. Winchester interrupted his thoughts. "Your wife, Mr. Houdini? She couldn't join us today?"

"Please, call me Harry. After I'd contacted you and asked if I could come calling I realized I'd neglected to ask if Bess could accompany me. I didn't want to impose any further."

Mrs. Winchester made a murmur of dismay. Harry patted her arm where it lay on his.

"It's really just as well," he said. "She's addressing a local Ladies' Auxiliary luncheon on our exploits and travels for me. She did take the carriage-ride out. She welcomes any opportunity to get out into the country and was delighted to see your property. I hope that's all right."

"Of course." The veil bobbed. "You love your wife very much, don't you?"

Harry was startled, then looked down at her and laughed. Just because he couldn't see Sarah Winchester's face behind that veil didn't mean that she couldn't see him clearly. He'd let himself be caught out by one of the oldest and simplest of illusions.

"Yes, I'm afraid I'm quite transparent on that score. I love Bess to distraction." His laughter trailed away as he remembered how much Sarah Winchester loved her husband. This bizarre mansion was direct evidence of that.

Mrs. Winchester appeared not to have noticed his change of mood. "We're almost there . . ." For a moment Harry thought he'd heard "Ehrich." But no, she must have said "Harry."

In the near distance, across the width of one small room, he saw the open door to the conservatory. In the far distance behind him he heard the blurred sounds of construction, coming closer. Harry felt cold again. He suffered a fleeting vision where he imagined himself to be a small boy, and the birds had mistaken his carefully dropped stones for crumbs and flown away with them.

Frances Merriman appeared in the conservatory door. Sunshine shone there in sheets of gold, warmly welcoming. A Chinese cook looked out, beaming, from a table he was arranging. Harry's brief panic subsided. Sarah Winchester pulled gently on his arm.

"Please, just one minute," he said, further distracted by a stained-glass window set in the small room that served as antechamber to the conservatory. Harry ran his fingers over it.

"Lovely, isn't it? I had Tiffany's design it especially for this room," Mrs. Winchester said.

"Yes, it is lovely," Harry said. This piece, with its ribbonlike flourishes, abstract floral patterns, and nuggets of quartz, was a match for anything he'd come across in the cathedrals of France or Germany. But that wasn't why it had caught his attention.

He turned back to his host, took her arm and escorted her to the waiting table. That window had been executed to be set in a south-facing window, where the sun's light would penetrate its colors, transforming the room with radiance as bright as a symphony. Why had Sarah Winchester exiled it to a northern wall, condemning it forever to a muted, silent existence?

Tea in a jungle, Harry thought, sitting down to the brunch. Ferns, palms, fleshy-leaved plants nodded over their shoulders as they nibbled dainty, butter-rich pastries shaped into sailors' knots, bowls of fruit compote, salmon mousse sandwiches cut and arranged on the serving platter to look like Moorish tile.

Harry wondered if Mrs. Winchester intended to eat with her veil on. But on sitting, the lady of the manor carefully rolled the black gauze up and away from her face.

Her hair shaded from silver to pure white. Harry could see that she'd been quite pretty in her youth, with high, wide cheekbones and well-balanced features. Even now, in her sixties, she'd be considered handsome.

They chatted on about polite subjects until the cook served them coffee in demitasse cups. Frances Merriman excused herself to go back to work updating household accounts.

"Now, Mr. Houdini..." Sarah Winchester said as she poured them both another minute cup of coffee.

"Harry," Harry interrupted.

"Harry," she agreed. "Perhaps now you'll explain why you went to all this trouble to ask for this audience."

He fussed with his napkin, leaned forward. "I came to offer you my help, on a matter in which I possess a certain amount of expertise. Please let me explain." He hesitated. "And I'm afraid my explanation is partly a confession.

"As you know, I'm a showman, a sort of conjurer. The role of a magician is to manipulate reality to create an illusion. The

Frenchman I took my name from—Robert Houdin—said that a conjurer is an actor playing the part of a magician. That is true for me. I play at being a magician.

"I'm quite proud of what I do, the way I differ from others in my profession. I talk directly to my audience, simply, and tell them exactly what I am going to do. In a way, opposite to my colleagues, who expect that the impossible be believed of them, I ask my audience to disbelieve me, then escape anyway. I feel that I am offering them an entertainment of wonder, based solely on my skill and honesty."

He picked up his napkin again and fidgeted with it, drawing it back and forth in his hands, twisting it into a knot. "Now for the part I'm not so proud of. Until I found my métier, I struggled for quite a while trying to survive by other, more standard tricks of the trade." Harry smiled wryly and pulled the napkin between the thumb and forefinger of his left hand. The white linen turned to crimson silk as he drew it through. But he felt that Mrs. Winchester's gaze never left his face. Harry looked down at his hands.

"I even dabbled for a while at holding séances. I told myself that it was lucrative, harmless, and usually amusing. When a client was bereaved and seeking to contact a loved one, I convinced myself that I was giving them comfort." Harry made himself look up into Sarah Winchester's eyes.

"I was wrong, Mrs. Winchester. It was a cruel, dishonest thing to do. I quit that line of work and vowed to launch my own crusade against this type of fraud. I have kept my vow."

He stopped. The next part was always hard, but in Mrs. Winchester's case he found it almost impossible to continue.

"May I go on? I'm afraid I'm about to tread on painful ground for you."

She nodded.

He gestured to indicate the expensive table service, the conservatory, the whole mansion around them. "I know, as does anyone who's heard of you, that the means by which you execute all this comes from your husband's family's estate. And that on the advice of so-called spirit mediums all of this is an expiation for what you believe to be the guilt of the Winchester family."

Unspoken, hanging in the air between them, were the hundreds and thousands of lives lost to the Winchester repeating rifle.

Harry knotted his fingers. "Mrs. Winchester, I lived in the world of the séance masters. I know their every device and trick.

"I also know a good deal about you. I know that you support orphanages, medical research, shelters for the homeless. You treat your servants so well, so humanely, that their loyalty to you is unswerving. You certainly don't deserve to have bald-faced liars and greedy hucksters sentence you to a lifetime of atonement and guilt. You didn't lose your husband and daughter because vengeful spirits laid a curse on the Winchester family name."

Harry thought with remorse of those he had deluded, thereby sentencing them to a lifetime obsession with death. "Please, while you have time left to you, rejoin the world of the living. When I heard of your story, I knew it was the most heinous crime I'd yet heard of perpetrated on the innocent by those monsters of fraud. To try to free you and others like you is my penance for having been one of them once."

Harry bowed his head. Was Sarah Winchester sitting there silently in shock, or grief, or fury?

He felt a soft touch. She was pressing his hand in the same way that he'd pressed hers earlier. She looked as though she were searching for just the right words.

"Mr. Houdini, do you think that you know exactly what goes on in the minds of your audience when you perform for them?"

Harry looked at her blankly.

"By that I mean, could you consider that they might perhaps derive associations, perceptions, or inspirations from your performance that you couldn't control or even particularly conceive of?"

Harry grudgingly admitted this might be so.

"Then please don't imagine that because yes, I did consult with mediums and attend séances, I necessarily took them at their word.

"I lost my daughter Annie at the age of only a month, to one of those mysterious maladies that strike so many infants. Later my beloved William died of tuberculosis, as do many other people every year, most of whom have nothing to do with rifles or slaughter.

"I admit I sought spiritual advice because I was grieving. It's true that I paid those scalawags too handsomely until I found and embarked on my own mission. I even followed their advice: to move out here to California and begin this strange building project. But please believe me, Harry, it was not for the reasons those mediums thought they'd provided me."

Harry's forehead creased. "But then why all this?"

Sarah Winchester placed her own napkin on the table and faced him squarely. "Harry, we have not been entirely honest with one another. You told me that when you put on a performance you speak to your audience directly and tell them exactly what you are going to do.

"Of course, you don't. I've seen articles where you've been quoted as saying that 'the secret of showmanship consists not of what you really do, but what the mystery-loving public thinks you do.' Therefore you don't tell them about the key your wife passes you from her lips in those poignant farewell kisses you and she share, or any of your other tricks."

Harry sat amazed before her sharp intelligence. "But—but I . . ." he started to protest.

Sarah raised her hand, halting him. "I'm not reprimanding you. I realize you practice the misdirection of apparent honesty for the audience's own good, to achieve the effect and response that they come to you for. What you commit is more a sin of omission that outright prevarication.

"Now I must make a confession of my own: I can hardly condemn you, since I practice those same methods. All that you see here is, like your escape act, not necessarily what it seems."

Harry hardly knew what to reply to that statement, since it inferred a logic to the mansion's appearance which was entirely lacking in the first place.

Sarah Winchester laughed, a delicate but merry sound—no doubt at the incredulous look on his face. "Yes, something is going on here," she said. "But it is entirely different from what you or the public supposes."

The laughter left her face. "Which leads me to confess further duplicity. I asked you why you'd requested an audience with me when I knew the reason all along."

Harry shrugged uncomfortably. Now that he understood how intelligent and well-informed the widow was, he realized she could have easily heard about his anti-spiritualist crusade and drawn the correct conclusion about his intentions.

Sarah Winchester rearranged the veil over her face. Her voice rang sibyl-like from behind it. "My source for that information is not what you think it is. You asked, if I didn't believe my spiritualist advisors, why did I take their advice? Why all this?" She copied his earlier expansive gesture. "Let me show you, Harry Houdini."

She reached out a hand to him. He helped her up and once more supported her on his arm. They took an elevator up another floor. She directed him down a hallway until they stood before a door. Sarah pointed to it. "Inside there is my séance room."

Harry looked for a doorknob. There was none. They passed two similarly nonfunctional entrances. Finally she led him on a circuitous route that ended at a door that did have a handle. Harry opened it and stood aside to let Mrs. Winchester enter first, then followed her.

Harry looked behind him. The door they'd come through had no handle on this side. The other walls hosted three doors and a cupboard, all with handles.

"That's correct." Sarah Winchester interpreted his glance. She'd drawn aside her veil again. "There is only one entrance, which you cannot return by. But there are three exits. This room reflects the structure of the entire building. You come into it in only one way, from wherever you are in your life. But you can depart through many exits, to a choice of lives, of possibilities. This is what I have been led to do in building Llanda Villa, Harry. Not to perform mere penance, but to right the wrong. To right many wrongs."

"I don't understand," said Harry, looking around him. "Who led you to this? The spirit mediums?"

Her séance room was plain. It had been painted blue and held a desk, several well-furnished bookshelves, and a chair. Robes of some sort hung from a set of thirteen coat hooks. The two windows were the most remarkable features. One looked out across fields and forests, the countryside surrounding the mansion. The other peered down onto an inner courtyard. Both were paned with clear but peculiarly thick and watery glass.

Sarah gestured to the single chair and smiled. "As you can see, I am both the client and the medium here. So if any money changes hands, nothing is lost.

"No, the voices I heard weren't the spiritualists, nor those of their fraudulent phantoms, cast by crude and obvious machinery. The voices that guided me belonged to William and Annie, to those slain by the Winchester rifles, and to others who will, or have already, died unjustly before their time. They told me how to build rooms for them to take up their lives once again, the doors by which they can reach those lives they should have had. I don't live under a curse, Harry Houdini, but a blessing, for there is room for all of them and their lives in this house that I have built."

Harry held his hand to his eyes, hiding his face, the hope he'd felt for Sarah Winchester crushed. Her intelligence and charm at lunch had only been one of those moments of intermittent lucidity that the delusional occasionally enjoy. "Sarah, you cannot hear dead voices. The dead are gone. You can't cheat death. Everyone has to die."

"Do you think I'm mad?" she said. She sounded amused. She gently pulled his arm down and looked up into his eyes. "The voices I hear are alive. I'm not trying to escape death here, Harry. Of course everyone has to die. There's nothing wrong with that. But what is wrong is to not be allowed one's allotted time. That's all that I'm accomplishing here."

Harry shook his head. She sounded so sane, her calm logic could match his own when he performed.

Sarah hobbled painfully over to the window that looked out over the inner courtyard. "I told you that I knew you were coming to visit me and why. And that you wouldn't recognize the source of my information. The source was one of my voices, Harry."

The hair on the back of Harry's neck prickled erect.

She looked over her shoulder at him. "The voice that told me about you belonged to a boy, Ehrich Weiss. He's a Jewish boy who was born in Hungary. He's very discouraged, Harry. His father is a rabbi—a prestigious position for your people, I believe—but he's a failure both religiously and as his family's support. Do you suppose that's why Ehrich has trouble with faith, with believing? Ehrich had to leave home when he was only twelve to find work so that he could send money home to his family."

Harry felt himself sweating under his elegant clothing. How could she know these things? His past was a closely guarded secret—not so much denied as obscured behind layers and layers of veiling and contradictory myth.

"In spite of his hard childhood Ehrich hasn't given up hope," Sarah continued. "He knew that there would be better times, even wealth and fame."

Harry felt himself teetering on some precipice, about to let himself go and plunge over.

Sarah's eyes gazing at him from across the room were clear, brilliant and sad. "He also knows of his possible fates. That's why he spoke to me. He might live, happy and healthy, offering pleasure and wonder to millions, well into his seventies. Or he might die needlessly, in his fifties, at the hands of callow youth. Now that I have heard him, it's my responsibility to help him escape that premature fate."

She nodded to the doors. "Choose, Harry Houdini. By allowing yourself to be ensnared by my home, you shall escape."

Harry was paralyzed. What was happening here?

Sarah limped to one of the doors. He found himself following. "You still hesitate," she said. "Let me show you what I have to offer before you choose."

She opened the door. Harry caught a glimpse over her shoulder of a sheer drop of four stories, broken only by a fragile latticework of struts far below. Sarah started to take a step out into the empty vacuum.

"No!" shouted Harry. He grabbed at her funeral-black sleeve. For an instant he thought they were going to plummet together down the airshaft. Then he pulled back and they were both safe. He slammed the door shut and whirled on his hostess in angry amazement.

She looked up at him with that preternaturally serene expression. Harry's furious words died away before he could speak them. There was no point. He recognized that the look in her eyes. It was the absolute calm of unsalvageable insanity. Harry finally accepted that his mission had been doomed before it began.

He took a deep breath. "That's not necessary. You needn't

show me anything." He shepherded her toward the wall cabinet. "I've already made my choice." As soon as he'd entered the room he'd recognized the cabinet door as one of the trick exits. It included part of the wall, its true boundaries blending in when the door was closed.

He pushed it open. His hands still shook. He bowed Mrs. Winchester through.

"That's a fine choice, Harry. Now that you've made it, I'm sure you're anxious to return to San Jose to prepare for tonight's performance." Sarah Winchester seemed subdued and more than willing to release him now.

But Harry didn't want to take his leave of her just yet. Who knew what she might do if left alone?

She seemed to sense his hesitancy. "I'll take you down myself, Harry. I'm sure if anyone could find their way about, it would be you, but I couldn't be that ungracious."

Their journey down through the mansion felt like an eternity to Harry. Where were the foreman, the servants, Frances, or any of the scores of workmen he heard moving all about them, like animals hidden in the walls? Where was someone, anyone, to whom he could deliver Sarah safely?

"Ah, there you are." Frances Merriman emerged from a pantry off a hallway. "Did you enjoy your visit, Mr. Houdini?"

"Very much so," Harry said stiffly.

"Frances, entertain Harry for a moment while I order the carriage to come round for him." Sarah slid into the pantry. Harry heard her speaking into a servants' callbox.

Harry drew Frances aside. "Your aunt is in grave danger."

Frances looked shocked. "My heavens, from whom?"

"From herself. She nearly fell down an airshaft, believing it to be a stairway. I barely pulled her back in time."

Frances Merriman turned pale. She put her hand to her mouth and gasped. "Aunt Sarah did what? Where?"

"In the séance room. I have a confession to make: I initiated a discussion—I was hoping to alleviate her suffering—but I fear our conversation propelled her over the boundaries of sanity instead." Would there be no end to his guilt? He mopped his brow with his handkerchief. "Whatever my culpability, I can tell you that the key is the séance room. You must keep her out of it at all costs. It only feeds her delusions. Have the foreman board the accursed place up immediately, and never let your aunt out of your sight."

Frances grasped his arm. "Mr. Houdini, I'm sure that the fault was not yours. Thank you for rescuing her. Thank God you were there! I had no idea she'd become so fragile. Now that you've alerted me, rest assured I'll take care of the matter."

"Take care of what, Frances?" Sarah had finished her call and emerged from the pantry to rejoin them.

"Take care of showing Mr. Houdini the rest of the way out, Aunt Sarah," Frances said smoothly. She and Houdini shared a glance.

"No, I insist on showing myself the door," Harry said. "I've imposed on your hospitality long enough."

Sarah Winchester looked doubtful, but acquiesced. "So, Harry Houdini, before you leave, tell me—what do you think of Llanda Villa?"

Just as she said that, Harry realized that at no point had he stopped hearing the hammering and sawing following along behind them. His ears had become inured to the noise.

"I've tested myself against the master locksmiths of the world and won, Mrs. Winchester. I'm not sure I'd care to test myself against your beautiful home."

Sarah Winchester nodded as if that were precisely what she was hoping he'd say. She raised her hand. Filled with pity, Harry took it and pressed it to his lips.

"You will come again," she said. Harry couldn't tell if that was meant as an invitation, command, or a promise. "And your lovely wife must join us."

Harry set off down the hallway. He glanced back over his shoulder. Frances had her arm around her aunt and was leading her away.

In spite of his bravado, Harry couldn't find his way out. The few landmarks he recognized seemed to be in different places than he remembered them. He chilled as the sweat saturating his clothes turned cold. Features that he'd learned of from his research appeared as meaningless tableaus. He passed the grand ballroom where no one had ever danced, the front doors no one had ever passed through, save for only once each by Sarah and the two carpenters who'd built them.

Finally, after skirting around an aviary filled with strange

144   Michaela Roessner

birds, Harry found that he'd come around by yet another route to the back carriage entrance. A carriage was waiting for him. Only as he stepped up into the coach did Harry allow himself to feel how hard his heart had been pounding.

The sounds of hammering faded in the distance as the coach drew farther and farther away from the mansion. Harry had a disoriented, diminished feeling, as if he'd just woken from a dream.

He thought of what he'd said about the master locksmiths of the world and wondered if one day the ingenuity of man would invent a lock that constantly shifted and changed the way that house did. He shuddered. A lock like that would be inescapable. A lock like that would resemble the tragic intricacies of Sarah Winchester's guilt-trapped soul.

From the séance room Frances Merriman watched the coach depart. The window there was set with an optical glass. Its inverting properties made it appear that the farther Harry receded, the closer he approached.

Frances sighed. "Why did you let him come? Why did you tell him everything?"

Sarah looked up from her desk. She had new plans for the mansion laid out before her and had been drawing in a new wing.

"You know why I let him come. I had to to save him. As for why I told him everything . . ." She sighed and began folding up the sheets of paper. "A moment of weakness, I suppose. I had so hoped that he would understand and believe. We're such kindred souls, practically inversions of each other. He spoke of magic as the manipulation of reality to create illusion. And what do I do here but manipulate illusion to create realities?

"Don't worry, Frances. He feels sorry for me. He won't tell anyone. The brash conjurer turned out to be a kind and earnest young man, fascinating in his work. I know that William will like him." She slid the revised plans into a desk drawer. "Will you assist me to the door, dear?"

Frances helped her aunt make her pain-racked way to the air-shaft door. "You're in so much pain here, I'm afraid that one of these days you'll decide not to come back to us."

Sarah Winchester patted her niece's arm. "I know my responsibilities, dear. I won't abandon you or anyone else who comes my way." She turned and opened the door. A stairway was barely outlined there, faint as smoke. A stairway Sarah's carpenters had never built.

Frances watched her aunt step out onto the empty air. Step by slow step the elderly woman receded down and away from her, fading bit by bit until she disappeared.

Sarah made her way down a floor. With each step the arthritis in her ankles and hips receded. By the time she reached the next floor landing she felt as though she could dance.

She walked across the landing to where it let into a little room. It was just the right time of day. The late-afternoon sun shone through the room's magnificent stained-glass window. The light from the ribbonlike flourishes and abstract floral shapes washed across Sarah like a wine made from jewels.

Through one of the quartz crystal nuggets she peered down on the inner courtyard. Harry Houdini was holding court there, entertaining other guests with card tricks. Eventually he would come to understand that this was the one place he could be glad he couldn't escape from.

Sarah heard the faint strains of the orchestra warming up in the ballroom. William waited for her in the Venetian study. And any minute Annie would come racing through the front door with one of her beaux, ready to waltz the night away again.

After a lifetime of good works, Sarah Winchester died at Llanda Villa peacefully in her sleep in 1922 at the age of eighty-three.

For years Harry Houdini went on to greater and greater acclaim. Among his other feats, he took challenges to his physical prowess. He claimed that anyone could punch him full-force in the abdomen to no ill effect. On October 21, 1926, a couple of college boys approached him in his dressing room after a show and struck him before he had a chance to contract his muscles against the blows. The assault ruptured his appendix and caused other internal injuries. Within a few days he lay dying.

Long before this, Harry and Bess had decided that if Harry should pass on before Bess, if there was opportunity, he would whisper into her ear a sentence that only she would know, so she could challenge the mediums to retrieve that message from Harry from "the other side." It was to be Harry's final refutation of the spiritualists' claims.

From his hospital bed Harry felt himself slipping away. Instead of the final darkness or light he expected, the corridors of a familiar and limitless mansion began to open up before him. Harry at last understood what Sarah Winchester had been trying to tell him.

He felt himself sliding into a Harry who'd never escaped Llanda Villa, who'd lived there since his visit. There was time left, perhaps years and years, before he'd face that last light or darkness. "Bess," he whispered urgently. "Bess."

Bess leaned toward him to receive the message she hoped she'd hear again from the great beyond. Proof, despite Harry's debunking, that there was a hereafter where they would be together again.

"Meet me back at the house, Bess. Go to the great house and meet me there. I'll be waiting," Harry said with his last breath, clutching at her. He kissed her. Then he slid away.

Bess frowned through her tears. It was a strange, strange message, but she memorized it word for word and committed it to her heart. And never understood it.

Afterword to "The Escape Artist"

I think it's normal when writing to find at the culmination of a project that one has an awful lot of "outtake" material from the research. I found this especially true after I finished my second book, *Vanishing Point*.

This novel was set predominately in the Winchester Mystery House (Llanda Villa) in San Jose, California—a mansion endowed with a wealth of eccentric history and detail. The detailing formed a central part of my novel, but due to the time frame in which the novel was set, and plot constraints, I could use little of its history. For the last year or so I've been nagged by ideas for short stories set in Llanda Villa based on its actual, and rumored, chronicles.

"The Escape Artist" is one of these. I brought it as an untitled rough draft to Sycamore Hill. The general critique consensus was that, as written, it made for a rather sweet story, a "valentine" (Maureen McHugh's insightful comment). In that first draft the tale ended with Sarah descending the stairs to meet William and Annie.

I had no objection to the story having that sort of impact, at least in part. But I'd wanted to convey a sort of sadness and poignancy besides. After the workshop I changed the ending to one of several that I'd had tacked up on my studio wall as possible alternatives or extensions. And of course, there were lots of other problems with the piece.

During Sycamore Hill we all wrote "magisterial comments" on each other's stories. I got useful comments from everyone, but Mark Van Name's covered all the bases for me the best, and was the one I kept checking back in on during the rewrite:

> "This story frustrated me deeply, because it is built on such rich material and yet does not hold together well as written. Houdini and the Winchester Mystery House form such a natural and intrinsically interesting pair that the story must provide an equally rich and interesting payoff. Houdini could be facing the house as a kind of escape test, or it could be a truly supernatural place whose authenticity he tragically fails to recognize, or he could recognize its true supernatural nature but be unable to tell anyone—many plots could work. The obvious but tough trick is to find the one that expresses the message you want the story to deliver."

Mark, I hope that this version comes up to both your and my expectations more fully.

I owe thanks to John Kessel for the title—thanks John, I think it's perfect.

Michaela Roessner

P.S. This story has already won an award, bestowed upon me by the ad hoc Sycamore Hill Awards Committee. It won "Character in a Critiqued Story that We'd Least Like to Have as an Editor"—Sarah Winchester, because of the way she'd endlessly tear down, build up, and rewrite your stories.

Body & Soul

ROBERT FRAZIER

KYUKI

CLIENT: Genobotix Labs
FILE: Dali.gx * report notes
From encrypted files I discovered on the Genobotix net:

"There is one physical characteristic shared by all of Dali's victims. They secrete hardened teardrops.

"The drop is of such hardness and resistance that it bears smart blows from a hammer without breaking. Yet if you grind the surface of a teardrop which has resisted the hammer, or if you manage to break the tip off the small end, or tail, the whole shatters to a powder. This shattering is attended with a loud report; and the dust or powder to which it is reduced is extremely scattered all around. If the experiment is made under fixed air pressure, the drop bursts with greater impetuosity, so as to sometimes break the container holding it; and its dust is finer than when done in open air. If burst in darkness, the drop produces a brief flash of light."

This passage affected me deeply. What was the so-called Dali stalker doing to the insides of these people? Did he think that by changing their physiology so drastically he could alter what they were deep down? Alter their humanity?

I didn't believe that was at all possible.

I couldn't accept it.

But he was out there. And if this Dali was the same man Genobotix hired me to find, the same "past employee" they desperately wanted to recover, then I felt compelled to confront him alone. Before other operatives got in the way. Especially the Feds (whose case files couldn't show up at Genobotix without collusion . . . collusion at a high level).

So I pressed forward with my search. Went undercover without a word to my contacts at the Labs.

I kept thinking—why would they keep Dali's identity a secret?

MURTAGH

From the past, from the constant and unbidden memories that discharge across my temporal lobes in epileptic waves, another voice sings to me. It's gruff and nasal and seems to caution that too much madness in this world is too much sorrow. But I'm bone weary and must finish yet another nostalgia piece on the roadside.

I know nothing is truly as it seems. Nothing.

This time it is a student hitching a ride from San Diego to Salt Lake. Big kid with eyes behind thick gold-rimmed glasses. Baby fat that squares his face with the look of a tired bulldog. He is a whiner. He whines about his beliefs, about the squeaky-clean goals of Mormonism, about holiness, about a future dictated by the righteous and the just; yet he triggers a fearful vision in me. I imagine Gothic tableaus informed by sound. Feet stamping out military anthems. Staccato volleys of gunfire.

Last night a full seizure overtook me. What Hughlings Jackson called a doubling of consciousness. An overlay of what Penfield termed in his experiments, "the brain's record of visual and auditory experience." I found it extremely difficult to hold the van to my lane on the highway. Yet the seizure held a miraculous sense of joy for me.

I felt time roll back, and there stood my mother in the flesh. Young and handsome with her auburn hair. Holding out her arms for me to run into. Singing Irish lullabies that drowned out the Gothic furor that the boy beside me—in the van—seemed to extrude.

I knew then that I must free this twisted soul from the blinders of his teachings, from his terrible demons, and I began to conceive the blueprint of the boy's change. I tapped out combinations of instructions. I encoded the commands that would rewire the mechanism of his human thoughts. All this from the keypad on the central pad of my steering wheel. While in the back of the van, my little nanocells began to queue up in their factory vats.

And now that it is over—the subject injected, the piece concluded by his vast metamorphosis—I drive away with a momentary feeling of quiet. No song, no furor.

Mother, I am at peace.

KYUKI

CLIENT: Genobotix Labs
FILE: Dali.gx * report notes

I ran the simulations a hundred times. Three days' worth. Had to. Variables compounded each day that Anthony Murtagh traveled under false identity, each week since he went rogue from the Labs (presumably with the routines and nano samples he developed).

And I narrowed it down to one pattern of credit fraud. This pattern was restricted to small-scale highway vendors without security cams. In 40 percent of the incidents, the perp was described as a woman. Usually a van, varying in color. Never the same plates: state or number. These elements may have thrown the Feds off the scent. If in fact they were as good as I was at sniffing out patterns and applying logic. Which I doubted.

Last two Dali incidents: Pocatello then two days ago at Barstow, California. Last series of fraudulent incidents that fit my pattern: Vegas then San Bernardino then Provo then Laramie, a fresh one.

The Feds thought Dali continued west into the quagmire of Southern California to hide. My guess, Murtagh doubled back to I-80. Headed toward Iowa, where he went to graduate school. I patched into the DOT Highwatch cams at Grand Island and found my suspect based on rate of travel and a million other fac-

tors that I'm capable of factoring. Then I prayed he (she) wouldn't change vehicles, or identities, before I got there.

I chose my stretch of highway, just after an on-ramp. Determined the best sites for first contact. Leased a security op to chopper me to the initial site, and arranged to have him hold at a distance, either to relocate me (site #2, West Branch exit) or to follow as a backup.

I changed clothes under a scrub oak and set up on fifty yards of wide shoulder, expecting to try further sites for most of the day and night.

The van slowed at my first raise of a thumb.

MURTAGH

Before me Interstate 80 runs straight as a ruler through the hills of eastern Iowa. Between two endless stands of corn I spot a figure in silhouette against an acid-washed seam of sky. Facing me, arm out, backbone stiff, thumb up. My memory shuffles to a phrase of austere, almost glacial jazz. Something off my mother's favorite late-night radio programs. I take this for a sign, a purer message from beyond. I brake and idle along the stony shoulder.

"Hey, thanks," the hitchhiker says through the open window. She hesitates then opens the door.

The song in my head is loud and I say, "What?"

"Thanks!"

I say, "No sweat."

"I'm chilly," she says as she settles in the passenger seat. "That wind is picking up." She rubs her hands together in front of the heater vents in the dash. I program a one-minute blast.

She's just a year or two older than my last rider, with a heart-shaped Oriental face, spaghetti-straight black hair, no bangs, no makeup, no jewelry or adornments. A plain cowhide jacket, tight black stretch pants, and red high-top sneakers with medallions of white rubber at the ankles.

"I'm headed to Chicago. You staying on Eighty?"

I nod.

She continues. "Thank God you're not a guy. I was worried, you know?"

"You've had trouble?"

"Kind of."

I slip the van back into the slow lane, accelerate. A new song blares in my head. I say, " 'Kind of.' That seems ambiguous."

"Well, my last ride tried to hit on me."

I lean toward her and say, "He hit you?"

"No. Ah, it was nothing much. I mean, I took care of it."

I'm not sure I heard her right. "You what?"

She raises her voice. "I told him I was a fan of Dali. You know, the guy who alters people into, like, sculpture. That shut him down."

And that's when I realize this girl is a real talker. Someone who'll run at the mouth about themselves and cute guys and the latest bit of media sensationalism.

"I'm Kyuki."

I let the music drown her out.

KYUKI

CLIENT: Genobotix Labs
FILE: Dali.gx * [direct feed]

I'm sub-vocalizing. Direct to microchip. But it isn't direct enough to capture what I'm going through.

This woman is Murtagh. I'm convinced of it. Not an ounce of earthy sensibility in her bones. She regards everything with the curious eye of a scientist. She stays aloof. This is no doubt due to Murtagh's history of deafness. Actually, to the deafening seizures of a "musical" epilepsy that plagued (or empowered) Anthony Murtagh's last brilliant months of research at the Labs.

I feel scrutinized and at the same time dismissed. Ignored. Only a man can accomplish that feat.

Murtagh must have injected himself with the nanocells to assume a disguise. Despite what those FBI files said, despite all the restricted reports I have scanned, his nanocells aren't dangerous and unpredictable. Somehow they perform minor genetic changes without running rampant through his body. If crossmorphing from man to woman can be called a minor *affair.*

MURTAGH

"Dali is this guy who's like this serial, ah, artist," Kyuki says with a shrug. "He doesn't really kill people. But he preys on motorists and travelers. He gets them away from their vehicles, and he changes them. It's a morphism. No, zoomorphism." She surveys all the equipment patched into the dash. "You must have HV in here somewhere?"

I tap a button that activates a flat black monitor inset at the center of the dash. I hate the violence of the news, so I use a screenblock code for rides just like her. "The signal's wonky."

Kyuki stares out the windshield as a blue truck glides even with us in the slow lane. Then she looks back at me. Her eyes have widened.

"That's him, for chrissakes."

"Who?"

"The guy who gave me a ride. Do you think he's following us?"

Before I get a decent look, the truck maneuvers into a charge-station-and-restaurant complex off the highway. We buzz past the turn-off.

I say, "Guess not."

"Don't you scan newspapers?" Kyuki asks.

"Not much. It's just me. I like it that way."

"Oh. A retro." She tenses. "Hey, this isn't a gas huffer, is it?"

"Hardly!" I exclaim for effect. "She's antique but fully converted. State-of-the-art electric."

Kyuki relaxes, convinced I am an odd bird, perhaps, but nothing from her categories of "dangerous." Then she starts fidgeting again.

"So maybe you've heard of nanotech?"

I nod. "Molecular machines," I say, giving the simplex view.

"Yeah, they say that's how this Dali does it."

I say, "I thought they cured the flu."

"Look, I don't know."

A new series of songs kick my head. A Sousa march. An ad jingle. A scronking sax. Then a soulless, restrained horn funneling notes across the rooftops of Las Vegas. Siesta hour for the lounge crowd. It's all terrible, but hopeless to ignore. It neutralizes our conversation.

Kyuki looks peeved with me. Then bored.

She starts up again. "You know what else is extreme? Jetboarding down K-2 and Everest. There's special coverage on HV."

"Times are a-changin'." I nod sagely. "Maybe that's what this is about."

"Huh? You've lost me."

"Just thinking. Maybe these are transition times. No more passé expression of rage. Or angst. You, well, you do something else."

Kyuki grins ear to ear. She's not saying anything but she's thinking real loud.

I say, "What? What is it?"

"At first I thought you were simple. An Earth Firster, maybe. But you're okay."

I laugh. "That's good to know."

And then a truck pulls up behind us, matches our speed for a while. Kyuki turns dead quiet. I floor the accelerator and try to keep ahead.

KYUKI

CLIENT: Genobotix Labs

FILE: Dali.gx * report notes

This was not a pleasant business, Murtagh's business. The one victim who could speak, though only for a short while, gave this account:

"I found myself in a half-awake state, wondering at my circumstance. I had been struck by a blow outside the rest stop, that much I remembered, but I could not determine where I was. My eyelids would not lift. Was I in my car? Another car?

"Soon after, I felt a burning sensation trickle up my arm, as if I had been injected with acid. My eyes smarted and filled with water. They finally flickered open. Darkness surrounded me and I tried to move.

"With a jolt I felt the fire seize my heart. My whole body experienced a prickling pain attended by fainting and shortness of breath, on which I fell into cold sweats. My belly began to swell to enormous proportions, followed by violent purgings that did nothing to reduce the swelling. I felt I was birthing a parasite or a demon."

*   *   *

When I realized what Murtagh had done to himself, I wondered if he went through this pain. Just to become a woman.

I would rather have died than suffer such an intrusion to my being.

Or wait for reports of another victim.

MURTAGH

The road snakes under our wheels, exfoliates behind.

Somewhere around Coralville, where the dam contains a reservoir as vast as the secrets we all withhold, I leave the back-and-forth with the truck and take an exit. It feeds south along the Iowa River. Time for a recharge and a long slow drink, ice cold. I ride on the crest of a drumming in my head, something African. Followed by a huge choir of women dissing their lot as mothers and wives. Stuff that eats right at my soul, keeps me quiet. Only the girl seems to be in a deeper funk than I am.

First we notice a square gray building where, according to the sign, American speech is tested against Iowan English as a norm. A bunker in the already hopeless war against illiteracy. Then a dairy farm with a yellow-and-black-striped feed silo that resembles a yellow jacket's ass. In close we wind through the city park, full of immense shade trees and pens with native buffalo and flightless birds the size of prize-winning hogs.

My passenger smokes a cigarette. Flicks the ash out the vent window by snapping her thumb against the filter.

I ask, "Ever been to Iowa City?"

"Nah. You kidding?"

"Not a bad university town. What would Austin be without students? What would Madison be?"

"Redneck."

I say, "Correct."

She smirks. "Like I really see somethin' different about this."

"But Iowa students recently showed the first holovids here at an experimental film festival. The university is progressive."

She brushes that jet hair from her eyes. I wonder what's playing in her temporal lobes, what buzzes through the peripheral fission of her brain.

She says, "Did I tell you? My name is Kyuki."

I say, "I'm Ana. Ana Murray."

"You want a cig? They're denics."

I say, "All the cancer, none of the fun."

"So. Did you go to school here?"

I say nothing. Chalk one for the girl. She's prying uncomfortably close to my personal life without exposing a whiff of her own.

She flicks her butt out the vent again and stares down the tree-lined streets like there's another place she suddenly wants to go.

KYUKI

CLIENT: Genobotix Labs
FILE: Dali.gx * [direct feed]

He (she) unsettles me. I believe firmly in statistics and probabilities, not fate. Yet didn't he stop on my first attempt at contact?

I am further distressed by my breach in ethics. I was hired to gather data on Murtagh's disappearance, make projections and run my sniffer programs. A simple armchair job (albeit with a large order of complication). But once I detected him, did I download my sniff to the Labs and upload my fee? Did I contact the different local authorities (who want him so badly)? Did I leave it to the FBI and their vested interests?

No.

Instead, I arranged this rendezvous for my own purposes.

And there is this—what will he do to me if he finds out the truth?

MURTAGH

You learn to survive for cheap on the road, dirt cheap. After acquainting myself with the changes in the downtown area, I pull into a fast-food establishment called Bar-B-Q, with the logo of a *B* above a *Q* separated by a branding iron that is stamping out the doughboy face of the chain's original owner—Garth or Billy Ray or whatever-his-name-was. There are creosote-treated picnic tables to one side, a life-sized bull for the garbage, but it's windy and cool out there as I connect the van's plugs to the remote recharger jacks in front of the restaurant. Juice first, eat in the van later. Back inside I use the dashboard fax instead of walking the ten yards to the order window, and I wait in the van for our order numbers to cycle across an LED display along the facade of the building. I access through my files for the proper alias to charge our stop to, but I decide on cash. I've been using the cards too much.

In my big California-style mirrors, I watch Kyuki cross the street to a drugstore and return with a newspaper on a ROM card the size of a gum stick. She hikes herself in, and I start the engine to blow some real heat into the front section of the van.

"Check this," she says as she plugs the card into the dash. "A big spread. It was previewing at the register."

"Wow!" I say. But the enhanced colors on the screen are grainy at best. Low-res dreams.

"This one." She scrolls. "This one's a real piece of gear. I mean, Max Ernst gone 3-D!"

"Hmmm," I say as I scan the captions. "Not very insightful text."

Her eyes widen. "Oh?"

"Well, look. It talks about this Dali character and the victim, who she was, the human-interest angle. What about meaning?"

She points. "You mean like tree limbs painted bloody and other weird stuff?"

"Yes." I zoom in on several features of the photo spread.

"Dali's signature? Or sick humor?"

"Why not both?"

She looks hard at me. "But you don't think so."

I shake my head. "That wouldn't communicate."

She brushes my hand off the controls. "This—" She zooms in and blows up the biggest picture in the center of the spread. "This is what you call communication?"

I'm hearing Midnight Oil.

The victim is clearly delineated. The lower torso is female. The upper torso looks like a huge cockatoo. It's strapped to a bed that has been burned down to charred mattress springs. Clearly in panic. The marks of huge tires mar the sand around the bed. There's a man-sized soft sculpture thermometer stuck on forty-five degrees Celsius. And red tree limbs overhang the dried creek bed where the person was recovered.

"This contains a message?" she says, loud enough to startle me.

"Well," I say. "So maybe I'm wrong."

I look away. Our order's been posted. I clear my throat and step out into the chill air. Later, when we've opened the food cartons and set them steaming on the tray between us, I remark, "Not the best food I've eaten."

Kyuki snickers. "I thought this town was a dump."

She irritates me as much as I her.

KYUKI

CLIENT: Genobotix Labs
FILE: Dali.gx * report notes

One innocent victim had already been infected by the technology Murtagh employed. That worried me. Could it happen again?

The doctor—who'd been infected through contact with a victim—said this:

"Since my hand and forearm are now altered by my handling of the patient, specifically during the cleansing of her wounds, I have been able to experiment with the phenomenon closely. Too close for comfort.

"When the epidermis is separated by cantharides (a drastic measure), or by fire (a stove burn), it is much thicker and tougher and more difficult to raise. The blue-green hue at first seemed to be a juice or fluid between the epidermis and cutis, in newly formed aqueous vessels perhaps, but when macerated I found my flesh gave off no color at all in warm water. The very nature of the organ is changed. The entire genetic blueprint.

"Thank God the transformation stops at my elbow. The duplicating action of branching DNA, and other nano-specific genomorphic alterations, can just as easily get out of hand."

Considering this, I could not touch Murtagh. Not even in passing.

I hoped I didn't have to face that.

MURTAGH

I'm quiet on the next stretch of highway. Mostly thinking to myself about what Kyuki's been saying. The girl jabbers for the both of us.

Simultaneously my head plays through a song list of Van Morrison, a favorite among my research colleagues. I ask Kyuki if she knows the singer.

"I like him," she says. "He's aware. You know, when Van talks about the Queen of the Slipstream, you just know who that is. She holds her tongue when secrecy is needed. She's one of the hidden people that makes the world turn."

Kyuki stares at me.

I'd prefer anything to that little Irish crooner gone bald.

At dusk we cross the Mississippi River at Davenport, where the interstate jumps to Moline and western Illinois. She gets bored as the miles tick by, and she works the keypad under the dashboard screen until she gets around my mute codes. The audio is tinny.

"The third victim was a man, doctors think. This particular metamorphosis was characterized by a totally alien form. The flesh shone orange when cut, and when all the lucid autopsy parts were surveyed at once, they made a very splendid show. Yet the blood did not yield a luminous quality of itself. Upon pressing a sliver of the flesh between glass slides, its light was not extinguished nor drained away. And no part yielded the least degree of heat."

She kills the screen, rolls the window down, fumbles in her pack for another cigarette. "Wow! That must have been something."

My body tenses.

"Hey," she says. "Do you suppose that if those buggers change enough of you that you're truly a different person? Does your soul change?"

I say, "Yes." There doesn't seem to be any other answer.

She gets real pensive then, and fiddles some more with something in her backpack. Just enough to create an extra double-strength buzz along the surface of my nerves. Enough to make me recall that she's had her hand in that pack all along. I'm ready to slam the brakes. And sure enough a truck rides up beside us, but it zips away and up an exit ramp. There's been no signal between them. And in the ramp lights I see the truck was red, not blue. I feel a trickle of sweat slide along the last rungs of my spine and drain away. I've been silly.

Another five miles up the road we approach a highway service area adjacent to a small dirt airport and more planted fields.

"Your van need juice?" she says. "I have to use the girl's."

"Fine," I say as I call up the battery levels. I can't avoid the stop; we're nearly drained and the emergency battery lasts only twenty minutes.

"Thanks."

I nod and ease into the left lane, then up the entrance feed.

I get out first, plug into the restaurant's jacks. The charge meter spins madly.

Kyuki says as she gets out, "Might be awhile."

I watch her carefully. She follows the RESTROOMS sign that flashes down the side wall to the back. She doesn't even look toward the office where the attendant is . . . and the phones.

A couple planes come and go, a loud chopper. Kyuki doesn't return.

Is Kyuki gone? Desperate for a quick ride? Probably more like spooked, I decide. I slip back behind the wheel and lay my hand on the friend I keep Velcroed to the underbelly of the steering column. A special. I tuck it in my waistband and round the corner to the back, to check the restrooms.

And that is when it happens, the moment I have both dreaded and longed for, and finally accepted as an inevitable consequence to my actions.

They snap my arms behind me, spread me against the wall like an unwashed heathen who might not know what he's done. But I do. I've lived more than anyone can imagine in this last year, seen more real estate burn in the flickering depths of all those eyes up close before they're altered forever. And that's what they're afraid of, why they hate me so much.

The unspeakable things that I have seen!

That I truly know.

KYUKI

CLIENT: Genobotix Labs
FILE: Dali.gx * [direct feed]

Almost got away. I'd called in my backup, but the Feds showed first.

They cuffed me and then quarantined me. Like I was another criminal. Like I was the bug, the wiggly under their microscopes.

I'm in the hospital wing that they've taken over to house Murtagh. Outside of Davenport. Not far from the Hoover historic site. Herbert, not J. Edgar.

The chance of infection has passed, yet they still find me useful. They know who I am. They won't listen to a single argument for releasing me.

I make the best of it by grilling their medicos. Making observations when I can. Asking to visit Murtagh, insinuating myself in this weird acting role they've given me. The near-victim-who-deserves-to-know-everything-as-they-see-it-through-to-the-end role.

In a way, the events have allowed me to observe Murtagh's obsession in a way my joy ride would never have allowed. For he's done it again.

My observation . . . Murtagh is perhaps the least changed of his own victims, yet perhaps the most. For he cannot yet be dismissed as an abomination. The woman's body has disappeared, but the remaining form still possesses the color of human flesh (gone gray, poor in oxygen). Though the organs are newly differentiated. Especially the heart, for the doctors have explained that it has but one ventricle, with only the vena cava and aorta that open into it; so by the aorta the blood comes out of his heart, which then branches a thousand times over the exposed bronchia that, in protective folds, comprise the entire upper surface of his body, only to be reunited. The reunion of these capillaries forms two large trunks, of which one proceeds towards the head, the surviving cranial area, and the other towards the lower parts. In other words, he breathes without lungs.

In other words he is simplified. Morphed to an original schematic, to the pure fish form we all evolved from. Is this all that Murtagh wants? To become some essential, some purity that has been lost to us all?

Shudder to think.

MURTAGH

I let go almost from the moment I am caught. I feel the release, like a great weight shifting and freeing an elevator car that rises to the heavens.

The inhibitor codes I used to stabilize them inside of me . . . I have wiped, flushed, booted, let go . . .

Let my nannies swarm through the body . . .

Let them conquer and be done with it . . .

Let the music end . . .

KYUKI

CLIENT: Genobotix Labs
FILE: Dali.gx * [direct feed]

My activities seem purposeless. A dog circling for just the right spot to lie down. Dreamlike flows. I walk where the echoes sound hollow, where lives have passed but left no impact that cannot be washed away. Hospital time runs at the same speed as the afternoon soap operas that play unwatched in the rooms. Each gesture paused. Unmeasured. Each scene played three times before the heroine's question is answered.

And what is my question here?

Why these smells? The antiseptics and astringents that waft like perfumes blowing off Dante's Inferno. Why these white white tiles? The brightness seems to twist and turn and fold back into itself, a Klein bottle effect.

Perhaps I should ask why I am here. Because I was caught in the web surrounding Murtagh's criminal arts? Because of my curiosity? Not precisely. But because his imprint is nearly identical to mine. Right down to the color blindness. To the gene markers at the very end of the digitized strips I uncovered in his medical files. He's Irish with a Japanese-American mom. I'm half Irish half Japanese.

Murtagh could be my blood.

Yet I find him abhorrent and unspeakable. My skin crawls to be in his mutageneous presence. I hate all that he represents. Still, there is nothing to prove that he is not my lost father.

Though of course he is not.

I end up in the bathroom at the end of the hospital wing, sit-

ting on the stall floor, crying because I am helpless. Blubbering. Helpless to leave. Helpless to stay. Helpless to make a difference.

A rookie nurse calls to me from outside the stall. She asks if I'm okay.

I am, but I'm without choices.

MURTAGH

The moments blur. . . . Not just because my eyes have changed, have oozed and reformed and thickened into lenses of small focus. . . . But because time has changed. . . . Not so much within me. . . . Not my inner center or my core clockworks. . . . But the outer workings that surround me as a context. . . . There is no day or night now. . . . I see one long stream of bright lights. . . . I sense a constant presence of machinery. . . . People bustle about me in an unending stream. . . . If I sleep, I have no memory of it. . . . But when the girl stands before me I see she has gone through time. . . . Losing it. . . . Gaining it back. . . . I feel sorry for her. . . . They used her to find me. . . .

KYUKI

CLIENT: Genobotix Labs
FILE: Dali.gx * [direct feed]

I am still sub-vocalizing. The Feds haven't suspected me of this. And tonight, they have further relaxed their security.

Perhaps the van yielded all the secrets they cared about. Perhaps they're waiting for Murtagh to die, or have resigned him to life as a root vegetable. But he is still awake, if that is a proper description. When I make a loud noise, he quivers then falls back into a stupor which lasts only as long as his next heartbeat. He tries desperately to move his neck, or what was once his neck. In order to be visible to him, I stand directly in his line of sight. I lean toward him and he reacts with a blink of his eyes. He hears me, I think. He can no longer speak back when I ask how he is.

I sit in the chair, but this time I move it close to his bed. He is so compact, so amorphous, he must be strapped in, but that is not enough. His bluish, oxygen-starved flesh seems to flow, and it threatens to drag him through the restraints and onto the floor. If that happens, I cannot help him. The thought of touching his flesh frightens me deeply. Just sitting this close frightens me.

I am shaking, and he is quivering. We are surely a pair.

I realize that no VIPs or doctors are hovering. We are a pair, at last, truly alone.

I say, "I am sorry. If I hadn't interfered, you would still . . . still be yourself."

And he somehow speaks back. His re-formed mouth-parts clack like busted piano keys. His musculature again strains to turn his head, a head without a tether. He grunts softly, the words repeat.

"Golk dhe."

His form heaves against his restraints and he shifts closer to me. . . . Flops next to me, almost touching.

"Olv dme."

Those liquid jelly eyes seeming to flow across his cheek, his skin, no actual cheeks, just this glowing gunmetal blue. This untouchable cobalt dull radium skin. Then . . . then the unspeakable gets spoken. I understand.

"Hold me."

I go rigid, my breath stops.

ANTHONY

My body is not a body anymore . . . it is a container . . . a mere tissue. . . . I am shapeless . . . surprised I can even focus a normal thought . . . with my synapses realigned . . . with this web of electricity . . . this nerve web . . . yet all holds to the same truth. . . . I hear only whispers . . .

KYUKI

CLIENT: Genobotix Labs
FILE: Dali.gx * [direct feed]

Again he squalls, "Hold me."

I find I can bend forward, and I reach out. I find myself undoing his restraints. I feel his heart's jittery tremolo as I pick him up into my arms. Surprised at the lightness of his being. Surprised that I embrace the unembraceable.

And I carry him out.

Past a weary guard.

Past the doctors who confer behind closed doors, and through the back entrance to the parking lot outside. Where I can go no farther with him. He is only this free. By a hundred yards. Yet the distance from only a day ago, or two days ago, seems immeasurable.

He or I? Who is it that has come farther to reach this place, this moment?

ANTHONY

I feel myself rising ... this time I am the elevator car ... my vision moves across a mosaic of white and chrome ... glare and wispy shadow ... it is a tiny window on the old reality ... a magnifier held over a document too detailed to read without it ... I feel the intimacy of her hands ... they press into me ... support me as I float ... carry a warmth that flows through the will of my reformation ... keeps the cold from shattering organs ... vessels ... melted bones ... all the beastly formed struts of my architecture ... something like a tear oozes from my eye ... time stretches each syllable of my plea ... "hold me" I say again ... "don't leave me" ... but do words come out if I cannot hear myself make them ... if there's no breath ... and somewhere ... yes ... somewhere another weight is shifted ... freed ... and a profound and utter silence floods in ... my mother's face fills me ... brightens ... flares ... pure light ... and I am accelerating with it as it leaves Earth for home ... for the spaces that rend the heavens ...

Workshop Comments

Karen said: "A curiously nostalgic story about the good old days when serial killers merely raped and ate their victims." Ouch. She also said, "Push the first-person view further." That felt good.

John said: "What is this story saying about randomness and control in our lives?" I stripped that to a basic.

Richard said: "Get rid of the 'Bob' music." I had songs in the margins, imaginary bands like Acid Bitstream and Cypher Optic.

Jonathan said: "Do cut some of the talk, musical especially." Do reassess the role of music in this, especially.

Carol said: "I like the murders offstage." But I still wanted some juicy details, Carol.

Alex said: "Focus on the nano-killer." *Focus* was the operative word.

Bruce said: "Don't flinch from the consequences of your own imagination." Eventually I looked and saw (instead) my mother, dying, unable to save herself.

Nancy said: "We need to see a foil to her and what her grisly 'art' is trying to do." Head click—two viewpoints are better than one.

Mark said: "I hate the secret-society stuff." Gone.

Maureen said: "The story cheats; it's a first-person p.o.v. where the narrator omits information." But I . . . but I worked hard at that.

M. R. said: "When you know where to go with this, smooth out the misdirection." Or just plain give it up.

Frost said: "All the cancer, none of the fun." Used that line.

Kelly said: "Maybe she morphs herself at the end." Another healing prescription from the story doctor.

Afterword to "Body & Soul"

That week in Raleigh started hot and ended hot. But sometimes I remember only the rain.

I'm used to it on Nantucket, where nor'easters slash sideways and eat the shoreline from under our summer homes. This seemed harsher. Walls of water. Vertical torrents that caught you walking back to the workshop building. They felt brief yet chilling.

In some way, the heat and the rain form an analog for my Syc-Hill experience. Foremost, the workshop sharpens my critical skills. *Numero uno* on the wired list. My drive is rekindled in just one week of sleep deprivation and serious talking about prose (leavened with plenty of bad snack foods and silly antics and partying, of course). That's the hot part, the constant. But there's a bucket of iced Gatorade in middle. The moment when all that high-octane perception is focused on your story.

Yes, I remember the rain. But most times it's the rest of the week I look back on with affection.

Kelly's house. Arrival night. Reading. Baked potato night. Rapping cynical anthology names. Emma's feet. Reading. Sitting around the tables. Reading. Standing out on the balcony. Mark's end-it party. Talking real and talking silly.

Getting the heat back.

Robert Frazier

The Fury at Colonus

ALEXANDER JABLOKOV

THE ONLY BLACK ambulance in the city stopped in the littered area at the rear of police HQ. The siren, unsuccessfully repaired many times, sounded like a sobbing infant, one too tired or despairing to cry properly. The dark-cloaked figure of the Fury rolled out of the back and fell to the pavement. Without seeing if his unwelcome passenger had landed safely, the driver gunned the engine, and the ambulance whimpered off.

"Nice to see you back, ma'am," the desk sergeant said from behind his bulletproof glass, scrolling a schematic smile across the LEDs of the overhead announcement board. The Fury peeled a flattened Coca-Cola cup from her dark coat and dropped it on the floor. It was a hot day, the sunlight molten on the worn squares of the floor, but the Fury kept her ankle-length coat buttoned up to her neck. Only the ends of her thick fingernails stuck out of the overlong sleeves. Her hair was long and stiff with dried blood.

She walked past the rows of desks and the whispers followed her.

"Back?"

"Long one, this time. Rough. Maybe next time she won't—"

"Shh! Bad luck. Did you hear what happened?"

"Popped Oedipus's head like a watermelon, when she finally caught up to him. Don't know why it took so long, with those bad feet of his. . . ."

"Popped his head?"

"Right between her hands."

"Oh, come on. A watermelon's impossible, much less a skull. Think you could do that?"

"Hey, I don't know. Maybe those empty eye-sockets made it easier, gave a pressure release or something. I saw the autopsy photos. Here, I got 'em in my desk."

"You *are* a swine. Can I see?"

The Fury opened the door to her office. She had already noted the absence of her name on the frosted glass, and so was prepared for the empty room with its cracked plasterboard and Burger King bag crumpled in a corner. Her heavy desk had left gouges in the floor. As she examined the abandoned space, the one fluorescent remaining flickered and went out, leaving a dismal residual glow, like crushed fireflies.

Her new office was five levels down into the substructure of the building, behind a stack of dented filing cabinets with hand-lettered labels, the black ink faded almost to illegibility. There were two windows, which implied a rise in status, but both revealed nothing but twisted layers of bedrock. They were the sides of aquarium tanks, displaying trapped seas of stone.

They'd moved her collection and arranged it in order on her walls: dangling jump ropes, crowbars bent by the frantic force of their homicidal use, pieces of stained cloth, even her favorite, a more-than-man-sized execution device made of two perpendicular wood beams. The drawers of her desk were still full of teeth and finger bones, and racks of organs in jars filled the shelves. The morgue kept demanding them back, but she always refused to recognize the validity of their paperwork. She was too attached to her souvenirs to let them go. Each was the memory of an avenged wound.

The precise arrangement of the office was all of a piece with the new Director's meticulousness, and indicated that the Fury's effectiveness could, and would, be destroyed without ever violating departmental regulations.

The Fury sniffed her desk. Clean as a looted tomb. A key

flick, and PENDING files appeared on the computer screen. Nothing flagged for her. Departmental statistics showed that a higher percentage of crimes was being solved. She wasn't interested in solving crimes. That wasn't her territory.

As a final indignity, her IN tray held a stack of sheets explaining the Department's new retirement plan. Glossy color photographs showed the green leaves of a place called Kindly Grove, with the legend *Gracious and Exclusive!* Using her fingernails, she spread them deliberately out on the ancient surface of her desk, tearing and shredding the paper. They would try to wall her in down here, she knew, until she was completely entombed in stone, as she had been before her existence.

As she sat, the trundle of document-laden carts, the flirtatious laughs, the anxious footsteps, the tense discussions, all the sounds of the office, continued, first abashed by her presence behind the door, then unrestrained, as her existence was forgotten.

A drop of liquid fell on the piled sheets, its smack loud in the silence of her office. She turned her head in time to see another blot of crimson appear on the investment options page. Then another, each drop thick, rounded, and shiny. The metallic scent of fresh blood filled the room. A desperate splatter obliterated most of the health benefits. The Fury put her fingernail in a drop, touched it to her tongue—and was out of the office and down the hall.

"Oh, an oversight, of course," Athena said from behind her garishly painted desk. Her hair was swept up above her head and held in place by rusting metal spikes pulled from some distant battlefield. Her wide gray eyes regarded the Fury calmly.

"You should have been copied on it. An oversight, as I said." Athena snacked on an ox's thighbone wrapped in fat, but didn't offer the Fury any. There had been a time, the Fury remembered, when sacrifices had been offered her as well. "It's nothing. All taken care of. No need to trouble yourself, it's just a family dispute, a problem stemming from the late war. . . ."

The Fury ran her fingernails across the desk's elaborately painted surface. Ten parallel lines of blood appeared, and began to soak in, ruining the colorful scenes painted there. With a casual air, as if she'd just spilled a little tea, Athena shook out the linen napkin in her lap and wiped up the blood.

Athena was an Olympian, a member of the new administration. A lot of irrevocable changes were being made. But the Fury was a key member of the Old Service. Athena could fiddle with the details of jurisdiction all she wanted, but she could not stop the Fury from acting.

Athena swiveled her chair and stared out of the window. Her office was high up, and looked out over the bronze towers of the city. Their edges were rosy now with what was either dawn or sunset. Abruptly rising mountains held in the sky.

"Well, fine. If you want to go, I can't stop you. As you obviously know. But . . . well, I do have to mention . . . there's no free money left in the travel budget. None at all. I don't know how it happened, something to do with how we calculate the quarter—"

The Fury turned and left the office. She could walk.

Most of the storefronts were boarded up, the fiberboard panels bearing the spray-painted names of their suppliers, the only businesses thriving in the neighborhood. Behind the stores were endless rows of apartment blocks, curtains hanging dispiritedly out the windows. Children peered out of the darkness, momentarily distracted from TV screens by the false promise of the world outside. A hand dangled a one-armed doll over a dangerously low sill, as if checking its urge to suicide.

One entire block had been torn down for an optimistic parking lot, now abandoned, grass coming up through the cracks, ailanthus trees growing against the wall of windowless brick next door. The Fury stared across it and imagined it covered with trees. She could see the roots shoving their way through the asphalt, cracking it and revealing the old soil beneath.

The Fury turned away, disturbed by this image of retirement, and crossed the car-tormented street. The funeral home had once been a comfortable mansion, from a time when people had lived here as a choice. It was the only structure preserved from that time. With its white columns and high windows it was solemnly beautiful. Its porch wrapped around two sides. Bright red awnings had been unfurled against the summer sun.

Right next door was a garbage-strewn vacant lot. Men in brightly colored warm-up suits squatted there, injecting drugs through disposable syringes from a pink box stolen from some hospital storeroom. The fat one in the canary yellow, his sneakers as clean as if he had been carried into the lot by slaves, seemed to be the leader. The others aped his gestures, desperate for his approval. The vacant lot ended in a corroded and half-toppled wrought-iron fence, beyond which was the overgrown cemetery.

Inside the funeral home, there were no mourners, no sign that anyone knew that Clytemnestra of Argos was dead. After she finally managed to pry the front door open, the Fury found herself there alone. She walked to the rear of the room, undid the catches, and slammed back the lid of the massive bronze coffin.

The embalmer had been careful to restore Clytemnestra to her appearance just before her death. Her gown was fine and looped with silver, jewels glittered around her neck and in her ears, her hands were raised up to ward off the blows, a look of terror deformed her face.

The Fury undid the gown and slid her fingernails into the body through the wounds. It took only a few minutes to determine that all relevant information had already been removed from the body during autopsy and embalming. The liver was a plastic child's purse filled with colored seahorses. The heart was a can of spackling compound. The ovaries, in a cruel joke by one of the male Olympians, were charcoal briquettes.

The actual autopsy results were closed to the Fury by the new regulations. The Olympians meant for her to be stymied, to scream out her impotent rage here, tear this irrelevant place apart.

But the Fury was not entirely without resource. She stood for a moment until the air from her nostrils no longer smelled like burnt hair. She stripped Clytemnestra's dress away completely, to reveal the knife-slashes through her sagging skin, so tattered that the embalmer had been forced to attach it to the underlying fat and muscle with safety pins. The attack had been brutal and unrelenting. Her neck was almost severed.

The Fury pushed her lips down on Clytemnestra's and exhaled gently. The wounds cried out in agonized chorus: "Orestes!" The name of her only son was a curse, Clytemnestra's last, and it was that curse that had brought the Fury out from her subterranean imprisonment. The Fury sucked in, tasted death and vengeance, and teased Clytemnestra's tongue out of the nest of her mouth. The taste was bitter, more bitter than the Fury remembered. As she inhaled, the wounds gasped, "Oedi—" She pulled her mouth back, and the wounds fell silent. She yanked Clytemnestra's tongue and flipped it out across the chin. She scraped a bar code across the pale, white-coated flesh, so that Charon would take Clytemnestra across the Styx without argument, payment provided by the Old Service.

"Are you ready?" someone said behind her. It was the leader of the warm-up suit–clad drug addicts from the vacant lot. His belly swelled proudly in his canary yellow. She stepped aside, already feeling the breath of loss. Clumsily, pupils dilated, muscles twitching, they picked up the heavy coffin and hauled it out the rear of the funeral home.

The sun was blinding after the darkness of the house. The Fury preceded the coffin through the cemetery, mourning, weeping desperately, the tears streaming down her face, carving paths through the ancient dried secretions on her cheeks. Clytemnestra now lived on within her, and she was sorrowing for her own death.

The pallbearers toppled the coffin off their shoulders. They had not bothered to dig a grave, but the bronze hulk sank down into the earth like a whale diving. Soon the weeds and grasses would grow over the spot, and it would be as if nothing lay beneath. They collapsed amid the weeds, weary with their great effort. Without looking back, the Fury walked out the other end of the cemetery and down the road toward Argos.

The gate guard hid within his mirrored kiosk and pretended not to see her. The Fury skirted the lowered security gate intended to bar entry into Argos and headed up the winding road that led between the lawns. The houses sat back behind their garages. Beyond them was the white wall, topped with a roof of red tile, that surrounded Argos and protected it from the desert.

An occasional car slid by her, drivers polo-shirt relaxed in their air-conditioning, but there was no other sign of life. The planned community centers, one in each quarter of the city, were empty, the bulletin boards devoid of anything but admonitions that notices would be removed after two weeks. A single toppled tricycle on a front walk seemed like a monument to a vanished race.

The Fury stalked to Agamemnon's house. Reporters were clustered around the front, outside the POLICE LINE tape, waiting for something to happen. Most sat in the back of the video van from a local TV station, crunching empty coffee cups in their hands and staring at the pavement. Some peered anxiously at the half-open front door, desperate for any sign of activity.

A murmur ran through them at the Fury's appearance. Camera and video lenses shifted in her direction, but there was no *click-whiz* of film advance or whir of videotape, just breathless peering through the viewfinders. The Fury kept her power because her image was never reproduced. Aside from vague rumors, the first sight of the Fury was always the first unforgettable sight. This was quite unlike the new Olympians, whose power depended precisely on the excessive reproduction of their externals, on the presence of a hieratic image of Zeus in every temple and automobile showroom, so that the actual appearance of the god was unnecessary.

Well, the Fury still did all her own stunts. The new gods would soon no doubt change this rule. There would be cover stories on the Fury, tabloid TV scenes of her office, Fury posters, Fury drinking cups, all the rest, and her effectiveness would vanish. These reporters would be instruments of that downfall, and they knew it.

That would explain why she was here, at this scene of an irrelevant sideshow. Clytemnestra had not died at Agamemnon's house. That the roots of her death could be found here should have been irrelevant, but somehow it wasn't. Agamemnon had been murdered by Clytemnestra on his return from the war, but since Clytemnestra was not his blood, but just his wife, the Fury had not been called to avenge him. A man chooses his wife, and thus cannot find her actions against him incomprehensible.

A nondescript sea scene hung askew on the wall of the living room, an unnecessarily coy symbol of violent events. One of the off-white armchairs, part of a coordinated set that included the curtains, was toppled over, and the vast TV in the walnut cabinet was shattered. The vacuum of the CRT had sucked most of the broken glass into itself, and the oatmeal cut-pile carpet was clean, except for the bloodstains. The victim had died watching TV, perhaps even a local report of his own recent activities.

Aegisthus lay on his back on the living-room floor. He wore a steroid-driven paramilitary police uniform, a large holster, and insignia of iridescent tantalum, a subtle sign of his ancestry, and perhaps a claim of legitimacy. That claim had done him little good. After his assistance in the murder of his cousin Agamemnon, Aegisthus had pushed Argos around for years, his power derived from Clytemnestra.

The security walls, the checkpoints, the tire-busting spikes at the entrance—these kept the outside world at bay, but did nothing to defend against internal tyranny, whose takeover was made easier by isolation. No one had struggled too hard against it. He'd reduced greens fees.

A young police lieutenant, his uniform already stripped of the more egregious insignia, seemed unconcerned by his one-time commander's fate. He knelt by Aegisthus's pulled-in right hand, tilted the wide, sightless face first this way, then that, and talked quietly into a tiny tape recorder. He had not noticed the Fury's entrance. He glanced occasionally at the open front door, to where the reporters stood, one or another of them pointing a camera at the only activity visible: the intent policeman doing his job.

He moved down the body, careful to stay in view of the door. Aegisthus had suffered as many knife blows as Clytemnestra. Orestes was clearly fit, and not a man to make the minimum necessary effort. Aegisthus had damage to every major organ, with an almost mathematical delivery of thrusts. He was a heavy, fleshy man, and it couldn't have been easy to find the pancreas, say. The Fury leaned forward to listen in on the police lieutenant's forensic observations.

"... then, sauté the shallots in the clarified butter," the lieutenant murmured into his tape recorder. "Take the shallots out and deglaze the pan with the white wine. Reduce the sauce by a half, and put the shallots back in, along with the mushrooms. Pour the sauce—"

For the first time, he saw the Fury, and clicked off his recorder. "I'm afraid I'll have to ask you to step back behind the police line."

The Fury leaned over farther. He blinked, then covered his face in horror, as the pus that came from her eyes dripped down into his face, burning and sending its rank stench into his nostrils.

He crawled to the partial shelter of the overturned armchair and held on to the legs for comfort. "No, no, no . . . it wasn't my fault, I was loyal, I did my job." His voice was muffled as he rubbed at the ooze on his face. "But now the Olympians are here, it's out of my hands, don't you think I'd do something if I could? Don't take me, I don't deserve it."

The Fury stepped over Aegisthus's outstretched legs and walked down the hall. The master bathroom was the most dramatic part of the house. It was all dark tile, mirrors, gold-plated taps and nozzles. It was here that Agamemnon was murdered by Clytemnestra and Aegisthus, just as he was stepping into the tub for a long-awaited bath. That case had been hushed up by an earlier administration, and Clytemnestra and Aegisthus had been permitted to run Argos for years. That reign was over. The new Olympians clearly had other deputies in mind.

The images of the blood-spattered tile had been widely reproduced, though without comment. No news service had been sure whether Agamemnon's murder was laudable or vile, and so the images had remained just abstract patterns, like a wallpaper design. Every square inch had been photographed before a quick hosing had returned the bathroom to its pristine state. A major advantage of modern bathrooms was their ease of cleaning.

Two workmen with paint-spattered caps were in the bathroom, spreading clear plastic sheets on the walls.

"Over to the left a little bit . . . no, too far. Now down just a hair . . . what kind of hair? Don't get me started. Did I tell you what she made me do last week? You wonder why I had to talk like I'd had a root canal all morning? Well—"

He sucked in his breath when the Fury entered, then had to cough.

The plastic sheet bore the pattern of bloodstains from Agamemnon's murder. Attached to the clean black tile, it brought the room back to that day. The other worker, unconcerned with the Fury's presence, calmly taped the top of the sheet. It matched exactly, with the straight lines of blood running just down the white grout between the tiles, forming a red-brown grid at the bottom of the wall.

"So that we can remember why," the gabby one said.

Clytemnestra remembered why. In her head, the Fury bore the entire toxic history of the House of Atreus, a stack of murder and violence so heavy that it would never be moved or sorted out. But the Fury could already see the Olympian solution. They would repaint the structure and turn it into art, a subject to employ television writers, advertisers, and directors. Agamemnon's father, Atreus, had served up his brother Thyestes's own children to him at a feast. Aegisthus, another of Thyestes's sons, had finally killed Atreus, only to be supplanted by Agamemnon. But these were merely the last chapters of an endless bloody tale, stretching back past Pelops to the ancient ancestor Tantalus.

In his last moments, Oedipus had warned her of what would happen. Rather than bloody, still-dripping crimes, these could be turned to stories, with Orestes's murder of Clytemnestra merely the last. But the Fury could taste Clytemnestra's death in the back of her throat. And despite all the Olympians, she would soothe that taste with the sweet flow of Orestes's blood. She had no interest in stories.

She could just see the tips of Aegisthus's polished boots from where she stood. And, for the first time in her existence, she asked herself a question. Could a man who murdered the driver of another car in a foolish traffic dispute—as Oedipus had murdered, all unknowing, his father Laius—ever be worthy of worship? She still heard his words.

Disturbed by her musings, and dismayed by her own distraction in coming to Agamemnon's house, she swept back out past the assembled reporters, who were all now clustered around the police lieutenant.

"We have all suffered long enough," he told them. "It was time for a change." The shiny lenses of cameras and videocams repeated countless distorted reflections of his face. A hundred whispered duplicates of his voice recorded themselves on the spinning tapes.

Clytemnestra had been murdered on the largest of Argos's three golf courses. It was the only real public space in Argos: the community centers were unused, and all the stores where the inhabitants shopped were in the strip malls on outside roads. Clytemnestra had just been teeing off. Typically, she had been at the blue tees, the men's, adding ten yards to her drive.

"It's not as if nothing grows there." A groundskeeper was taking his lunch at the spot, in the shade of an intensively watered sycamore. "Nothing would be okay, we'd just put in a sand trap, move the tee over a bit, difficult but no real problem. No, people say that, but they don't actually come here to look." He vaguely held out a silver thermos, not really wanting her to accept, then poured himself another cup of lemonade. He swirled it in his hand to hear the cold ice click.

The place where Clytemnestra had died was barren, with a few remnants of dead grass around the edges. Extravagantly spiked cacti sprouted from the dry soil. The gray-brown surface was already covered with miniature black stacks of cryptograms, the dry microscopic plants that held the desert soil together. For all the efforts of the green grass to make it seem dead, the desert was deeply alive. That was what made it so frightening.

"A hazard's supposed to be clean sand, not this stuff. It's a reminder they don't need, and no one wants to rip his Sansabelts on a damn Joshua tree while digging holes with his wedge. And who do they blame? You got it."

The groundskeeper had not gotten up with the Fury's arrival. He was an old man, brown and sagging from years of the desert sun, and wore the trim blue uniform of the Argos Golf Course.

"I served with the old man, you know. In the war. Only saw him from a distance. Never up close. I was at Aulis. . . ." He tried to hurry past the thought. "I always did my duty. So did Agamemnon. That's what got him into all the trouble." He peered up at the Fury. "That's what I like about you. You do your damn job, and don't jaw about it."

The Fury didn't move, and he shifted position so that she gave him a little extra shade, as if she was just some sort of topographic feature. Most people feared the Fury, but there was no reason for it. The Fury was not arbitrary. He had done his duty, lived well, and had nothing to fear.

"The boy had to kill her, you know. He really did. Things couldn't go on the way they were. Not that I don't understand her. Boy, I know why *she* had to do what she did. Like I told you, I was there." He looked past the Fury at the mountains. "I was there, waiting with everybody else. Aulis AFB was never meant to hold so many troops. We were triple-stacked in what barracks there were, camped out in the hangars, piled up all over the place, cooking in the sun. We were getting sick. And mad. We wanted war, not waiting around. Of course, if we'd been given a choice later, we might have changed our minds."

The golf course was also the town graveyard, the Fury now saw. Tiny stone squares were everywhere, almost invisible in the grass. Each one bore a name, a location, and a bar code for inventory control. She looked over the names while the groundskeeper spoke. Troy was the most frequent place of death.

The groundskeeper was almost crying. "We had to go. We *had* to. The old man knew his job, his responsibilities. The new administration didn't want to take over the useless projects from the old, and Artemis demanded . . . Well, you know what it was." The old man's voice took on the singsong tones of a long-rehearsed but never-told story. "Iphigenia, Agamemnon's daughter, Clytemnestra's daughter, had to be sacrificed. It's in the regs, how you do it. Eighteen paragraphs of it. They raised her up on the rack in the repair garage, cut her throat. She looked around, meeting each of us in the eyes, and there were hundreds of us there. As her blood fell on the oil-stained concrete, the C-5As were finally able to start their engines. They thundered up into the smoky sky behind us. You shake when those engines go, all the way to your heart. But none of us turned to look. Each of us looked at her, remembering her eyes, the way she'd looked at us. Her hair hung down over the end of the lift, the ends trailed in the oil sump. Then they formed us up, and we went off to the war." He passed a hand in front of his eyes, clearing the scene. "Clytemnestra never forgave any of us for that. I could feel it when she saw me mowing the grass. I was an Argos employee. She wasn't going to kill me. But when it came to Agamemnon . . . well, as I said, I know why she did it. Did him."

The groundskeeper looked off across the course at the distant wall.

"He didn't go back, you know. After he killed his mother. Orestes didn't go back into town. . . ."

That was as much as he was going to give her, and it was enough. She walked off across the grass. Behind the clubhouse, an arroyo dug down under the wall, passing through a high concrete culvert. Teenagers had cut through the grating with torches and bent the corrugated iron bars back. The culvert itself was filled with broken bottles and old cans, blackened in ritual fires. Beyond was the eternal desert, sere and serene in the light of late afternoon.

The soft sand left from the last cloudburst was marked by a single line of footprints.

The mobile homes in the park had been there so long that they were almost invisible under spreading vines, untrimmed shrubs, abandoned leaning bathtubs. Strings of Chinese lanterns hung above picnic tables. The street sides of yards were marked by truck tires painted white, filled with flowers. And everywhere were the mystic silver globes on their stands, sign of the cryptic Orphism of country folk. In each of the trailers a TV glowed, many tuned to the same channel. Some joke on an old sitcom caused a thunder of canned laughter through the trailer park, like a coming storm.

A burly man with a yellow beard sat at a picnic table in work-stained coveralls, several drain pans in front of him on the green-checked plastic tablecloth. He scrubbed carburetor parts with an old toothbrush dipped in solvent, shifting them from one pan into another as he decided they were clean enough.

"If I had known, I never would have let them into the house," he said. He held a needle valve up to the light, shook his head, and discarded it and its housing into a drain pan with a flick of his thumb.

"Oh, *your* fine house." A woman in a dragon-embroidered house robe appeared in the trailer door. She was beautiful, with bitter lines to her face. Her dark hair was long and wild, and her lipstick was smeared on her lips, probably deliberately, with a thumb. "Orestes and Pylades. Their hands were so . . . clean. So soft. I noticed it as soon as they arrived. Do you really think they wanted to come in here?"

She leaned against the jamb and crossed her arms under her breasts. She irritably examined the kitchen witch that spun slowly under the lintel. One elegant leg stretched out of her robe. She wore velvet high-heeled house pumps. This was Electra, Orestes's sister, Agamemnon and Clytemnestra's daughter. She had been compelled to marry the auto mechanic while Aegisthus and Clytemnestra ruled Argos. His name was Waldemar, and it was clear from the way he looked at her that he loved Electra desperately.

"His hands aren't clean anymore, that's for damn sure." Waldemar took a certain gloomy satisfaction in that. He looked up from his work and saw the Fury where she stood, silent in the road. Her presence didn't seem to surprise him. Silently, he gestured her to sit on the bench opposite him. She did not move.

"He's not here, damn you!" Electra teetered in the trailer door on her high heels, but did not quite dare to fly at the Fury.

"True enough," Waldemar said. "Didn't come by this way, far as I know. Only on the way in, on the way to Argos." He shook his head. "If I'd known what those two butt-heads were up to . . . Well, Pylades is in jail now, though he's got a fancy lawyer and will be out pretty soon, smart word says. He was just helping out a friend, after all. What could anyone do? Want some chili? It's what we're having for dinner. Out of a can, though, I should warn you. Electra's a sweet thing but she's never been much of a cook. . . ."

"Stop chattering with her," Electra said. "You know you're just doing it to bug me."

"Well, you got your chance to talk with those TV guys." For the first time, the Fury noticed the tracks of the media vehicles all over the grass. A shrub had been broken next door by a van backing up, several of the trees had clamp marks on their bark where cameras had been attached, and the flowers were turning back to the glow of the setting sun, having been temporarily seduced by the brighter sun of the TV lights.

"I couldn't get a word in edgewise." Waldemar had finished his carburetor and set the drain pans in a neat row against the side of the trailer.

"Oh!" Electra bit back the retort that he wasn't important enough to be listened to, though it hung, almost visible, in the air.

The TV was on inside. War scenes flickered on the screen: explosions, miles-long lines of refugees, burning cities, tanks roaring across fields and smashing through the corners of farmhouses already tilting with age. Agamemnon was alive again, sitting behind a table and stabbing a pointer at a chart covered with symbols. He was a bland functionary of death, not a warrior, and this made him sad. Somewhere, hidden deep, never reflecting the light of day, was a bronze helmet with a bobbing plume, a helmet he had never been permitted to wear. On the TV he was suddenly a tragic figure, unfairly removed from a life in which he had never really participated. His beseeching eyes looked out toward Electra, Waldemar, and the Fury. In the corner of the screen was the tiny outline of a running figure: the logo of Orestes In Flight, symbol of this news coverage.

The scene cut to a vast traffic interchange crammed with cars, all stalled with their windows shattered, bodies hanging out of the doors and dangling over the railings, Agamemnon's great victory in the war, then to a perfume commercial. Beautiful hands with long fingers delicately opened a crystal bottle.

The Fury kept staring at Electra. It was starting to make her nervous. The Fury stood in her long dark coat like a funeral monument, an old one, something ancient, put up because of the real fear that the body beneath might rise up if not held fast by the weight of the stone. Flies buzzed in the heavy air.

"It wasn't my fault," Electra gasped. "I didn't have anything . . . that is, I didn't know, I didn't know what Orestes was going to do!"

Waldemar stood and put himself between the Fury and Electra, though the look on his face revealed that he had no idea of what he could do if the Fury chose to act. The Fury knew that Clytemnestra had never truly loved Electra, who was too much Agamemnon's daughter, while she dearly loved Orestes, and Electra knew it too.

"If you had any brains, you'd be able to figure it out for yourself," Electra jeered, as a way of excusing her fear, her betrayal. "And I can tell you because it doesn't matter. He's on his way to Delphi. Good luck with getting him once he's there."

Delphi. Apollo's home base. They weren't making it easy.

"Climb back into your hole!" Electra hooted behind the Fury as she walked off. "You've bitten off more than you can chew."

Orestes stopped in an ice-cream shop for a soda. The place was decorated in a deliberately Olde Tyme style, with ceiling fans over the curlicue tables and chairs, and a picture of a gentleman in a straw boater, wearing what looked suspiciously like a butcher's apron.

Orestes was just reaching for the large paper cup when the Fury came up behind him. He tried to be cool, to pretend that her presence didn't matter at all to him, but his hand shook as he tried to pay the bored high-school girl behind the counter, and he dropped the change.

"I . . . I think I'm going to be sick." He ran for the bathrooms in back. There was a door there, leading to the gravel parking lot. The screen door flopped loudly.

The Fury scooped up the change and handed it to the girl behind the counter. "Thanks." As she turned indifferently back to the magazine she had been reading, the Fury recognized where she was. A rack of newspapers displayed to one side said *Thebes Advertiser.*

Thebes was the home of Oedipus, the Fury's last victim, the one who had come closest to destroying her, and the one whose voice still spoke to her. The counter girl did not recognize the executioner of her great ruler, never having seen her on TV, or in the magazine she had now turned her attention to. Her eyes were as blue and vacant as the sky, and the Fury had the sudden urge to remove *her*, this innocent and chance-come-upon young woman, as guiltier than Electra, Orestes, Agamemnon, or Clytemnestra, to drag her screaming through the streets and sacrifice her in the main square beneath the monuments to old wars.

The Fury dug her nails into the counter. She had never before thought of killing anyone but the one designated for punishment. Indifference and ignorance were not crimes, not to her. They weren't. The Formica peeled off its fiberboard backing with a sound like dry leaves. The girl looked up from her magazine, annoyed.

"Hey, is there something else?" As she looked more closely, fear seized her face. Her skin tightened and her thick pancake makeup seemed about to crack and fall to the floor.

It was that fear that saved her, and saved the Fury from an impossible swerving from duty. Some trace of her old power was still left her.

She left the shop and strolled the streets, seeing the scene of

Oedipus's history. Thebes had a pleasant green, and rows of old brick buildings, many of them now gone. The building, she thought, where Jocasta had hanged herself, and Oedipus had put out his eyes with a pin from her dress, was a smooth expanse of improbably white gravel, as was the old hotel at which Tiresias had stayed. Thebes was determined to have no memory of the great. Perhaps the girl was not alone to blame for her ignorance.

The Fury walked past the strip malls and video-rental stores at the edge of town, and found the remains of the Sphinx where they lay, on a bluff above the creek, near a railway embankment. The iron-heavy lion paws lay embedded in the soil, their claws extended, as if the Sphinx had grabbed at the sky as she fell. The wings leaned against the trees, most of their feathers gone, the skin beneath shredded into thin strips. The serpent tail was just visible in the brown, tannic water of the creek. The head with its face, austere and beautiful, lay half toppled, kept in its place by tree roots partially washed out of the soil. Soon it would loosen and fall into the water, to be buried in the soft green mud of the creek bottom. The Fury looked at the gently smiling enigma, now disfigured with spray-painted graffiti, and wondered about the true story of her death. For the Sphinx had been, like her, a member of the Old Service.

Surely an answer to that silly riddle about the ages of man had not been enough to cause her suicide. The Sphinx had had an infinite number of riddles, and no man—not even Oedipus, whose entire life was a riddle—could have answered any of them. The Fury looked up into the sky. Afternoon cumulus clouds stacked themselves up until they hit the top of the air and turned into thunderheads. The Sphinx had flown high up into the clouds, until she was nothing but a speck, then had hurtled downward, screaming, and smashed to the ground here, killing trees and sending stones flying.

Perhaps Oedipus had revealed the future to her, as it was slowly being revealed to the Fury, and the Sphinx had realized that she had no place in it, *could* have no place in it. So she had, by her own will, ignored the rules of the Old Service and destroyed herself.

And it was Oedipus who had started uncovering that future to the Fury. She remembered the last time she had seen him, at the suburb of Colonus, near Athens. She had stood on a parking lot in front of an old brick warehouse, its former windows gone, sealed with paler, shoddier bricks than those of the elaborate facade. A stretch of green-painted freeway had hemmed them in close, crowded with motionless trucks rumbling and belching smoke, their drivers featureless figures, uncaring of the drama that went on below them.

Oedipus had left his daughter/sister Antigone at the rusted chain-link fence and shuffled forward on his deformed feet, the feet through which his father Laius had put a steel pin when he learned the prophecy that his son would eventually kill him. His blank eye-sockets seemed to stare piercingly at the Fury, who had not even had to pursue him. He had, instead, come to her.

"Well," he said, as he felt the tips of her rough fingernails reaching out for him, "I feel myself becoming a story." And thus he lived, long after he should have been dead, and would influence the thoughts of those yet unborn.

Corn fields, vivid green, thriving unnaturally under the hot sun, stretched out on the other side of the creek. Beyond them, on the two-lane blacktop, the Fury could see the figure of Orestes, heading toward Delphi, his shape deformed by the hot air rising from the pavement until he flickered in and out of existence. He was desperate, fearing doom, yet his gait still retained something of the football star's insouciance. The Fury looked at him with Clytemnestra's eyes, with mixed rage and proud love, as an archer might look at a fresh-shot arrow flying heartbreakingly at exactly the wrong target.

The Fury got to her feet.

The clouds crashed to earth with the coming of night. Tree branches creaked in the high wind. The Fury walked on the edge of the road, rain sluicing down her coat. Glowing yellow windows floated in the darkness. A spotlit sign on a fake-rustic stone wall said PARNASSUS. For the first time in her memory, she was tired. It was a desperate, terrifying weariness, one that spelled her eventual doom. Cars whipped their headlights across her, then sped on, sliding their wheels on the wet leaves, desperate to leave her behind.

She stepped off the road and waded across a swirling drainage ditch. Apollo's house, Delphi, sat on its impossible width of smooth lawn, just the other side of a thin stretch of what was left of the forest. The house was gigantic in the darkness. The Fury walked up on the flagstone patio and peered in through a window. She could see the monitory red blinking of the security system as it waited for her. The rain drove heavily on her, and she felt that she would slip and sink into the patio stones, to be found in the morning as nothing but a few shreds of dark, stinking cloth. Apollo would laugh and rake her into a Hefty bag.

She worked her way along the slope on which the house was built, seeking downward with the water running through the grass.

The Olympians were new, but they always built on the old. They lacked the courage, or perhaps the imagination, to raise their proud structures on virgin soil. She thought she might . . . She slid down the mud to the lowest level of the house. Sure enough, Apollo had used a preexisting foundation, massive blocks that had once supported a wooden barn. She pulled the old metal-bound door open and slipped in under the house.

She could smell the animals that had once been kept here, the cattle and sheep, lowing and baaing, knowing that they were bound for sacrifice. The ground was still littered with the rotten remains of the ties and hobbles that had held them.

Moving blindly, the Fury worked her way up the stairs out of the subcellar, into the upper reaches of the house. There was no sound save the gentle whirring of the ventilation system, and the crash of the rain outside. The carpet was soft and silent under her feet.

Orestes slept in an upstairs bedroom, facedown on the bed, his arms thrown around a vast pillow. The Fury ran her nails down his back. He muttered and shifted, but did not wake up. Incredibly tired, the Fury lay down on the bed next to him and went to sleep, too.

"You're asleep?" The Fury stirred and blinked her encrusted eyes. "I didn't even know you *could* sleep. And what does that leave me? I'm dead, and those I've killed are down here with me. I am dishonored even in the grave. They mock me. My heart is full of holes . . . look, I can put my fingers right inside of it." The

Fury whimpered at the lash of Clytemnestra's voice. "And Orestes is gone already. He's got connections, he knows he won't suffer. Not while you're snoozing. Will you wake up?"

The Fury snorted and jerked, finally coming awake. The bed-sheets were bunched up around her, and Orestes had disappeared. The shade of Clytemnestra stood at the foot of the bed, seeping blood. She held the shreds of her skin apart to show her heart.

"You lay down right next to him," Clytemnestra shrieked. "You went to sleep. Here in Apollo's house, like it's some sort of rest stop."

The Fury looked down at where her nails protruded from her sleeves. The white tips seemed to glow in the dark bedroom. By now they should have been encrusted with Orestes's blood. She was black and hollow. She no longer understood what it was she was trying to do. Oedipus had cursed her. Her old rules did not compel her any longer.

"Go! Get up, and go. I don't care what gods you have to face. You have my vengeance on your tongue, and you cannot swallow until you have Orestes. Go, you dismal thing, so that I can lie on my stone without feeling the sting of contempt from those other miserable dead, who mock me for the way I died."

The Fury stumbled to her feet. Clytemnestra's shade vanished with a last anguished shriek. Bright sunlight slanted through the window past the carefully tied-back curtains. As softly as she had come, the Fury went back down the stairs.

The house was packed with offerings. Stacks of stereo receivers, microwaves, CD players, computers, Cuisinarts, many in their original packages, piled up to the ceiling. More exotic donations: ion implanters, CAT scanners, auto emission diagnostics, precision gyroscopes from B-1 bombers, high-energy lasers, stood in places of honor under the overhead lights. A stack of VCRs and gigantic color-TV sets made up one wall of the living room. Each TV showed a repeating tape loop of an honored donor to Delphi, scenes of domesticity and business, an eternal repetition that earned Apollo's blessing. The Fury ducked under the wheels of the titanium mountain bikes that hung from the ceiling, and went out the front door.

Apollo polished a bright green BMW M5 in the circular

driveway in front of the house. He spread wax on it with fierce intensity, then buffed it so that he could admire his own face in the finish.

Apollo saw the Fury, and snapped his polishing cloth at her contemptuously.

"Get out," he said. "And stop persecuting Orestes. He's under my protection. He's only done what's necessary. You operate by primitive rules, like a flatworm, so I don't expect you to understand. Leave it up to us in the new administration to deal with the subtleties."

The Olympian was crisply handsome, with flowing golden hair, bright blue eyes, a cleft chin. He'd had opponents flayed alive and broken a lover's skull with a flung discus, but he now made the law.

"You don't care anything about the life people want to lead, do you? You don't want to understand the reasons they have for what they do. If you looked into their hearts you wouldn't be so obsessed with enforcing your obsolete regulations." The Fury did not respond. The pleading left Apollo's voice and his face grew hard. "You have no idea what you're up against. A heat-seeking missile could take you off the road like a bug. Zeus can hit you with a restraining order and forbid you to come within ten yards of anyone who has murdered a parent or sibling. You'll feel those barriers against your face." The blood flowed close under his pale, perfect skin. "You'll burn like the foul fat drained to the bottom of a crematorium."

The Fury gained strength from Apollo's contempt, though even that was a defeat, for she had never before had to worry about her resolve. She rested her hand on the enameled fender of his BMW. The paint blackened and blistered, the metal beneath corroded in an instant. The car groaned as some strut deep inside failed. The front wheel tilted, loose.

Apollo, one hand on the tire to keep it from falling, shaking with rage, let her walk down his driveway and out of Parnassus.

"All right, all right." Orestes stood on the buckled asphalt of the parking lot, raising his voice to be heard above the din of the motionless trucks on the expressway. "I'm here. You're here. Let's get on with it."

He was guilty, ragged, near defeat, but he still bore irritating remnants of his frat-boy arrogance. The Fury stared at him, feeling Clytemnestra's reluctant love for him, her only son, Agamemnon's son, joyful in youth, proud in manhood.

She did not move. Why did the bricked-in windows of the warehouse in Colonus rise up again behind her? Why the green-painted expressway, the trucks apparently still unmoved, their drivers embalmed monarchs untoppled from their thrones? Here, where she now stood, Oedipus had gladly met his end. The dark columns of the expressway stood by her like tree trunks. The smoky sun did not touch her now. She stood in shade, and did not reach out to enfold Orestes. Within her, Clytemnestra gave one last anguished cry.

"You can't touch me, can you?" Orestes was wearily proud. "I did what I had to do. Apollo and Athena recognize that. Their law will take it into account."

The Fury's only argument was herself, tall in her black coat, her hair crunchy with dried blood, her eyes seeping poisonous pus, her fingernails sharp and ready to pull the heart out of Orestes's chest.

But that argument was no longer sufficient. The cool shade of the steel-and-brick grove was banished by the glare of spotlights hoisted up on gantries by cursing, overall-clad grips with TV-station logos smeared across their backs. A camera floated serenely by overhead on the end of its crane.

Torn newspapers spun across the pavement in a vicious prop-wash. Athena strode into the lot to the thunder of the helicopters. Over her hair she wore a CBW hood. It was thrown up casually, as if nerve-gas protective wear was in this year. The eyeports gazed lugubriously, like the eyes of a basset hound, and the huge cylinder of the air filter bobbed above her forehead.

"You had your chance," she said sadly to the Fury. "But you thought too much, waited too long. I'm afraid you've finally lost jurisdiction. Here." She gestured with a brochure. "Take this. I think you can use it."

Behind her television vans jockeyed for position along the curb. Police had blocked the ends of the street, and it was criss-crossed with power cables. Workers finished affixing white columns to the facade of the building opposite. Lit from the side, the

Areopagus Courthouse looked perfect. TV anchors stood in front of it and talked earnestly into the lenses of their cameras, setting the scene for the viewers sitting in their rooms at home.

The brochure suddenly in the Fury's hand showed a picture of a green shade: the Sacred Grove of the Eumenides, the last home of the Fury tamed. There she could rest, and reassure the Athenians that their world made sense. Human beings were close to inert and not given to transformations for the sake of mere art, save it was backed with gush of fire straight from hell. The Olympians would use her sticky, blood-covered claws, as they had used the willful sin of Oedipus before her, to give their feeble stories weight.

Athena, who had allowed the Fury this last futile mission precisely in order to finally defeat her, escorted Orestes into the glare of the lights, her arm around his shoulders, and faced the barrage of questions. The Fury turned from the glow of the monitors for fear of seeing herself, though she knew it was worthless. She had met her end when she listened to Oedipus. It had taken this long just to realize that she no longer had a reason to exist.

Orestes ascended the long steps of the white-columned courthouse, accompanied by the gray mass of his lawyers, their briefcases gleaming like polished shields, and disappeared through the high bronze doors.

The Fury turned and crawled her slow way into the deep cellars beneath the bricked-up warehouse, there to lose herself among the foundation stones with Oedipus's shade. The columns of the expressway were to be her Sacred Grove, where those who sought justice—few enough in an age that preferred mercy—could make their way to feel the goddess's sharp nails against their souls.

Afterword to "The Fury at Colonus"

The workshop session on this story began with a procession of cloaked and hooded figures pointing accusatory fingers and intoning, "Doom!"—guerrilla critiquing theater, right there in the sterile confines of the Merry Monk lounge. Then Jim, Mikey, Bob, Richard, and Greg pulled the bedsheets off their heads, got out their scalpels, and went to work on the story, along with everyone else.

Kelly: "This is a relentlessly, mordantly witty tale without a resolution. Too long, too long"—I cut ten pages.

Lethem: "Great, crazy writing. Cut it, and fix the end."

Roessner: "This is kind of long, but I couldn't tell you where to cut it because it's all so wonderful."

Fowler: "A tour de force. It's a bit long."

Emshwiller: "I think you should cut some *wonderful* things."

Butner: "The story sprung almost fully formed from the forehead of Jablokov. Kill your darlings, but don't kill the amazing evocative weirdness."

Van Name: "Clever and entertaining. Does drag in many places. The ending is also a big problem, because the trial is dull and does not stand up to the rest of the text."

Kessel: "Sometimes your prose is great, and at others it is clunky. I don't think the Greek myth and modern settings and moves are, in the end, integrated. Could you forget more about the allegorical meanings? Too long! Cut."

Do we see a consensus developing here? Absolutely right, at least on the subject of length. The version you have just read (unless you are just browsing through the book reading afterwords, an evil practice) is nearly 3,000 words shorter than the one I submitted to the workshop. I got much good advice on paragraphs, sentences, and excessive adverbs and adjectives to cut. I tend to write long, think it's all wonderful, and find myself loath to cut. A good workshop like Sycamore Hill provides not only advice on what to cut, but why. And also cautions on not going overboard. After hearing the discussion, Jonathan Lethem wrote on his sheet: "DON'T CUT TOO MUCH." I hope I didn't.

Frazier: "There can be sleep-deprived short-story moments at Sycamore Hill when you find yourself unwillingly and unwisely misappropriating the critical mondo-isms of others. So here's my Kelly headline in a Sterling hyper-verbiage loop: 'Jablokovian Electric Kool-aid Proto-Gasoline Punk Fear & Loathing Kill Riff on Greek Tragedy and the Joe Friday Empiricism of the American System . . . Hot Damn.' But Alex, don't forget the deballing part."

That one had to be quoted in its entirety. It's a big risk when playing ball with the pros at Sycamore Hill: sometimes the critiques end up being more interesting than the stories to which they are addressed.

Sterling: "Any story with a giant broken Sphinx covered with urban graffiti gets my vote. Great imaginative concentration, fine visionary intensity, eyeball kicks galore. Work some on the 'ecology of the supernatural.'"

Aside from the excessive length, the other concern was the ending. "The Fury at Colonus" is a retelling of the Oresteia from the point of view of the Furies sent to pursue Orestes. For dramatic purposes, I reduced the gang of Furies to one. Most of the great tragedians and poets of ancient Greece used the House of Atreus as a theme. All of the actions of the Fury are outside the confines of the classical narrative, though connecting with it, until she arrives at Delphi. This is directly based on the first half of Aeschylus's *Eumenides.* My original ending also used the second half: the trial of Orestes at Athens. It didn't work. All the energy I had built up in the story was dissipated. A free-for-all discussion after the written comments led me to the ending you have here, largely achieved just by chopping the last three pages off the story.

McHugh: "One gets the idea you would not be pleased if O.J. is found not guilty. This is a weird mix, a satirical salad that, after a stumbling start, takes on a life of its own. A wild ride."

Frost: "The Fury combines a Dirty Harry aesthetic with an image smacking of the Sea Hag in the old Thimble Theater comics from the twenties and thirties and the coat was reminiscent of both a spaghetti-western duster and a trench coat."

Greg also drew a nice picture of the Fury in a margin, which I am sorry I cannot reproduce for you.

Kress: "'... and the old gods die and pass away,' replaced by the tinny new. Done as stylishly as anyone ever has, and as entertainingly, and as poignantly."

Though the story has a strong anchor in Greek myth, and involved a lot of thought and preparation, the actual writing was done in a deranged state, with images slamming down on the page right from the nether regions of my brain. That made it hard to edit and correct, but Sycamore Hill handled it gracefully.

Alexander Jablokov

Homesick

MAUREEN F. MCHUGH

OUTSIDERS KNOW THAT if someone has been selected to dance at
Sah, they are a very good dancer. But inside Sah, when you have
grown up inside that old house, there isn't any outside. When I
was seventeen I was a very fine dancer, but so was every other
dancer there. When you are seventeen you compare yourself a
lot. You look at the size of another girl's hips, at her extension.
You feel ugly.

They were going to announce who would dance *Charn*. I
thought I might be cast. The instructors never told you if you
were going to be cast. At Sah you could be punished for asking.
So we watched the instructors all the time to guess what they
were planning for us. They were our weather, and how they
treated you in class was an omen. They were very hard on me at
that time, I remember. I couldn't get the feeling of flirting, I was
cocking my head the way I'd been shown, or I was spacing the
steps too evenly—this wasn't a musical in a play. Girls would say
to me, after class, that it wasn't fair to me. I thought I was being
tested, so I would just shrug.

I'd tell Thrella, my roommate, though. She thought the same
thing, that they were getting ready to cast me in something.

Charn is a small dance. Only eleven people.

I threw myself on my bed and stared at the ceiling until Thrella finally said, "What's wrong?"

"What if they cast me in *Charn?*" I asked.

"They might," she said.

"But what if they cast me in a male role?" I asked.

There are six male roles in *Charn*. I could dance a male role, I'm tall. And I'm strong, I can do lifts. Male roles are dramatic.

"You won't," Thrella said. She sat on the end of her bed. She was fine-boned, with tiny, delicate hands. When she danced, she was all sinew and cable.

"Sure, I might," I said. I ticked off the roles on my fingers. We knew who would be cast in some of the roles. They would be danced by principals, or by people who had danced them, or roles like them, for years. "For the female roles, Mov for lead, Kirtsa, Hevihai and Terez for the sisters." That much we all pretty much knew. "Grace for Mad Calliope."

"No," Thrella said. "They wouldn't cast Grace."

"They like Grace," I said. Grace and Thrella and I were all of the same age, the same class. We had been among the seven people from our class to be accepted as senior students. Everyone else had left Sah House to go out in the world and dance, but we could stay.

"Grace would be better for a male role," Thrella said. "She can do broad. She *is* broad. Her tightwork sucks."

I always said her tightwork sucked. Actually, her tightwork was orthodox, adequate, even clean.

"She makes things look difficult," I said.

Such a damning thing to say at Sah House. *"She makes things look difficult."* When you perform, you can get applause if it looks as if what you are doing is difficult. I thought that was cheap. We were dancers first, we were performers second, or at least that is what I thought when I was seventeen. It was my goal to make the difficult look effortless. You should be so good that you didn't advertise how good you were.

Male roles were the opposite of that aesthetic. Male roles were dramatic, strong. They were, I thought, a dead end. Lying there, on the bed, I thought that if I got cast in a male role, I would refuse it. I thought, quite clearly, that if I were given a male role, I would kill myself.

I would not have been the first girl at Sah House to kill herself. I'd be another ghost, another pale-faced girl who had hanged herself in the shower, someone to speculate about, someone to remember. Someone for whom dance had mattered more than life itself. The idea of joining those ranks of ghosts didn't seem very different from being cast in a dance. I was seventeen, and when you're seventeen, you think that the way your life is now, that's your whole life.

"You could dance it badly," Thrella said, "then maybe they'd never give you another male role."

"Then maybe they'd never give me another role at all," I said.

"They have to give you a role," Thrella said, answering so quick, I realize now, answering her own fears. "We all have to have roles eventually."

Thrella would probably not be cast this year, maybe not even next year. I didn't think anything about the fact that I was a better dancer than Thrella. We didn't talk about that because we both just knew. Young people are so arrogant, so insecure. In my secret self, I knew I was very good, and I expected to be adored. It was nice to have Thrella to talk to about dance.

I was, for a brief instant, honestly surprised when I was cast to dance Mad Calliope. I think I can remember that I was surprised before I decided that I deserved it. I want to have been surprised.

When I was twenty-seven I was chosen to go out of Sah House to Leihani to archive a dance. The dance was *Bottom Line,* a solo work which was something of a signature piece for me. It's a whimsical, difficult thing to make look easy. Before *Bottom Line,* most of the dances I did weren't whimsical. I'm not a character dancer; I don't play aunties or old women or witches. *Bottom Line* was frightening to do, and exhilarating. It is just a little over twenty minutes long.

I was not surprised when Sah sent me.

Leaving Sah was a little like dancing *Bottom Line.* It isn't that I had never left Sah House before; I've performed all over the world. But when we performed, we traveled as a troupe.

I'd performed in Leihani. It's a beautiful little artificial city, the quasi-capital of the Pacific. It was established fifty years ago, on a tiny island right smack in the middle of the Pacific. It wears its newness and its artificialness quite well. The buildings all seem to have hallways that turn a corner and are suddenly outside, without a door or even a screen. Apparently Leihani doesn't have mosquitos. There are plants and huge, improbably red-and-orange flowers. I had the feeling, the first time I was there, that the city barely managed to sustain its cityness. A little push and it would become island, and everyone would stop going to work and go to the beach instead.

When I came to Leihani alone, it was night and it was raining. I have flown alone to Sydney, to stay for a while with my parents, but I'd never landed in a city and not either been with people I knew or had people I knew waiting for me.

There was a stranger from the archiving people waiting for me, a very very young island woman, with a long flag of black hair down her back. "Ms. Banalong," she said. "I knew you from the performance of *Cloves and Cinnamon.* I've seen it so many times. I love your dancing."

It's a good thing it's hard to be mean to these young people. I wanted to be perfunctory. I smiled and said thank you, that it meant a lot to me when people told me. As if it meant a lot to me when I was tired out of my mind. I knew it should have meant a lot to me.

She chattered as she took me out to the car, talking about the schedule, and how she hadn't had this job very long, and how she studied dance and she danced for a little troupe on the island. The car wasn't one of the long limos, but a bright little yellow thing, barely big enough for two or three, so little that when we climbed in it bobbed under our weight.

We rushed through the rain, the streets shining back at us. My flat wasn't near the water or the big buildings of the center of town, it was out, where people lived. When we flew into a city to perform, we would pass over kilometers of streets and houses and blue swimming pools that reflected, briefly, blindingly upward like mirrors in the grass. My apartment was in a white building that loomed suddenly through the rain. I carried my bags up one of those staircases that didn't seem to have decided if it was an indoor space or an outdoor space. The door at least knew that it marked a boundary, it was some heavy, tropical-looking wood. The front room was apricot, too bright, too airy, to fit this cold rain.

She chattered more, now that she wasn't concentrating on ferrying me home through the rain. And then she left me, and I realized I couldn't remember her name. I wished I was home with Thrella. But this was the last time it would ever be my first night here, I told myself. Two months until I could go home.

The first nights I travel I always sleep badly. I'm always afraid that I'll miss some important connection. I wake up in bed not knowing where I am.

I woke up tired but full of nervous energy. It was time to start. When I finished my two months here, I would be changed, and that would show itself in my dancing. My dancing would be more mature, as I would be more mature from the two months of living on my own. Sah was too close, too much a mother. I was twenty-seven.

I was ready when my bright-eyed girl showed up in her little yellow car to pick me up. And I managed all the way to the archiving studio without letting on that I didn't remember her name.

The archiving would take months because archiving is a kinesthetic record. Historically choreography was transferred by word of mouth. Then someone invented a dance notation but dance notation was not even as exact as a musical score. And then there were visual records, but visual records lie.

The archivist in Leihani is a man named Christian Fedland. Christian Fedland is one of the best archivists in the world. Fedland's name led me to expect someone European, but he was an islander, with a broad round Polynesian face.

"You are Wae Banalong," he said. "I'm pleased to meet you. Have you ever done any archiving?"

I had not.

He is a large person. Not physically—although he is broad and stocky and he wears shirts in vivid yellows and reds, big Pacific prints that just fill a room. But he is big in a room. Sometimes he is a Buddha, you know, and sometimes he is a conductor.

Making a kinesthetic record is difficult, because you can't record all the muscles, so an archivist's skill lies in where he puts the sensors.

Fedland made me dance. He made visual recordings of me doing the same diagonal from *Bottom Line* over and over again. I danced for Fedland for three days and although in some ways it was very strange—he never corrected me, of course, he was trying to record what I do—it was the same thing. You rehearse, people watch, you do it again.

The fourth day he came in and I thought we would rehearse some more but he said, "I'm ready." And he got out his sensors and his gels and his recording devices and I took off my clothes.

I pulled off my tard, and everyone was nonchalant.

"You could all get naked, too," I said. And people laughed, the tension was broken and the bright-eyed girl who was my babysitter said it wouldn't be a bad idea.

Fedland knelt down in front of me and said, "Flex the big muscle." He meant the big muscle of my thigh. So I put my foot forward and flexed like a bodybuilder and he studied the way my ligaments insert, and smeared clear gel-glue on my pale leg and stuck on a little sensor, tiny and light as paper. I've danced naked before but it was hard to stand in front of this man and have him gel me up and attach the tiny discs to my skin. There are some places every archivist uses. Always the large muscles of the legs, and the diaphragm and the shoulders, but Fedland archived me way down at the base of my spine. "People think that since you dance off the vertical that it is all here," he touched my hip, "and here," he touched the long laterals across the rib cage. "There is a lot of stress on the hips, the way you dance, but it is not where your movements originate. This is what we'll do for this movement." He was as clinical as a doctor or a customs inspector.

He didn't care about the order of the dance. He had a tape of me doing *Bottom Line* and he had decided the order we would archive long before I ever came to Leihani. I don't think he cared about the dance itself at all. It was an archiving problem to him. "I would like to put a sensor on your heel," he said after I had danced the first line for him. "But it wouldn't stay. We'll try low on the Achilles tendon."

The more I was around him, the more I liked him.

*   *   *

I liked it the first time I went to shop—all the possibilities—I went in and I was surrounded by all the choices. And I would stand and look at the, say, soap. Gold packages, like gold bars, green packages like the ocean, packages that open like flowers, and two, three, four varieties of each type. They looked so valuable, those bars of soap. They are soap. The shopping women reached past me, confident and sure, and took a package and I thought, That's the right one. And then another woman took another, just as certain. But what if one of the women was buying for her husband, and another because her skin is too dry? How did they know which was best? All this thinking about food and things, it was exhausting. It was stupid. I was supposed to dance.

At the end of the first week, they wanted me to sit the rough record. They were so proud of themselves. I don't like kinesthetic records. I did when I was in my teens. I absorbed as many of them as I could. Now I think they make me self-conscious in the wrong ways. But a kinesthetic record of myself should be, well, clear.

Fedland fussed around. "The editing booth is just like a regular playback system," he said. "It just has more things, but you don't have to worry about all those things, you just have to press this, right here, the yellow one."

I sat down and he taped the leads to my wrists. I wouldn't let him put on the blind, I did that myself. It was heavy on my cheeks, and in the darkness, I saw patterns on light on the inside of my eyelids.

"Do you dream in color?" Fedland asked me.

I was sitting there, quite blind. "I think so," I said.

"You know, when you absorb a kinesthetic, it is a dream."

"It's like a dream," I said. It wasn't really a dream. It deactivated the same parts of your brain that sleep did, so you wouldn't really move as you "danced," but dreams you controlled. In dreams you were the agent; in kinesthetic records you were passive.

I sat there. "Can I start?" The yellow button was on the armrest, by itself, so that you could find it while you were wearing a blind. Fedland edits without the blind. I don't know how people can do that.

It was short, just the one diagonal cross of *Bottom Line*. I felt myself do the steps, sweep, sweep, cat, thrust the hip out, turn, turn—no music, no sight yet. I felt the muscles of my back. I felt muscles moving all over the place. I didn't feel that when I danced. When *I* danced I felt my body. Nobody can dance and not feel their body. I knew what I felt when I did that diagonal, God knew I'd done it enough times this week. I felt the knee I was going to have to have worked on when I went back to Sah. I felt the alignment. I felt *entirely different things than this*. It was a lie. It was outrageously ugly.

I took the blind off and they were all smiling at me, all happy, all proud. Isn't it great, they were saying.

"I've never done that before," I said.

They thought I meant a kinesthetic, and I had to explain that I meant one of myself. But it was enough. They were all chattering and nobody ever realized that they hadn't asked me if I liked it.

I should have said, Stop. This isn't what it is like to dance. But then I thought, maybe a teacher can use this. Maybe you can get things out of all this. The kinesthetic records I had absorbed as a girl, they had helped me dance, hadn't they?

What if I had to be here for two months to create a lie?

"Come to dinner," Fedland said. "You eat dinner? I won't eat in a restaurant with a woman who doesn't eat something." He had a big grin that said, Don't be offended.

"I eat dinner," I said.

So he picked me up in his car, which was barely bigger than my babysitter's and no easier to climb into. But it was red, not yellow.

I have been out with men before. When I go to visit my parents, I've sometimes gone to dinner or gone dancing. Men are very interested in a woman who lives only with other women. They want to know if I'm bisexual or if I have a lover but usually they won't ask. It's hard to explain the way things are in Sah House, so I never explain about Thrella. Or sex. Or what it means.

He took me to an expensive Indian place, the kind where you eat with your fingers.

Fedland didn't seem to care about Sah House. He didn't mention it at dinner. Mostly he talked about the archiving he had done. He had stories. Not gossip, not exactly, more like anecdotes about trying to archive work by people who didn't speak English or people who were drunk or arrogant. He had a broad way of talking. Scooping up curry and rice with his poori bread, he described the French dancer Philip Devereaux as "serotonin deprived" and said he was an example of someone whose testosterone-soaked brain was not just compartmentalized but "full of hermetically sealed little spaces."

He was amazingly smart. So smart it took me most of dinner to realize he didn't have a clue how to talk to me.

I assumed it wasn't just me, but people in general. He watched me when he talked, and when I kept appearing interested, or even more when I occasionally contradicted him, he seemed to relax.

I was flattered that he bothered. He was one of the few people I had met who seemed to take my dancing for granted. I had the suspicion that except for the fact it gave us people in common to talk about, dancing didn't matter at all. I liked that.

He took me back to my little apricot flat. I didn't know what he would do after that, or what I was supposed to do, but in fact, he did nothing at all. He sat in the red car until I was on the stairs and that was all.

There was a charming little tram that came past my house. The trams in Leihani look like amusement-park rides. On some streets, like mine, they are all dark, glistening English hunting-green trimmed in gold. Farther along they all seem to be claret-colored, and downtown they are all Dutch blue trimmed in white. It's all as if Leihani had some sort of colonial past (which it doesn't).

In the morning I got up early to allow plenty of time to get to the studio. I had my dance things in my bag, and I was down the whitewashed concrete steps, into the tropical morning. I stood on the walk, back a bit from the street. I waited. I studied my toes in my sandals. I studied the grass; broad flat stuff growing out of white sand. I felt the breeze and thought no particular thoughts and then worried about how long I had stood there. Would I be late?

After I had stood for ten minutes, it seemed to me that I saw the trams all the time, so why didn't I see one now? Should I call and ask someone to pick me up? It would be embarrassing if I couldn't figure out how to catch a tram. Children did it. And then finally it came gliding up the street. I stepped out into the grass. (I'd never seen anyone actually step on the grass. I should have stayed on the drive into the parking area. I would tomorrow.)

The tram passed me.

For a moment I couldn't think anything. Then I wondered what I had done wrong. Was I supposed to signal? I would have to call. How awful to have to call and make my poor babysitter make the long drive out to collect me.

But the tram was slowing up at the corner. So I held my bag and ran, foolish and flat-footed in my sandals.

The driver was holding the door. "You have to get on at the stop, miss," he said. "I'm not allowed pickups between the stops." He seemed cross with me, but no one had told me. How was I supposed to know?

Fedland. Fedland. "Where did you get a name like Fedland?" I asked, standing naked with my back to him while he studied my musculature.

"Dutch," he said. "I had an ancestor who was a missionary. Or one who was taken by the idea of missionaries. Or something like that."

"I didn't know that there were Dutch colonies in the Pacific."

"My family is from Indonesia," he said. Not paying much attention to what I was saying, because he was not interested in me just now.

Such concentration. I do not think anyone has ever known my body the way Fedland knew it. There was no intimacy to his gaze, no caress. I thought there was maybe some affection. The kind of affection you would expect of a racehorse owner.

He told me once, "You should not be able to dance this dance, it is all broad comedy, all mime. Your strengths are different, your strengths are extension and balance, not the short wiry strengths of a character dancer. But there are little accidents of your body that happen that allow you to cheat. You know you have ruined this dance."

"Ruined it," I said, startled.

"Certainly," he said. "This will become the standard, people will think you are the defining type for this role. They will think it is meant to be danced off the vertical, always falling, the way you do. But you have made it that way."

It is my strength as a dancer that he is talking about. Dance is all about forces counterbalancing for that moment of suspension. In dance, the dancer comes ever back to true, to the vertical alignment of spinal column and head. The tension of dance is moving away and back to that, stepping through imbalance to balance while your internal gyroscope spins, always telling you where to come back to. But I do not have to come back, I can sustain the tension of imbalance for a long time, moving around the vertical true point so that when I am too far one way I go too far another way. It is because I am strong, and it is because of something else that I can't explain, that is just the way I dance. If I could explain it, other people could do it and it wouldn't be special, and then I would not be Principal Dancer Wae Banalong, from Sah House. I would not be here archiving this dance.

He gelled a place at the outside of my thigh and the cool air was briefly colder on that spot before he tapped a sensor there.

"Do the flashy part you don't like," he said. "Do the part where you put your hand on your hip."

What would it be like to be in love with Fedland? When I was an adolescent, for about a year all I wanted was romance. All the tapes I watched, everything I read, was romance. I planned to run away from Sah House, where I would never know what it was like to be really loved by a man. I resented the choices that had been made in my name.

I found myself explaining this to an interviewer who asked me about dancing *Cloves and Cinnamon*. It didn't really have anything to do with *Cloves and Cinnamon* which is an abstract dance and not a story dance at all. And I didn't mention Christian Fedland, or going out to dinner in connection with this. Because we went out to dinner now about once a week, and there was never any romance at all.

"And now?" the interviewer asked, the red light of her recording unit remorselessly on.

"It was adolescence and the wash of hormones," I said,

laughing. It was a good laugh, a real laugh. "I met men who came to choreograph and dance at Sah, and found out that they really weren't these selfless, passionate creatures from the books, but that they were just as egotistical and driven as all the women I knew."

She asked me if I still ever thought about relationships and about sex at Sah House and I told her Sah House was not a nunnery but that it was about dance.

"Will you ever leave Sah House?" the interviewer asked.

"I might," I said. "People do."

But all I wanted when I went to the apricot flat each night was to go home.

And I was so sick of *Bottom Line* I couldn't stand it. I had never done just one dance for so long in my life. I thought it would never, ever end.

A month went by. I wasted the hours on the tram. I danced a half dozen steps of *Bottom Line* for two days. I watched myself for signs that I was different, but I wasn't. Nothing happened and I did not change.

I wished I were home.

On Saturday, we all went to the beach. A long string of bright little bobbing cars. I rode with Lily, and with Tomi, who was the person who played the music for me to dance to, and who would eventually integrate the music into the kinesthetic record.

Tomi wanted to stop and get some wine and I didn't mind. The little car was playing Shanghai pop and Lily was keeping time, which kept the little thing bobbing along. (Lily was my babysitter; I had finally learned her name.) I had drunk more wine in Leihani than I had probably drunk in the year before I came here. After lunches out and dinners with Fedland I was probably fat and I didn't know that I cared. When I got to Sah I would pay. Dance Mistress Hannah would put me on a regimen.

"Wine sounds good," I said. It was nice not to care.

We turned left, away from the shining beach, out of the string of cars. I was in back where there was only room for one, held in the little backseat like a sling that wasn't really meant to hold anyone. I couldn't really see much, just Lily and Tomi's heads and some space between them. Out the little windows beside me it was the same as always, whitewashed flats and palm trees and whitewashed walls covered in green. Then an open stretch with little houses on one side and nothing but rough grass and trees on the other.

Tomi said something I didn't hear and slammed on the brakes, turning. We weren't going that fast. The car slowed to the right, towards the grass and away from the houses, and I felt myself pushed forward until my nose was almost at the front seat and I was hung in my harness.

Then we hit something, a thump, and between Tomi and Lily's heads I saw the silhouette of a child bloom in white on the windshield, the glass cracking like frost from the impact, a child running. And the child was gone, and still we were skidding, oddly slow it seemed, off the road, bumping between the trees, and then with exaggerated care, the car went up on the right, maybe over a hillock or something, rising up in the air on the right, past the point where it would balance back down.

This is serious, I thought.

And in the same strange, slow way, the car fell over on its side.

And everything was still.

I felt the silence and nothing else.

Strange moment, waiting to see if you have been changed or passed over.

"Are you all right?" said Tomi. His voice very close in the tiny car.

"I'm all right," I said, and then decided that, yes, I was.

"I've hurt myself," Lily said, her voice tiny.

The windshield was gone, we were looking at grass and trees. The silhouette of the child was gone with it and, maybe I imagined it, the tiny cracks where the child hit and the spiderweb of great cracks around it. Maybe I made that up after the crash, I'm not sure.

"Can you get out?" Tomi asked Lily. His door was pinned against the ground. Lily was lying on top of him. "What's hurt?" he asked.

"My arm is hurt," she said.

"We have to get out," he said. "I think I hit a little kid."

Lily couldn't use her right arm because it hurt too bad, and her shoulder and back hurt, too, she said, but Tomi could wriggle out from underneath her and climb gingerly through the place where the windshield had been. Lily closed her eyes and cradled her arm while Tomi's legs moved out of my view. I was in the backseat.

I couldn't get out. I was on my side, wedged in the seat with the beach things. I couldn't get out until Lily got out. I didn't want to make her move if she was hurt, particularly if her back was hurt.

Her eyes were closed so I didn't say anything. If I turned my head I could see window and sky.

I was all right.

I had no idea what to do. I didn't know exactly how to help.

Tomi came back with two other men and a woman, and together they all lifted Lily out. She didn't want to lie down, so she sat on the grass, crying and holding her arm. I climbed out through the passenger-side door to avoid the bits of broken windshield. One of the men who lifted Lily out had a cut on his arm. I hoped the fact that Lily was sitting was a good sign.

I walked over to where the boy was lying in the street. He was moaning, which was good, because I was afraid he was dead. People were standing in a kind of semicircle around and I stood there for a moment. Someone had gone to get his mother.

She has four children, someone said, and around me, everyone shook their head. Only irresponsible people have four children in this day and age. No wonder he was running in the street, someone said.

People said the boy just darted into the street, there was nothing Tomi could have done. He looked about six, dark and wiry, his face lined around the mouth with pain as he moaned. He looked prematurely middle-aged, all leathery and lined.

I think, It isn't his fault if his mother is irresponsible. Tomi looked stricken.

I didn't know what to do so I went back and sat with Lily. I stroked her hair, like I would have Thrella's. It comforted me as much as it did her. "You're so nice," she said, which wasn't true.

It seemed like a long time until medical people came and took the boy and then Lily. And the police gave Tomi and me a ride to the hospital.

The boy had broken a hip. His mother was young, she looked barely twenty, so I don't know if she really had four children or someone just said that. Or maybe she looked young for her age.

The boy had a broken hip and a concussion and they had to do a lot of work on his hip. Lily had sprained her back and her wrist, but she was okay.

And I was okay.

I think Tomi was the only one who wasn't okay, because all his life he would remember hitting the child. I could see it in his face. He was changed. I was not, but he was.

I was stiff in my shoulders and back the next day, but the day after that was Monday and I was okay to dance. So I went and Tomi was there, and Lily came, chattering and normal, with her arm in a sling.

"It's good you're okay," Lily said. "I would rather you were okay than me. For someone like you to get hurt would be terrible, because you couldn't dance."

"No, no, no," I said. "Best if no one would have gotten hurt."

When I danced I would think of what had happened, remember lying cushioned against the beach towels and the bags of food. When I thought of it, that was when I remembered the boy against the windshield.

Fedland seemed embarrassed by the whole thing, as if it were his fault somehow, and it made him gruff for a while. But then he got all right.

We finished *Bottom Line*. I said I was so sick of it I could barely stand it.

Fedland said, "Last year we did *Plus ça change.*"

"Oh God," everyone said. "That went on forever."

Plus ça change has twenty-one roles. Could I have done this for nine months instead of two? Maybe if there had been more people from Sah House.

I was so tired of being alone.

"Oh my God," Thrella said, "what have you done to your hair?" She covered her mouth to hide a smile.

"It's just long," I said. In Leihani it had looked short, not long. It had just begun to look normal. I was embarrassed, which was stupid because I had been dancing naked in front of strangers for months, and hadn't been very embarrassed, and now here I was letting Thrella get to me about my hair.

"I'll cut it for you," she said. "Let me have a bag. How was it, was it fun? Were you homesick?"

"I'm fat," I said.

She looked around, momentarily critical, and didn't say anything. That meant that I was, indeed, fat. About three kilos' worth of extra fat.

Sah House looked like it always had, and it looked older. It had a vaguely institutional air that I hadn't really noticed before.

"I can't believe how curly your hair is," Thrella said.

"Don't worry," I said, "it will all come off."

My father had curly hair. In Leihani, most people had straight hair.

Oh, I was tired. I was so tired.

I sat down in our room, on my bed.

It was a little room, compared to the apricot flat that I'd had in Leihani. I hadn't ever thought about how small it was. But it didn't matter that it was small, it felt like home.

"Come on," Thrella said. "I'll wash your hair, then you can shower. It'll make you feel good. It'll relax you. You don't travel well, you never did."

I didn't want a shower, I didn't want anything. I was out of time, still rising and falling with the sun at Leihani.

The bathrooms in Sah were long echoing places, not really private at all compared to the apricot flat. Thrella sat me down on a stool and leaned me back so that my head was in the sink. The ceiling was black and white, as familiar as my own hand.

It was soothing to have my hair washed.

"Your hair is so curly," Thrella said. "I never knew your hair curled." Her strong fingers felt good.

"Who cut your hair while I was gone?" I asked.

"Tern."

I felt a lurch. Tern was such a strong dancer.

"Okay," Thrella said, "you're you again."

I turned and looked in the mirror. It was my own self in the mirror.

Not familiar at all. It will come back, I told myself. You've come back to Sah.

But for no reason at all I started to cry.

Afterword to "Homesick"

I've had an idea for a story for years about a group of dancers who are like a religious order—that is, their lives are completely organized around dance the way a religious order is organized around prayer—because it seems to me that the demands of professional ballet or gymnastics are about as great as the demands of being a Benedictine nun. And there is something really wonderful and really frightening about a life of such purity.

The story didn't come easily, and in the first draft the protagonist, Wae, got sick and it wasn't clear if she would ever be able to dance again. I thought this would give me the dramatic crisis that would illustrate the conflicts I hoped would come out in the story. I wasn't really sure what those conflicts are because I often write to discover what I really think about something.

The language of the first draft was pretty effective, but the characterization and structure weren't. Bruce Sterling found Wae emotionally infantile and said, "I want this richer, blunter and messier and bolder and far, far more adult."

Sah House dominates the story, but was too indistinctly drawn. Almost everybody commented on how much more they needed a sense of Sah. Jonathan Lethem said, "I credited your workshop draft of this story with being a subtle but devastating *critique* of Sah House. Right or wrong?" Karen Joy Fowler said, "But for me, the issue of Sah House begins to dominate my attention." She saw Sah as utopian. So I thought I needed to establish Sah more clearly, something I am not sure I have yet worked out.

Jim Kelly wanted to know if she danced again or not after being ill, and his question made me realize that I didn't want that to be an issue. So I rewrote the entire story and got rid of the illness. There are perhaps five paragraphs from the original draft in this version.

Finally, I originally saw this as some sort of far-future, traditional SF interstellar empire, and everyone said that only distracted from the story. So that Eridani is gone, guys.

It's a better story, but I don't know if I really pulled it off or not.

Maureen F. McHugh

from *Ledoyt*

CAROL EMSHWILLER

Oriana

FAYETTE WAS TWO and a half when they had Christy, and the minute Oriana laid eyes on that baby that looked so much like herself, she understood how that rape wasn't her fault at all. Not any part of it. She would kill if anybody tried such a thing with this girl-child. She would make up to Christy in happiness for what had happened to herself. She wouldn't be distant and scary like her own parents. Christy would come to her right away with anything, there'd be that much closeness.

Beal hadn't told Oriana much about his sister, Christianne, except that she'd died at twenty-three and that he'd tried to save her but couldn't. Tibo had told her more than Beal had about how much they'd depended on Christianne. Oriana had suggested the name Christianne in case it was a girl and Beal had said he liked that. She thought he might, as she was, be undoing something—making up to Christy for what he hadn't been able to do for Christianne.

He stayed close by as much as he could. He'd done that when Fayette was born, too. The way she'd heard it and seen it, men didn't usually care that much for tiny babies. She'd even heard Tibo say, "They're not worth their feed till you can set 'em on a horse." (Of course, they sat them on horses when they could just barely sit up.) Tibo brought over their tiny saddle when Fayette was born. He said they'd not be needing it anymore. She'd wondered about that. Henriette was still young.

When Tibo needed Beal's help he didn't want to go. He even thought to say no, but the brothers never refused each other, so he went. But then he tried to come home almost every other day until Oriana asked him not to—for his own sake. All he did was sleep anyway, usually with Christy sleeping on his chest and Fayette snuggling up beside him. But Beal said, even so, he wanted to be there with all of them. Once he went to sleep at the table and fell out of his chair.

They had the perfect family. They both felt it though they never spoke of it. They could see it in each other's eyes. Here they were, lucky at long last; first they'd had each other, and now these perfect children, and this new house, built, mostly, by his own hand, his new-bought land up in the hills where his beeves fattened. And their children were safer than other children because they were so isolated. Lotti had never had measles or mumps or chicken pox or diphtheria. All she'd ever had was whooping cough. Fayette hadn't had anything. Christy, though she looked as if she'd crept out from under some rock in their sparkling river, was more vigorous and healthy than she seemed, and she was, now at nine months, out of the danger zone— though who ever really was? Jacob always said, "We're all just hangin' by a string." ("Strang," he said.) She should have been thinking of that.

Christy's first word was "Pa." She said it over and over, along with "Papa" and "pop-pop." When Beal came in she sounded like a series of little explosions. She'd hold up her arms to him and screech and he always picked her up. He called her *"Mon coco"* and *"Mon p'tit poussin."*

They looked strange together, the pale-skinned, pink-headed baby girl and the weathered dark man. Oriana would look at them and think: Mother, look, our little girl . . . look at her pulling on this dark man's moustache, even on his bushy eyebrows, even on the hair of his chest. . . . But of course Mother would be wondering why he had his shirt unbuttoned and where was his tie? And Christy pulled too hard. Oriana said she'd never learn not to if he didn't stop her, but he said she'd learn all too soon. Oriana knew she said this when she felt left out of their closeness, but she knew, too, that he needed all those "Papa"s, and he needed how Christy's eyes—how her whole self—lit up when he came in. He needed it more than she did.

She died of blood poisoning. They hadn't even noticed the scratch on her foot or the red line along her leg—not in time—only how fussy she was. Perhaps if they'd noticed. . . . They burned her foot with alcohol bandages. When the doctor came he said that's what he'd have done, too.

Two days after the doctor came, Oriana went out to get ice so as to cool the water for bathing the baby. They thought she might be about to have convulsions again. Usually Oriana hated to go into the ice cave because the sawdust in front, where it was warmer, was full of odd-shaped, rubbery eggs. She had no idea what they were, but now, if she'd come across a whole nest of newborn rattlesnakes, she'd have hardly noticed or cared.

When she came back, Beal was on his knees on the floor, sitting back on his heels, hand over his mouth, and she knew. He looked almost as if praying, though, knowing him, she knew he wasn't. He'd once said, if he hadn't prayed for Christianne, he wouldn't pray for anybody. Seeing him on the floor, clutching his jaw like that, she went to hold him and be held. She couldn't bear *not* holding him, and *not* being held, but he warned her away with a fierce gesture and left.

All night long he hammered and sawed and sanded, making an extraordinary coffin, fine and smooth and varnished, with mitered edges and offset nails. . . . Such a little coffin.

While he worked, she washed and dressed Christy and then sat listening to Beal, out in the tool-and-buggy barn. Lotti had bolted herself in her room as usual. Oriana thought she ought to go tell her, but then Lotti could climb out the window anytime she felt like it. Oriana hardly had the energy or inclination to go find her. And she must have heard. There wasn't much that Lotti didn't know almost before it happened.

Even Fayette knew. She was holding Christy's hand when he crept out and climbed into her lap. He pulled her hand away from Christy and cuddled up, sucking his thumb and patting the line of lace at her breast. She was wishing for the warmth of Beal close to her, but Fay in her lap was the next best thing. Rocking him, she dozed off herself.

Beal was as if struck dumb and half blind. He did chores—

any chores—his, hers, Lotti's—whatever he happened to see to do, as if thinking or planning was too much for him. Nobody dared talk to him. Tibo came over, but even he didn't dare talk to him, either. Tibo kept saying, "I don't know. I don't know what." Oriana wasn't sure what he meant, but she thought he must be wondering, as she was, what Beal would do next. Even Henriette hardly said a word. Henriette kept hugging her. At least there was that.

Oriana had sent Lotti, nine years old then, to tell them. She could see Beal was of no use for anything of that nature (God knows where he'd have ended up), but she wondered if Lotti could do it and if she knew the way. Lotti said, "Of course I can. I've been almost all the way over there lots of times and you didn't even know it. I never went on in, though. I didn't want to get talked French to. They're just trying to make me feel bad. I *don't* feel bad, but I don't like it anyway." Oriana didn't say, as she usually would have, "It's not on purpose to tease you. That's how they talk."

Henriette arranged for the funeral. It was not to Oriana's liking, but she was glad it was done for them. The talk of God was comforting, even though she'd have liked more about nature instead. And she always loved the old songs: "Rock of Ages," "Gather by the River" . . . (Someone she'd never met came and played on her organ. They had moved it outside under the Lombardy poplars.) But when they sang the children's song, "Jesus Loves Me," she couldn't listen anymore.

Tibo was so good to her, as if to make up for his brother's lack. The way he hovered over her was so like Beal used to do, but why couldn't Beal have brought himself to be a little bit closer? Even if he'd just held her hand through the service. But anger was useless and unladylike—immoral at a time like this. She wouldn't let herself feel it. She'd hold herself together by herself if that's the way it had to be. She had thought, so often, and even before they'd married, I'll just take whatever he has to give, but this time all he had to give was nothing. In fact it felt like less than nothing—as though his presence was an empty hole where a person should have been.

It was a comfort to know that Tibo and Henriette had been through it. She hadn't understood till now how it must have felt.

And four times! All their boys except Henri. Jacob, too. He'd lost his whole family a long time ago. Wife and three sons. He often spoke about how he didn't have a single child left to leave his ranch to. He always said Oriana's family was his only family now.

Then . . . and there were no preliminaries. . . . (They were in bed the night after the funeral.) The first she knew he grabbed her arm. Grabbed her with a crazy man's grip. So cruel she couldn't believe it was him and she called out as if for his help. He rolled her over, jerked at her nightgown, pushed her legs apart with his knees. It was just like that other time—the man who'd fathered Lotti. He pinned her arms up over her head as if she was fighting him, but she wasn't. She would have come to him willingly, glad to be close in any way. Besides, it was her duty as a wife and his right as a husband, though she hadn't ever thought of that in terms of the two of them before. Rights and duties had nothing to do with their love. Except now.

Before the funeral he would lie every night staring at the ceiling. She couldn't tell if he slept at all, but probably not. They hardly slept, both of them lying tense and alone. She did want to touch him and be touched, but this shocked her—that he could do as that man had done, forcing her, pounding at her. . . . She had to keep thinking again: It's you, it's Beal, as she had that first time when it had worked out finally, and she could, after all, do . . . be a real woman to him. (Sometimes, before, he had been violent with desire. Always tender at the start and always tender after, but wild in the middle, though never this wild. She had liked that wildness. It gave her a sense of power—woman-power—over him and his body. This was different.)

But then, in spite of herself . . . and she shocked herself: Christy dead, the funeral just this morning, and she felt this dreadful, shameful pleasure, his rage as if her rage, his energy and fury, hers. Even the pain, a relief from that other pain, but she was ashamed, both of her rage and, especially, of her desire.

Afterwards he fell asleep instantly. On top of her. His wet breath in her ear. Dead weight, but so alive. The feverish, beating, breathing life of him. . . . Stomach to stomach so that she couldn't breathe any other way but in rhythm with his own.

She knew, for sure, at last he slept. She pulled her arms out from under him, held him, one hand on the sweating back of his neck, one hand on the sweating small of his back. She slept finally, too, uncomfortable but comforted. They would be all right. Time would heal. Everybody said it would.

The next morning he was gone. She didn't even know if he'd left soon after, or in the middle of the night, or when—she'd slept that deeply for the first time since Christy. And he left without a horse or bedroll or any extra clothes. Left with no food and not the heavy sweater she'd knit for him. The nights were cold. Didn't he want anything along to remind him of her but the patches in his pants? She had bruises and soreness to remember him by every time she moved. She had the marks of his fingers on her arms where he'd held her so tightly, and—and she hardly dared let herself think about them—teeth marks.

Always before, when she was angry with him, she could tell herself she had no right to feel that way since she knew very well who she'd married and had married him anyway. Henriette . . . even Tibo had warned her this was not a man who had ever—since his sister's death—stayed in one place for more than a month. But he *had*, of course. More or less, anyway, and she'd been grateful for it, but now, no matter how hard she tried, she did feel angry. She couldn't talk herself out of it.

First thing that morning she walked all round the house and saw his tracks heading straight out into the desert—into the middle of nowhere—and her anger left her and she feared for him, in his state. She set Lotti to cleaning the lamp chimneys with old newspapers. Lotti said it was a girl's job. Normally Oriana would have said, "I know it," or, "Beal does it," and there would have been an argument, but this time she didn't answer, and this time Lotti started right in. Oriana saddled up, sat Fay in front of her and followed Beal's tracks, but lost them where the ground got hard and salt-crusted.

After two weeks, post-office money orders began to come. No letter, of course. She couldn't imagine him ever writing a letter even under normal circumstances. The first came all the way from Gardnerville, and the next from Virginia City, and after that they came from Winnemucea, five hundred miles away, and she knew he hadn't gone by the narrow gage. Every week, fifteen dollars. Sometimes twenty. That had to be all his pay. What was he living on? And did it mean he was never coming back? She could tell Tibo was worried, too. He kept saying, "It'll maybe take him a little while." But Tibo didn't know about that night and how Beal might be feeling about it.

"Tibo, he always disappears. Why does he have to do this?—except I *do* understand it this time. But you didn't run away when your children died. Never once."

"No, but I never was like him. He and Christianne, you know. They were so close. I wasn't in that. And then, after everybody died, I grew up having him to help me. He had nobody."

Tibo called him Béal. He and Henriette always said his name that way when they felt most intimate and most loving. When Christy died, they called him that a lot. When Oriana and Beal had married, Beal had said to the lawyer who married them, "It has to be Béal. Call me Béal for the ceremony."

Lotti left a drawing in plain sight for a change. She always kept her drawings secret except for Fayette. She let him watch her as she drew and he never got tired of it. For that bit of time, Lotti would leave off pestering him and Fay would go so far as to lean against her shoulder.

This drawing she had propped up against the kitchen cabinet where it not only couldn't be missed, but was in the way. Oriana moved it aside out of harm's way. She wasn't sure if it was a gift or not or if she was just supposed to see it and say something. It had a complete background: their long, low house and the flower garden and in the distance, snowcapped mountains, each with a cloud trailing out from the peak. In the foreground was Lotti's mustang, Strawberry. Lotti had cleverly smeared charcoal marks to simulate the roan color. It couldn't be a gift. Not with Lotti's mustang. Or could it? She ought at least to say something, but she hardly had the energy or the inclination. Well, she would. She would find a minute and say, "Very nice," sometime when she felt better and could think, but not right now.

* * *

After nine weeks the money orders stopped. She hoped it meant he was on the way home, though she feared the opposite. But walking and hitching rides . . . Even if he really was coming home, it would take a long time.

Then, walking . . . and it was almost exactly like the first time she'd seen him, this thin—as thin and tired and ragged as he'd looked on her first view of him. He looked so bad, she thought, My God, he's done nothing but work hard and drink hard and smoke and not eaten at all!

She was hanging up the clothes. She had two clothespins in her mouth and two in her hand along with Fayette's nighttime diapers. She must have looked a sight, just like that first time he came walking in, but he was all cleaned up and freshly shaven. He'd probably stopped and washed at his pond—for her sake. She thought, all over again: What a funny-looking man. He took off his hat in that exact same gesture as before, respectful, honoring her, but this time without the self-mocking smile. He looked cautious. Unsure of how she would receive him.

The clothespins fell from her mouth. She dropped the diapers in the dust and then stepped on them, she felt so wobbly. They stared at each other. It seemed for a long time. She was thinking somebody should say something.

Finally she said, "I'll have to do these over," and he said, "Yes."

She said, "I got the money," and he said, "Yes."

She said, "Thank you," and he said, "Yes."

She bent to pick up the diapers in order to avoid his stare and because she was trembling and didn't want him to know. She shook the sand from them, shaking harder than she needed to. Why didn't he say something? She'd tried. Or why didn't he reach out to her? Even in rage? Except there was no rage left in him.

Then she said the exact thing to turn him from her, and she knew it would, and would hurt him. It seemed to pop out of her mouth by itself. "We're . . . having another baby."

He turned his back, but she could see the muscles of his jaw working. She shouldn't have said it like that, and she shouldn't have said it now. She should have waited for another month or so. Maybe even more. He already felt bad enough.

And she ought to know by now that she was the one who would have to say the first words and make the first move. She was married to a man who easily told other men what to do, but who was so tentative with her he could hardly make a move until he knew for sure she wanted him to. Even "that"—except for the night before he left—he always found some way of asking.

She could faint and he would pick her up and she would be in his arms and nobody would have to say anything. That occurred to her not only because she was reminded of that other time when she thought she should have pretended to faint—that time when she knew for sure he would reach out to touch her, except he didn't, but it occurred to her mainly because she felt so dizzy and nauseous she thought she might be going to anyway. But feeling nauseous made her think of the time she'd held his forehead when he threw up after losing the fight with Big Andy. That was the very first time she'd put her arms around him. So she said what she'd said to him then, and it was almost as hard to say now as it had been, but she wanted to just as much. She said, "My dear," and she said, "My love," and she took a step towards him. But then, and for the first time in her life, she *did* faint.

She woke on their bed with him putting cool cloths on her forehead and saying, "Please." And when he saw she had come to, he said, "You went down *so* hard. I tried to catch you. Are you all right?"

But she had his rough, sandpapery fingers pushing her hair from her forehead. She had his lips on her eyelids, her neck, her earlobes. How could she not be all right?

He said, "I'm the one that hurt you. I'm always the one."

"You were in pain."

"So were you. My God. I've done . . . I bit you. Did I really bite you? And this baby!"

She said, "We'll get through it," and she thought, if they could do it together, they would—she would, anyway, as long as he stayed.

After a while he went to make her fresh coffee and then he finished hanging up the clothes. Lotti and Fayette came back from playing cowboy on the half-grown lambs. When Fay saw Beal he started jumping and yelling . . . shrieking really, and running around in circles. (Beal said he'd done the same when he was little.) Strange, though, happy as Fay was, he wouldn't go near Beal. As though he thought he'd disappear again. Oriana knew how he felt. Lotti acted as though he'd never left and as though nothing had happened—kept her distance and looked watchful, just as she usually did.

That night he said—for about the fourth time over the years they'd been together—exactly what he'd said on their wedding night: "Don't leave me. Please don't ever leave me. *Ne me quitte pas.*" And she thought, as she had each time: What an extraordinary thing for *him* to be saying to *her*. Perhaps he thought he'd come back someday and find her gone. Perhaps he thought it would serve him right if she was. She always said, "I'll never leave you. You know that," but this time, though she said it, and right then, in his arms, she felt it, she wasn't quite so sure she might not, someday, go. While he was gone, Henriette had said, "It's about your turn, isn't it? You maybe surprise him one of these days and turn up missing." Then she'd said, "*Certainment* he's a pretty good man, as men go, and when he's not in some mood of his, he's more fun than most (not counting T-Bone, of course) and I do love him dearly, but Oriana, I don't know why he hasn't yet driven you completely loco."

Except Oriana could never bring herself to leave Fayette. If she ever ran away, she'd have to bring him along. Not a bad idea actually, but she couldn't run away from this new baby, on its way no matter where she went, though she wanted to.

He had brought her dried apricots. For once something useful. When she told Henriette, Henriette said, "And finally something with good taste, too."

Those first days after he was back, he couldn't seem to get enough of touching her, helping her, and she thought: Things will be all right with him now. Not all right with Christy dead, that would never be all right with either of them, but he'd be ready to go on and they'd comfort each other, and after a time the pain might fade some, though right now she didn't want it to. As if for Christy's sake, she kept thinking, I will never, ever, ever forget you. I will always feel the pain—except that sharp, sudden agony that caught her unawares. . . . How long would that last?

But things were not all right at all. He hovered. When he wasn't working, he was underfoot. He watched her—almost as he had in the beginning. He asked, over and over, "What can I do?" and, "Is there anything you want?" It seemed he wanted her to ask of him some Herculean task. It made her think of the time he'd climbed the tree up into the tiny, top swaying branches, so high it scared her and she had wished he wouldn't do that, and of the time he built the dam for no reason, though it turned out to be a good thing after all. Those were the sorts of things—she was sure of it—he wanted her to ask of him. Or even fight. Maybe fight Big Andy and get beaten up all over again. She did know what she wanted, but it wouldn't be hard enough to suit him, and it might not help anyway.

He had taught her what loving was all about after she had spent so many years hardly able to look at a man. He had taught her to like being close and to need being close and now he wouldn't. At first she thought he wouldn't and then he tried and couldn't, and after failing twice, he didn't try again.

He had used to look at her with secret signals, little half-winks or tiny raisings of the eyebrows. Now he looked as though just seeing her pained him. It was too bad she still had the mark of his bite on her shoulder. She knew he'd seen it. One more thing to make him wince. (She wondered if she would carry the scar to her grave.) Sometimes at night it seemed he might be trying not to cry, but it could just be coughing.

She told him what she wanted. "A second honeymoon," she said. "It doesn't have to be more than a couple of days, but I want the two of us away alone, and I want a bed of pine boughs and for us to be looking up at the stars and you naming them and telling me about them and about Coyote."

"I'm finished with the stars."

"But can we go? Jacob would love to come over. He loves being Grandpa." She hoped that when they got out where they'd been when they'd first married, and before that, too, and where he'd been so . . . so the opposite of now, it would make him able to be . . . a husband again.

On their honeymoon they'd seen rattlesnakes dance. She had started to hurry away as fast as she could, but he grabbed her, held her tight, whispered, "Wait," stood behind her and put his cheek against hers. They watched the two snakes rise up, coil their bodies together, sometimes their heads touching just as their own were, and dance, weaving back and forth—they, as hypnotized by it as if the snakes were the snake charmers. Even snakes, then, caught up in—just as they were—"ecstasy." A word she'd never thought about till then and never would say out loud, but that's what came to mind. Snakes, and she, and he holding her tight. Who would have thought, she of all people? And with this funny man, nothing to him but sinew and bones and those crooked teeth of his and a mustache. In spite of what the books said, how could it be wrong if all of nature . . . ? All!

The People's Common Sense Medical Adviser
by R. V. Pierce

The health of the reproductive organs can only be maintained by a temperate life. . . . Lascivious thought should be displaced by cultivating a taste for literature which is elevating in its nature.

Excessive sexual indulgence not only prostrates the nervous system, enfeebles the body, drains the blood of its quickening elements, but is inconsistent with intellectual activity, morality, and spiritual development. . . . Hence the gratification of sexual instincts should always be moderate.

They had not been moderate. Neither on their honeymoon nor before.

"Remember the rattlesnakes?"

Ah, there was the look in his eyes she liked to see, and a bit of that old down-turning grin. She'd thought maybe it was gone forever.

One sunset up there on the mountain, he'd lain with his head in her lap, his fingers smoothing back her pink-red hair, looking at her instead of the colors in the sky behind her. He said, "The sun's gone down, but you're still out and shining." That was on their honeymoon, too.

So Beal went and fetched Jacob. Even before he and Oriana left, Lotti was jabbering at Jacob in a way she seldom did anymore at home. And she was listening, too. She liked his tales of the olden days, of Indian fights and soldiers and such, right here on their land. Lotti was sorry the Paiutes weren't on the warpath anymore, and sorry everything was so settled up now. Jacob said the Indians were much better off being civilized. He said everybody was better off civilized, but Lotti said she didn't think so, because who would want to do other people's laundry or work in other people's fields and eat potatoes?

Before Beal had come, Lotti said she wished her mother would go ahead and marry Jacob. She said it after Beal had come, too. Sometimes Oriana thought that might have made everything a lot easier. She never would have had to learn what love really was all about. But maybe it wouldn't have been easier because, sooner or later, she'd have met Beal, and she had loved him almost at first sight. (She always wondered why, and what that meant. She didn't even believe in love at first sight.) Except, knowing she was Jacob's wife, if she had said yes, Beal wouldn't have looked at her as he did. Knowing she was Jacob's wife, he never would have come close. He almost hadn't anyway, with nothing in his way but himself.

They had horses now, and two mules. Beal rode his big mule, Matou, and Oriana rode Lotti's little mustang. They took the pack mule and, just in case, the tent, but they didn't use it. They did lie, looking up at the stars and the moon and sometimes into the tops of trees. In the moonlight she was even more aware of how much gray hair he'd gotten just in the last few months. He was so streaked with silver in that light. So beautiful.

But she could see that Beal, looking up, wasn't seeing anything. He had said he was through with the stars and that looked to be true. She said, "You're still staring at the ceiling, aren't you? Do you sleep at all?"

"It's better when I'm with you."

She thought: Well, why not stay here with me, then? But she said, "I wish I knew what to do to help you."

"I'm the one who did it."

"But you hardly knew what you were doing. You were in such a state. I never saw the like."

"If everybody went around saying they didn't know what

they were doing, it would be a sorry world. It was a terrible thing I did, 'specially to you, 'specially since I know what you've been through. I wanted to be the one to help you and keep you safe and all I've done is hurt you more." And he made one of those coughing noises.

"You're hurting me now, Beal. Besides, remember when I couldn't and I thought I'd never be able to, and when you tried, I hit you. You were already so bruised from that fight and I couldn't stop hitting. I've always felt bad about that. I'll forgive myself if you'll forgive yourself."

"That's the one thing I can't do. What I did is different."

"You taught me love and now you're taking it away."

"Not love."

She was surprised he could bring himself to use the word at all.

He turned, took the pins from her hair as he always liked to do. He always said that was his job. His hands were all over like they used to be. The moon . . . It was so bright she could see his eyes were shut. And all that white hair! He started, but he couldn't keep on. And then he cried and it didn't sound like coughing anymore. He said the same thing he'd said when he got drunk by mistake on their wedding night—more from not eating than from drinking. It had taken both her and Tibo to get him upstairs to bed. *"J'ai tous gater."* Tibo had told her what it meant: "I've spoiled everything."

She thought, after he'd let himself cry himself out at last, that he might be better, but he wasn't. It took her almost dying to bring him back in all the ways she wanted him. That was six months later when they lost that other baby that neither of them wanted. Stillborn. Dead, Aunt Jenny said, maybe days before her first labor pains.

She was so sick she hardly remembered anything of that birth but a fog of pain—much worse than with Fayette. Aunt Jenny didn't let her see the baby. She said it would be bad for her and she wouldn't say its sex. Later Beal said it was a boy, and when she wanted to know more, he finally said it looked all right, but he wouldn't say anything else.

Aunt Jenny was there for a long time after that, but Beal was always there, too. Every time she opened her eyes, there he was; sometimes he was holding her hand; sometimes he was asleep, leaning forward in the chair, resting his head on the edge of the bed; sometimes he was standing in the doorway, lost in thought, it seemed. She thought she remembered his whispering, "I love you," into her ear, and not just once, though it might have been a wishful dream. She wouldn't ask him about it. He wouldn't like her to. If he waited to say it when she was awake, that was for him to decide. And maybe it hadn't happened anyway.

Beal

She didn't know he was there. He was by her bed most every minute, but Oriana thought he wasn't. She'd look right at him and say, where was he? She called Aunt Jenny over and over to ask her, "Is he coming back?" and he'd be right there, holding her hand. Once she looked straight into his eyes and said, "Aunt Jenny, I can't bear to see him so unhappy." It was no use saying, "I'm here," and, "I'll not leave you." He even said, "I'll be happy."

She would toss and turn and say how tired she was and yet not be able to lie quietly. "Everything's falling apart," she said.

"It's not. I'm holding it together."

"It's ended. I knew he'd go someday."

"It's just begun. We'll have a hundred honeymoons."

"I'm scared. Hold me."

"I've got you. I'm holding on."

He, like Oriana, turned to Aunt Jenny. "What'll I do? Have I really been gone so much?"

"When a person wants you here, a little bit of 'gone' goes a long ways."

"She never says a word."

"Well, that's Oriana. She won't push."

It wasn't until he and Aunt Jenny put her into the big zinc bathtub of warm water that she finally came to herself, stopped her restlessness, held on to him, said, "I thought you weren't ever coming back."

For modesty's sake, in the bath, Aunt Jenny had partly covered her with wet towels. They clung to her body. She looked like the pictures in her fancy art book—like a Greek statue. A Diana. Even after these children. . . . Hard to think three and only Fayette to show for it. No four. He forgot about Lotti. And even at her age, still looking like a young girl. Didn't matter what had happened to her. Didn't matter what he'd done to her himself, she always looked so innocent. And was.

As he held her and helped to bathe her, he said, "Aunt Jenny, without her I couldn't."

"I expect you'd do what we all do."

"No!"

"You have Fayette and Lotti to look after. You'd do what we do."

"Maybe."

"But she'll be all right now."

Lotti

Lotti writes:

I had not thought to set myself on fire and I'm not sure why I did it. I decided at the last minute when sparks had already burst onto my skirt. I didn't wear skirts that often, even back then. They were always in the way. I suppose, partly, I wanted to burn that skirt up. I only had one other. First I brushed the sparks off and then I took the little fireplace shovel and put them back on. I don't remember thinking much of anything. I was only ten and didn't think things out as I do now. I know I was desperate but I don't even know why. I guess I wanted to change things—in any way. I had to do something big and important. But really I didn't think at all.

Old You-Know-Who was just outside, and the little one (I always think of Fayette as the little one of him) was right there by the fireplace. I wanted Fay to see me do it. (He was three then.) I wanted to hear him scream, and he did scream. I didn't. I'm always braver than Fayette and I always will be. No matter how old he gets to be, I'll be braver. I suppose it was Fayette's screaming that saved me. Without him I'd have burned up for sure because the fire burned faster than I thought it would. It was as if my whole skirt was tinder. It went up all at the same time once it got started.

I'd like to do something sort of like that over again now—now that I have bosoms. I would feel like a woman to him as he lay on top of me. Of course, I couldn't do that exact same thing. And the pain lasted a long time. Much longer than I thought it would. A whole year. More, in fact. I thought it would be like a kitchen burn. Just last a few days. Old Him was in pain, too. Ma and Fay had to do up his buttons.

He was *so* quick—*so* strong. It all went *so* fast I hardly realized what was happening. I made no sound at all, Fayette screamed, and he was there before I knew it, tore off my burning dress (bits of burnt cloth and buttons scattering away). He knocked me down, rolled on top, his jacket pulled around both of us. I felt his body against me. He seemed all ropes and knobs and knots and . . . so naked under his clothes. I felt . . . well, strange. Embarrassed, kind of. I didn't like it. I didn't think I'd feel that way.

Afterwards I covered my bare breasts with my hands—or, rather, where my breasts would have been if I'd had any. I covered them because they weren't there. If I'd had them, I'd not have been so quick to cover myself up.

Beal

She did that on purpose. He saw it in her face. Just let herself burn and didn't say a word or raise a hand to save herself. Jealous of Oriana—they knew that already, but so jealous of Christy, too, she would have died to be like her. Almost did. And out of her head with . . . Hard to say what it was she felt for him, and he, old enough to be her father. *Is* her father for heaven's sake.

She didn't like it when he fell on her and rolled. She jumped away as soon as he let her go, as if being close to him was worse than burning up. He'd not forget the look on her face. Surprise and outrage and fear. As if he was about to hit her though he'd never spanked her, except that one time when she shot arrows at him. She pushed him away like he was the fire. Ran off, naked, to her room. Bolted the door. Why had he let her put in that damn bolt? First thing, she gets a real room of her own and that's what she does. Made it and nailed it up all by herself. Well, she'd have to make another. Trust Lotti to make a good strong one, too, but he managed to break through.

She lay on the floor, still silent. Skinny little stick-figure, trying to cover up what wasn't even there. He wanted to help her, comfort her, though when had she ever let anybody do that? She was huddled by her bed, hugging herself and shaking. In shock most likely. She didn't want him near. He threw a blanket over her. He could see she wanted that. She must have been in pain but you couldn't tell. Maybe she wasn't feeling it yet. He didn't either, until later. He'd rubbed the burned skin clean off his hands slamming at her door before he took his shoulder to it and didn't even feel it. Oriana came. At first Lotti wouldn't let her near, either, but finally she let herself be looked after. But no hugging. Of course, with Lotti, no hugging allowed, even then. He ended up having to comfort Fayette instead. Or maybe it was Fay who was comforting him.

Echinacea, comfrey, sweet butter, marshmallow on the burns. Meadowsweet, white willow, valerian, hot gooseberry wine for the inside. It made him sick, but Lotti kept it down and slept.

Couldn't hold reins, let alone saddle up. Couldn't milk a cow. Couldn't turn the pages of a book. Could just barely hold a cup, two-handed. Wedged a spoon into his bandage to feed himself. Stopped smoking so at least he wouldn't have to bother Oriana with that. She offered to help him do it but he wouldn't let her. Couldn't touch her. Even her warmth near his hands hurt.

Afterword to "from *Ledoyt*"

I know workshopping a section from the middle of a novel—especially this sort of novel—is a bad thing, but this is all I've been working on for three years. I wanted to bring to SycHill something current that I cared about. My earlier writing seems so alien to me I don't want to deal with it.

I know, too, that workshopping parts of an unfinished novel can be dangerous. Workshopping finished—or more or less finished—short stories is great. I was so used to doing that it took me a long time to realize how destructive criticism could be to such a bulky, lumpy, only partly conceived thing as a novel—or as this sort of novel—is. Even too much praise can lock in things that shouldn't be locked in. And God forbid somebody should say you ought to cut out something that, unknown to you, might be a clue your subconscious had left you for something that might happen farther along in your book. Maybe the clue doesn't belong where you put it, but it has to go someplace where you can find it and notice it, not hidden away with notes you seldom look at.

But nothing destructive happened at SycHill. Everybody there has written novels and they know the problems. I got only good, important-for-the-book help. I was wishing I could have had the whole book critiqued by the workshop.

Most important was the advice (unanimous, I think) that Lotti needed to be in this section a lot more than she was. Though she's the main character, I had almost forgotten about her, I was so wrapped up in the problems of the lovers.

John and Mikey (others, too) gave me a lot of specific help on how to make this section stand alone. I don't think it does, even now, but because of their help it almost does.

The group (also just about unanimously) said too much happens in too few pages. I hope my additions help with that some.

One of the problems with a section out of the middle of this kind of novel (and I didn't realize this until I took it to SycHill) is that details—especially details of characterization—have more weight than they do in the novel as a whole. By the time the reader gets to this section, he already knows the people pretty well and so knows when a character is acting uncharacteristically. But when a section is the reader's first view of the characters, the reader laps up all the clues that appear, as avidly as if it were the beginning of a short story. They don't know, for instance, as here, that the "hero" and "heroine" really do love each other.

One of the things I wanted to do in this book was to show younger people than myself (and most people are) how women of my mother's and grandmother's generation lived. I got angry at TV and movies. They almost all give the wrong impression of how it was here in America around the turn of the century. Women of my mother's and grandmother's generations tried to be what they thought of as "ladylike," as, for instance, a good woman always defers to her husband. (My mother and grandmother tried to make me that way, too.) Oriana has been called passive. She tries hard to be that way, as my mother did. People seem to have already forgotten how women used to be before women's lib, and even during the first women's lib (which went right by my mother). Women of that period either succeeded, as my mother and grandmother did, in being, or at least seeming to be, passive, giving, "angels," or they became hellions—harpies. A lot of them went crazy. I mean a lot! Seems to me everybody's family had a crazy woman in the background. Or, at least, people called them crazy and put them away where they wouldn't make trouble.

And I wanted to show how talk of sex was taboo. Nakedness also. Oriana doesn't have any words for bodily functions just as my grandmother had no words. My mother finally came to use "BM" for "bowel movement," but that wasn't until my littlest brother came along fourteen years after me. (The Scots, at least, were like this. Not everybody was. I brought in the French characters for a lot of reasons, actually, but partly so I'd have more sexual freedom in some of the characters.) Of course, Lotti, the main character, is far from being either passive or prudish.

Carol Emshwiller

The Miracle of Ivar Avenue

JOHN KESSEL

INSIDE THE COAT pocket of the dead man Corcoran found an eyepiece. "Looks like John Doe was a photographer," the pathologist said, gliding his rubber-gloved thumb over the lens. He handed it to Kinlaw.

While Corcoran continued to peel away the man's clothing, Kinlaw walked over to the morgue's only window, more to get away from the smell of the dissecting table than to examine the lens. He looked through the eyepiece at the parking lot. The device produced a rectangular frame around a man getting into a 1947 Packard. "This isn't from a camera," Kinlaw said. "It's a cinematographer's monocle."

"A what?"

"A movie cameraman uses it to frame a scene."

"You think our friend had something to do with the movies?"

Kinlaw thought about it. That morning a couple of sixth-graders playing hooky had found the body on the beach in San Pedro. A man about fifty, big, over two hundred pounds, mustache, thick brown hair going gray. Wearing a beat-up tan double-breasted suit, silk shirt, cordovan shoes. Carrying no identification.

Corcoran hummed "Don't Get Around Much Anymore" while he examined the dead man's fingers. "Heavy smoker," he said. He poked in the corpse's nostrils, then opened the man's mouth and shone a light down his throat. "This doesn't look much like a drowning."

Kinlaw turned around. "Why not?"

"A drowning man goes through spasms, clutches at anything within his grasp; if nothing's there, he'll usually have marks on his palms from his fingernails. Plus there's no foam in his trachea or nasal cavities."

"Don't you have to check for water in the lungs?"

"I'll cut him open, but that's not definitive anyway. Lots of drowning men don't get water in their lungs. It's the spasms, foam from mucus, and vomiting does them in."

"You're saying this guy was murdered?"

"I'm saying he didn't drown. And he wasn't in the water more than twelve hours."

"Can you get some prints?"

Corcoran looked at the man's hand again. "No problem."

Kinlaw slipped the monocle into his pocket. "I'm going upstairs. Call me when you figure out the cause of death."

Corcoran began unbuttoning the dead man's shirt. "You know, he looks like that director, Sturges."

"Who?"

"Preston Sturges. He was pretty hot stuff a few years back. There was a big article in *Life*. Whoa. Got a major surgical scar here."

Kinlaw looked over Corcoran's shoulder. A long scar ran right to center across the dead man's abdomen. "Gunshot wound?"

Corcoran made a note on his clipboard. "Looks like appendectomy. Probably peritonitis, too. A long time ago—ten, twenty years."

Kinlaw took another look at the dead man. "What makes you think this is Preston Sturges?"

"I'm a fan. Plus, this dame I know pointed him out to me at the fights one Friday night during the war. Didn't you ever see *The Miracle of Morgan's Creek*?"

"We didn't get many movies in the Pacific." He took another look at the dead man's face.

When Corcoran hauled out his chest saw, Kinlaw spared his stomach and went back up to the detectives' staff room. He checked missing-persons reports, occasionally stopping to roll the cameraman's monocle back and forth on his desk blotter. There was a sailor two weeks missing from the Long Beach Naval Shipyard. A Mrs. Potter from Santa Monica had reported her husband missing the previous Thursday.

The swivel chair creaked as he leaned back, steepled his fingers, and stared at the wall calendar from Free State Buick pinned up next to his desk. The weekend had brought a new month. Familiar April was a blonde in ski pants standing in front of a lodge in the snowy Sierras. He tore off the page: May's blonde wore white shorts and was climbing a ladder in an orange grove. He tried to remember what he had done over the weekend but it all seemed to dissolve into a series of moments connected only by the level of scotch in the glass by his reading chair. He found a pencil in his center drawer and drew a careful X through Sunday, May 1. Happy May Day. After the revolution they would do away with pinup calendars and anonymous dead men. Weekends would mean something and lives would have purpose.

An hour later the report came up from Corcoran: There was no water in the man's lungs. Probable cause of death: carbon monoxide poisoning. But bruises on his ankles suggested he'd had weights tied to them.

There was no answer at Mrs. Potter's home. Kinlaw dug out the L.A. phone book. *Sturges, Preston* was listed at 1917 Ivar Avenue. Probably where Ivar meandered into the Hollywood hills. A nice neighborhood, but nothing compared to Beverly Hills. Kinlaw dialed the number. A man answered the phone. "Yes?"

"I'd like to speak to Mr. Preston Sturges," Kinlaw said.

"May I ask who is calling, please?" The man had the trace of an accent; Kinlaw couldn't place it.

"This is Detective Lemoyne Kinlaw from the Los Angeles Police Department."

"Just a minute."

There was a long wait. Kinlaw watched the smoke curling up from Sapienza's cigarette in the tray on the adjoining desk. An inch of ash clung to the end. He was about to give up when another man's voice came onto the line.

"Detective Kinlaw. How may I help you?" The voice was a

light baritone with some sort of high-class accent.

"You're Preston Sturges?"

"Last time I checked the mirror, I was."

"Mr. Sturges, the body of a man answering your description was found this morning washed up on the beach at San Pedro."

There was a long pause. "How grotesque."

"Yes, sir. I'm calling to see whether you are all right."

"As you can hear, I'm perfectly all right."

"Right," Kinlaw said. "Do you by any chance have a boat moored down in San Pedro?"

"I have a sailboat harbored in a marina there. But I didn't wash up on any beach last night, did I?"

"Yes, sir. Assuming you're Preston Sturges."

The man paused again. Kinlaw got ready for the explosion. Instead, Sturges said calmly, "I'm not going to be able to convince you who I am over the phone, right?"

"No, you're not."

"I'll tell you what. Come by the Players around eight tonight. You can put your finger through the wounds in my hands and feet. You'll find out I'm very much alive."

"I'll be there."

As soon as he hung up Kinlaw decided he must have been a lunatic to listen to Corcoran and his dames. He was just going to waste a day's pay on pricey drinks in a restaurant he couldn't afford. Then again, though Hollywood people kept funny hours, as he well knew from his marriage to Emily, what was a big-time director doing home in the middle of the day?

He spent the rest of the afternoon following up on missing persons. The sailor from Long Beach, it turned out had no ring finger on his left hand. He finally got through to Mrs. Potter and discovered that Mr. Potter had turned up Sunday night after a drunken weekend in Palm Springs. He talked to Sapienza about recent mob activity and asked a snitch named Bunny Witcover to keep his ears open.

At four-thirty, Kinlaw called back down to the morgue. "Corcoran, do you remember when you saw that article? The one about the director?"

"I don't know. It was an old issue, at the dentist's office."

"Great." Kinlaw checked out of the office and headed down to the public library.

It was a Monday and the place was not busy. The mural that surrounded the rotunda, jam-packed with padres, Indians, Indian babies, gold miners, sheep, a mule, dancing señoritas, conquistadors, ships, and flags, was busier than the room itself.

A librarian showed him to an index: The January 7, 1946, issue of *Life* listed a feature on Preston Sturges beginning on page 85. Kinlaw rummaged through the heaps of old magazines and finally tracked it down. He flipped to page 85 and sat there, hand resting on the large photograph. The man in the photograph, reclining on a soundstage, wearing a rumpled tan suit, was a dead ringer for the man lying on Corcoran's slab in the morgue.

Kinlaw's apartment stood on West Marathon at North Manhattan Place. The building, a four-story reinforced concrete box, had been considered a futuristic landmark when it was constructed in 1927, but its earnest European grimness, the regularity and density of the kid's-block structure, made it seem more like a penitentiary than a work of art. Kinlaw pulled the mail out of his box: an electric bill, a flyer from the PBA, and a letter from Emily. He unlocked the door to his apartment and, standing in the entry, tore open the envelope.

It was just a note, conversational, guarded. Her brother was out of the army. She was working for Metro on the makeup for a new Dana Andrews movie. And oh, by the way, did he know what happened to the photo album with all the pictures of Lucy? She didn't have a single one.

Kinlaw dropped the note on the coffee table, took off his jacket and got the watering can, sprayer, and plant food. First he sprayed the hanging fern in front of the kitchen window, then moved through the plants in the living room: the African violets, ficus, and four varieties of coleus. Emily had never cared for plants, but he could tell she liked it that he did. It reassured her, told her something about his character that was not evident from looking at him. On the balcony he fed the big rhododendron and the planter full of day lilies. Then he put the sprayer back under the kitchen sink, poured himself a drink, and sat in the living room. He watched the late-afternoon sun throw triangular shadows against the wall.

The *Life* article had painted Sturges as an eccentric genius, a man whose life had been a series of lucky accidents. His mother, a

Europe-traipsing culture vulture, had been Isadora Duncan's best friend, his stepfather a prominent Chicago businessman. After their divorce Sturges' mother had dragged her son from opera in Bayreuth to dance recital in Vienna to private school in Paris. He came back to the U.S. and spent the twenties trying to make a go of it in her cosmetics business. In 1928 he almost died from a burst appendix; while recovering he wrote his first play; his *Strictly Dishonorable* was a smash Broadway hit in 1929. By the early thirties he had squandered the play's earnings and come to Hollywood, where he became Paramount's top screenwriter, and then the first writer-director of sound pictures. In four years he made eight movies, several of them big hits, before he quit to start a new film company with millionaire Howard Hughes. Besides writing and directing, Sturges owned an engineering company that manufactured diesel engines, and the Players, one of the most famous restaurants in the city.

Kinlaw noted the ruptured appendix, but there was little to set off his instincts except a passing reference to Sturges being "one of the most controversial figures in Hollywood." And the closing line of the article: "As for himself, he contemplates death constantly and finds it a soothing subject."

He fell asleep in his chair, woke up with his heart racing and his neck sweaty. It was seven o'clock. He washed and shaved, then put on a clean shirt.

The Players was an eccentric three-story building on the side of a hill at 8225 Sunset Boulevard, across Marmont Lane from the neo-Gothic Château Marmont hotel. Above the ground-level entrance a big neon sign spelled out *The Players* in easy script. At the bottom level, drive-in girls in green caps and jumpers waited on you in your car. Kinlaw had never been upstairs in the formal rooms. It was growing dark when he turned off Sunset onto Marmont and pulled his Hudson up the hill to the terrace-level lot. An attendant in a white coat with his name stitched in green on the pocket took the car.

Kinlaw loitered outside and finished his cigarette while he admired the lights of the houses spread across the hillside above the restaurant. Looking up at them, Kinlaw knew that he would never live in a house like those. There was a wall between some people and some ways of life. A lefty—like the twenty-four-year-old YCL member he had been in 1938—would have called it *money* that kept him from affording such a home, and *class* that kept the people up there from wanting somebody like him for a neighbor, and *principle* that kept him from wanting to live there. But the thirty-five-year-old he was now knew it was something other than class, or money, or principle. It was something inside you. Maybe it was character. Maybe it was luck. Kinlaw laughed. You ought to be able to tell the difference between luck and character, for pity's sake. He ground out the butt in the lot and went inside.

At the dimly lit bar on the second floor he ordered a gin and tonic and inspected the room. The place was mostly empty. At one of the tables Kinlaw watched a man and a woman whisper at each other as they peered around the room, hoping, no doubt, to catch a glimpse of Van Johnson or Lisabeth Scott. The man wore a white shirt with big collar and a white Panama hat with a pink hat band, the woman a yellow print dress. On the table they held two prudent drinks neatly in the center of prudent cocktail napkins, beside them a map of Beverly Hills folded open with bright red stars to indicate the homes of the famous. A couple of spaces down the bar a man was trying to pick up a blonde doing her best Lana Turner. She was mostly ignoring him but the man didn't seem to mind.

"So what do you think will happen in the next ten years?" he asked her.

"I expect I'll get some better parts. Eventually I want at least second leads."

"And you'll deserve them. But what happens when the Communists invade?"

"Communists schmommunists. That's the bunk."

"You're very prescient. The state department should hire you, but they won't."

This was some of the more original pickup talk Kinlaw had ever heard. The man was a handsome fellow with an honest face, but his light brown hair and sideburns were too long. Maybe he was an actor working on some historical pic. He had a trace of an accent.

"You know, I think we should discuss the future in more detail. What do you say?"

"I say you should go away. I don't mean to be rude."

"Let me write this down for you, so if you change your mind." The man took a coaster and wrote something on it. He pushed the coaster toward her with his index finger.

Good luck, buddy. Kinlaw scanned the room. Most of the clientele seemed to be tourists. At one end of the room, on the bandstand, a jazz quintet was playing a smoky version of "Stardust." When the bartender came back to ask about a refill, Kinlaw asked him if Sturges was in.

"Not yet. He usually shows up around nine or after."

"Will you point him out to me when he gets here?"

The bartender looked suspicious. "Who are you?"

"Does it matter?"

"You look like you might be from a collection agency."

"I thought this place was a hangout for movie stars."

"You're four years late, pal. Now it's a hangout for bill collectors."

"I'm not after money."

"That's good. Because just between you and me, I don't think Mr. Sturges has much."

"I thought he was one of the richest men in Hollywood."

"Was, past tense."

Kinlaw slid a five-dollar bill across the bar. "Do you know what he was doing yesterday afternoon?"

The bartender took the five note, folded it twice and stuck it into the breast pocket of his shirt. "Most of the afternoon he was sitting at that table over there looking for answers in the bottom of a glass of Black Label scotch."

"You're a mighty talkative employee."

"Manager's got us reusing the coasters to try to save a buck." He straightened a glass of swizzle sticks. "I paid for the privilege of talking. Mr. Sturges is into me for five hundred in back pay."

Down the end of the bar the blonde left. The man with the sideburns waved at the bartender, who went down to refill his drink.

Kinlaw decided he could afford a second gin and tonic. Midway through the third the bartender nodded toward a table on the mezzanine; there was Sturges, looking a lot healthier than the morning's dead man. He saw the bartender gesture and waved Kinlaw over to his table. Sturges stood as Kinlaw approached. He had thick, unkempt brown hair with a gray streak in the front, a square face, jug ears and narrow eyes that would have given him a nasty look were it not for his quirky smile. A big, soft body. His resemblance to the dead man was uncanny. Next to him sat a dark-haired, attractive woman in her late thirties, in a blue silk dress.

"Detective Kinlaw. This is my wife, Louise."

"How do you do."

As Kinlaw was sitting down, the waiter appeared and slid a fresh gin and tonic onto the table in front of him.

"You've eaten?" Sturges asked.

"No."

"Robert, a menu for Mr. Kinlaw."

"Mr. Sturges, I'm not sure we need to spend much time on this. Clearly, unless you have a twin, the identification we had was mistaken."

"That's all right. There are more than a few people in Hollywood who will be disappointed it wasn't me."

Louise Sturges watched her husband warily, as if she weren't too sure what he was going to say next, and wanted pretty hard to figure it out.

"When were you last on your boat?"

"Yesterday. On Saturday I went out to Catalina on the *Island Belle* with my friends, Dr. Bertrand Woolford and his wife. We stayed at anchor in a cove there over Saturday night, then sailed back Sunday. We must have got back around one P.M. I was back at home by three."

"You were with them, Mrs. Sturges?"

Louise looked from her husband to Kinlaw. "No."

"But you remember Mr. Sturges getting back when he says?"

"No. That is, I wasn't at home when he got there. I—"

"Louise and I haven't been living together for some time," Sturges said.

Kinlaw waited. Louise looked down at her hands. Sturges laughed.

"Come on, Louise, there's nothing for you to be ashamed of. I'm the one who was acting like a fool. Detective Kinlaw, we've been separated for more than a year. The divorce was final last November."

"One of those friendly Hollywood divorces."

"I wouldn't say that. But when I called her this morning, Louise was gracious enough to meet with me." He put his hand on his wife's. "I'm hoping she will give me the chance to prove to her I know what a huge mistake I made."

"Did anyone see you after you returned Sunday afternoon?"

"As I recall, I came by the restaurant and was here for some time. You can talk to Dominique, the bartender."

Eventually the dinner came and they ate. Or Kinlaw and Louise ate; Sturges regaled them with stories about how his mother had given Isadora the scarf that killed her, about his marriage to the heiress Eleanor Post Hutton, about an argument he'd seen between Sam Goldwyn and a Hungarian choreographer, in which he played both parts and put on elaborate accents.

Kinlaw couldn't help but like him. He had a sense of absurdity, and if he had a high opinion of his own genius, he seemed to be able to back it up. Louise watched Sturges affectionately, as if he were her son as much as her ex-husband. In the middle of one of his stories he stopped to glance at her for her reaction, then reached impulsively over to squeeze her hand, after which he launched off into another tale, about the time, at a pool, he boasted he was going to "dive into the water like an arrow," and his secretary said, "Yes, a Pierce-Arrow."

After a while Sturges wound down, and he and Louise left. At the cloakroom Sturges offered to help her on with her jacket, and Kinlaw noticed a moment's skepticism cross Louise's face before she let him. Kinlaw went back over to talk with the bartender.

"I've got a couple more questions."

The bartender shrugged. "Getting late."

"This place won't close for hours."

"It's time for me to go home."

Kinlaw showed him his badge. "Do I have to get official, Dominique?"

Dominique got serious. "Robert heard you talking to Sturges. Why didn't you let on earlier you were a cop? What's this about?"

"Nothing you have to worry about, if you answer my questions." Kinlaw asked him about Sturges' actions the day before.

"I can't tell you about the morning, but the rest is pretty much like he says," Dominique told him. "He came by here about six. He was already drinking, and looked terrible. 'Look at this,' he says to me, waving the *L.A. Times* in my face. They'd panned his new movie. 'The studio dumps me and they still hang this millstone around my neck.' He sat there, ordered dinner but didn't eat anything. Tossing back one scotch after another. His girlfriend must have heard something, she came in and tried to talk to him, but he wouldn't talk."

"His girlfriend?"

"Frances Ramsden, the model. They've been together since he broke with Louise. He just sat there like a stone, and eventually she left. Later, when business began to pick up, he got in his car and drove away. I remember thinking, I hope he doesn't get in a wreck. He was three sheets to the wind, and already had some accidents."

"What time was that?"

"About seven-thirty, eight. I thought that was the last I'd see of him, but then he came back later."

"What time?"

"After midnight. Look, can you tell me what this is about?"

Kinlaw watched him. "Somebody's dead."

"Dead?" Dominique looked a little shaken, nothing more.

"I think Sturges might know something. Anything you remember about when he came back? How was he acting?"

"Funny. He comes in and I almost don't recognize him. The place was clearing out then. Instead of the suit he'd had on earlier he was wearing slacks and a sweatshirt, deck shoes. He was completely sober. His eyes were clear, his hands didn't shake—he looked like a new man. They sat there and talked all night."

"They?"

"Mr. Sturges and this other guy he came in with. Friendly looking, light hair. He had a kind of accent—German, maybe? I figure he must be some Hollywood expatriate—they all used to all hang out here—this was little Europe. Mr. Sturges would talk French with them. He loved to show off."

"Had you seen this man before?"

"Never. But Mr. Sturges seemed completely familiar with him. Here's the funny thing—he kept looking around as if he'd never seen the place."

"You just said he'd never been here before."

"Not the German. It was Sturges looked as if he hadn't seen the Players. 'Dominique,' he said to me. 'How have you been?' 'I've been fine,' I said.

"They sat up at Mr. Sturges' table there and talked all night. Sturges was full of energy. The bad review might as well have happened to somebody else. The German guy didn't say much, but he was drinking as hard as Mr. Sturges was earlier. It was like they'd changed places. Mr. Sturges stood him to an ocean of scotch. When we closed up they were still here."

"Have you seen this man since then?"

The bartender looked down the bar. "Didn't you see him? He was right here when you came in, trying to pick up some blonde."

"The guy with the funny haircut?"

"That's the one. Mr. Sturges said to let him run a tab. Guess he must've left. Wonder if he made her."

It was a woozy drive home with nothing to show for the evening except the prospect of a Tuesday-morning hangover. He might as well do the thing right: Back in the apartment Kinlaw got out the bottle of scotch, poured a glass, and sat in the dark listening to a couple of blues records. Scotch after gin, a deadly combination. After a while he gave up and went to bed. He was almost asleep when the phone rang.

"Hello?"

"Lee? This is Emily." Her voice was brittle.

"Hello," he said. "It's late." He remembered the nights near the end when he'd find her sitting in the kitchen after midnight with the lights out, the tip of her cigarette trembling in the dark.

"Did you get my letter?"

"What letter?"

"Lee, I've been looking for the photo album with the pictures of Lucy," she said. "I can't find it anywhere. Then I realized you must have taken it when you moved out."

"Don't blame me if you can't find it, Emily."

"You know, I used to be impressed by your decency."

"We both figured out I wasn't as strong as you thought I was, didn't we? Let's not stir all that up again."

"I'm not stirring up anything. I just want the photographs."

"All I've got is a wallet photo. I'm lucky I've got a wallet."

Instead of getting mad, Emily said, quietly, "Don't insult me, Lee." Her voice was tired.

"I'm sorry," he said. "I'll look around. I don't have them, though."

"I guess they're lost, then. I'm sorry I woke you." She'd lost the edge of hysteria; she sounded like the girl he'd first met at a Los Angeles Angels game in 1934. It stirred emotions he'd thought were dead, but before he could think what to say she hung up.

It took him another hour to get to sleep.

In the morning he showered, shaved, grabbed some ham and eggs at the Indian Head Diner and headed in to Homicide. The fingerprint report was on his desk. If the dead guy was a mob button man, his prints showed up nowhere in any of their files. Kinlaw spent some time reviewing other missing-persons reports. He kept thinking of the look on Louise Sturges' face when her husband held her coat for her. For a moment she looked as if she wasn't sure this was the same man she'd divorced. He wondered why Emily hadn't gotten mad when he'd insulted her over the phone. At one time it would have triggered an hour's argument, rife with accusations. Did people change that much?

He called the Ivar Avenue number.

"Mrs. Sturges? This is Lemoyne Kinlaw from the LAPD. I wondered if we might talk."

"Yes?"

"I hoped we might speak in person."

"What's this about?"

"I want to follow up on some things from last night."

She paused. "Preston's gone off to talk to his business manager. Can you come over right now?"

"I'll be there in a half an hour."

Kinlaw drove out to quiet Ivar Avenue and into the curving drive before 1917. The white-shingled house sat on the side of a hill, looking modest by Hollywood standards. Kinlaw rang the bell and the door was answered by a Filipino houseboy.

Once inside Kinlaw saw that the modesty of the front was deceptive. The houseboy led him to a large room at the back that must have been sixty by thirty feet.

The walls were green and white, the floor dark hardwood. At one end of the room stood a massive pool table and brick inglenook fireplace. At the other end, a level up, surrounded by an iron balustrade, ran a bar upholstered in green leather, complete with a copper topped nightclub table and stools. Shelves crowded with scripts, folders and hundreds of books lined one long wall, and opposite them an expanse of French doors opened onto a kidney-shaped pool surrounded by hibiscus and fruit blossoms, Canary Island pines and ancient firs.

Louise Sturges, seated on a bench covered in pink velveteen, was talking to a towheaded boy of eight or nine. When Kinlaw entered she stood. "Mr. Kinlaw, this is our son, Mon. Mon, why don't you go outside for a while."

The boy raced out through the French doors. Louise wore a plum-colored cotton dress and black flats that did not hide her height. Her thick hair was brushed back over her ears. Poised as a *Vogue* model, she offered Kinlaw a seat. "Have you ever had children, Mr. Kinlaw?"

"A daughter."

"Preston very much wanted children, but Mon is the only one we are likely to have. At first I was sad, but after things started to go sour between us I was glad that we didn't have more."

"How sour were things?"

Louise smoothed her skirt. Her sophistication veiled a calmness that was nothing cheap or Hollywood. "Have you found out who that drowned man is?"

"No."

"What did you want to ask me about?"

"I couldn't help but get the impression last night that you were surprised at your husband's behavior."

"He's frequently surprised me."

"Has he been acting strangely?"

"I don't know. Well, when Preston called me yesterday I was pretty surprised. We haven't had much contact since before our separation. At the end we got so we'd communicate by leaving notes on the banister."

"But that changed?"

She watched him for a moment before answering. "When we

met, Preston and I fell very much in love. He just swept me off my feet. He was so intense, funny. I couldn't imagine a more loving husband. Certainly he was an egotist, and totally involved in his work, but he was also such a charming and attentive man."

"What happened?"

"Well, he started directing, and that consumed all his energies. He would work into the evening at the studio, then spend the night at the Players. At first he wanted me totally involved in his career. He kept me by his side at the soundstage as the film was shot. Some of the crew came to resent me, but Preston didn't care. Eventually I complained, and Preston agreed that I didn't need to be there.

"Maybe that was a mistake. The less I was involved, the less he thought of me. After Mon was born he didn't have much time for us. He stopped seeing me as his wife and more as the mother of his son, then as his housekeeper and cook.

"Sometime in there he started having affairs. After a while I couldn't put up with it anymore, so I moved out. When I filed for divorce, he seemed relieved."

Kinlaw worried the brim of his hat. He wondered what Sturges' version of the story would be.

"That's the way things were for the last two years," Louise continued. "Then he called me Sunday night. He has to see me, he needs to talk. I thought, he's in trouble; that's the only time he needs me. A few years back, when the deal with Hughes fell through, he showed up at my apartment and slept on my bed, beside me, like a little boy needing comfort. I thought this would just be more of the same. So I met with him Monday morning. He was contrite. He looked more like the man I'd married than he'd seemed for years. He begged me to give him another chance. He realized his mistakes, he said. He's selling the restaurant. He wants to be a father to our son."

"You looked at him last night as if you doubted his sincerity."

"I don't know what to think. It's what I wanted for years, but—he seems so different. He's stopped drinking. He's stopped smoking."

"This may seem like a bizarre suggestion, Mrs. Sturges, but is there any chance this man might not be your husband?"

Louise laughed. "Oh, no—it's Preston all right. No one else has that ego."

Kinlaw laid his hat on the end table. "Okay. Would you mind if I took a look at your garage?"

"The garage? Why?"

"Humor me."

She led him through the kitchen to the attached garage. Inside, a red Austin convertible sat on a wooden disk set into the concrete floor.

"What's this?"

"That's a turntable," Louise said. "Instead of backing up, you can flip this switch and rotate the car so that it's pointing out. Preston loves gadgets. I think this one's the reason he bought this house."

Kinlaw inspected the garage door. It had a rubber flap along the bottom, and would be quite airtight. There was a dark patch on the interior of the door where the car's exhaust would blow, as if the car had been running for some time with the door closed.

They went back into the house. In the backyard the boy, laughing, chased a border collie around the pool. Lucy had wanted a dog. "Let me ask you one more question, and then I'll go. Does your husband have any distinguishing marks on his body?"

"He has a large scar on his abdomen. He had a ruptured appendix when he was a young man. It almost killed him."

"Does the man who's claiming to be your husband have such a scar?"

Louise hesitated, then said, "I wouldn't know."

"If you should find that he doesn't, could you let me know?"

"I'll consider it."

"One last thing. Do you have any object he's held recently—a cup or glass?"

She pointed to the bar. "He had a club soda last night. I think that was the glass."

Kinlaw got out his handkerchief and wrapped the glass in it, put it into his pocket. "We'll see what we will see. I doubt that anything will come of it, Mrs. Sturges. It's probably that he's just come to his senses. Some husbands do that."

"You don't know Preston. He's never been the sensible type."

* * *

Back at the office he sent the glass to the lab for prints. A note on his desk told him that while he had been out he'd received a call from someone named Nathan Lautermilk at Paramount.

He placed a call to Lautermilk. After running the gauntlet of the switchboard and Lautermilk's secretary, Kinlaw got him. "Mr. Lautermilk, this is Lee Kinlaw of the LAPD. What can I do for you?"

"Thank you for returning my call, Detective. A rumor going around here has it you're investigating the death of Preston Sturges. There's been nothing in the papers about him dying."

"Then he must not be dead."

Lautermilk had no answer. Kinlaw let the silence stretch until it became uncomfortable.

"I don't want to pry into police business, Detective, but if Preston was murdered, some folks around here might wonder if they were suspects."

"Including you, Mr. Lautermilk?"

"If I thought you might suspect me, I wouldn't draw attention to myself by calling. I'm an old friend of Preston's. I was assistant to Buddy DeSylva before Preston quit the studio."

"I'll tell you what, Mr. Lautermilk. Suppose I come out there and we have a talk."

Lautermilk tried to put him off, but Kinlaw persisted until he agreed to meet him.

An hour later Kinlaw pulled up to the famous Paramount arch, like the entrance to a Moorish palace. Through the curlicues of the iron gate the sun-washed soundstages hulked like pastel munitions warehouses. The guard had his name and told him where to park.

Lautermilk met him in the long, low white building that housed the writers. He had an office on the ground floor, with a view across the lot to the soundstages but close enough so he could keep any recalcitrant writers in line.

Lautermilk seemed to like writers, though, a rare trait among studio executives. He was a short, bald, pop-eyed man with a Chicago accent and an explosive laugh. He made Kinlaw sit down and offered him a cigarette from a brass box on his desk. Kinlaw took one, and Lautermilk lit it with a lighter fashioned into the shape of a lion's head. The jaws popped open and a flame sprang out of the lion's tongue. "Louie B. Mayer gave it to me," Lautermilk said. "Only thing I ever got from him he didn't take back later." He laughed.

"I'm curious. Can you arrange a screening of one of Preston Sturges' movies?"

"I suppose so." Lautermilk picked up his phone. "Judy, see if you can track down a print of *Miracle of Morgan's Creek* and get it set up to show in one of the screening rooms. Call me when it's ready."

Kinlaw examined the lion lighter. "Did Sturges ever give you anything?"

"Gave me several pains in the neck. Gave the studio a couple of hit movies. On the whole I'd say we got the better of the deal."

"So why is he gone?"

"Buddy DeSylva didn't think he was worth the aggravation. Look what's happened since Sturges left. Give him his head, he goes too far."

"But he makes good movies."

"Granted. But he made some flops, too. And he offended too many people along the way. Didn't give you much credit for having any sense, corrected your grammar, made fun of people's accents and read H. L. Mencken to the cast over lunch. And if you crossed him he would make you remember it later."

"How?"

"Lots of ways. On *The Palm Beach Story* he got irritated with Claudette Colbert quitting right at five every day. Preston liked to work till eight or nine if it was going well, but Colbert was in her late thirties and insisted she was done at five. So he accommodated himself to her. But one morning, in front of all the cast and crew, Preston told her, 'You know, we've got to take your close-ups as early as possible. You look great in the morning, but by five o'clock you're beginning to sag.'"

"So you were glad to see him go."

"I hated to see it, actually. I liked him. He can be the most charming man in Hollywood. But I'd be lying if I didn't tell you that the studios are full of people just waiting to see him slip. Once you start to slip, even the waitresses in the commissary will cut you."

"Maybe there's some who'd like to help him along."

"By the looks of the reactions to his last couple of pictures, they won't need to. *Unfaithfully Yours* might have made money if it hadn't been for the Carole Landis mess. Hard to sell a comedy about a guy killing his wife when the star's girlfriend just committed suicide. But *Beautiful Blonde* is a cast-iron bomb. Daryl Zanuck must be tearing his hair out. A lot of people are taking some quiet satisfaction tonight, though they'll cry crocodile tears in public."

"Maybe they won't have to fake it. We found a body washed up on the beach in San Pedro answers to Sturges' description."

Lautermilk did not seem surprised. "No kidding."

"That's why I came out here. I wondered why you'd be calling the LAPD about some ex-director."

"I heard some talk in the commissary, one of the art directors who has a boat down in San Pedro heard some story. Preston was my friend. There have been rumors that's he's been depressed. Anyone who's seen him in the last six months knows he's been having a hard time. It would be big news around here if he died."

"Well, you can calm down. He's alive and well. I just talked to him last night, in person, at his restaurant."

"I'm glad to hear it."

"So what do you make of this body we found?"

"Maybe you identified it wrong."

"Anybody ever suspect that Sturges had a twin?"

"A thing like that would have come out. He's always talking about his family."

Kinlaw put the cinematographer's monocle on Lautermilk's desk. "We found this in his pocket."

Lautermilk picked it up, examined it, put it down again. "Lots of these toys in Hollywood."

The intercom buzzed and the secretary reported that they could see the film in screening room D at any time. Lautermilk walked with Kinlaw over to another building, up a flight of stairs to a row of screening rooms. They entered a small room with about twenty theater-style seats, several of which had phones on tables next to them. "Have a seat," Lautermilk said. "Would you like a drink?"

Kinlaw was thirsty. "No, thanks."

Lautermilk used the phone next to his seat to call back to the projection booth. "Let her rip, Arthur."

"If you don't mind," he said to Kinlaw, "I'll leave after the first few minutes."

The room went dark. "One more thing, then," Kinlaw said. "All these people you say would like to see Sturges fail. Any of them like to see him dead?"

"I can't tell you what's in people's heads." Lautermilk settled back and lit a cigarette. The movie began to roll.

The Miracle of Morgan's Creek was a frenetic comedy. By twenty minutes in, Kinlaw realized the real miracle was that they had gotten it past the Hays Office. A girl gets drunk at a going-away party for soldiers, marries one, gets pregnant, doesn't remember the name of the father. All in one night. She sets her sights on marrying Norval Jones, a local yokel, but the yokel turns out to be so sincere she can't bring herself to do it. Norval tries to get the girl out of trouble. Everything they do only makes the situation worse. Rejection, disgrace, indictment, even suicide, are all distinct possibilities. But at the last possible moment a miracle occurs to turn humiliation into triumph.

Kinlaw laughed despite himself, but after the lights came up the movie's sober undertone began to work on him. It looked like a rube comedy but it wasn't. The story mocked the notion of the rosy ending while allowing people who wanted one to have it. It implied a maker who was both a cruel cynic and dizzy optimist. In Sturges' absurd universe anything could happen at any time, and what people did or said didn't matter at all. Life was a cruel joke with a happy ending.

Blinking in the sunlight, he found his car, rolled down the windows to let out the heat, and drove back to Homicide. When he got back, the results of the fingerprint test were on his desk. From the tumbler they had made a good right thumb, index, and middle finger. The prints matched the right hand of the dead man exactly.

All that afternoon Kinlaw burned gas and shoe leather looking for Sturges. Louise had not seen him since he'd left the Ivar Avenue house in the morning, he was not with Frances Ramsden or the Woolfords, nobody had run into him at Fox, the restaurant manager claimed he'd not been in, and a long drive down to the San Pedro marina was fruitless: Sturges' boat rocked empty in its slip and the man in the office claimed he hadn't seen the director since Sunday.

It was early evening and Kinlaw was driving back to Central Homicide, when he passed the MGM lot where Emily was working. He wondered if she was still fretting over the photo album. In some ways his problems were simpler than hers; all he had to do was catch the identical twin of a man who didn't have a twin. It had to be a better distraction than Emily's job. He remembered how, a week after he'd moved out, he'd found himself late one Friday night, drunk on his ass, coming back to the house to sit on the backyard swing and watch the darkened window to their bedroom, wondering whether she was sleeping any better than he. Fed up with her inability to cope, he'd known he didn't want to go inside and take up the pain again, but he could not bring himself to go away, either. So he sat on the swing he had hung for Lucy and waited for something to release him. The galvanized chain links were still unrusted; they would last a long time.

A man watching a house, waiting for absolution. The memory sparked a hunch, and he turned around and drove to his apartment. He found the red Austin parked down the block. As he climbed the steps to his floor a shadow pulled back into the corner of the stairwell. Kinlaw drew his gun. "Come on out."

Sturges stepped out of the shadows.

"How long have you been waiting there?"

"Quite a while. You have a very boring apartment building. I like the bougainvillea, though."

Kinlaw waved Sturges ahead of him down the hall. "I bet you're an expert on bougainvillea."

"Yes. Some of the studio executives I've had to work with boast IQs that rival that of the bougainvillea. The common bougainvillea, that is."

Kinlaw holstered the gun, unlocked his apartment door, and gestured for Sturges to enter. "Do you have any opinion of the IQ of police detectives?"

"I know little about them."

Sturges stood stiffly in the middle of Kinlaw's living room. He looked at the print on the wall. He walked over to Kinlaw's record player and leafed through the albums.

Kinlaw got the bottle of scotch from the kitchen. Sturges put on Ellington's "Perfume Suite."

"How about a drink?" Kinlaw asked.

"I'd love one. But I can't."

Kinlaw blew the dust out of a tumbler and poured three fingers. "Right. Your wife says you're turning over a new leaf."

"I'm working on the whole forest."

Kinlaw sat down. Sturges kept standing, shifting from foot to foot. "I've been looking for you all afternoon," Kinlaw said.

"I've been driving around."

"Your wife is worried about you. After what she told me about your marriage, I can't figure why."

"Have you ever been married, Detective Kinlaw?"

"Divorced."

"Children?"

"No children."

"I have a son. I've neglected him. But I intend to do better. He's nine. It's not too late, is it? I never saw my own father much past the age of eight. But whenever I needed him he was always there, and I loved him deeply. Don't you think Mon can feel that way about me?"

"I don't know. Seems to me he can't feel that way about a stranger."

Sturges looked at the bottle of scotch. "I could use a drink."

"I saw one of your movies this afternoon. Nathan Lautermilk set it up. *The Miracle of Morgan's Creek.*"

"Yes. Everybody seems to like that one. Why I didn't win the Oscar for original screenplay is beyond me."

"Lautermilk said he was worried about you. Rumors are going around that you're dead. Did you ask him to call me?"

"Why would I do that?"

"To find out whether I thought you had anything to do with this dead man."

"Oh, I'm sure Nathan told you all about how he loves me. But where was he when I was fighting Buddy DeSylva every day? *Miracle* made more money than any other Paramount picture that year, after Buddy questioned my every decision making it." He was pacing the room now, his voice rising.

"I thought it was pretty funny."

"Funny? Tell me you didn't laugh until it hurt. No one's got such a performance out of Betty Hutton before or since. But I guess I can't expect a cop to see that."

"At Paramount they're not so impressed with your work since you left."

Sturges stopped pacing. He cradled a blossom from one of Kinlaw's spaths in his palm. "Neither am I, frankly. I've made a lot of bad decisions. I should have sold the Players two years ago. I hope to God I don't croak before I can get on my feet again."

Kinlaw remembered the line from the *Life* profile. He quoted it back at Sturges: " 'As for himself, he contemplates death constantly and finds it a soothing subject.' "

Sturges looked at him. He laughed. "What an ass I can be! Only a man who doesn't know what he's talking about could say such a stupid thing."

Could an impostor pick up a cue like that? The Ellington record reached the end of the first side. Kinlaw got up and flipped it over, to "Strange Feeling." A baritone sang the eerie lyric. "I forgot to tell you in the restaurant," Kinlaw said. "That dead man had a nice scar on his belly. Do you have a scar?"

"Yes. I do." When Kinlaw didn't say anything Sturges added, "You want me to show it to you?"

"Yes."

Sturges pulled out his shirt, tugged down his belt and showed Kinlaw his belly. A long scar ran across it from right to center. Kinlaw didn't say anything, and Sturges tucked the shirt in.

"You know we got some fingerprints off that dead man. And a set of yours, too."

Sturges poured himself a scotch, drank it off. He coughed. "I guess police detectives have pretty high IQs after all," he said quietly.

"Not so high that I can figure out what's going on. Why don't you tell me?"

"I'm Preston Sturges."

"So, apparently, was that fellow who washed up on the beach at San Pedro."

"I don't see how that can be possible."

"Neither do I. You want to tell me?"

"I can't."

"Who's the German you've been hanging around with?"

"I don't know any Germans."

Kinlaw sighed. "Okay. So why not just tell me what you're doing here."

Sturges started pacing again. "I want to ask you to let it go. There are some things—some things in life just won't bear too much looking into."

"To a cop, that's not news. But it's not a good enough answer."

"It's the only answer I can give you."

"Then we'll just have to take it up with the district attorney."

"You have no way to connect me up with this dead man."

"Not yet. But you've been acting strangely. And you admit yourself you were on your boat at San Pedro this weekend."

"Detective Kinlaw, I'm asking you. Please let this go. I swear to you I had nothing to do with the death of that man."

"You don't sound entirely convinced yourself."

"He killed himself. Believe me, I'm not indifferent to his pain. He was at the end of his rope. He had what he thought were good reasons, but they were just cowardice and despair."

"You know a lot about him."

"I know all there is to know. I also know that I didn't kill him."

"I'm afraid that's not good enough."

Sturges stopped pacing and faced him. The record had reached the end and the needle was ticking repetitively over the center groove. When Kinlaw got out of his chair to change it, Sturges hit him on the head with the bottle of scotch.

Kinlaw came around bleeding from a cut behind his ear. It couldn't have been more than a few minutes. He pressed a wet dish towel against it until the bleeding stopped, found his hat and headed downstairs. The air hung hot as the vestibule of Hell with the windows closed. Out in the street he climbed into his Hudson and set off up Western Avenue.

The mess with Sturges was a demonstration of what happened when you let yourself think you knew a man's character. Kinlaw had let himself like Sturges, forgetting that mild-mannered wives tested the carving knife out on their husbands and stone-cold killers wept when their cats got worms.

An orange moon in its first quarter hung in the west as Kinlaw followed Sunset toward the Strip. When he reached the Players he parked in the upper lot. Down the end of one row was a red Austin; the hood was still warm. Head still throbbing, he went into the bar. Dominique was pouring brandy into a couple of glasses; he looked up and saw Kinlaw.

"What's your poison?"

"I'm looking for Sturges."

"Haven't seen him."

"Don't give me that. His car's in the lot."

Dominique set the brandies on a small tray and a waitress took them away. "If he came in, I didn't spot him. If I had, I would have had a thing or two to tell him. Rumor has it he's selling this place."

"Where's his office?"

The bartender pointed to a door, and Kinlaw checked it out. The room was empty; a stack of bills sat on the desk blotter. The one on the top was the third notice from a poultry dealer, for $442.16. PLEASE REMIT IMMEDIATELY was stamped in red across the top. Kinlaw poked around for a few minutes, then went back to the bar. "Have you seen anything of that German since we talked yesterday?"

"No."

Kinlaw remembered something. He went down to where the foreigner and the blonde had been sitting. A stack of cardboard coasters sat next to a glass of swizzle sticks. Kinlaw riffled through the coasters: On the edge of one was written, *Suite 62.*

He went out to the lot and crossed Marmont to the Château Marmont. The elegant concrete monstrosity was dramatically floodlit. Up at the top floors, the building was broken into steep roofs with elaborate chimneys and dormers surrounding a pointed central tower. Around it wide terraces with traceried balustrades and striped awnings marked the luxury suites. Kinlaw entered the hotel through a Gothic arcade with ribbed vaulting, brick paving, and a fountain at the end.

"Six," he told the elevator operator, a wizened man who stared straight ahead as if somewhere inside he was counting off the minutes until the end of his life.

Kinlaw listened at the door to suite 62. Two men's voices,

muffled to the point he could not make out any words. The door was locked.

Back in the tower opposite the elevator a tall window looked out over the hotel courtyard. Kinlaw leaned out: The ledge was at least a foot and a half wide. Ten feet to his right were the balustrade and awning of the sixth-floor terrace. He eased himself through the narrow window and carefully down the ledge; though there was a breeze up at this height, he felt his brow slick with sweat. His nose an inch from the masonry, he could hear the traffic on the boulevard below.

He reached the terrace, threw his leg over the rail. The French doors were open and through them he could hear the voices more clearly. One of them was Sturges and the other was the man who'd answered the phone that first afternoon at the Ivar house.

"You've got to help me out of this."

" 'Got to'? Not in my vocabulary, Preston."

"This police detective is measuring me for a noose."

"Only one way out, then. I can fire up my magic suitcase and take us back."

"No."

"Then don't go postal. There's nothing he can do to prove that you aren't you."

"We should never have dumped that body in the water."

"What do I know about disposing of bodies? I'm a talent scout, not an executive producer."

"That's easy for you to say. You won't be here to deal with the consequences."

"If you insist, I'm willing to try an unburned moment-universe. Next time we can bury the body in your basement. But really, I don't want to go through all this rumpus again. My advice is to tough it out."

"And once you leave and I'm in the soup, it will never matter to you."

"Preston, you are lucky I brought you back in the first place. It cost every dollar you made to get the studio to let us command the device. There are no guarantees. Use the creative imagination you're always talking about."

Sturges seemed to sober. "All right. But Kinlaw is looking for you, too. Maybe you ought to leave as soon as you can."

The other man laughed. "And cut short my holiday? That doesn't seem fair."

Sturges sat down. "I'm going to miss you. If it weren't for you I'd be the dead man right now."

"I don't mean to upset you, but in some real sense you are."

"Very funny. I should write a script based on all this."

"*The Miracle of Ivar Avenue?* Too fantastic, even for you."

"And I don't even know how the story comes out. Back here I'm still up to my ears in debt, and nobody in Hollywood would trust me to direct a wedding rehearsal."

"You are resourceful. You'll figure it out. You've seen the future."

"Which is why I'm back in the past."

"Meanwhile, I have a date tonight. A young woman, they tell me, who bears a striking resemblance to Veronica Lake. Since you couldn't get me to meet the real thing."

"Believe me," Sturges said. "The real thing is nothing but trouble."

"You know how much I enjoy a little trouble."

"Sure. Trouble is fun when you've got the perfect escape hatch. Which I don't have."

While they continued talking, Kinlaw sidled past the wrought-iron terrace furniture to the next set of French doors, off the suite's bedroom. He slipped inside. The bedclothes were rumpled and the place smelled of whiskey. A bottle of Paul Jones and a couple of glasses stood on the bedside table along with a glass ashtray filled with butts; one of the glasses was smeared with lipstick. Some of the butts were hand-rolled reefer. On the dresser Kinlaw found a handful of change, a couple of twenties, a hotel key, a list of names:

Jeanne d'Arc		Carole Lombard	X
Claire Bloom		Germaine Greer	X
Anne Boleyn	X	Vanessa Redgrave	
Eva Braun	X	Alice Roosevelt	X
Louise Brooks	X	Christina Rossetti	
Charlotte Buff	X	Anne Rutledge	
Marie Duplesis		George Sand	X
Veronica Lake			

Brooks had been a hot number when Kinlaw was a kid, everybody knew Hitler's pal Eva, and Alice Roosevelt was old Teddy's aging socialite daughter. But who was Vanessa Redgrave? And how had someone named George gotten himself into this harem?

At the foot of the bed lay an open suitcase full of clothes; Kinlaw rifled through it but found nothing that looked magic. Beside the dresser was a companion piece, a much smaller case in matching brown leather. He lifted it. It was much heavier than he'd anticipated. When he shook it there was no hint of anything moving inside. It felt more like a portable radio than a piece of luggage.

He carried it out to the terrace and, while Sturges and the stranger talked, knelt and snapped open the latches. The bottom half held a dull gray metal panel with switches, what looked something like a typewriter keyboard, and a small flat glass screen. In the corner of the screen glowed green figures: 23:27:46 PDT 3 May 1949. The numbers pulsed and advanced as he watched. . . . 47 . . . 48 . . . 49 . . . Some of the typewriter keys had letters, others numbers, and the top row was Greek letters. Folded into the top of the case was a long finger-thick cable, matte gray, made out of some braided material that wasn't metal and wasn't fabric.

"You have never seen anything like it, right?"

It was the stranger. He stood in the door from the living room.

Kinlaw snapped the case shut, picked it up and backed a step away. He reached into his jacket and pulled out his pistol.

The man swayed a little. "You're the detective," he said.

"I am. Where's Sturges?"

"He left. You don't need the gun."

"I'll figure that out myself. Who are you?"

"Detlev Gruber." He held out his hand. "Pleased to meet you."

Kinlaw backed another step.

"What's the matter? Don't tell me this is not the appropriate social gesture for the mid-twentieth. I know better."

On impulse, Kinlaw held the case out over the edge of the terrace, six stories above the courtyard.

"So!" Gruber said. "What is it you say? The plot thickens?"

"Suppose you tell me what's going on here? And you better make it quick; this thing is heavier than it looks."

"All right. Just put down the case. Then I'll tell you everything you want to know."

Kinlaw rested his back against the balustrade, letting the machine hang from his hand over the edge. He kept his gun trained on Gruber. "What is this thing?"

"You want the truth, or a story you'll believe?"

"Pick one and see if I can tell the difference."

"It's a transmogrifier. A device that can change anyone into anyone else. I can change General MacArthur into President Truman, Shirley Temple into Marilyn Monroe."

"Who's Marilyn Monroe?"

"You will eventually find out."

"So you changed somebody into Preston Sturges?"

Gruber smiled. "Don't be so gullible. That's impossible. That case isn't a transmogrifier, it's a time machine."

"And I bet it will ring when it hits the pavement."

"Not a clock. A machine that lets you travel from the future into the past, and back again."

"This is the truth, or the story?"

"I'm from about a hundred years from now. Twenty forty-three, to be precise."

"And who was the dead man in San Pedro? Buck Rogers?"

"It was Preston Sturges."

"And the man who was just here pretending to be him?"

"He was not pretending. He's Preston Sturges, too."

"You know, I'm losing my grip on this thing."

"I am chagrined. Once again, the truth fails to convince."

"I think the transmogrifier made more sense."

"Nevertheless. I'm a talent scout. I work for the future equivalent of a film studio, a big company that makes entertainment. In the future, Hollywood is still the heart of the industry."

"That's a nice touch."

"We have time machines in which we go back into the past. The studios hire people like me to recruit those from the past we think might appeal to our audience. I come back and persuade historicals to come to the future.

"Preston was one of my more successful finds. Sometimes the

actor or director or writer can't make the transition, but Preston
seems to have an intuitive grasp of the future. Cynicism combined with repression. In two years he was the hit of the interac-
tive fiber-optic lines. But apparently it didn't agree with him. The
future was too easy, he said, he didn't stand out enough, he
wanted to go back to a time where he was an exception, not the
rule. So he took all the money he made and paid the studio to
send him back for another chance at his old life."

"How can you bring him back if he's dead?"

"Very good! You can spot a contradiction. What I've told
you so far isn't exactly true. This isn't the same world I took him
from. I recruited him from another version of history. I showed
up in his garage just as he was about to turn on the ignition and
gas himself. In your version, nobody stopped him. So see, I bring
back my live Sturges to the home of your dying one. We arrive a
half hour after your Sturges is defunct. You should have seen us
trying to get the body of the car and onto the boat. What a
comedy of errors. This stray dog comes barking down the pier.
Preston was already a madman, carrying around his own still-
warm corpse. The dog sniffs his crotch, Preston drops his end of
the body. Pure slapstick.

"So we manhandle the ex-Sturges onto the boat and sail out
past the breakwall. Dump the body overboard with window
counterweights tied to its ankles, come back and my Sturges
takes his place, a few years older and a lot wiser. He's had the
benefit of some modern medicine; he's kicked the booze and cigarettes and now he's ready to step back into the place that he escaped earlier and try to straighten things out. He's got a second
chance."

"You're right. That's a pretty good story."

"You like it?"

"But if you've done your job, why are you still here?"

"How about this: I'm actually a scholar, and I'm taking the
opportunity to study your culture. My dissertation is on the effects of your Second World War on Hotel Tipping Habits. I can
give you a lot of tips. How would you like to know who wins the
Rose Bowl next year?"

"How'd you like to be trapped in 1949?"

Gruber sat down on one of the wrought-iron chairs. "I probably would come to regret it. But you'd be amazed at the things you have here that you can't hardly get in twenty forty-three. T-bone steak. Cigarettes with real nicotine. Sex with guilt."

"I still don't understand how you can steal somebody out of your own past and not have it affect your present."

"It's not my past, it's yours. This is a separate historical stream from my own. Every moment in time gives rise to a completely separate history. They're like branches splitting off from the same tree trunk. If I come out to lop a twig off your branch, it doesn't affect the branch I come from."

"You're not changing the future?"

"I'm changing your future. In my past, as a result of personal and professional failures, Preston Sturges committed suicide by carbon monoxide poisoning on the evening of May 1, 1949. But now there are two other versions. In one, Sturges disappeared on the afternoon of May 1, never to be seen again. In yours, Sturges committed suicide that evening, but then I and the Sturges from that other universe showed up, dropped his body in the ocean off San Pedro, and set up this new Sturges in his place—if you go along."

"Why should I?"

"For the game! It's interesting, isn't it? What will he do? How will it work out?"

"Will you come back to check on him?"

"I already have. I saved him from his suicide, showed him what a difference he's made to this town, and now he's going to have a wonderful life. All his friends are going to get together and give him enough money to pay his debts and start over again."

"I saw that movie. Jimmy Stewart, Donna Reed."

Gruber slapped his knee. "And they wonder why I delight in the twentieth century. You're right, Detective. I lied again. I have no idea how it will work out. Once I visit a time stream, I can't come back to the same one again. It's burned. A quantum effect; 137.04 Moment Universes are packed into every second. The probability of hitting the same M-U twice is vanishingly small."

"Look, I don't know how much of this is malarkey, but I know somebody's been murdered."

"No, no, there is no murder. The man I brought back really is Preston Sturges, with all the memories and experiences of the man who killed himself. He's exactly the man Louise Sturges married, who made all those films, who fathered his son and screwed up his life. But he's had the advantage of a couple of years in the twenty-first century, and he's determined not to make the same mistakes again. For the sake of his son and family and all the others who've come to care about him, why not give him that chance?"

"If I drop this box, you're stuck here. You don't seem too worried."

"Well, I wouldn't be in this profession if I didn't like risk. What is life but risk? We've got a nice transaction going here, who knows how it will play out? Who knows whether Preston will straighten out his life or dismantle it in some familiar way?"

"In my experience, if a man is a foul ball, he's a foul ball. Doesn't matter how many chances you give him. His character tells."

"That's the other way to look at it. 'The fault, dear Brutus, is not in our stars, but in ourselves. . . .' But I'm skeptical. That's why I like Preston. He talks as if he believes that character tells, but down deep he knows it's all out of control. You could turn my time machine into futuristic scrap, or you could give it to me and let me go back. Up to you. Or the random collision of atoms in your brain. You don't seem to me like an arbitrary man, Detective Kinlaw, but even if you are, basically I don't give a fuck."

Gruber sat back as cool as a Christian holding four aces. Kinlaw was tempted to drop the machine just to see how he would react. The whole story was too fantastic.

But what if it wasn't? There was no way around those identical fingerprints. And if it were true—if a man could be saved and given a second chance—then Kinlaw was holding a miracle in his hand, with no better plan than to dash it to pieces on the courtyard below.

His mouth was dry. "Tell you what," he said. "I'll let you have your magic box back, but you have to do something for me first."

"I aim to please, Detective. What is it?"

"I had a daughter. She died of polio three years ago. If this thing really is a time machine, I want you to take me back so I can get her before she dies."

"Can't do it."

"What do you mean you can't? You saved Sturges."

"Not in this universe. His body ended up on the beach, remember? Your daughter gets polio and dies in all the branches."

"Unless we get her before she gets sick."

"Yes. But then the version of you in that other M-U has a kidnapped daughter who disappears and is never heard from again. Do you want to do that to a man who is essentially yourself? How is that any better than having her die?"

"At least *I'd* have her."

"Plus, we can never come back to this M-U. After we leave, it's burned. I'd have to take you to still a third branch, where you'd have to replace yet another version of yourself if you want to take up your life again. Only, since he won't be conveniently dead, you'll have to dispose of him."

"Dispose of him?"

"Yes."

Kinlaw's shoulder ached. His head was spinning trying to keep up with all these possibilities. He pulled the case in and set it down on the terrace. He holstered his .38 and rubbed his shoulder. "Show me how it works, first. Send a piece of furniture into the future."

Gruber watched him meditatively, then stepped forward and picked up the device. He went back into the living room, pushed aside the sofa, opened the case and set it in the center of the room. He unpacked the woven cable from the top and ran it in a circle of about ten feet in diameter around an armchair, ends plugged into the base of the machine. He stepped outside the circle, crouched and began typing a series of characters into the keyboard.

Kinlaw went into the bedroom, got the bottle of scotch and a glass from the bathroom and poured himself a drink. When he got back Gruber was finishing up with the keyboard. "How much of all this gas you gave me is true?"

Gruber straightened. His face was open as a child's. He smiled. "Some. A lot. Not all." He touched a switch on the case and stepped over the cable into the circle. He sat in the armchair.

The center of the room, in a sphere centered on Gruber and limited by the cable, grew brighter and brighter. Then the space inside suddenly collapsed, as if everything in it was shrinking from all directions toward the center. Gruber went from a man sitting in front of Kinlaw to a doll, to a speck, to nothing. The light grew very intense, then vanished.

When Kinlaw's eyes adjusted, the room was empty.

Wednesday morning Kinlaw was sitting at his desk trying to figure out what to do with the case folder, when his phone rang. It was Preston Sturges.

"I haven't slept all night," Sturges said. "I expected to wake up in jail. Why haven't you arrested me yet?"

"I still could. You assaulted a police officer."

"If that were the worst of it I'd be there in ten minutes. Last night you were talking about murder."

"Since then I had a conversation with a friend of yours at the Marmont."

"You— What did he tell you?" Sturges sounded rattled.

"Enough for me to think this case will end up unsolved."

Sturges was silent for a moment. "Thank you, Detective."

"Why? Because a miracle happened? You just get back to making movies."

"I have an interview with Larry Weingarten at MGM this afternoon. They want me to write a script for Clark Gable. I'm going to write them the best script they ever saw."

"Good. Sell the restaurant."

"You too? If I have to, I will."

After he hung up, Kinlaw rolled the cinematographer's monocle across his desktop. He thought of the body down in the morgue cooler, bound for an anonymous grave. If Gruber was telling the truth, the determined man he'd just spoken with was the same man who had killed himself in the garage on Ivar Avenue. Today he was eager to go forward; Kinlaw wondered how long that would last. He could easily fall back into his old ways, alienate whatever friends he had left. Or a stroke of bad luck like the Carole Landis suicide could sink him.

But it had to be something Sturges knew already. His movies were full of it. That absurd universe, the characters' futile attempts to control it. At the end of *Morgan's Creek* the bemused Norval is hauled out of jail, thrust into a national guard officer's uniform, and rushed to the hospital to meet his wife and children for the first time—a wife he isn't married to, children that aren't even his. He deliriously protests this miracle, a product of the hypocrisy of the town that a day earlier wanted to lock him up and throw away the key.

Then again, Norval had never given up hope, had done his best throughout to make things come out right. His character was stronger than anyone had ever given him credit for.

Kinlaw remembered the first time he'd seen his daughter, when they called him into the room after Emily had given birth. She was so tiny, swaddled tightly in a blanket: her little face, eyes clamped shut, the tiniest of eyelashes, mouth set in a soft line. How tentatively he had held her. How he'd grinned like an idiot at the doctor, at the nurse, at Emily. Emily, exhausted, face pale, had smiled back. None of them had realized they were as much at the mercy of fate as Sturges' manic grotesques.

He looked up at the calendar, got the pencil out and crossed off Monday and Tuesday. He got the telephone and dialed Emily's number. She answered the phone, voice clouded with sleep. "Hello?"

"Emily," he said. "I have the photo album. I've had it all along. I keep it on a shelf in the closet, take it out and look at the pictures and cry. I don't know what to do with it. Come help me, please."

Workshop Comments

Kelly: "Needs tightening. Sturges is a success in the future and has bought his way back into the past. Don't forget that Kinlaw is your main character. There should be some parallel between Kinlaw and Sturges. When Kinlaw realizes that time travel is possible, his first reaction is to fix his life using it. When Detlev escapes, Kinlaw realizes the trick is not time travel, but actively trying to change the course of your life."

Sterling: "This divertissement is no big stretch for a writer of such ability, but what a pleasure to see a real pro work his favorite theme. Gruber's explanation becomes a tad tiresome. Sturges should return from the future not because he failed, but because he wants to go back to a more naive world, live with his wife and child and have a life."

Lethem: "First half of the detective story is much too convenient. Kinlaw has this case thrown at him again and again—either alter this or make it a running joke. Kinlaw needs to compete for our sympathies better than he does or else he becomes just a framing device for an essay on Sturges."

Butner: "Glistering lambent pearls of prose cheek-by-jowl with lumps of research. If it ain't broke, don't fix it."

Van Name: "The ending just didn't register enough emotionally. Without more information about Kinlaw and his past, Sturges will dominate the story, and Gruber will also overshadow him."

Frazier: "I can't believe that Kinlaw doesn't distrust Gruber. There's a sweetness here that overpowers the dark undercurrent. Then again, it's probably meant to be a romp, and is pure velvet scotch whiskey. And without more pleading phone messages from Emily, showing more of their broken relationship, you don't really earn the epiphany on which the ending turns."

Fowler: "Only one serious complaint: you've dangled the technology of time travel in front of a man with a dead child without thinking of the consequences."

Afterword to "The Miracle of Ivar Avenue"

My big question going in was whether my interest in Preston Sturges warranted a story for those who never heard of him. My big question afterward was whether giving Kinlaw a dead daughter was a mistake in tone. I had not seen this story as the lighthearted romp some read. I thought about eliminating Lucy, but eventually realized that Kinlaw's loss was the thing that made Sturges' history interesting to him. So that the story of a director who had it all and lost it might speak to him personally, instead of downplaying Kinlaw's trouble I brought it more into the fore-ground—drinking, divorce, lost child.

Yes, Richard, Bruce, Jim, I did need to digest that research, discipline those explanations. Jonathan Lethem's comment that the mystery's solution was handing itself to Kinlaw on a plate was too embarrassingly true, and in this version I worked to make it arise more out of Kinlaw's efforts. Jim Kelly was dead-on about the need to make Kinlaw's and Sturges' situations parallel. Bob Frazier is responsible for the phone call from Emily. Karen Fowler saved me from a gaping hole in Kinlaw's reaction to the possibility of time travel.

I thought about it, Jonathan, and Kinlaw's getting assigned the case of this unknown drowned man *is* a framing device for a meditation on Sturges' career, and on chance and fate and charac-ter, subjects which I seem to come back to again and again. I think all stories are occasions for us to examine the things that obsess us. But it's also supposed to be Kinlaw's story, too, and to the extent he was overwhelmed by Sturges and Detlev he needed to be brought forward.

This is the kind of invaluable deconstruction you can't get anywhere but from a group of gimlet-eyed writers at a place like SycHill, and I think my story is better for it.

After you've been to a few workshops, you begin to see that the critiques are not the most important part, though you couldn't have a good workshop without them. They are the foundation, but not the house.

The house is everything else that happens. The drinking game a bunch of us played late one night. Washing dishes after meals. Walking down to the CharGrill to eat greasy hamburgers for lunch. Sitting on the balcony in a nighttime thunderstorm talking about movies. We spend most of our year with our families, in our day jobs, alone in a room with the word processor or the notebook. At SycHill, for one week, the part of you that is a writer comes first. You are in an atmosphere where certain things—things difficult to explain to nonwriters, and that per-haps you can't explain even to a sympathetic listener—are taken for granted.

Because the people you spend this week with are so much the

same as you, differences matter. Voluntarily or not, guards are let down. This is a dangerous thing, but on the whole a good one. I have gotten as much from my disagreements at SycHill as I have from my agreements. You learn from your differences, not always pleasant things, but they give you the chance to grow as a person and writer.

From this year's workshop I'm going to remember taking Bruce Sterling to the top of the North Carolina State University library to shoot a scene for a low-budget movie. This required climbing a steel ladder from the air-conditioning deck twenty feet up a brick wall to the roof. There, at the foot of a radio tower, undoubtedly bathed in every frequency of electromagnetic radiation, a sunburned crew was shooting the last scenes of *The Delicate Art of the Rifle,* in which a sniper is picking off pedestrians in the plaza below the library tower.

Against the background of a majestic thunderhead, Bruce, as a TV weatherman, read a speech about how predicting the weather is impossible because of chaos theory, and any desire to know for sure what's going to happen tomorrow is doomed to frustration.

I don't know how they decided to put exactly these words in Bruce's mouth, but there you have it—the world of science fiction.

Greg Frost gave me a line of dialogue that belongs somewhere in my story, but which I couldn't fit. Still, in the Platonic ideal of "Ivar Avenue" someone must say it, so I give it to you here:

"It's a big harbor. Anybody could wash up there."

John Kessel

Missing Connections

Mark L. Van Name

SHE WAS FIFTEEN minutes late. She was never late. Johnny checked the monitor again: 3:15, no incoming mail.

Nick intently watched the porn groaning and thrashing on the TV. Johnny said, "Don't say a word. Not a word."

Nick laughed. "Why don't you call her?"

"I can't," Johnny said. "I don't know her real name. I know she's at Duke, but so are thousands of other women. We were going to meet in person for the first time today."

Nick switched off the TV. "You don't know her name? You told me you guys had been talking for months."

"We have, sorta. We've been e-mailing and chatting over the Anarchist's anonymous remailer. I asked a friend of mine there to run down her name, but she comes in from a remote anonymous site." He sighed. "Of course, so do I. See: that's what's so perfect about her. About us."

"Yeah, right," Nick said. "I'd love to hear more, but I have to pack. Dear Father demands I spend the first weekend of spring break at the Cloisters."

"You're really going?"

"You bet. It's either that or watch my tuition vanish. Father shows up Monday morning to collect me. If I haven't spent a full three days drying out from the network evils of the modern world, I can kiss Duke good-bye."

"They caught you again?" Johnny said.

"Yeah. One of Mother's anti-porn league cronies had a niece on my list. Just my luck."

"You are such a pervert," Johnny said.

"At least I meet some of the girls I send mail to. Besides, a lot of women enjoy net porn. It's like fishing: pick a good spot with a lot of live ones, throw in a big net, and you'll always catch something."

"I hate fishing. And, I can't believe any women fall for your porn mail."

"Quantity's the key," Nick said. "Get a long-enough mailing list, and someone will always bite."

"So what went wrong this time?"

"The niece told Mother's friend, who had a daughter on the same list. How am I supposed to know everyone my mother knows?" Nick grabbed a suitcase from the closet and started laying clothes in it.

"You shouldn't complain," Johnny said. "Half the people on campus are trying to get into the Cloisters. It's the hottest resort in the world."

"It's hot—as long as you don't mind living in the middle of a Florida forest completely cut off from the entire universe." He pulled a brochure from the suitcase and read. "The Cloisters offers all the comforts of home, electronic and otherwise, but none of the hassles. No e-mail, no incoming or outgoing telephone lines, no deliveries, no broadcasts of any kind, not even messengers. The outside world simply cannot reach you. From guards to a broadband white-noise generator surrounding the entire hundred-acre compound, the Cloisters provides the ultimate in data independence.' " Nick tossed the brochure in the trash.

"That doesn't sound too hard to take for three days."

Nick grunted and kept packing.

Johnny scanned the network status update on the monitor: the mailer was up, but he had no mail. His eyes hurt. He went in the bathroom and took out his contacts. Without them, from more than six inches away from the mirror his face was a dull blur. He rubbed his eyes and wondered if he was the only person on campus who couldn't afford corrective eye surgery.

The mail gong sounded. He grabbed his glasses and ran to his system. "One new message from Ursula," flashed on the monitor. He opened the message.

Shocker,
I'm not late. I'm not telling you my real name. We're not meeting. See the attached file.
You are total scum.
Ursula

He couldn't believe it. He opened the attachment. It was a log of e-mail messages. The first was from his Shocker ID to a Diana. Huge type filled the bulk of the screen:

BUT DO YOU WANT IT?

Beneath that, normal 12-point text began:

Tired of always being in control? Ready to surrender to the right master?
A tall man, strong, sensitive—but stern. Picture black leather. Picture

Johnny exited the message and clicked on the next. It was to a Jackie but otherwise identical. It was also from Shocker.

He quickly reviewed the rest of the log. Twenty-six messages, all from Shocker, all the same. The last was to Ursula.

He tried to open a chat connection to Ursula, but she wasn't online. He quickly mailed her:

Ursula,
I didn't send those messages. Please talk to me. Please.
Shocker

One chance, that was all he needed. If she was sitting by her system, if she would read the message and chat, he could explain, he could find out what had happened.

The gong sounded again. A message from Ursula. His trembling hands made it difficult to position the trackball pointer on the message. He opened it.

It's break time!!
This is Ursula's auto-mailer. Ursula is on her way to a vacation at the Cloisters, and she hopes your spring break is as nice. She's looking forward to a respite from the creeps that prowl the net. When she returns, this ID will vanish and most of you will get her new one.
Except you, of course, Shocker. You jerk.

Someone must have hacked his account. He had a password, and he never told it to anyone. He couldn't even think of anyone who knew he was Shocker. He was so careful he almost never logged on as Shocker outside this room.

This room.

"Nick?"

"Yeah?"

"You wouldn't happened to have used my Shocker account, would you?" He stood.

Nick closed his suitcase. "No. Why would I?" He glanced at his watch. "Gotta run. My plane leaves around nine, I've got some shopping to do, and I want to make sure to be there early."

Johnny caught Nick at the door and spun him around. He stared into Nick's eyes. They were almost exactly the same height, a little over six feet, and had similar slender frames. Nick, though, was so blond and light that he looked pale next to Johnny's black hair and olive skin. "You used my Shocker account. It had to be you, you son of a bitch."

Nick tried to turn, but Johnny pushed him back.

Nick looked at the floor. "Hey, they were monitoring my account, and I couldn't get a new one, so I figured, you know, what's the harm? I wasn't going to use it for long, just until this Cloisters thing blew over."

Johnny wanted to hit him, but what good would it do? He went to his bed and sat. "Great. You go to the Cloisters. Ursula goes to the Cloisters. She and twenty-five other women I don't even know think I'm a jerk." He curled into a ball. "If you could have read her mail, seen the talks we had. She was smart and strong and clever and full of attitude and so much fun. She was beautiful, I know she was. I loved her, or at least her mail. Now I'll never get to meet her."

"I'm sorry," Nick said. "I really didn't mean to cause you any trouble." He left.

Johnny lay on the bed. He felt closer to Ursula than any girl he had dated in high school, any of the few women he had seen at Duke, any friend he had ever known. Now she was gone.

Nick walked back into the room.

"I know I've got this problem, and I'm trying to work on it. I shouldn't have used your ID."

"Thanks for thinking of this now," Johnny said.

"I've thought of something else," said Nick. He held up what looked like a credit card. The word *Cloisters* covered its face. "This is my Cloisters ID. With it, you're Nick Potter. We're the same size and the same age, and they don't have a photo of me. All you need to get in is this. It's good from when the plane lands tonight until Monday morning. You said Ursula is going there. You were supposed to meet her today, so she's got to be on one of the evening flights to Florida. Mine's the last, so she'll either already be there or maybe even be on the same plane as you. If she's so important, follow her and find her." He pulled an airplane ticket from his left jacket pocket. "The plane leaves at nine-fifteen. I can buy another ticket and meet you at the Ocala Hyatt at ten on Sunday night. You'll have Friday and Saturday and most of Sunday to find her. Charge anything you need to the room; dear Father is buying."

Johnny stared at the badge and the ticket. A hundred acres, the brochure had said. God only knows how many people, and he had never seen her. He would never find her.

He had to try.

He grabbed the tickets and ID. "You're still an asshole, Nick, but thanks."

Johnny had never flown first-class before. He tried out Death Games III on the video-game console built into the seat in front of him and eyed the seat's modem jack wistfully, wishing he could connect to Ursula. He didn't normally drink, but the champagne was free and he was nervous, so he chugged the glass

274 Mark L. Van Name

the attendant offered. The man refilled it seconds later, but Johnny let the glass sit. One social drink was his usual limit.

When the plane was airborne, the food started: warm nuts, a salad, then cold salmon on a bed of lettuce. Johnny hated the smell and taste of most fish. Salmon, while not a dish he would order on his own, was one of the few fishes he could tolerate, and he was hungry. He cut off a small piece.

"Not a proper American fish, if you ask me," said the man seated next to him.

"Excuse me?"

The man pointed at Johnny's plate. "Salmon. Not really American, you know what I mean? Oh, sure, you get 'em from Alaska, but that might as well be Canada anyway, know what I mean? Not a bright fish, either. Any fish with a lick of sense, any American fish, would swim with the river, not against it." He leaned closer. "You want a one-hundred-percent American fish, a fish you can trust, one that'll give you a good fight then fill you up and never leave you wanting, you're talking only one breed: bass. Am I right?"

"Sure." Johnny didn't know a bass from a blowfish, but he was stuck on the plane for the next hour and a half.

The man laughed. "That's the spirit." He opened his vest, a fishing vest Johnny now noticed, to reveal a red T-shirt that proclaimed in large black letters, BASS IS BEST. He extended his hand. On its back gleamed a silver-and-blue tattoo of a fish in mid-jump. "Bob Blackston's the name, bass fishing's the game." Johnny shook hands. Blackston turned in his seat, and Johnny read the back of the man's vest: "North Carolina Bass Champions."

Johnny hunched over his food.

"Of course, not everybody's as enlightened as us, son. Take your airlines for instance." He waved his arm to take in the whole plane. "They'll serve your salmon. They'll even serve your tuna, not a bad fish but not a scale off the fin of a bass. But will they serve you bass? I ask you." He shook his head. "Not on your life." He bent over and pulled a large silver bait bucket from under the seat in front of him. "Which is why"—he paused as he fumbled in the bucket and then with a flourish produced a baggy full of sandwiches—"I bring my own." He pulled out two sandwiches and offered one to Johnny. "Basswich?" A strong fish smell flooded the cabin.

Johnny fought the urge to gag. He put down his fork, the cold salmon too disgusting to eat. "No, thank you, I'm already full."

"Suit yourself. More for me."

Blackston chewed loudly. Johnny knew he would never last the flight sitting there. Time to search for Ursula. He waved off the attendant's offer of dessert and instead downed the champagne glass to fortify himself. Then he went searching for Ursula.

She was a big Duke fan, so he looked for women with Duke T-shirts or bags. She was also a senior. She knew every act playing every punk club in a twenty-mile radius. She loved tech as much as he did, so he looked for pierced noses, scrolling message implants, portable computers, lit hair, or anything else distinctively tech.

No one on the plane was even close. There were only twenty or so women, most of them middle-aged and three easily over sixty. None were anywhere near the right age. Most of the passengers on the lightly loaded plane were heavyset men wearing fishing vests just like Blackston's. Waiting in line for the plane's lavatory, one told Johnny they were heading south for a major bass-fishing tournament, big money.

Johnny returned to his seat.

"Meet any of my boys?" Blackston asked. "Damn fine crew. I'm the president, you know."

"I'm not surprised," said Johnny. "I picked up a couple of clues." He checked with the attendant; forty-five minutes to go. When the man offered champagne, Johnny accepted a fresh glass, drained it quickly, and held it out for a refill.

By the time he reached Ocala, Johnny had used the credit-card number on the plane ticket to sign up Nick Potter's father as a Scale Breaker sponsor of the Bass Club. As a token of the club's appreciation, Blackstone had given Johnny a red BASS IS BEST T-shirt and his own silver bait bucket. Johnny was wearing the shirt, which he thought looked quite dashing. He had crammed his previous shirt into the bait bucket. He was a bit dizzy and had to concentrate to walk. He was also much more optimistic about

his chances of finding Ursula. How hard could it be? Nothing
could stand in the way of love.

As he walked out of the terminal, he realized he had no clue
how to get to the Cloisters. He checked the back of his ID, hoping for instructions. A small light strip displayed in red letters,
Brown 18. He wished he had taken Nick's brochure out of the
trash.

A man and a woman in severe dove-gray suits walked up to
him. Both were shorter than he, about five-eight, very slender,
and well-tanned. Both wore their hair cropped close to their
heads. The woman checked a small wrist display. "Good evening, Mr. Brown," she said. "I'm Jeeves 47. This is Jeeves 52."

Johnny clutched his bait bucket and stared. They smiled
pleasantly and stared back. Jeeves? Mr. Brown? When in doubt,
keep it simple: he stuck his right hand out to shake each of theirs.
A temporary tattoo of a bass decorated the back of his hand. It
was a lovely silver-blue that nicely matched the bait bucket. He
couldn't quite remember when Blackston had given it to him. If
they looked at it, he did not catch them. He could handle this.
"I'm Nick—"

"Yes, you're Mr. Brown. Brown 18," the woman said. "You
haven't stayed with us before, so let me explain. You're resident
18 in our Brown quadrant, hence your name. We also have Smith,
Lee, and Sato quadrants. All residents are anonymous, even
within the compound." She cleared her throat. "As I'm sure you
can appreciate. We, like all of the staff, are Jeeves. Any time you
want anything, use one of the in-compound phones to call for a
Jeeves, and one will appear."

Johnny's throat was suddenly quite dry. "Got any champagne?"

"Certainly, sir," the man said. "In the limousine. If you'll follow us."

The man rode in the back opposite Johnny. The woman
drove. The champagne tasted stronger than that on the plane.
Johnny swallowed two quick glasses. He had never realized alcohol could go down so smoothly. He fell asleep holding a third
glass.

He awoke as the car pulled in front of a long, low white
stucco building with a peaked red-tile roof. Stained-glass depict-

ing forest scenes filled its windows. The champagne glass was no longer in his hands. The Jeeves was still smiling. Johnny watched out the rear window of the car as a large metal gate swung shut behind them. The gate was set into a white stucco wall that had to be thirty feet high.

The male Jeeves opened the limo door. As Johnny stepped out, he was instantly struck by the sounds and the air that smelled damp, alive. The slight breeze gently played the branches of the pine trees scattered around the building and crowded together outside the compound's walls. The branches soughed a gentle background to the peeps of crickets. Wide walkways led around either side of the building.

The male Jeeves opened the building's door. Johnny entered, still carrying his bait bucket and trying to walk a straight line. The female Jeeves followed with his suitcase.

A registration counter on the opposite side of the room faced him. To his right, a dozen or so people sprawled on sofas as another man in a gray suit—another Jeeves, he assumed—spoke softly and pointed several times to a map on the wall. His male Jeeves whispered, "Optional orientation," and motioned Johnny to the counter. The people on the sofas stood.

A young woman behind the counter said, "May I help you, Mr. Brown?" She wore the same gray suit as the other Jeeveses, but her skin was almost paper-white and dusted with freckles that made her look too young to be working there. A tangle of red hair fought a winning battle with several frobs. Her eyes were small, round, and light blue. Johnny couldn't decide whether she was cute. It didn't matter: he was on a mission.

He put his bait bucket on the counter and pulled out his Cloisters ID. "Yes, I'd like to check in."

He tried to hand the young woman his ID, but dropped it when his hand hit the counter. Bending over to get it, he saw the last few people in the orientation group leaving through a side door. A young woman was carrying a Duke gym bag.

Thick blonde hair with orange stripes fell in razor-straight lines to her shoulders. Strong, brown legs. A tank top. As she turned to leave, Johnny saw three earrings in her left ear, one a skull. Ursula.

Johnny lunged forward and cried, "Ur–" but tripped on the

suitcase the first female Jeeves must have placed by his side. Both the man and the woman rushed to help him stand. The redheaded Jeeves asked, "Are you all right, Mr. Brown?"

He leaned over the counter. "Who is that girl?" He noticed then that this Jeeves wore a small triangular cobalt pin with the number 18 over her heart. Glancing back, he saw now that the other Jeeveses wore similar pins. "Please, 18, Jeeves. What's her name?"

She smiled pleasantly. "I'm sorry, Mr. Brown, but all guests are anonymous. You are, of course, free to ask her yourself, but we do discourage it."

Johnny leaned closer to 18. Her nose wrinkled slightly and she backed up a step. "At least tell me her name here, where's she staying." He looked around wildly. He couldn't afford to get this close and lose her again. He grabbed the bait bucket. "I'll give you this bucket. It's a great one, Bob Blackston, the president of the club, told me so."

She blushed slightly. "I'm sure it's an excellent bait bucket, sir, but all gratuities are included in your residence fee." Her mouth was twitching. "I'm not a big fishing fan."

Johnny realized he was being an ass; a bait bucket, indeed. "Look, I'm sorry. I don't normally drink, but I was having a hard time on the plane and I thought the champagne might help and the drinks were free and I've already lost her once and I just didn't want to do it again." He had trouble stopping talking. "I'm sorry. Really. I shouldn't have hassled you." His stomach grumbled, and he was thirsty again. "I won't bug you anymore. May I have my room key?"

The young woman regarded him for a moment. She typed on a keyboard he could not see, then said, "Your ID opens your apartment. Have a good stay, Mr. Brown."

He grabbed the bait bucket. "Thanks." The male Jeeves held open the side door and studied a small display in his palm.

Before Johnny reached the door, the young woman called, "Mr. Brown! You forgot your orientation booklet." She opened a door beside the counter and brought him a paperback-sized booklet with an embossed white-on-white cover. "You'll want to study it when you have a moment."

The two Jeeveses climbed into the front of a golf cart that was waiting outside the building. Johnny settled in the back. The female Jeeves drove the cart down wide paved divided walkways. Yellow globes hanging from tree branches lit the way.

Johnny opened the booklet. On the inside cover large script in black pen read, *She's Brown 12. I put you in the apartment above hers.*

"Yes!" Johnny yelled.

The Jeeveses looked over their shoulders at him.

Johnny smiled. "Just glad to be here." He couldn't stop smiling.

Johnny's apartment was easily five or six times as large as his dorm room, with a living room, kitchen, bathroom, and bedroom. The walls were a muted coral, the floors a light, natural oak. One wall of the living room was filled by a huge TV screen, a bank of speakers, and shelves of CDs and laser discs—all selected, the male Jeeves had said as they loaded the wall, according to the list Nick had supplied. They apologized for the change in room assignments and for not having everything already fully stocked. They even cued the laser disc and CD they said Nick had requested. Surround-sound speakers were set in the ceiling and the other walls. A single remote controlled everything.

If the room had only held a computer with an e-mail link to Ursula, it would have been perfect. There was a phone, but when he punched the speaker button a Cloisters operator answered instantly.

Johnny didn't feel very well and thought food might help. The Jeeveses had offered to bring him anything he wanted, but he didn't want to deal with them again. Besides, they had shoved a few boxes of food into the kitchen shelves and refrigerator, again supplies they said Nick had ordered.

The supplies proved to be two cases of Dos Equis, two boxes of Pop-Tarts, a dozen chocolate-glazed donuts, a quart of orange juice, and, in the freezer, a large plastic bag of frozen fish sticks. He would definitely order new food in the morning. For now, though, it was make do or deal with a Jeeves. He settled on the orange juice and three of the donuts.

He ate in the living room. He wanted to run downstairs and burst into Ursula's apartment, but it was after midnight. He could wait until morning, make a better impression. He had to be in the best possible shape, and his reflection in the television's screen told him he was nowhere near that. The whites of his eyes were more red than white. His hair stood at odd angles. He hadn't shaved that morning, and his face looked it. He was afraid to check a real mirror.

His stomach throbbed like an overworked heart. He did not feel at all well. He grabbed the remote and sat on the sofa. Perhaps music would help him relax. He punched the CD button.

A thousand cats screamed from the front speakers as Stompin' Kittens, a North Carolina indie band Nick loved, launched into their regional hit, "Red Pulp." As Johnny fumbled for the volume button, guitar feedback joined and merged with the cat wails. Johnny's head and stomach were going to explode. He pushed more buttons, barely able to keep his eyes open against the churning in his gut. The TV burst to life and a fanfare swelled from the ceiling and rear speakers. A booming male voice announced, *"In the days after the last great war, it crawled from the seething sea. Radiation was its past; human women its future. Half man, half fish, all stud: The FishMaster!"* The fanfare mutated into a series of wet sucking sounds as a man wearing a latex fish suit ripped open his shorts to reveal an enormous finned penis.

Johnny lurched toward the bathroom.

Johnny awoke in bed but couldn't remember getting there. The alarm clock on the nightstand read 7:20 A.M. He rolled over, then realized where he was. He sat up, and his head detached from his body and went bouncing down the concrete steps to Hell. He didn't move. When the pain abated, he carefully checked himself and the room. He was definitely in the Cloisters apartment; so far, so good. He was fully dressed, still wearing the BASS T-shirt, which was another vaguely comforting relief. The bedroom curtains and door were closed. Tendrils of light snaked from the edges of the windows and under the door. They hurt his eyes.

Next to the alarm clock a small note sat propped against a pharmacy bottle. It read:

May we suggest two of these pills, sir? They should help.
Jeeves.

Johnny shook two pills from the bottle and gently stood. His head took a few seconds to catch up with his shoulders. He walked gingerly to the door, covered his eyes with his right hand, and opened it. The morning sun assaulted him even through his hands and closed eyes. He rested against the door frame.

The apartment was still. All was as it had been. There was no trace of the night before. "Thank you, God, thank you," he said.

In the bathroom he filled a small cup with water and tossed it back. He could barely walk. In the bedroom he stripped, climbed slowly into bed, and pulled the covers over him.

The next time he awoke, the clock read 4:00 P.M. He was weak but better. His contacts were gummy, so he trashed them and found his spare set. He brushed his teeth, then stood under a hot shower until his skin was red. The water pressure was wonderfully strong. A no-fog mirror was set into one wall of the shower, and he used it to shave. The bass tattoo on the back of his right hand had faded a bit, but he could not wash it off.

The food choices in the kitchen had not changed. He toasted two of the Pop-Tarts, broke them open, scraped off the filling, and ate the bread with a small glass of water. He took small bites and chewed carefully.

After dressing in a white linen shirt and black jeans, Johnny decided it was time to see Ursula. You could never go wrong with flowers, so he picked up the living-room phone.

A male Jeeves answered immediately. "Yes, Mr. Brown. May I help you?"

"Thank you, yes. Do you have a florist?"

"Of course, sir."

"I'd like to send a dozen red roses." Johnny thought of Nick and all the trouble he had caused. "No, two dozen roses to the young woman in the apartment below me."

"I'm sorry, sir," said the Jeeves, "but there is no young woman in the apartment below you."

"What?" Johnny screamed, then realized what he had done. "I'm sorry. I didn't mean to yell."

"That's quite all right, sir."

"It's just that there was a young woman there last night when I checked in."

"Sir, the former occupants of that room moved to another location late last night. It seems there were noise problems in the apartment above them. Sir."

Damn! She was gone again. Right below him, and then gone before he even had a chance to talk to her. "Where are they staying now?"

"All guests and guest locations are, as you know, sir, anonymous," the Jeeves said. "May I do anything else to help you?"

"No," Johnny said. "No thank you."

He leaned back against the sofa and wanted to cry. So close, he had been so close.

Still, the Jeeves did say she had moved, not checked out. Ursula was somewhere in the Cloisters, so he could find her. The problem was no different than the one he had faced the night before. If only there were e-mail, a way to reach her and explain. He knew how to talk to her there, how to say the things he felt. She had always been right there, a mere electron's-throw away.

He picked up the phone.

"Yes, Mr. Brown?"

"Is there an in-house e-mail system I could use?"

"Of course not, sir."

"Right. Thanks." He hung up.

He spotted the white orientation booklet on the end table beside the sofa. It must have maps. He opened it, saw the note, and hazy memories of checking in crawled through his brain. Perhaps the redhead who had helped him then would help him now.

A golf cart was charging in a slot labeled *18* on the side of his apartment house. Following the map in the booklet, he drove to the main building.

The redhead was behind the registration counter again, perky but also clearly bored. There were no other customers around.

"And what can I do for you, Mr. Brown?" she said.

"I have a problem."

"Yes, I heard about last night." He felt himself blush, and she clearly noticed. "You don't have to worry. We don't broadcast the confidential business of our clients."

"I don't drink, not really," Johnny said. He looked her straight in the eyes. They were an amazing blue. "That won't happen again. Really." His hands tapped the counter as if it were a keyboard.

She pointed to his right hand and with a barely suppressed giggle whispered, "Nice fish."

He blushed again. "Yeah, I don't remember much about that, either. Just that the bass-club guys were very friendly. Anyway, I need your help. Again."

"To do what?"

"To find that girl. See, last night I accidentally made a lot of noise and then I passed out and it must have bothered her family and—"

"—they moved," she said. "Yes, I know. Look, I helped you last night. In return, you had a one-man porn party. You blew it." She shook her head. "Typical male."

"I wasn't watching that disc! I didn't even know it was in there. I turned it on by accident."

"Well, you requested it."

He wanted to tell her the truth, but he couldn't without losing all hope of finding Ursula. "This girl could be *the one,* okay?" he said. "This is no joke. This isn't my hormones taking over. She and I have been talking for months, and we—" He didn't know how to explain what had happened. "—had a misunderstanding. I just need to talk to her for five minutes. That's all: five minutes. Will you please help me?"

She stared at him. He did his best not to flinch. "Maybe all men aren't scum. I go on break at eight o'clock. Meet me at the staff door in the back of the building, and I'll see what I can do. Don't be late."

"Thank you, thank you! If I can do anything for you—"

"Don't be lying to me. And, when you see her, be a man, not just a guy. Now I've got to get back to work."

Two huge gardenia bushes flanked the staff door. Their rich smell hung over the walkway. Johnny arrived almost fifteen minutes early, determined not to miss her.

At exactly eight o'clock, the redhead stepped out. "We can talk here," she said. "I only have an hour break, and I need time to eat. You've got a real problem."

"Why? I just need to know her apartment."

"It's not that simple anymore. She's not in an apartment. She's in the special guest house in the Brown quadrant."

"All right, so I'll go there."

She laughed. "Did you read that booklet I gave you?"

"Not all of it," Johnny said. "I don't really plan to do much while I'm here."

"Well," she said, "if you *had* bothered to read it you would know that each quadrant has one special guest house. These houses are each twice the size of the building that holds your apartment and the one below you, and each is dedicated to a single guest or family. Premium territory, premium prices. Each is surrounded by a privacy wall and has its own pool, ponds with fountains, and staff. The staff includes a twenty-four-hour-a-day gatekeeper. The ultimate in Cloisters privacy. Get the picture?"

"Oh, shit," Johnny said.

"Exactly." She regarded him for a moment. "What exactly do you want to do when you see this girl?"

"She's mad at me for something she thinks I did," Johnny said, "but I didn't do it. I know she'll understand if I can tell her the real story."

"And then what?"

"I don't know. Maybe we live happily ever after. Maybe she dumps me. Whatever it is will be better than having her vanish from my life without me ever even having a chance."

"Sometimes," she said, "the best thing to do is to vanish."

"Maybe, but not this time. This time there's no reason to go away, not really."

The night sky was clear. A sliver of moon hung over the trees. Spring was already in full force, and every tree and bush seemed ripe.

"All right," she said, "here's the deal. The mom's a health-food freak—you met her yet?"

"No. I haven't met any of her family yet."

"Every scrap of food in that house is healthy, healthy, healthy. Sprouts, beans, you name it. The dad's a big-time meat-and-potatoes guy with your typical middle-aged gut, but the mom's got him on the health-food diet. Except he's paying the bills, so every night at eleven, after she's in bed, he gets a special delivery. Last night it was steak, tonight's a huge Carolina barbecue and fish platter, tomorrow it's a down-home Texas brisket and sausage barbecue combination. You're going to make tonight's delivery."

"How?"

She handed him a small map and pointed to a dark square. "That's the Brown quadrant's central kitchen and staff area. I can arrange to have the back door unlocked around ten-thirty tonight. You grab a Jeeves suit—there are racks full of pants, white shirts, and jackets, pretty much every size, and lots of our standard-issue shoes—then pick up the order. You can walk from there to the guest house in about two minutes."

"What about the normal delivery man? What if he catches me?"

"He won't. I help with the nightly system backups, so I've got some network administrator privileges. This job will still appear on the kitchen's worklist, but as far as the rest of our scheduling systems are concerned, it won't exist."

Even this snippet of computer talk made Johnny realize how much he missed the real, online world. "Are they logging admin account activities?" he asked. "Can't they use that to catch you?"

"Yeah, they could—if editing the logs wasn't so easy." She checked her watch. "I gotta run. Good luck."

Johnny spent the day hanging out near Ursula's guest house, walking the pathways around it, watching for people coming and going, trying to stay out of sight of the gatekeeper. The wall around the place was more white stucco, a little taller than he was, rough and firm. The front gate was light pine, wide enough to permit a golf cart to pass. No one came or went. In the afternoon he heard people laughing and splashing in a pool.

At ten, he changed into a tank top and running shorts to make getting into the Jeeves suit as quick and easy as possible. Deliver the food, climb the stairs, visit Ursula in her room. No reason to be nervous; he could do this.

The back door of the central kitchen was unlocked, as promised. He pulled some 34/34 pants from a labeled shelf, grabbed a 16-long shirt and a 44-long jacket. The pin on the jacket identified him as Jeeves 42. He repeated the number a few times, hoping he would respond correctly if someone called it. He checked his look in the mirror of the adjoining bathroom and decided he could pass.

At ten-fifty he picked up the order, a huge heavy platter with a sealed plastic lid. Ursula's father had to be some kind of eater.

He carried the platter on the shoulder between him and the guard sitting in the small gatehouse at the entrance to Ursula's house. The guy yawned and waved Johnny through without a word.

A long wide walkway ran from the gate between two large ponds to the front of the house. Cupid fountains shot arrows of water in the center of each pond.

A fat, balding fiftyish man in shorts and a tank top opened the front door before Johnny could knock. He looked lovingly at the platter, then whispered, "Ssssh" and motioned to Johnny to follow.

A stairway opposite the door led to Johnny's goal, but he had to be patient. He followed Ursula's father down a long hall and into the kitchen. He noticed a back stairway led from the kitchen to the second floor. A breakfast table in the kitchen's corner held a serving fork, a large spoon, and a single place setting. A slight breeze blew through an open window above the table.

"Let me take that from you, son," the man said.

As Johnny held out the platter, his bass tattoo sparkled briefly in the light.

"Bass man, eh?" the man said. He took the food and set it on the table. "Good for you. I've done a bit of fishing now and again myself, though mostly deep-sea, not much bass." He pried off the platter's lid. Rich smells rushed out. "For pure eating pleasure, though, I'll stack the simple catfish, cooked right, against any of your fancy fishes." He set the lid aside. A pyramid of shredded-pork barbecue sat in the center of the platter. Surrounding it were bowls of hush puppies, Brunswick stew, fried chicken, and fried whole catfish. The man speared the barbecue with the serving fork and stuffed it into his mouth. With his free hand he grabbed a catfish and offered it to Johnny. "Try one?"

The fish was revolting, yellow and smelly and dripping fat. "No thank you," said Johnny.

"I understand," the man said. "No eating on the job. I can respect that." He sat down and began spooning food onto his plate. "Thank you, son. I'll leave the empties outside in about an hour. You can pick 'em up then. Mind letting yourself out?"

"Not at all," Johnny said. He retraced his steps but stopped at the front door. Through its peephole Johnny verified that the gatekeeper wasn't coming his way. So far, so good.

He climbed the front stairs slowly, moving as quietly as he could. Four doors opened off the small hall at the top, two on either side. The second on the right was a bathroom with a small nightlight burning. The first room on the right was dark, as was the room opposite the bathroom. Light spilled from under the door of the remaining room.

Ursula. Of course she was still awake. They had often chatted late into the night. He knocked lightly on the door. Nothing. He cracked open the door. She was lying on her side, facing away from him and toward the reading lamp that illuminated the room.

He whispered, "Ursula." No response. He said it a bit louder.

"Huh?" The woman spoke. Her voice was surprisingly low. She rolled over and sat up. Short black hair and a set of red velvet eyecovers made her look like a bee caught in the light. Ursula's mother! In a sleepy but loud voice she called, "Vernon, is that you?"

Johnny stepped out of the room.

From the kitchen Ursula's father said, "Oh, shit!"

Johnny turned back to the bedroom, but Ursula's mother was pulling off her eyecovers and standing. She sniffed the air like a blind dog.

"Vernon, are you eating meat again? Do I smell barbecue? Catfish? What did I tell you about that terrible food?"

Dishes rattled in the kitchen. Johnny ducked into the bathroom and climbed into the tub. He hid behind the shower curtain. Through a small opening he watched as Ursula's mother headed down the rear stairs.

"Vernon!"

A light snapped on in the bedroom opposite the bathroom.

Ursula! He had to be bold. He crossed the hall and threw open the bedroom door. A young boy facing the opposite direction was pulling on a pair of gym shorts.

"Can't I have any privacy around here?" the boy said.

Ursula's mother and father started up the rear steps, both talking at once.

"Look, dear—"

"I can't believe—"

"—it was just one moment of—"

"—you have any respect for me or—"

Johnny ran down the front steps and out the front door. He forced himself to walk at a normal pace until he was through the gate and out of sight of the gatekeeper. Then he chanced a look back. A light appeared in the front right bedroom. Ursula's silhouette moved across the curtains.

Saturday was almost over, he had less than a day to go, and he still had not found a way to talk to her.

Johnny was waiting by the staff door of the main building when the redhead came out a little after midnight. He had changed back into the running clothes. The night air chilled his skin.

"Nice legs," she said. "How'd it go?"

"It didn't." He told her.

When he was done, she said, "So what are you going to do now?"

"I don't know. What would they do to me if I stood outside the house's gate and yelled at her?"

"Haul your ass away. Nicely, of course."

"That's what I thought. My next-best idea is to climb over the wall and break in. It's probably not legal, but it shouldn't be hard; that wall's not much taller than I am."

"Real smart. The tops of those walls are lined with sensors. The gatekeeper can tell when a fat ant crawls two inches on that wall. You'll be lucky to make it five yards before security grabs you."

"You got any better ideas?"

"You could give up."

"No, no I can't," he said. "I have to try. I have to figure out a way. If I could talk with her for even a minute, it might be enough." Fatigue and disappointment washed over him. "I really appreciate all you've done. I'm going to get some sleep. Thanks again—" He stopped as he realized he didn't know her name. He didn't know Ursula's name. Was the world entirely full of women whose names he didn't know? "I feel really weird trying to thank you without knowing your name. Names have been bugging me a lot lately. Could you tell me your name, even your first name? I'll be out of here tomorrow one way or the other, and I won't cause you any trouble."

She crossed her arms. "Lucy. Lucy Case."

"Thank you, Lucy Case, for all you've done." He was tired of lying to her. "My name is Johnny Warriner."

"But your file says Nick Potter!"

"Keep your voice down, okay? I know what my file says, but it's not right. Nick's my roommate. That's how I got his key. He let me borrow it so I could talk to this girl. I could never afford this place on my own."

"I know what you mean. The prices here are insane."

"Nick's father can afford it, and Nick didn't want to be here anyway." Neither of them spoke. He didn't want to leave, didn't want to go back to the apartment and be alone, but he also didn't have a good reason to stay. "Thanks again, Lucy." He headed back.

Johnny slept fitfully, his dreams permitting little rest. He fell through endless tunnels, screamed as angry mobs of women chased him across campus, stood helplessly as the man in front of him in the cafeteria line took the last non-fish plate, ran as fast as he could after Ursula only to watch her draw away easily and then vanish.

At seven he stopped trying to sleep, showered, dressed, and walked to Ursula's house. He stood across the front walkway and hoped for a sign of her. No luck. The crisp morning air formed a light dew on the hairs of his arms. He caught the eight-o'clock changing of the guard outside the house. The two gate-keepers spent a few minutes filling out paperwork in the cramped gatehouse. If anyone in the house was awake, Johnny couldn't tell from outside.

He had to get into the house. Once he had talked with Ursula, it wouldn't matter whether the guards caught him.

He once again considered climbing the wall, but he wasn't sure he could beat the gatekeeper to the house. The man looked almost as young as him and much more fit.

A golf cart whizzed by on the walkway in front of him, going too fast for safety. A guard, probably late for his shift, was driving.

Johnny stared after the cart.

* * *

He spent the rest of the morning driving his golf cart all through the Cloisters, past apartments and houses and tennis courts and a shared swimming pool. On a few long stretches on strips parallel to the rear wall of the complex he floored it and was pleased to see the speedometer crawl over thirty miles per hour.

At noon he returned to his apartment and plugged in the cart. He ate a sandwich in a Cloisters deli, then went shopping in the gift shops. He picked up a complete set of logoed bicycling accessories: helmet, elbow pads, knee pads, and gloves. He also grabbed a pair of mirrored blue wraparound Oakley shades. He charged everything to the room.

At three-thirty he dressed: his thickest jeans, a flannel shirt, and all the cycling gear. He knocked his elbows, knees, and head against the apartment wall; he was as safely padded as he could manage.

A few minutes before four he drove past Ursula's house. He stopped about a block and a half away, as far from the house as he could get and still have a clear run, and turned the cart around.

He had to hand it to the gatekeepers: they were punctual. The second appeared right at four, and the two of them crammed into the gatehouse to do their paperwork.

Johnny floored the golf cart. He looked back and forth between the speedometer and the gatehouse. Ten. Both men had their backs to him. Twenty, over halfway there. Both guards were still busy. As he drew parallel with the start of the house's fence the speedometer hit thirty and Johnny turned the cart right, off the walkway and onto the grass. One guard turned but it was too late.

Johnny held tightly to the wheel as the cart hit the gate. The cart broke through the pine easily and Johnny yelled as loudly as he could, "Ursula!"

He tried to straighten out and head up the walkway, but the front tires snagged in the grass and the steering wheel squirmed in his hands. He was headed right for one of the ponds. He hit the brakes. The cart skidded past the walk, nosedived into the pond, and rammed the fountain. Trying to keep the steering wheel from impaling him, Johnny lost his grip on it and cannonballed over the cart's hood, past the cupids, and into the pond.

He sat there stunned, raising his hand through the pond lilies to smear scum on his aching forehead. He seemed to be in one piece. The guards splashed in behind him. He looked up from the carp that were butting his legs and saw Ursula standing in the doorway of the house. Before he could yell again, a guard clamped a hand over his mouth, twisted his arm behind his back, and dragged him to his feet. As the other guard pulled off Johnny's gloves and slapped on handcuffs, he noticed the tattoo on Johnny's hand. "Looky here, Charlie," he said.

Charlie shook his head. "Son," he said, "I surely do hate to see a bass man do so perfect an imitation of a horse's ass."

One guard stayed with Johnny in his apartment while the others and an apparently senior Jeeves took his ID and left. By the time they returned, Johnny had showered and changed.

"We've talked with your father," the senior Jeeves said, "and he's agreed to pay for all the damages. He'll collect you in the morning."

Johnny wondered how Nick would talk his way out of this one.

"Until then," the Jeeves said, "you're free to stay or leave as you choose, but a Jeeves must accompany you when you leave this apartment. For your convenience, a Jeeves will wait outside your door. Clear?"

"Yes."

The Jeeves handed back Johnny's ID, and the men left.

Johnny packed quickly and headed for the registration area. The waiting Jeeves, a very large man wearing number 53, had politely insisted they walk.

Johnny went straight to Lucy at the counter. "Can you take a break?" he said. "Just for a minute? Please."

Lucy shook her head no, but then said, "Yeah, all right. Fifty-three, will you please cover for me for a few minutes? I'll be responsible."

The man looked skeptical but nodded.

Lucy motioned Johnny behind the counter and led him into a back room. Once they were alone, he started telling her what had happened, but she interrupted.

"I know," she said. "Everybody knows. You're the talk of

the town." She shook her head again but this time laughed. "What possessed you to try that stunt?"

"I thought it would work. I was desperate. And stupid. Obviously."

"I hope this girl appreciates this craziness, and I'm sorry you never got to talk to her." She put a hand on his shoulder. "Hey, you gave it your best. You can always call her next week."

"No," Johnny said, "that's the whole problem. I can't." He owed Lucy the truth for all her help. "I don't know her real name. You see, we've been talking over e-mail for months, and . . ." He told Lucy the whole story. It was good to tell someone, to share his frustration.

As he talked, she moved closer. When he got to the part about Bob Blackston, she put her hand on his arm and said, "Come inside for a moment. I have something I think you'll like."

Behind a keycode lock in the back room a row of dark monitors on standard white computer desks filled a space barely bigger than a walk-in closet. She typed a password on the nearest keyboard. The monitor above it sprang to life. "You know Max-Comm?" she asked. He nodded. "Okay, this is an outgoing line. You can use it to dial into your net server and send her e-mail."

"I told you: Ursula's turned off that ID."

"What have you got to lose?" Lucy asked. She sat in front of a keyboard and monitor at the other end of the room. "I'll give you a little privacy and check my own e-mail down here." When he hesitated, she said, "Go ahead. You might as well."

"Yeah, what the hell." He logged into his node, opened a new message, and stopped as he realized he had counted on being able to see her, to talk to her. No matter; this was how they had started. He typed:

Ursula,
I tried to reach you at the Cloisters, but it never worked. I was the fool in the apartment above you who kept you up all Friday night. I was the idiot who snuck into your mother's bedroom, and I was the ass in the golf cart. Nick, my roommate, sent those messages using my Shocker ID. If you get this, please respond and give me a chance.
Shocker

P.S. My real name is Johnny Warriner. I wish I knew yours.

He sent the message, leaned back in the chair, and closed his eyes.

A small gong sounded at the other end of the room. Moments later, a gong sounded in front of him. He opened his eyes and saw, "One new message from Ursula." He clicked on it, every bit of him focused on the screen.

Shocker,
I'm sorry for the misunderstanding. I'm still at the Cloisters.
Turn around.

Lucy was standing there, smiling.
"Disappointed?" she asked.
In the reflection of the monitor she was beautiful, not the image in his mind, but different—more. "No," he said. "Are you?"
She laughed. "Not even a little."

Afterword to "Missing Connections"

The conflicting feelings you experience before a workshop are often one of the most educational aspects of the entire process. You want to relax and simply *write,* but at the same time you cannot help but hope to impress your colleagues. You want to take risks, to stretch and grow, but in a pressure-packed situation your natural tendency is to turn to the story types you know best. You want to receive the most probing, accurate critical input possible so you can polish your story into a fine gem, but you also want to waltz in, plunk down your manuscript, and have everyone fill the critique session with praise for your genius. And so on.

Most of the writers with whom I've attended workshops over the past decade have possessed the maturity to keep these conflicts from unduly influencing them or their work, and the sensitivity to not discuss the pressure with those obviously feeling it more.

I have demonstrated neither. In fact, in the more than a decade since the first Sycamore Hill, I have let the feelings grow into internally crippling mind games. I have been so frozen prior to my last four workshops—two at Evergreen that Tom Maddox and friends ran, then the last two Sycamore Hills—that I have been unable to finish a story before any of them. Instead, I have ended up writing my story in the evenings at each workshop. The critique sessions then, quite naturally, and quite justifiably, pointed out the obvious first-draft problems of the stories, problems that I took as signs of my own ultimate inability to be a good writer. I spent months after each workshop anguishing over whether I could ever write fiction again, whether I should rewrite the workshop story or trash it, and so on. Of the four stories from those workshops, one sat a year before I rewrote it, two I have never rewritten, and one—this one—was presold. Each workshop has clearly brought me an enormous amount of almost totally self-induced pain.

So why do I keep going to Sycamore Hill?

The answer, as you might expect, is multifaceted.

At one level, I attend Sycamore Hill because it helps me become a better writer. At every Sycamore Hill I have been one of the most junior, least accomplished, fiction writers. Despite that status, my colleagues have always granted me, my work, and my comments on their work, all the respect they have accorded to each other. They have also never failed to tell me when and where a story needed work. I have learned from every aspect of this process, and my writing has improved as a result.

I also attend Sycamore Hill for the work itself: it helps me make my stories better, usually much better. Consider this one, for example.

The first draft of "Missing Connections" that I workshopped is significantly different from the one in this book. The clear messages I took from the critique session were that the draft was simply not funny enough for its length and that it lacked the escalating difficulties and continuing motifs that are the hallmarks of the best romantic comedies. Everyone hit these points in one way or another, but of the magisterial comments I received, I think Karen Fowler stated the key points most clearly when she wrote:

The level of zaniness is not sufficiently high. Although the character he believes is Ursula fades further and further away, still you are missing the sense of the plot thickening. Every move Johnny makes should not only not succeed, but should make the task measurably harder to accomplish. The key sentence to post over the word processor is, "Johnny has a problem and *it's getting worse.*"

Karen, I didn't post that sentence over any of my computers, but I did memorize it and repeat it to myself often.

I also owe a debt to John Kessel for harping on the need for continuing motifs and for a simple solution to a pacing problem.

The story as you see it here reflects my best efforts to incorporate the feedback I received at Sycamore Hill. I believe the story is much stronger for the critique it received, and that's another good reason for attending the workshop.

(I would be remiss if at this point I did not mention the incredible level of assistance and support I received from David Drake, a fellow writer who did not attend Sycamore Hill and who has no interest in such workshops. David helped me with the basic plot skeleton and was unyielding in his support during the story's construction. Thanks, David.)

The sheer fun of the week of Sycamore Hill is another reason I go. Nowhere else in my normal life do I have the opportunity to live writing with fellow writers. It's a blast. We talk writing, often learning more from the unofficial, unplanned discussions than from the critique sessions. We hang out a lot, indulging in the old-fashioned and currently undervalued art of conversation. We get silly, sometimes real silly. We make a pilgrimage to Bullock's Barbecue on Friday night and revel in plates of food too tasty to be as bad for us as they undoubtedly are.

Finally, I attend Sycamore Hill because it's just so damn intense I can't resist it. At one point or another, the workshop process exercises just about every emotion I possess—and I don't have to do anything more physically dangerous than overindulging in junk food for a week.

Growth as a writer, a better story, great times, and intensity; so what if it hurts a bit? It's a deal I'll take every time.

Mark L. Van Name

That Blissful Height

GREGORY FROST

"Populus vult decipi . . . decipiatur!"

I.
Post Trance

"THINK OF ME," the child's voice fades, "as you do a gentle moon-beam. . . ." The medium's arms spread as wide as her dark hoop skirt and she sinks down until her head presses against the rose-wood breakfast table. Its tip-up top wobbles slightly from palm to palm as if the securing bolt has loosened and is about to flip it vertically. Mercifully—not for the woman, but for the couple who hang upon her every gesture—it does not.

They are young, early in their twenties, still struggling to make their way in the world of 1850. The loss of their six-year-old daughter has been as cruel as anything can be; as cruel, thinks Robert Hare, as the loss of his own sister so long ago. Their misery has driven the poor couple, named Howitt, out of the objective sphere: their need to believe has become their universe. Is it truly the voice of their daughter that has emerged from the seemingly unconscious medium? How can anyone be certain when the girl has been dead so many months?

Hare recalls the words of the great Scottish philosopher Sir William Hamilton: "Is it unreasonable to confess that we believe in God, not by reason of Nature which conceals Him, but by reason of the supernatural in Man which alone reveals and proves Him to exist?"

If that question needs proving, here the proof lies. The weeping wife supplicating the Deity while her husband, pale and teary-eyed but determined to be the rock against which she can lean, gathers her up. The shoulder seam of his coat has begun to unthread.

At the sound of rustling skirts, the medium stirs. Her hands slide together and she pushes herself upright, disheveled hair wisping her forehead, her eyes shifting as if to reestablish her surroundings. Hare watches her with a skeptical eye. She composes herself in time to collect her fee from the dazed Mr. Howitt before he can maneuver his wife through the door.

Once she has led the couple from the room, Hare glances at his friend, Joseph Hazard, positioned opposite him on the far side of the table in order to have a clearer view of the medium during the performance. Hazard cocks an eyebrow and shakes his head sadly as if to say, *"Those pitiable people."*

Hare rises from the mahogany side chair, what they call a wheelback chair, although the design it has pressed into his frock coat looks more like a spider's web than a wheel. All the chairs in the room bear this design.

The medium, Margaret Fox, returns from the foyer. She's a small woman, of shy and genteel character—not a low-class trickster, as many of her peers seem to be. Because of this alone he finds it hard to dismiss her. Her color has lost its flush. She is composed as she takes her seat at the table, and smiles to both men with a sympathetic serenity. "They know now," she says, "that their girl is well and they need not be concerned." She clasps her hands, "Praise God, and it's as much as I ever hope for."

"You've helped them, you mean," says Hare.

"Can I do less, Professor Hare?" Her blue eyes sparkle.

"Retired, ma'am, near six years," he corrects her, although it's nice to hear the title now and again.

"I think it a good thing that one such as yourself—a scientist, one who seeks for great truths—should open yourself to our small society."

"The society of spirits? Well, and I wish to believe, Miss Fox, that all this which Mr. Hazard and I have witnessed *is* real."

Her brow creases for a moment, no more. "You entertain doubts even now."

He bows slightly, his knees stiff from so long being seated.

He is over seventy. "As you say, Miss Fox, I'm a scientist. For me there can be no absolutes."

"What about death, sir? Is that not an absolute—the certainty of death?"

"Yet," interjects Hazard, "while he must play the skeptic, I know he was moved, as was I, Miss Fox, and I'm certain he will return for another session with you."

"As will you?" she asks, a hint of coquetry beneath the words, so slight as to be disregarded given the absolute decorum she has maintained. She is so young, her gentle tease is but a trick played upon old men's vanities.

"Mayhaps, ma'am, another day." He adds, "Alas, *I* am not retired, and still must perform."

For an instant Hare stands apart from these two, and seems to hear them speaking some cloaked language, full of amatory import; but he knows better than to act on such indistinct supposition. He wouldn't even ask. Hazard would be shocked, and what can Hare know but that what he has inferred comes from within himself and not without? No, he can say nothing.

"Robert, come, I've my afternoon appointments yet to keep." Hazard turns.

The two men are shown out onto Arch Street. It's warm in the sun, positively an August heat on this late April day in Philadelphia. The door closes behind them and they climb down the five steps to the walk, as a carriage passes. Hazard signals to one farther up the street and its reins flash. He won't allow Hare to walk anywhere, so concerned is he over his friend's condition. He is, Hare thinks, more like a mother hen than a lawyer.

Hazard turns to him. "Now you must tell me, you suspect what of Miss Fox?"

"Everything. The spiritualist is artful, perhaps by nature. Whether or not deceitful has yet to be established, but when I witness such a performance, when I see her come to her senses before her clients can elude her in their misery, what am I to make of it? I cannot *help* but suspect. There's not enough here to trust."

Hazard nods. "I tell you, Robert, I have seen tables caper, and ghosts display impossible knowledge through the use of alphabetic cards such as she manipulates, but in the face of it all remains the niggling doubt that some cunning is at work. I can prove nothing. Nothing in Margaret Fox's actions evinced deception. How, other than by supernatural means, *did* she know so much about the daughter, when I could find nothing near as much about the child through legal process? Yet I began to wonder in the midst of the child's appearance if those people would have confirmed anything she said, however far it might be from true. Out of their suffering. And so—"

Hare takes hold of his arm. "Precisely, Joseph. What can you know from a woman pointing her fingers at a cardful of letters?" He smiles conspiratorially. "To which end I have ordered materials for construction."

The carriage rolls to a stop before them. Hazard turns to help his friend, but Hare grabs hold of the splashboard rail and pulls himself up. "Materials? What would you do, Robert—box in your spirits?"

Hare takes his seat. "What would I do? Know absolutely the fate of"—his smile falls slack—"of them all." The carriage jerks forward and Hazard drops into the seat beside him.

It's the age of the supernatural. Ever since Walpole's *Otranto* ninety years earlier, Gothic subjects have freighted the literature, and matters wholly fantastic have been embraced by the greatest minds. Hare knows well that he's in good company.

As Man is enveloped in systems of weather, he may also be surrounded by invisible and wondrous forces, most as yet undetermined save that their presence is detected. Mesmer's magnetic fluid; Franklin and Kinnersley's electricities; somnambulism, clairvoyance, mediumship—all are squintings into the inexpressible. Hare's own concentration—chemistry—promises similar revelations one day, and perhaps will tie the disparate elements of mind, body, and energies together. Not simpleminded alchemical transubstantiation, no. More remarkable discoveries, which a generation other than his will behold—energies he can but imagine. And who knows but that a doorway will open between the corporeal and spirit realms? Are they alive who have gone before? Is his sister there, waiting for him? Dear, dear Anna—he must know.

He thinks: *As Mrs. Crowe argued in her wonderful book—*

The Night Side of Nature—*all phenomena must be open to the proofs of science, even if the means to prove do not yet exist. Not yet. But I have within me the capacity to change that. When I return to the world of the spiritualists, I will shake that world till the truth falls out. One way or the other, I will know.*

Enquiries thus far have already estranged former colleagues from the University of Pennsylvania, where he once chaired the School of Chemistry. What he proposes to investigate is deemed unworthy of serious contemplation. Not, mind you, blind acceptance; on the contrary, the mere contemplation of *possibility*.

When he plunged concentric coils of copper and zinc into troughs of muriatic acid, producing not only electricity but a heat intense enough to consume charcoal, they were not shocked, although the specifics of what was happening and why, were not immediately known. Yet, when he turns to something that may be no less explicable, they turn their backs. Well, he's old, and has pried at one time or other into everything from chemistry to meteorology to banking, and don't forget the brewing of porter. He'll address former colleagues as he does the Christians, who have no trouble swallowing the camels of Scripture, and yet dismiss Spiritualism, about which they know nothing. In the end, in print he'll declare his findings and let the findings speak. Proof he will offer, the requirement of science.

Of those scientists who once called him friend, only Seybert and Silliman remain allies. Seybert inadvertently pushed him in this direction years ago with questions regarding the afterlife. Silliman he has regrettably alienated because Hare refuses to countenance divine revelation: How can anyone—Silliman in particular—accept on blind faith the validity of his religious inclinations while demanding absolute proofs about everything else? There can be no dichotomy of thought. *Everything* must submit to testing. Still, for all that they differ and will neither yield, he loves and respects Silliman. Though they don't speak any longer, it's to Silliman that his proof will be, however obliquely, proffered. Whatever the outcome, he must sway *someone*.

In the carriage, he surprises Joseph Hazard as he suddenly blurts out, "It's precisely as you say: The cards by which these guides communicate with their audience are unreliable under the best of conditions. Pushing a finger from letter to letter to spell out any word one chooses—how can rational men such as we countenance that? It requires a leap of faith across too vast a chasm. No more defensible than Bechworth's absurd argument that six to eight people gathered around a table produce an electric current capable of causing everything that's attributable to spirit phenomena." He laughs. "Do you think Bechworth ever in his life *beheld* an electric current? 'A dry wooden table,' I responded in my letter in the *Inquirer*, 'is very nearly a perfect nonconductor.' That fool."

Hazard agrees, somewhat edgily.

"You mention table motion—I'll tell you the substance of table motion: accumulated muscular force. It's as Faraday suggests: The hands upon the table do the actual moving. So long as there are hands upon the table, you and I and the rest will harbor doubts. I say: No hands upon the table, then, no fingers upon a card." He waggles his own finger to emphasize.

Hazard ponders, lulled by the clopping of the horse's hooves. He remarks, "You would think, on the face of it, that Christians would *wish* the afterlife legitimized, wouldn't you?"

"Fah. The truth is they only want it to conform to what, without a shred of evidence, they already hold that it is. If anything, the Christians are worse than Bechworth. *They* ascribe all these goings-on to Old Nick. If there is anything imaginary in the whole of these proceedings, it is the supposition that the phenomena are brought on by the interference of the Devil. That—*that*—is the sage opinion of a church that extirpated the Canaanites, the Albigenses, that created the auto-da-fé, the Inquisition, the massacre of St. Bartholemew, set the fires of Smithfield, roasted Servetus, and have persecuted even here Quakers and witches!" He could list many more examples, but speaks to the point: "What could be more devilish than for God the Creator to have created the Devil? The Devil is nothing more than a means for small men to disavow their own evil passions and disguise their own villainous handiwork."

Jumping from thought to thought like a child leaping stones to ford a stream, he then abruptly announces, "Comté is a fool to think that reliance upon Scripture will magically shrink as science grows. Science would have developed already on this ghostly front and resolved it had not the entanglements of biblical intolerance confounded every effort." He falls then into silence, his features flushed.

Hazard keeps still, but gives his friend a sidelong glance.

Hare's keen dark eyes smolder with the inner fire of his contemplation. His chin juts, the jaw clenches. It's a formidable profile—one befitting a Roman statue—and one that has kept more than a few men from voicing unworthy opinions. Hazard knows him well enough to know such fear is groundless.

He has been friends with Robert Hare for many years. No less hostile or arrogant man exists. Hare has always been so vivacious and agreeable in his conversation that he willingly gives opponents any opportunity for rebuttal while he soundly defeats their every objection as though he had run through it all before them. After which the opponent is respected for his attempt to scale the heights. There seems to be no subject with which he is unacquainted; but this one is different. This dark investigation stirs the old man's blood in ways that voltaic chemistry does not.

Hare has had his enemies—the early ones, like the Englishmen Clarke and Maugham, who tried to appropriate credit for his oxyhydrogen blowpipe, were thieves and ultimately revealed as such. Hare had only to hold his ground and let others vindicate him. That won't work here, Hazard knows.

This time, the people on his side are the ones about whom there are questions.

II.
The First Device

On a hot June morning two men unload from the back of their wagon a canvas-draped object that ends in four beautifully turned table legs. Unlike a table it bulges on one side, where the canvas is pushed up in an off-center hump. A woman holds open the door at 178 North Tenth Street to let them carry it up the steps and into the rowhouse.

Mrs. Margaret B. Gourlay is of medium height, with dark hair pulled back into a large bun. She has a broad, handsome face just beginning to lose its definition. Her eyes are brown and warm: gentle and honest eyes. She is dressed very plainly in dark green, although the fullness of her brown skirt over cage-crinoline requires her to retreat from the door far enough to let the freightmen inside. They carry their burden into the parlor where her clients come.

Her husband, Dr. Gourlay, stands in the doorway from the dining room and looks on in some bewilderment as the twine is untied and the canvas lifted, revealing an arcanely cobbled device. He watches the men tie a sinker weight to a vertical cord so that it hangs a few inches above the floor. A second, larger weight they tie to the end of a second line and set forward of the table like a small iron doorstop, the line stretched taut.

Finished, the men gather up the canvas and ropes, then wait for money, although Hare has paid them at the loading. Dr. Gourlay reluctantly tips them, not generously by any means, and, feigning indignation, they depart. His wife's voice echoes from the foyer.

He approaches the device with grave caution.

It is a lovely satinwood needlework table—or once was. Now, attached to the top, marring more than half of the veneer, sits a tall metal box with a steeply angled lid, a kind of enormous bread box. From the back of this emerges the cord on which the sinker weight ultimately dangles, but first the cord wraps around the spindle of a large wheel. The wheel hangs off the side of the table. It has letters inscribed around its rim: ZJWKERUCFH &ALUSMOP around the top half, GTNXOBIVD around the bottom. Where the spindle protrudes through the center of the wheel, the line from the iron counterweight attaches. There is also a thin metal rod that sticks up to mark which letter is to be read. At the moment it rests upon the letter *F*.

The doctor circles the table. Around behind the wheel, the metal box is open. Inside it is some sort of lever. Gourlay leans on the table, bending slightly, and reaches to put his hand in the box and press the lever.

From the doorway, his wife says, "Don't."

The doctor straightens. "I was going to—" He stops, for he does not know what he intended. "Did you know of this . . . this contraption of his? How it works?"

"No," she replies. "I've put my trust in Professor Hare as he has in me."

Her husband brushes his hand across the table as if in defiance of her. He turns smartly on his heel, sweeps up his gray stovepipe hat from the chairback settee where his wife's clients usually sit, and marches out of the parlor. "I shall refrain from interfering, of course, in *spiritual* matters," he tells her, then leaves the house. Mrs. Gourlay waits until the vibrations of the front door have ceased reverberating before she sets foot in the parlor.

When Hare arrives some hours later, Mrs. Gourlay meets him at the door in an excited state. "She's spoken to me," she tells him. "Come see, come see." And she leads him by the hand into the parlor. She has drawn a dining-room chair to the table, on which she settles, her skirts billowing around her. "Look," she says. Hare takes a seat where he can read the wheel and watch the medium.

For a time she sits in seeming contemplation, her gaze unfixed. Then her eyelids flutter and close. She leans forward as her hands, within the box, begin to press upon the lever. The wheel answers her pressure, rolling clockwise in sluggish rotation. Around and around on its axle the wheel spins, stopping briefly, sometimes with difficulty, upon each letter in sequence, having to rotate around a full turn to spell the same letter twice. By then he knows; a cold apprehension suffuses him like a chemical reaction overflowing a flask. The medium doesn't seem to be aware. Her head is down. He can't see her eyes at all. She cannot be watching the wheel, and as she is behind it, she couldn't see the letters on its face in any instance.

The wheel spells out the fourth letter, the name ANNA. His sister's name. Mrs. Gourlay's head remains lowered.

The wheel continues to spin another quarter hour, until he has recorded the message: ROBERT WELCOME. At that point, Mrs. Gourlay exhales sharply and draws back from the device. Her head circles, coming upright. She opens her eyes and looks at him. "It is so difficult, so draining, to use this machine. But she came, did she not?"

"Who?"

"Your sister, Professor Hare."

"My sister?" He tries to seem unenthusiastic.

"Yes, that was her relation to you, I'm sure of it. A sister." She glances at the wheel. "You hadn't told me of your sister."

Had he, though? No, he's quite certain he withheld everything. He replies, "I hadn't thought—" He had not dared hope.

"Your device is a most cumbersome thing to use. Levers and wheels."

Here's something he can speak to. "Cumbersome, yes. And yet you succeed in demonstrating its merit, Mrs. Gourlay. More than that, I believe you've made a case here for the truth of your claims and those of other mediums. This is a great stride forward, do you have any idea? The first scientific validation of your craft, Mrs. Gourlay. Exhausting or not, please apply yourself again to the spiritoscope, if you would be so kind."

"Spiritoscope." She stares apprehensively at the thing before replying. "I must tell you, sir, that it takes *all* my energy to maneuver it."

"*Your* energy?"

"Indeed, sir. 'Tis after all mine that the spirits utilize. Look how quickly I was drained. How quickly she withdrew from me—one message and no more. A card is very easy for them, as you can imagine. It takes but a finger." As she says this, she raises her index finger.

Precisely. That was the point. But now the point impedes. He wants only to hear from Anna again. He contemplates the machine awhile in silence.

Mrs. Gourlay doesn't begin, and instead pushes her chair back from the table. "Might I offer you some tea, Doctor? I'm, myself, quite thirsty just now."

"Please," is all he says. His gaze does not shift from the table, even after she has risen and gone away.

He reconsiders the design of his spiritoscope. He has reengineered everything he ever constructed—he modified the oxyhydrogen blowpipe a dozen times in twenty years to make it more efficient, even though the original was already the hottest heat source in the world. Nothing that is humanly engineered cannot be improved upon.

His father, the senior Robert Hare, was a brewer. Hare's American Porter was a superb ale, the most popular in Philadelphia at the turn of the century; yet he was forever working with the formula, experimenting with different roasts of malt, the further to enhance the flavor. His son, apprenticed to him, assisted

in much of the experimentation, from whence came his fascination with chemistry but also with sources of heat, with all that
heat could do. The slightest increase or decrease in the tempera-
ture or duration of roasting of the malt changed the characteris-
tics of the finished porter significantly—in many instances
beyond drinking. The younger Hare's mind raced along as it contemplated variables and cobbled a device to roast the malt faster,
thus enabling his father to increase his output. The process
worked; he refined it. As he will do here.

The problem served up by Mrs. Gourlay is how to make
working the spiritoscope easier without sacrificing the safeguards
built into it. He can't communicate in two-word dribs and drabs
like this. He dwells upon it to such an extent that he barely notices her return, doesn't see the china cup and saucer set before
him, hardly recollects the tea, and only returns to his senses when
she says to him, "You know, Professor Hare, I must tell you a
thing I've sensed about you since first Miss Fox introduced us."

He finds he's perched on the edge of his chair. Tea steams out
of his cup. "What you sense about me," he repeats, as if the repetition will explain what she has said.

"Yes, sir."

He regards the tea as a fortune teller might before sipping it,
as if it might yield a secret, and compresses his lips as he swallows
the bitterness. "What would that be, ma'am?"

"Why, that you share the spiritualist's gift."

Whatever he thought she might say, this isn't it. "I'm sorry, I
don't know that I understand you. Do you mean to imply I
should be able to speak to them?"

"And they to you."

"How, then, do you explain that I have never in my life received any communication whatsoever from the spirit world?
Even as I would have hoped and prayed to hear of the continuance of my sister, there was no rapping on walls, no shifting of
furnishings." He abhors the suggestion. Hands trembling, he sets
aside the cup. "Indeed, it is outrageous, madam."

"Oh, but, *sir,* you would not be aware. You have no training
in the spiritualist's art. Your faculties lie dormant, untapped and
untried. I and my spirit guide do both sense about you such powers, restrained, awaiting release, that with training—"

"Please, Mrs. Gourlay, *no more!*" He waves her to silence. "I have in my time been a brewer, a chemist, a professor, an economist, and an inventor in all of these rôles." The thought slides in below his words: *And a neglecter of her in all of them.* "I believe I have quite enough talents for a lifetime without adding spiritualism to the list. Especially—" He hesitates, wrestling his ire under control. "—especially as the city is quite well populated with such-like already. Inventors seem far less procurable." He stands, leaning upon the table for support. "And now, as the demonstration has exhausted you, Mrs. Gourlay, I will be on my way. You've set me a fine challenge, to improve upon my invention. I'll consider it. But, I would like you to utilize the spiritoscope as much as possible. You may find it easier to maneuver as time goes on. Also, as I intend to publish my findings, you will likely find yourself with a clientele desirous to witness its demonstration."

Her smile as she sees him off is stiff—no doubt, he thinks, as a result of what he has said of her spiritualist compeers. But it's true: Philadelphia is a haven for spiritualists. There must be one for every street in the city. Mrs. Gourlay has a reputation as one of the more upright of her kind . . . which is to say that no one has ever caught her in a deception. That's why he chose her to receive the first machine. It was to be Margaret Fox, whom he no longer entirely trusts. But to suggest that he ought to practice spiritualism himself is—

Is what? he asks himself.

By the time he has been coached safely home, he has the answer.

Terrifying. It is terrifying.

III.

Expansionism

He has dreams after his meeting with Mrs. Gourlay in which his sister visits him. In one, she divides like a cell, becoming three of herself, in wide-striped skirts and puff-sleeved blouses, her long chestnut hair crimped and coiffured into chains encircling each of her heads. The nineteen-year-old sisters knock wooden balls across the lawn of the chemistry building with croquet mallets.

He has a mallet, too, but the multiplicity of sisters play their game around him, never offering him a turn, as though they don't notice him in their midst. Annas enclose him; the wickets trip him up and like bear-traps catch his ankles. The mallets crack familiarly as they strike. The croquet balls roll up against the posts and stop; there are three posts, and he thinks that this is wrong, there should be only two. The sisters pause over the balls, leaning on their mallets as they stare straight through him to one another in silent communion. If he could only move, if he could reach one and warn her, protect her. The wickets are driven through his legs, and when he tries for her, he totters and falls.

The instant he hits the ground he opens his eyes. His heart-beat hammers, his nightshirt is stuck, twisted, to him. He wipes spittle from his cheek, and sits up in the darkness.

She was so close that he heard her skirt swishing as she strode about. What if she is always as near as that? He has no way to know.

For days and weeks afterward, intense dreams interrupt his cerebration and render him incapable of invention. He broods upon her, turns her over like a coin, each turn a painful remembrance.

She grew up a tomboy, fearlessly investigating what she was not supposed to see, what girls were supposed to stay out of. She made him teach her conkers, a game that only boys ever played. They picked out chestnuts together, he advising her on the quality of each one she brought to him. He took the acceptable chestnuts, soaked them in vinegar awhile, and then nailed a hole through the light caps of six of them. After tying a bootlace through each, he left them dangling from a clothespeg beside her bed. Then he waited. The thrill of her squeal as she discovered what he had made for her still sped his heart. She came out of her room, the conkers clacking together, and she kissed him. With that kiss she transformed from the tomboy sister into Anna. Anna, the perfect jewel. Who married late and died young; who survived the yellow-fever plague of 1793, only to surrender to consumption before she had even borne a child of her own. When he thinks of her, he thinks of those clacking chestnuts swinging like simple pendulums on their laces—a moment suspended in time to which all other memories lead . . . because he, from the moment he began to help their father at the brewery, became so bound up in his researches that he barely noticed her, eventually losing sight of her. He thought she would always be there. As if, had he paid her more attention, she would have lived. His guilt coils into a wall of thorns around the spiritoscope.

He turns to other, less cumbered fronts.

There are some improvements he has wanted to make to his deflagrator, and another paper to deliver upon the caloric properties of weather systems: For some years he has studied the possibility that warm water from the Gulf of Mexico charges the air above it with such heat that, as the heat meets the cooler inland air above the mountains, it produces violent weather such as tornadoes, which are themselves—so he has determined—comprised of electrical currents of air. That study returns him to his calorimotor, and its production of heat in tandem with electricity. The circle of phenomena with which he's familiar ever expands, ever merges.

Through the sciences he finds he can approach the subject of spirits again. Might the realm of the spirits incorporate such things as electricity and heat? Are spirits cold? Mediums often describe a chill that settles upon them, and he once gripped a medium's hand that had gone ice-cold in an instant, but that is hardly the sort of proof he can use. Are they electrical in nature, the souls that guide Mrs. Gourlay's hands? It seems fitting that they should be—they would add another layer to what he already knows of electricity. Why shouldn't it be the unifying principle? All the world and all the energies, driven by electrical forces.

Hare recalls when he was twenty-two and fused strontianite for the first time with his oxyhydrogen blowpipe. Silliman assisted. Woodhouse and Seybert were practically beside themselves with excitement and wasted no time pushing through his election to the Chemical Society. He remembers thinking that his future would be like this. He would continue to invent, continue to win praise. Nothing could stop him. He had no inkling then of spiritualism—Seybert's fascination was not expressed until so much later—or that he would run up against such ignorance and prejudice within his own society. They forget that it's he who first fused heavy spar and threw platinum, gold, and silver into a state of ebullition. He whose process, under names such as "Drummond light" and "calcium light," illuminates lighthouses the world over. He whose *Compendium of Chemical Instruction* is the standard text to which all chemistry students are referred. He who possesses the Rumford Medal for his discoveries. He who is a life member of the Academy of Natural Sciences. It isn't arrogance. He *has* accomplished all these things. And he's not done yet.

With renewed purpose, he completely redesigns his spiritoscope.

Invited to speak in New York, he loads the new version onto a wagon and has it carted there.

He's allowed to choose the nature of his talk in New York—they know how broad is his range; nevertheless, the audience of professional and amateur scientists gathers in anticipation of a discourse related to chemistry.

Instead, Hare pounces upon the infinite chimeras of Scripture, blasting the Bible, and then describes the possibilities of spirit communication. Finally, like a stage magician who has saved his best trick for last, he offers a brief demonstration of the new, improved spiritoscope. He wants them to appreciate the mechanics of the machine.

It's a rectangular dining table now. The same revolving wheel hangs off one of the long sides of the table, facing the audience. He, as acting operator, sits across from them. On his left the two table legs end in small truckles, whereas on the right they're fitted with larger wheels connected by an axle. Rolling the table back and forth turns the axle, which drives the lettered wheel. His maxim remaining "No hands upon the table," he has placed a small wooden tray on casters of its own. The operator moves the table by rolling the tray back and forth upon it. Cumbersome once again, but less so, he feels, than the earlier version Mrs. Gourlay is mastering; and if it works it removes the medium even farther from direct contact with the wheel.

But when Hare attempts to demonstrate it for the audience, he can't move the table at all. Discouraged, he finally sets the tray aside and pushes the table back and forth manually. The wheel turns, but spins without any inclination to stop. He can spell out nothing. So much, he thinks, for his latent powers. So much for the proof of his claims. Even though the presence of a medium would have given his audience an easy excuse to dismiss him, he sees he has been stupid not to bring one. Something remarkable might have happened. He can see that the people don't care what he's doing. They can't wait to get out of the hall.

His reputation saves him from direct humiliation. So exhausted is he from trying to wrestle the table back and forth that he disregards the disappointment in the voice of the professor who arranged the talk—"That was a most singular performance, Dr. Hare"—and falls asleep in the carriage that takes him to his hotel.

Within the month of his appearance a letter arrives from a man named Isaac T. Pease of Thompsonville, Connecticut. Pease has learned of the spiritoscope. Perhaps he attended the New York lecture or knew someone who did. In ingratiating language he explains that he has experimented with a similar device at the urgings of local spiritualists and redesigned it on a much smaller scale than Hare's grand spiritoscope. He includes schematics of his devices, which he has dubbed "Pease's Dials." Looking them over, Hare doesn't know whether to be pleased or furious, remembering how the British attempted to steal his credit for the blowpipe.

He admits that Pease has made one or two improvements: Rather than the wheel, he has the index needle spin, which seems much easier to accomplish, once considered; the activator operates by a spring rather than a system of cables and weights and axles, and directly affects the index. The smaller disks, which can be adjusted for the medium to see, incorporate phrases as well as letters. The needle can point to "Think So" or "Must Go," "Yes" or "Doubtful," "I'll Spell It Over," "Done," "I'll Come Again," and even "Good-bye"—all spread around the wheel, written as if along the spokes. Ultimately, Hare is too impressed at the ingenuity to be angry. He admires invention too much to discount it even when accompanied by apparent hubris: "Pease's Dials" indeed. He'll catalogue them in his book, but otherwise, with their simple mechanisms, they return too much control to the medium for his necessary proof.

For the summer Robert Hare departs Philadelphia and travels with his household staff to the Atlantic Hotel on Cape May Island. The New York spiritoscope makes the journey with him, to be set up in the salon of his suite where he essays it from time to time in solitude. For all that he denies it, Mrs. Gourlay's pronouncement on his powers has burrowed into him. Silently, he turns over and over the question: Where does the supernatural mechanism dwell? And is it likely we all possess it?

Throughout the month of June he sits before the table at night, often with a cellar-chilled pint of Hare's American Porter—his private stock—and rests his fingers upon the sliding tray. Night after night, when he lets his thoughts drift, the back-and-forth pushing of the small board on casters begins to move the table and the wheel. He can't see the face, but what the wheel is spelling doesn't matter. It's moving now under his impetus, if not control.

Finally, he watches in awe as the table rolls from side to side as if loose upon the deck of a rocking ship and the wheel stops, moves, stops, reverses. The back of his neck prickles with the electricity of terror.

"I cannot be doing this," he says to the empty room. Therefore he is not. Something else—unseen—is there with him. The table stops.

He retracts his hands from the tray and retreats to his bed, where he lies for hours, alone, nervous and awake. Night surf on the cape roars in the distance and salty ocean breezes swirl through the stuffy room. Trees outside the windows hiss. The moonlit shadows of their dancing branches anthropomorphize the wallpaper and furnishings. The branches slap together: "clack, clack, clack." Dark ghosts whirl about him. The whole room tilts and spins. "Anna," he sobs, and drifts into a fitful sleep.

He meets at the hotel a number of people, including a Dr. Thomas Bell from Somerville, Massachusetts, who will later contribute much information to his book. Bell, a thin, dark man, is a head taller than everyone around him and speaks with a twisted curve to his words somewhere between Cockney and Bostonian English. He asks, then finally demands to see the spiritoscope and, when Hare takes him to the salon, insists on a demonstration. Other men and women present in the public dining room drift after Bell, coming to see, spilling in through the foyer past

Hare's surprised servant, Gilhay. They hang in the doorway.
Some have snifters in their hands, and cigars, and whisper to one
another. This is so casual for them, a lark to pass the evening.

He determinedly takes his place, ponders for a moment, then
closes his eyes. His fingers begin to push the tray on casters back
and forth, and even forward. Sluggishly, the table begins to roll,
the wheel to rotate.

"It's spellin' out something," whispers a woman, and he
opens his eyes. She's a large, fish-faced creature, but he tries not
to see, not to think.

Bell has his notepad out and a stub of a pencil. It takes ages for
each roll of the table, for the wheel to stop on each letter. The
crowd stands silent, motionless, until the sixth letter, and the
table comes to a stop. "W–A–R," says Bell, "U–E–N. What's
that, then, Dr. Hare? Waruen?"

Hare settles his hands palm-up in his lap. He stares at them
uncomfortably. "Warren," he replies, "the *U* and *R* are side by
side, it was supposed to be another *R*, I'm sure."

"Who might 'e be?"

Hare's eyes glitter bright. "Mr. Warren was my father's partner in business before I was born. He left Philadelphia and sided
with the British in the war—that's who he is."

Bell and the others seem unable to put this together with anything—their expressions betray what's missing from his answer.

He explains, "I was asking, don't you see. Asking the spirits
to give me some information only *I* knew. And they spelled out
his name, didn't they?"

"I suppose," says the fish-faced woman, and she glances sidelong at others. Gilhay, his manservant standing beside the door,
looks no less troubled by this revelation.

Hare wants them all gone now. "Well, thank you. I didn't
know what was being spelled out, if it was an answer to anything.
I've no idea when it works, if it works. That's the way I've designed it."

"Oh, continue, please, sir," Bell insists. "Let *us* ask something."

Hare dismissively waves his hand and falls back on Mrs.
Gourlay's excuse. "It's too enervating. One answer—a single
word—exhausts me. I'm not a skilled practitioner." He can see it

in their faces—the same look he has given to spiritualists, to Margaret Fox—skeptical smiles, the identical doubts expressed by the audience in New York and by the look in Gilhay's eyes, embarrassed on his behalf. Oddly, the doubt is harder to take from strangers. But there's nothing like doubt on Bell's face. Bell is thrilled.

Seeing that the performance is truly over, people begin to withdraw, all save Dr. Bell.

Gilhay lingers uncertainly behind him. He's an Irishman. His people know about spirits and demons, ghosts and *ban sidhes,* know the treacheries they can perform. Even dead friends will play tricks upon the living now and again—Hare's heard countless supernatural tales from him since undertaking this project. Also, it might be that Gilhay despises Bell as an Englishman. That would be enough to set him scowling at the intruder's back. He looks to Hare for a signal to eject Bell, but Hare shakes his head and Gilhay finally abandons the open door and retreats to his own small quarters.

Bell says, "Doctor, I'd like to contribute to your investigations. Already, I've looked into the matter substantially on me own. In Boston there are practitioners of remarkable skill who I've met. Once I stood at the end of a ten-foot table and watched a small woman sitting beside it put out her hands above without touching it, like someone working a puppet, and make it move, glide a foot or two at a time, this way and that. We set an iron rod in between folding doors at the bottom, and the table clambered over the rod into another room. Then it come back, right over the rod again. I noted in me journal that if the medium raised her hands above two foot from the table, all movement ceased. Whatever it was driving that thing, it was coming through her. I'm a tall man, you'll mark, and I could see down the whole length of the table that nobody was touching it. Not a soul—well, not a corporal one." He smiles. "There's much more that I could describe for you if you'd let me further my investigations and add them to the weight of your own."

Hare sits dumbfounded. A colleague in this business? "Dr. Bell, I should be most honored," he hears himself say, as if listening to the conversation from another room. "I'm compiling proofs to present to the scientific community. I would well appreciate yours, if they're objective."

Bell smiles once more. His teeth aren't very good. "I understand too well the rejection of traditionalists. No imagination in 'em. Have you read Poe, sir? *There's* a soul who understood the nature of life beyond death."

"Poe, yes." He recalls that name vaguely: He doesn't follow the careers of sensationalist writers. "Very good, Dr. Bell," he says, and moves forward, effectively urging Bell out the door. "Compile all you like. I'll certainly consider whatever you have to show. And of course we'll talk again here at the hotel."

"Of course, sir." He steps back into the hallway, bows formally. "I bid you good night, then."

"Good night." Hare shuts the door. He turns, leans against it and stares at the spiritoscope, expecting almost to see it rear up on its hind legs and caper through the salon. The table remains at rest.

Thereafter Hare takes his meals in his rooms or at off-hours to avoid Bell's company. He can't say why exactly, but he doesn't want to share his work with Bell. Maybe not with anyone else. Having accepted the role of iconoclast he's unwilling to part with it. He is his own hair shirt, he thinks, and chuffs at the inadvertent pun.

By the end of June he has improved his skill upon the spiritoscope. His mind drifts, the wheel spins freely.

He has established communication with Anna. It's as if she sits out of sight in another room, listening to his questions and writing him notes in response. If only it were true and he could look round the corner and find her.

Gilhay transcribes what the wheel dictates. One time he writes down a slightly misspelled *pulsatque versatque,* and Hare snatches his hands off the tray in amazement. "My *father* is with us! That was one of his favorite phrases. It referred to the beating Entellus gave Dares in the *Aeneid,* beating him so that he spun. My father used to recite it to me to warn me what I was about to get if I didn't behave. It can't be anyone else! Who else would know?" Gilhay glances around the room uncomfortably.

Although the manifestations of Anna and his father delight him, Hare comes to realize that he must produce something more by way of proof for others, else he is no different than any performing medium. The truth of what passes through him to operate the wheel can't be determined by this exercise. It has meaning for him alone. Spirits come and talk to him, but who else would recognize them?

He would dearly like to speak with Franklin and Washington, both of whom he admires so, if only he could draw them about himself like some great incorporeal cloak.

A few weeks later he's taking a late supper of cold chicken and leeks in the dining room when Dr. Bell appears, towing behind him a severe blonde woman named Miss Julia Hayden. She's from New York, and wears a dull black dress as if in mourning. Bell says, "She was 'ere on holiday. A remarkable medium, you must let her try your device." And so, pressed to it, he has to yield. They let him finish his meal, then he leads them up to the salon and the spiritoscope.

To his surprise (and delight), Julia Hayden is incapable of using the thing. The wood tray rolls back and forth on its casters. The table budges not an inch.

Eyes closed, she grimaces, twists her features, contorts her lips in a gruesome spectacle. Her face fades the color of a winding sheet. Her hands tremble on the tray, slide off and lie slack upon the table surface. Her head lolls, her expression gone loose. With a sharp breath, she opens her lips and the words commence: "Brother beloved, I am here."

It is not Miss Hayden's normal voice, but creaky and burbling. His sister died with her lungs full of liquid. The sound puts him back beside her as she failed, his hands wrapped tightly around hers as he desperately, uselessly, willed his life into her weak body. He doesn't want to hear this.

"Please." He indicates the table. That's how she's supposed to communicate.

The medium's head shakes as if someone is clutching the back of her neck and twisting. "Not physical . . . vocal. She has no skill here," she says, nodding at the wheel.

"Who are you?"

"You have to ask?" The words come slow as molasses dripping from a jar. A small bright drop of blood appears on her lip.

A sudden frost coats his lungs.

"Robert. You seek a proof you cannot receive from the table. I'm present to deliver it."

"Deliver? How do you intend?"

"Give me a message."

"A message for whom? I don't—"

"To Gourlay."

His jaw stiffens. He peers at Bell, at the medium, as if betrayed. How could her name be known to them? He hasn't mentioned it. She never came up in his brief conversations with Bell. No, this must be real.

What sort of message will do, then? Something involving other people, not Mrs. Gourlay alone. Proof beyond the medium and the devices, that's what he requires, his spirit sister is right about that. He must involve someone who doesn't believe. He casts about and the answer comes of its own free will.

"Go to her, then, and tell her to instruct her husband to proceed to the bank at one P.M. tomorrow, find out when the note is due on the brewery property and report what he has found to me at home at three-thirty." This will prove everything. There's no telegraph between Cape May Island and Philadelphia, no way for the message to make the journey any quicker than he can.

There comes no reply, no confirmation. The medium suddenly draws a breath, sits stiffly upright, then sags. Within a minute, color floods her cheeks as if she has just performed something strenuous. She raises her head. He is amazed at this transformation. It isn't something she could induce—the suffusion of blood into her cheeks. Eyes enclosed in sickly darkness, she glances from Bell to Hare, blankly. Then at the spiritoscope. "Did I . . ." she begins, removes her fingers from the tabletop, folding her hands before her throat.

She glances at Bell for confirmation. He leans solemnly forward. "You were directed, ma'am, by someone else."

Hare remains silent, looking for any hidden messages passing between these two. He finds himself asking how he can continue to suspect them when he has been operated by the same unseen forces in that very chair and endured the same suspicions from others.

He thinks, *We are all of us in uncharted waters.*

When no one speaks or moves for an interminable moment, Hare asks, "Do you know if she received my message, Miss Hayden?"

The woman—strange how severe she first appeared and how timid, helpless and confused she now seems—replies with her own question: "Message? For whom?"

Hare asks nothing more. The medium wishes to retire and Bell escorts her out of the apartments. He turns back at the door to offer an apologetic, "I hope this hasn't proved an intrusion, Dr. Hare. I sensed immediately you'd want to meet her. We strive to maintain open minds about all forms of spirit communication, do we not, sir? We must consider the nonphysical a legitimate expression, too, and this clever proof you've devised will establish her defense as well as yours. Please do contact me at your earliest convenience as to its outcome."

"Of course. Another time, Dr. Bell. I will have to leave early on the morrow." Hare nodes to Miss Hayden beyond Bell, who rewards him with a weary smile. "Rest, ma'am."

Bell gives him a final, troubled glance, as if sure he's going to miss a critical event here.

As he closes the door, Hare hears behind him Gilhay's door bump closed. Hare smiles to himself. The ever-protective retainer.

Although he will eventually use much material uncovered by Bell in his book, he never meets with him again. They communicate thereafter through the mail.

IV.
Proofs

Upon his return to Philadelphia, Robert Hare sits through an edgy, sweltering hour and a half of waiting until the appointed time. Three-thirty arrives. His appointment does not. He has failed, his communication was not received. He rises from the French settee. The clothing that he has worn for the hasty journey from Cape May sticks to him everywhere like a wet sausage-skin and is discolored by large patches of perspiration. Sweat from his brow stings his eyes. He looks out upon the tree-lined street where no breeze blows. Below him, roses stand, dappled with sunlight through the maple tree across the way. He hears the hooves of horses on the stones of nearby Chestnut Street. The carriages rarely come past the front of the house, situated as it is on a close.

A woman's figure passes by. It looks— But she has turned into his yard, and he leaves the window, nearly runs out of the room as the knocker raps like a musket-shot through the front hall. He opens the door upon Mrs. Gourlay.

The look on his face must perplex her. She says, "But surely you were expecting me."

"I did so, but—well, please come in. I despaired as the time passed."

"Oh, it has? Our mantle clock is not reliable. It runs both fast and slow, and the doctor takes his continental watch with him."

He seats her on the red Empire sofa there in the entrance hall below the stairs. "Tell me," he says.

She does. She had been working with his device when her contact was interrupted by an errant spirit, his sister, with an urgent message. Receiving it, she sent her brother to find her husband, and the two men went to the bank together. They determined that the note was not due for more than a year—which Hare knew already but anticipated no one else would, as it was so far outside the range of what anyone—even someone who had researched his family—would investigate. But there is more. She unfurls a piece of paper on which she has scrawled a poem in stiff handwriting.

> *Brother beloved, it begins, of ardent soul,*
> *Striving to reach a heavenly goal;*
> *Wouldst thou attain the blissful height*
> *Where wisdom purifies the light . . .*

He folds the sheet of foolscap and lowers his moist gaze. He has never seen the poem before, but its authorship is clear; nor can he can read further just now. His joy is inexpressible. "Thank you, Mrs. Gourlay. More than you realize, you've sped away the clouds of my doubt. I must now endeavor to show the world what you and I recognize in our hearts."

"Let me help," the medium says.

"I shall. Believe me, I'll require all your assistance. We've much to undertake now."

*   *   *

He begins work on his book in earnest as accounts come trickling in. Bell reports that entities who've spoken to him through verbal mediums are able to read his thoughts and see what he can see, yet lose their knowledge when answering what he and the medium do not know, a supposition he tests by asking them to duplicate a signature in a folded letter that he hasn't seen. They can't. But the moment he opens the letter and looks upon it, the medium's hand begins to write in imitation of what he beholds. Bell proposes that what he has uncovered is more than mere spirit communication, but a form of clairvoyance. He writes: "What the questioner knows, the spirit knows; what the questioner does not know, the spirits are entirely ignorant of." It's a provocative observation, one for which Hare has no answer.

Inquiries made earlier to acquaintances on the continent have also begun to bear fruit.

He receives a report that the Archbishop of Paris attended a séance and witnessed communication via rappings on a table. The spirit identified itself as Sœur Françoise, deceased the week before in a Paris convent. And when an abbot present demanded in the name of Christ the woman manifest, she did appear to them and answered questions. All the participants were afterward several days indisposed, as if the spirit had drawn upon them for her energy.

From Germany a Dr. Geib communicates to him about table-moving phenomena, giving a name to the spirits responsible: *klopferle,* for "rapping specter."

It's generally believed, says another correspondent, that this phenomenon has arrived, like some plague, off ship from America. One day there's nothing, the next, with an American medium present, tables turn, hats swivel on heads, and chairs spin on one leg. The news agencies, fearing for their reputations, refuse to report on these initial events. Even Hare has to wonder at what sounds on the face of it like a great fraud.

To his amusement, French scientists attempt to explain it with no more logic than Bechworth applied. They claim electricity is the culprit, or imperceptible muscular action, moving the tables. "Humidity of the palms" is responsible, asserts another expert, an explanation that takes its place beside magnetisms and polarities, and even "two interacting nervous atmospheres." However perversely, the press now turn their sights not on the phenomena but on the accepted theorists. In response to the comment about nervous atmospheres, one French journal suggests that, given the dullness of the theoretician, "the nervous system of the table (disgueridon) must be *very* sensitive." The journal later describes an episode where French scientists attempted to move a table by use of those proposed magnetisms while a spiritualist sat aside and watched in bewilderment. When they failed utterly and retreated outside, the table, left alone, began to buck.

From England, a Mr. Robert Owen writes to him of an apron untied from a woman and passed around a group at séance, and which was then ripped away from them by invisible hands. These same hands passed Owen a flower. His handkerchief was snatched from his pocket and formed into a hat. One spirit shook his hand, "and, sir, I could feel the individual fingers." In a passing remark, Owen's report mentions a spirit stating what Owen believes to be true but which later proves to be false—information which seems to have come from his own thoughts, much as Bell has suggested. Both observations he will include in the book. Let readers draw their own conclusions.

Hare has become a magnet for spiritualist data. Every day brings more letters, many impossible to use, some impossible to comprehend. Meanwhile, he routinely visits a coterie of spiritualists to whom he has been introduced by Mrs. Gourlay.

In the presence of local medium Henry Gordon, he watches a table float into the air.

When he takes his seat in the salon of Mrs. Ann Leach Brown, he finds his name written on a scrap of paper lying beside him on the carpet. Mrs. Brown denies all knowledge of it and, when she applies herself to one of Pease's Dials, through her a spirit explains that an old friend, William Blodget, has written it. Blodget is some six years deceased.

While Mrs. Brown communicates, a table against the wainscoted wall over a foot away from her begins to slide back and forth on the floor like one of his trays on casters. Both he and the medium sit in stupefaction.

"I've never seen the like," she confesses to him when the activity has stopped. "It is you, sir, causing this." And though he doesn't express it to her, he does feel uncanny energy pervading the air, like a huge bubble filling the room.

Phenomena spring up on all sides, as if casting him headlong toward some explosive event. Darkness is at his back. Friends have fallen away. In his absence he's either pitied or scorned, but he notices none of it. His whole world has become the spirit one.

In January Joseph Hazard returns from Rhode Island. His reason for visiting: "I have to check up on my old friend now and again, and business at present is sluggish." Hare refrains from admitting that just now he finds Hazard's appearance intrusive, like a distraction concocted by his enemies to slow him down, just as Hazard refrains from confessing that mutual friends whom Hare might currently consider enemies have urged him to come.

Hazard intrudes further when he insists on accompanying Robert Hare to spirit meetings, two or three a week.

In various parlors they sit apart as they did with Margaret Fox. With Hazard present tables don't dance and caper but rattle only mildly in corners or shift under the spiritualist's hands. If Hazard spots trickery or harbors doubts, he says nothing, only watches. His presence acts as a damper to Hare's elation as well as to the proceedings themselves, wherever they go. Yet Hare can't bring himself to ask his old friend to leave. Silliman's an abstraction, Hazard concrete; and if he can convert Hazard, the exemplar of a rational mind, that may silence the naysayers once and for all.

The first week of February of 1855, Hare goes to a sitting alone, returning late in the evening. Gilhay lets him in.

Hazard awaits in the dining room, and pours a mug of hot buttery cider to warm him. Two other mugs on the table indicate that Gilhay and Hazard have been sitting together awhile.

Still wrapped his heavy coat, Hare sits heavily and sips the steaming cider. A few minutes pass in uncomfortable silence. Then he says, "There is to be a convocation of spirits at the home of Mrs. Gourlay. This is what I've been flung toward, Joseph, and could not see in advance—all the strange events that have led me this far—this is where they were leading."

"To a gathering of the tribes," Hazard comments, then apologizes. "I don't mean to make it sound trivial. But how else does one describe it?"

Hare waves at the air. "Describe it however you choose. But this event *you* must attend. Many from her group will be there, adding the strength of their energies to Mrs. Gourlay's, calling upon the spirit world to come and speak and inform. They're about to reveal everything of the afterlife to us. Everything, Joseph! Say you'll accompany me. I need you to transcribe for me. My hands shake too much in the presence of the spirits. And there must be more than one witness to so incomparable an event. It might never happen again."

"Of course, of course I will," Hazard assures him. He would have it no other way.

After finishing his cider, Hare retires to his study and writes furiously for two hours as he does each day, compiling his notes, his arguments, his proofs, his rebuttals into what he has now titled *Experimental Investigation of the Spirit Manifestations.* The gathering of the tribes, as Joseph put it, will be the climax.

V.

The Convocation of Spirits

At 9:00 A.M. on February 18, Hare and Hazard sit in Mrs. Gourlay's parlor, surrounded by mediums and believers. Word has gotten out. There is Miss Fox, who breaks into a demure smile each time Hazard glances her way; Mrs. Brown, solemn and nervous; Henry Gordon, who looks to have steadied himself with drink for the event; Julia Hayden, sent by Dr. Bell. There are even people such as the Howitts.

As Mrs. Gourlay lowers her head and rolls the tray upon the table, the dial spins and spins, and Hazard writes down each name as it is spelled out. More spirits than corporeal forms surround the two men at the center. The spirits sign in: George Washington, John Quincy Adams, William H. Harrison, W. E. Channing, H. K. White, Isaac Newton, Andrew Jackson, Henry Clay, Benjamin Franklin, Lord Byron, Martha Washington—the list goes on and on, like the signatories of the Declaration of Independence coming forward one by one to take up the quill. The cataloguing seems to last for hours. Hazard fills two entire pages with names, having written too large at first. He couldn't have known.

When the wheel does finally come to rest, the entire room seems to sigh as one. Hazard sits back from his writing board and flexes his hand awhile before taking up the steel-point pen again.

After first offering a welcome to the invisible guests, Hare begins the questioning. "How do we arrive where you are?" he asks.

The wheel spins, and with it the story.

After death, the soul awakens from a profound sleep into a state of consciousness very like dreaming. Bright and shadowy forms appear to it, as does the body it has left. These forms soon solidify into spirits, usually those of departed friends. They greet the nascent spirit with affection and conduct it to a celestial abode in accordance with its moral state at the time of death.

He ponders briefly, then asks, "How is the spirit world composed?"

The answer comes: Between Earth and moon lie seven concentric rings, the regions of the spirit world. These have terrestrial scenery—mountains, streams, plains, rivers, birds, beasts—but all of greater beauty, and at each successive, ascending level, more lovely. The last is so glorious, it cannot be described.

Then, as if someone else of a slightly different opinion has wrested control, the answer is revised. Earth is the first level. The remaining six spheres compose the spirit plane. They commence about sixty miles up, rising out into space.

"The sun, then, illuminates your world as it does ours."

No, comes the answer. A black sun shines upon the spirit world, although its nature cannot be satisfactorily explained to mortals. Its rays consist of an all-pervading ethereal fluid. *We live in a realm of perpetual day, full of aromatic flowers, herbs, fountains, and rushing water underfoot. And singing floats through the air.*

"Then how do you see yourselves? What are you like, how do you appear differently that you make a distinction from the body cast off?" he asks. Hazard nods encouragingly as he writes. He was wondering the same thing.

The reply: *We are luminiferous. Like lightning bugs we glow.* Each spirit has a circumambient halo passing from dimness to effulgence as the spirit moves to higher planes.

"These spheres. How do you move to higher ones?" he asks,

trying to grasp this. Is it fair? Does it seem reasonable? It sounds upon the face of it like a caste system, which is not how he wants heaven to be. Underneath his questions, he wonders, too, which of the great and famous men is speaking to him.

Each ascends as he or she improves in purity. Purity, which can take two forms: love, and love/wisdom.

George Washington resides already in the seventh sphere, as Hare anticipated. Infants—which are considered blessed in their untimely death—ascend directly to that sphere, where they're instructed and grow up. They then return to earth to watch events unfold. Hare recalls the Howitt child whose spirit told its parents to think of it as a "gentle moonbeam," and glances over his shoulder at them. The husband nods to him, a painful joy inscribing his features.

"Angels," remarks Hazard as he writes this down.

Hare turns around. "Just so, Joseph, angels."

Hazard looks at Mrs. Gourlay with her head bowed. "But I'm troubled," he says before Hare can think of another question. "What of those who aren't in the seventh level?"

Degradation, the wheel spells out, *is an inevitable consequence of vice.* Not punishment—there's no punishment necessary, for God is all-love. The afterlife follows the apostles' injunction: Hold fast that which is good. They exist in what can only be called a republican order.

Too, some crimes occur in the lower spheres, and punishments are meted out in accord with these.

Hazard's brow knits as he writes this seeming contradiction down.

Hare, too, tries to understand. "How can one expect to rise in such a place?"

Love is the simplest way. Those who know unfettered love rise immediately. For the rest there are teachers on each level who impart wisdom to those who seek it—wisdom that, conjoined with love, advances them.

"Can we not see anything of your world?" Hare asks. "We're here to establish proof that we can show to anyone, so that they'll understand without having to come as far as I've done to arrive at enlightenment."

The wheel falls silent for so long that Hare fears contact has been broken. When it moves again, he leans forward as if to hear more clearly that which is said in silence.

The wheel spells out J–U–P–I–T–E–R.

The spectators exchange confounded glances. Hare, who has seen the night sky through a reflecting telescope, suspects he's hearing now from Isaac Newton. He says, "Please explain further, sir."

The wheel tells him: *The bands that can be seen around Jupiter are the spirit spheres of that world. Look upon Jupiter for evidence of our realm.*

Hare nods, slowly at first but with increasing effusiveness. Hazard, who also has astronomical knowledge and has many times looked upon the Jovian sphere, raises his head sharply from the page and asks, "How then do you account for the changes in the appearance of those bands? For they do change. I know."

The wheel hangs, then spells out simply: *optical delusions.*

Hazard sits grim-faced for a moment before he dips the pen and writes down these two words. He is unaware of shaking his head as he does so.

Late that same night, in the dining room of Hare's home, the two men sit divided by the dark table. Steam from a bowl of hot cider and their individual mugs floats between them. They're bundled up, though they returned nearly an hour earlier. The fire in the hearth softens the edge of the cold, but not its heart.

Hazard has done little more than murmur since the convocation ended. He took copious notes—Hare rejoices at the precision of the transcription. But a chasm has opened between them that was not apparent even as the event began—broader than the chasm between the living and the dead.

Hare takes the transcript between his hands and straightens it, tapping the sheaf against the table. "It's marvelous, Joseph, it truly is. I need add nothing to your words."

"Not mine," mutters Hazard, not looking at him.

Hare hesitates, almost asks what he means, but thinks better of it. Hazard won't meet his gaze however hard he stares. "Mmm," he adds finally, a noncommittal assent, but he must say something more than that. They ought to be celebrating. "Still marvelous, whoever's words—"

"Good Christ, Robert! Whose do you think they were? Monsieur Valdemar's?"

Hare doesn't know the name, but it doesn't matter. The doubt he's cast off threatens to ignite and consume everything.

Hazard continues to stare at the surface of the table, where his hands lie flat. "You genuinely believe you sat in the presence of Washington and Franklin and Newton," he says, and glances up finally, his eyes squinched with the pain of awareness. "You know what you've done? You've become the Howitts. You're as possessed as any medium ever claimed."

"Joseph, stop this."

"Because you'll lose Anna if you admit it? Robert, you lost her decades ago."

Hare's jaw sets and his brown eyes catch fire. "And I found her again."

"Where, in the bands of Jupiter?"

"And I am to gather you know for a fact what those bands are?"

"No, of course I don't know. No one knows. That's besides the point."

"I thought, Joseph, you weren't like the others, that you were capable of contemplating things considered unnatural, that you could see through their fog of superstition and religious eyewash. I hoped . . ." He breaks off.

Hazard leans closer. "Old friend, you say yourself that I copied the details of the dialogue perfectly. That being the case, look at the descriptions both of the spirit realm here and there. Seven concentric rings or spheres rising into space with the Earth at their core—the physical realm at the bottom. That's how the spirit world was described. Not as latitudinal bands, do you understand? The two explanations are contradictory. They look nothing alike at all." Hare seems puzzled, doubtful. "Oh, think, Robert. Look at it, read it."

"No." He slaps down the pages. "I've thought everything through, eliminated all possibility of treachery. The spirits are confused, nothing more. Or we are. I've spoken to Anna, I've used the spiritoscope, I know. Who's to say that the spirit world here wouldn't look the same to someone on Jupiter as theirs does to us? We can't be sure."

Hazard stops arguing. Anna occupies the heart of him; he can't win against her. Robert Hare created the perfect device to defeat spiritualist trickery, and so of course what comes pouring out of it must be true. Confused, misunderstood, perhaps, by the very audience of experts gathered round, but not an outright lie. Anna could never lie.

He might have thought as much himself had they not hauled in the planet and violated their own definitions. Optical delusions, indeed. The bands of Jupiter do change form. It's well-enough documented, and a scientist would know that. Hazard can no longer pretend to believe, as he can do nothing for his old friend. He climbs to his feet and says, "Good night."

Hare sits awhile longer, wounded, confused, and angry. Then he gets up and retires to his study to write up the convocation while it's still fresh in his mind. The work is what matters.

When Hazard departs the following morning, he lies asleep at his desk upon the document.

Five months later, Hare has assembled all his notes into a coherent volume, and threaded throughout it, his opinions on the unreliability of Scripture.

He points out for instance that we have only Moses' testimony of his communication with God—a report that has God slaying three thousand who were led astray but sparing Moses' brother, who *made* the golden calf. Hare calls the Old Testament a "pernicious idol" that patronizes men of a chosen seed, though they are guilty of robbery, fraud, and murder, and quotes St. Jerome's preface to the Gospels wherein the saint complained that no one copy resembled another, the translations were so poor.

His final act is to attach a preface including a letter from his spirit father that he receives only days before he turns in the manuscript. The spirit says: "Ask yourself how much happiness you have found in the contemplation of the fact which has been demonstrated, not only to your wishes but to your senses, that the thinking mind *never dies* . . . that it lives on, lives ever, and must throughout the ceaseless ages of eternity continue to unfold its power."

With the book at the publishers, he offers to exhibit his

spiritoscope to a convention of his own clergymen and is rebuffed. In November, invited again to New York, he gives a lecture on the evidence he has compiled. It's well attended, if only by those already converted.

After the book comes out, there follows no upheaval, no slanderous assault, no clear enemy at which to take aim. He's not vilified, he's disavowed.

Not one to sit idle even then, he turns his attentions to other subjects. Spirits continue to warn him to prepare himself, and he continues secretly to await the attack, but it never comes.

In 1857, not long before his death, he exhibits at the Franklin Institute an apparatus for determining whether phenomena attending the attrition of pieces of quartz, when rubbed briskly together, have anything to do with the new substance described by Schönbein as "ozone." His reception is cool. Some noise is made about the apparatus, but most of the dialogue is traded as if he were not in the room among them, or they cannot see him. Forlorn, he goes home.

Maple leaves blow in through the door before he can close it. He drops his cloak upon the Empire sofa in the entrance hall, and drifts to his study through the silent house. He stokes red embers in the hearth and adds new wood to the fire, then takes his seat before one of Pease's Dials he has set upon his desk.

He opens his glass inkwell and places beside it a steel-nibbed pen, inadvertently bumping a large anomalous chestnut he uses as a paperweight—actually two grown together into a single mass—hard enough that it tumbles off the side of the desk and rolls beneath his feet, where he can't reach it.

With a resigned sigh he lets it go and turns to the device. He adjusts the wheel so that he can see clearly anything spelled out there.

He presses his fingertips to the sprung plate that operates the machine and, thus poised, awaits his Anna.

VI.

Epilogue: The Seybert Commission

In 1883, Henry Seybert, a descendent of the same Seybert who once urged a young Robert Hare to consider the afterlife, endows a Chair of Philosophy upon the University of Pennsylvania, conditional on the university investigating the truth of modern spiritualism. A commission is assembled, including William Pepper, Provost of the University, and Joseph Leidy, the anatomist. Horace Howard Furness chairs the committee and writes up its findings. His wife died relatively young and he has good reason to want the continuance of the soul proved true.

Seybert himself dies before the commission can even begin its investigation, but the money is set aside and the work goes forward. The commission examines the subject for three years, inviting the most prominent mediums to conduct séances before it. Those who accept include one Mrs. Margaret Fox Kane, who is truly celebrated within her ranks. Furness finds her small and genteel, and so unassertive that she immediately wins him over. Yet, as the evening progresses, he slides into doubt.

She communicates with spirits through raps on the table. The spirits, while appearing to have intimate acquaintance with family affairs of some of those present, send Furness's brother a message from his spirit father. Except that his father is still alive. Later, the rapping is determined to be the product of Mrs. Kane's ankle striking the table while she seems to sit away from it, her hands in plain sight. She is, it would appear, usefully double-jointed.

The devices of Robert Hare are neither used nor mentioned, nor is his work cited. His work, in this arena, is forgotten.

The commission's report, published in 1887, causes a great stir in that it finds not a single fact upon which to base any belief in spiritualism. In summing up, Furness reports that no truth could be established because the whole business is so clouded with trickery that no phenomenon can be trusted. Filled with regret, for now he can know nothing of his wife's continuance, he confesses how desperately he wished to be converted by "these shabby charlatans."

Afterword to "That Blissful Height"

When I was twelve or thirteen years old, I read compulsively books about the supernatural—not fictions (although I was possibly rabid about Shirley Jackson)—but books purporting to describe true, if bizarre, events: *Stranger Than Fiction* by Frank Edwards comes to mind, and ghost books by Hans Holzer. The fantastic has always appealed to me, to a degree that probably borders on schizophrenia. But over time—and due in no small part to icons and institutions such as presidents and congresses and religious schemata that have proven to be as untrustworthy as any crackpot notion of a Von Daniken or a Velikovsky—I've lost the youthful ingenuousness that readily accepted the most improbable things.

And so, as this story evolved, I found myself ensconced in the role of Joseph Hazard. He was a real person, but his skepticism herein is my own. Because of this, I think, I initially kept him entirely in the background, with the result, as Bob Frazier put it, that "Hare and Hazard's friendship and effect on each other is not concluded." I had to free Hazard from artificial restraints. The place to do this was easy enough to locate: In researching the writings of Robert Hare, I gave up the ghost, as it were, the moment the spirits offered Jupiter as the physical proof of their unseen reality. And the perception of this as the moment of truth in the story was echoed nearly unanimously in the workshop critiques.

Bruce Sterling pointed out that what is ultimately revealed at the convocation is that the spirits are thoroughly useless; they can't tell you a damn thing. Bob Frazier, again, likened Hare's downfall to that of Percival Lowell with his unfortunate proclamations of life and canals on Mars. Most intensely of all the group, perhaps, Maureen McHugh declared that as she began the story she hoped the supernatural element would be real, saying, "I wanted it to be true." No more so, Maureen, than I.

Gregory Frost

Horses Blow Up Dog City

RICHARD BUTNER

HANES WAS REPAINTING the front window of the store, filling the thick black outlines of the letters in sparkling candy-apple red, when Carlos came back from lunch with the news. It had been a quiet day: no sales all morning, just dirty looks and double-takes from passersby. The new logo looked good, but red and black stains spotted the sidewalk beneath his feet. Metalflake paint was hard to get, but Hanes got it from the same sources as all the other junk that populated his shop, Changes: Antique Technology and Silver Salts. Retro chic, and therefore the painted front window. It was there not just to attract the collectors he lived off of. Mainly he just liked the way it made the store look. Stable.

Carlos was running and his new hair flapped against his skull with every clunky step. So the news, which Carlos brought back every day from the decidedly unstable front window of the Flower Ball burger stand, must've been pretty important.

"Grover's dead. They found his body in the desert. He just walked out into it and died."

Carlos was breathing hard and after those three sentences the urgency drained out of him. He slumped his shoulders, looked away, across the street in the direction of the crystal blue waters of the Hudson. Then he grabbed Hanes tight around the biceps for a second before walking into the store.

California Joe was just making his way down to the end of Washington Street, waving his laminated permits and chanting his usual midday rant. It was something Hanes heard every day. "Fire it up! Hey, killer, spare some change? Fire it up . . ." It was directed at no one in particular.

Hanes carefully closed up the paint tin, pushed his way into the store, and announced, "We're closed," to the three Malaysians who were scrutinizing the Gunfight game machine in the corner. They didn't complain. They'd been in town for a week, staying with family, wheedling Hanes daily for a deal on the thing.

Carlos had wisely retreated upstairs, leaving the downstairs photography vault empty for Hanes, who entered and sealed that door behind him and thought about how dumb he was for crying about a death that, in sudden retrospect, he should have seen coming a long time ago.

The photo vault, a grey room usually filled with the non-smell of polypropylene and stainless steel, now smelled like paint, even through the tears. His sinuses, relined over a year before, were still sensitive. It wasn't enough contamination to worry about; the purifier could handle it. He sat for a moment on the ledge next to the tinted Acrylite window, waiting for the tears to subside, checking his hands for wet paint flecks. Then he opened his personal drawer in the big Neumade cabinet, pulled out the box labeled *2004–2005*. He picked up the stack of positives he'd taken with the old Mamiyaflex, tossed them onto the light table. The colors still bugged him, skewed towards cyan because he had to process them himself. Everyone looked slightly ghoulish.

He took the photos up and one by one they showed just how small his world had been in the past two years: Grover surrounded by his puppet menagerie, the first publicity photo, one Hanes had done for free. Grover in the store, pretending to dance with the Omnibot 2000. A blurry shot Carlos took, of Hanes with his arm around Lexene, which should've been filed in an earlier box. Grover and Lexene returning from the first tour, goofing with movie-star sunglasses and scarves.

The boxes, the vault, the whole store, were about preserving things. The photo-positives and their surreal colors would be around for another hundred years, easy, and they were the originals, silver and dyes, not some high-res scans.

It surprised Hanes that Grover's image hadn't vanished from all the slivers of celluloid in the store.

She wouldn't have heard the news. Hanes spent a lot of time in the past because that was his job; Lexene was just plain disconnected. Grover's management wouldn't try to contact her, Hanes knew that too. They'd been on the outs since the last tour fell apart. They'd lost her Synaptic Six, her lighting and video rig, in transit from Mexico City. To them it was a worthless piece of junk, dead-end neural technology. They had offered to buy her a current model, but she turned them down. The Synaptic was what made Lexene's lights unique—too old to be of much use to anyone else, too young to be an antique.

Hanes stacked the plastic-clad slides together, locked them in his drawer, and then he locked Carlos in the store.

He'd have to walk to her place—Lexene didn't wear a phone, she wouldn't pay for most tangle channels, just had a little one-way box of Grover's, one possession out of the small pile he'd left at her place when he moved to L.A. Mainly she sat in her tiny walk-up, drafting designs which would never get produced, reading books. Even though she tried hard to be chronically unemployable—"difficult"—she still had to say no more often than anyone else Hanes knew. No to the managers, directors, and A&R goons who blundered out through the tunnel to track her down on her home turf. Yes to a select few, yes to people or shows or bands or ideas she loved, and that was her living. She could've had a nice life in an apartment in a restricted part of Manhattan, wall-to-wall design work, never have to touch a lighting panel or a video camera again. Instead she lived in Jersey and burned up a lot of time hanging out with Carlos and Hanes, going out on the road a few months out of the year to operate the Synaptic by hand.

Her place was a short walk. Hanes got there, did the mudras to get in the front door, and then, later, her door. A book about *fin de siècle* fads and fashion trends that he'd downloaded for her the week before was lying flat open on the enormous kidney-bean drafting table, almost finished. Hanes had skimmed it. The book was a shuck, written by one of those shyster profs at University Online, but it was full of raw data and good photos, and was therefore interesting. The text, though—it had taken the au-thor six years to digest and analyze what Hanes and Lexene had lived through and worn like skin.

Lexene was on her bed, staring coolly at the tangle box be-tween her boots, twisting her straight red hair in knots with her left hand.

Neither one talked. The box wasn't on a news channel. It was a live feed from a public-access show in San Diego. The emcee, a droll fourteen-year-old with crenellated ears, notches big enough to see even on the tiny screen, was talking about how learning the true names of Jesus had saved him from a life of crime. Behind him, another shape, less definite. A face just over the left shoulder of the Christian boy. Someone was mimicking his earnest sermon on the wonders of religion and linguistics. That someone was Grover.

Hanes hadn't planned any big speech for Lexene in the first place. He'd planned to tell her, "He's dead," and so he did.

"Really?" Lexene said, clicking her boots together over the screen. "He's right there. He's been making fun of this kid for the past fifteen minutes."

Back out in the street, Hanes and Lexene remained silent as foot-age of the recovery of Grover's body flashed across the front windows of bakeries, bars, markets. His adopted hometown was awash in the event, looping it over and over from every possible angle, cutting in shots of distraught fans all over the world. One Russian boy was dressed as the Sad Little Jester, the puppet that came out and explained the moral at the end of "Horses Blow Up Dog City."

"God, I met that guy when we played St. Petersburg," Lex-ene said. "He came to the show in that same getup. Grover made him come up onstage."

Then Grover plodded in front of the crowd of Russian kids gathered to mourn his death. They didn't seem to notice.

"This sucks," Lexene announced. "This is really going to suck if they start tagging Grover all over the place."

The prank wasn't anywhere near the first of its kind. The En-quirer Channel said it was space aliens, but their transmissions never seemed to get tagged.

Common knowledge was that this anonymous group of Belgian grad students was behind it, sampling images from the tangle into this big diamond block of storage, cobbling together moving images that had never occurred in reality, spitting them back out to invade channels at random. The year before, they'd sent out snippets of world leaders engaged in various marginally legal sex acts, and the TSA had to go public on their inability to shut all of the transmissions down. No one could detect the source of the rogue packets; they just showed up and superimposed themselves, unannounced and unwelcome. Mainly it was just showing off: The images attacked other packets that were encrypted with a supposedly uncrackable algorithm. There was nothing political about it. No demands, no manifestos, no public claims of responsibility.

"Stupid kids," Hanes said, assuming his role as the gruff middle-aged man. "They'll get tired of it soon, especially with Grover saturating the legitimate channels."

As it turned out, the Belgians were bigger fans of Grover than Hanes had predicted.

Hanes had met Grover a couple of months after returning from a long shopping trip to Australia. He was one of Lexene's discoveries. She always needed folks to eat out with, because she never cooked, and with Hanes out of town that meant she had to find another dining partner. Grover simply appeared to fill the void. After Hanes got back, the dining party numbered three.

Grover met them at the door of the storage space he was living in, and Hanes thought he looked all of seventeen or eighteen. A frail, curly-haired kid, hunched over. Lexene told Hanes later that he was twenty-six.

Inside, there wasn't a square inch of bare cement. Everything had been decorated—the walls, the floor, the ceiling, the bed, even the tangle box and the chemical toilet—covered over in sky blue and white. It was like being suspended in a bubble in the air. Clouds all around. And on top of this substrate sat the marionettes. They came in all sizes, some with two legs, some with four. The biggest was an eagle with a human head, lifelessly crumpled on top of the worktable. They were all people or anthropomorphized animals: rabbits, a mouse dressed up like a chef, two horses, some beasts which Hanes couldn't identify. All done in those same shades of bone gray and blue. Some actually were just skeletons, all were fragile looking.

"Hi," Grover had said, in that nervous, quiet voice. "Do you like the puppets?"

Lexene and Hanes walked aimlessly for a while, and finally she said, "Can I make some calls at the store?" Hanes nodded, and they turned back down Washington. That was when the surface tension in Lexene finally burst.

"It was so obvious. It was such a dumb cliché, no one ever figured it would come true. Remind me never to work with disturbed geniuses who can't handle fame, okay? How fucking cornball . . ." Lexene was getting as emotional as she ever got in front of other humans, which meant she was walking even faster than normal, fidgeting obsessively with her hair.

In the window of the bagel place, Grover was pogoing like a bunny through the middle of a show on the Catastrophe Channel—a fleet of plankton harvesters churning through water the color of rust. Opposing-view text scrolled up the bottom half of the display, carefully timed to deflate all the statements the main announcer was making. From the outside it was just nonsense, mirror writing. Grover's image hopped all around the window. Boing, boing, boing. To Hanes, the wide, toothy smile on his face, a smile that had never existed outside of the tangle, was utterly unconvincing.

The day after their first dinner together, all three went on a local shopping trip. They drove down to Englishtown, to an open-air market that Hanes knew about. "Most collectible stuff for the best prices, the shortest distance from New York." Grover seemed fascinated by the rolling countryside so close to the urban sprawl of New Jersey/New York. He said it reminded him of growing up in Georgia, but he didn't say anything else about Georgia. Still, he opened up fast, faster than Hanes was accustomed to. He ended up crouching between the front bucket seats, so his squeaky voice could be heard over the roar of the van.

He seemed to have an encyclopedic knowledge of the most trivial subjects: breakfast cereals and which had the optimal flavor, kung fu fighting styles (from the old flicks where you couldn't pick whether the good guys won or not), and cartoons—why the endless Looney Tunes remakes of the Singing Frog episode weren't half as good as the original. He'd watched a *lot* of tangle, but it didn't affect his mind the way the Surgeon General said it would. All the useless facts, the endless permutations of the same old sitcom plot elements, Grover cobbled all that detritus together and it became fascinating to hear him talk about it.

That day in Englishtown they found the Omnibot 2000, the robot that you programmed with old magnetic tapes.

"Cassettes," the Greek said.

"Little boxes," Grover said.

The Greek had a stack of the tapes in the back of his station wagon, most of which, surprisingly, hadn't melted or lost their fragile oxide coating. That was the hardest part, getting software for the old machines. It was a goldmine if you found tapes and disks that still worked. The robot was in perfect condition, too, and the Greek only wanted sixty for it. Hanes talked him down to forty just for the hell of it, and convinced him to throw in an old Atari too.

"Don't they understand what this stuff is worth?" Grover asked, walking back to the van with Hanes, who cradled the Omnibot like a newborn child.

"Collectors never drive to Englishtown," Hanes said. "They'd rather give me the money."

"My dad had an Atari like this one. I wasn't supposed to touch it." His face got dull. " 'Sixty-four bits!' That's what he'd yell at me when he caught me playing with it. 'Get your hands off of them sixty-four bits!' He could play it for hours, until his wrists got sore."

That was the only time Grover mentioned the existence of his father.

Hanes tried to stay busy the next few days, working through a backlog of mail-order business, checking and re-checking inventory. Carlos worked the register and stayed out of his way. Lexene was staying in a Manhattan hotel, running up an enormous room-service bill, so she could avoid the press and have a phone. The press was choking hard on the question, "Why does a child-

like millionaire, famous puppeteer, walk out into the desert and
die of exposure?" and filling up airtime with footage from the last
show at Madison Square Garden, the one that started with "Mr.
Sloth's Underwater Birthday Party." There was talk of starting a
Grover channel but his management sat on the rights to the rest
of the footage they owned.

Lexene walked into the store a week later, a week in which the
press had related that Grover's mother died of cancer five years
before, his father was in a private penal institution in Colorado,
and his management was "deeply saddened by the recent
events."

"I'm hungry," Lexene announced.

The first tour was originally just Grover and Lexene, road cases
for the puppets and her lighting board, a van. They stopped in at
the store before getting on the train to the rental place in Pater-
son. Because it had a phone, the store had become their base of
operations; they had to stop in to get the final tour schedule.
After a barrage down the East Coast, there were a lot of days off,
marked on the schedule with *Drive, drive, drive.* As it happened,
after Atlanta they ended up playing a show every single night.

At that point Grover had only played in small theaters in
Manhattan, and the actuality of leaving for tour made him chatter
even more nervously than usual. "I'm going to miss my tangle
box. If we make money, can we buy a battery-powered one for
the van?"

"We *will* make money," Lexene said, "and it will go straight
into the accounts your managers set up."

Carlos came downstairs with a stack of disks. "All done," he
said, disgusted, and he handed them to Grover, who tossed them
into the laundry bag he was using for a suitcase. "I don't know
what you get out of that noise. . . ."

Grover had coaxed Carlos into recording Hanes's entire collection of lute music from 1998, when the fad had been in full
swing, spurred on by the constant media presence of Gerhardt
Hess, the famous seven-foot-tall lutist. He toured the world
with a single graphite lute and a road case full of scans of mezzo-
soprano clef music. Hanes had a stack of hardcopy press on the
guy, too, all carefully encapsulated, waiting for the right collec-

tor. The amazing thing was how similar all the articles sounded. They all had headlines like, "UndiLUTEd!" or "Hess Takes Lute To New Heights," but the body text was mostly the same. A year and a half later, after an appearance on "Lifestyles of the Media Presences," the listening public suddenly became embarrassed at its own taste, and Hess's product vanished.

Grover, of course, remembered Hess. "He looked like a big insect, grappling with that lute."

Lexene would later report that every day in the van, Grover carefully played all ten discs, in chronological order. Her earplugs, which she normally carried when she ran her designs for bands, were unfortunately left sitting in their plastic case on her drafting table.

Lexene and Hanes went to the Indian place on Willow Street. It had been the last restaurant without tangle in the front window, until the family that owned the place gave in and installed a secondhand Sony. They still ate there for tradition's sake.

The news was on. General Foods execs testifying before Congress, denying that they purposely made their designer fats addictive. The Supreme Court declaring automated facial recognition unconstitutional. The usual wars.

Then, a "new development" in the ongoing babble about Grover, which turned out to be an interview with his high-school art teacher. "I always thought Grover was one of my most talented students."

Then Grover's head filled half of the screen, covering the old woman in her affected velvet suit. "We have this to report: Puppeteer Grover McKay is still dead."

Another head appeared. "I'm not dead yet," it chirped.

"Awww," said Lexene. "Can we get our stuff to go?"

"There's no escaping it," Hanes said. "You might as well get used to this. Anyway, it looks like it was triggered by the news. Maybe the Belgians are trying to send the press a message."

In the window, the two heads argued about whether or not they were dead. The tall Punjabi waiter came out and cycled through a few channels, but the heads were tagged onto every one.

"Maybe not," Lexene said.

* * *

By the time that first tour hit San Francisco, Grover's managers had run through three A&R people. They'd also rebooked the dates, each venue getting bigger and bigger until Grover sold out the Warfield three nights in a row, two shows a night. In New Orleans, the van became a tour bus, which just as quickly turned into a private jet. Grover christened the jet the *Gravy Dog*.

Every night, Lexene would call and relate the latest details on Grover's rapid ascent. Every night was "amazing." The first real press on the tangle was a bit from the Baltimore show. It snowballed from there, to a familiar scene that Lexene would relate:

All the kids in their seats, chattering away in a dull roar around Lexene at her light board. All the puppets hanging from their racks on the stage. Then Grover would shamble out onstage in his black coveralls, pick up the first two characters, and Lexene would announce his presence with a big flash of white light and a close shot of Grover's wide-eyed face on the monitors. Silence from the crowd, probably amazement at the big image of the tiny little man they'd come to see.

"Hi. How are you?" Grover would say into his headset mike, then he'd launch into the story of "Mr. Magic Teeth." For the rest of the show, Lexene's hands moved automatically across the board, helping it improvise on her basic program, as the puppets danced in front of Grover.

Before the tour, when Grover was explaining the show to the management team that Lexene dug up, they couldn't understand why he didn't want to be hidden—that much they could remember about how puppet shows were supposed to be done. He couldn't explain why. The management didn't want to know anything about breakfast cereals, or kung fu movies, or cartoons. Lexene had to convince them that it was really an elaborate deconstructionist riff, having Grover stand there with his puppets. They bought that.

At first, with no roadies to help out, he had to pause every time he wanted to switch puppets from the two he could manage. By San Francisco, there was a two-person crew just to hand him the right puppets. The People Channel gave him an honorable mention as their Best New Media Presence of the Year, since even they admitted that it was a necessity to see him live.

*   *   *

Lexene dumped all three sauces on her samosas, making the waiter cringe. She took a big bite and talked around it as she chewed.

"Well, I'm embarrassed to admit it, but this past week, holed up in the Great Northern, I spent a lot of time watching tangle. Not that crap where they tag Grover; that's creepy. But I clicked around, trying to get all the news I could. Trying to find out how much the management lied to us about what was going on. . . ."

"It's their job to lie. That's why people go into that line of work—they're uniquely suited to constant dissimulation as a way of life."

"Well, yeah."

The waiter reappeared to refill the water glasses. "I am quite sorry about the malfunctioning window," he said. He'd given up on the channel selection and simply shut the sound off.

" 's okay," Hanes replied. Because it was there, they both took sips of water.

"So why did he do it?" Hanes asked the tablecloth.

"You saw that last tour. He was over the edge, and there was no one around him to say no.

"The first few dates, everybody was up. Then Grover just started going sideways. First he wanted to cancel the tour, but he couldn't explain why. They smoothed that one over by tweaking the one last responsible nerve he had in his body: They reminded him how many people's livelihoods depended on him. By that time we had a roadie for every single puppet, five caterers, a masseuse, and that glorified babysitter who thought he was a road manager. Hell, I had my own crew; I didn't have to lift a finger until the show started. But it was stupid for them to remind Grover of just how responsible he was supposed to be.

"He got enthusiastic about the tour, but then he kept wanting to change things. He had all these ideas, and none of them sounding like the Grover I knew. Then, in Mexico City, when he came out and sat on the front of the stage and just started talking to the people in the front row . . . god. They didn't tell us until we were already on the jet after the show that we were headed back to New York, not on to Guatemala. And Grover was headed back to a team of therapists and his new house in L.A.

"Why did he do it? I don't know. Maybe he was just trying to walk away from everything. . . ."

"Yeah."

"It just doesn't seem real that I knew who that was," she said, pointing at the heads in the window, "let alone actually rode around in a van with him."

When the waiter brought the main course, Grover's images vanished from the front window, uncovering the news.

"Try not to think about why, Hanes. Leave that up to the Enquirer Channel; they'll figure it out and the world will still be the same crappy place." She elbowed him in the ribs, trying to take his attention away from the newly uncluttered window.

"Get out of town, take a trip. I'm going back out on this hip-hop reunion tour; that's what I set up while I was staying in Manhattan. Small places, mostly, but the gig's enough to keep my bank account from absolute zero."

"Where to?"

"Pac Rim, Japan, Oz. Starts there. You should think about doing the same. You got time. You've got money."

The last tour. Hanes rode down to D.C.; he'd been busy for all the New York shows. The opening act was Gerhardt Hess. Grover's managers didn't want to book the lutist, but at that point they didn't have much choice. If Grover had asked to tour the country on a fleet of chrome tricycles, they would have said yes.

He had dinner with Lexene, then once they got back to the arena, she stalked off to check the work her crew had done. Hanes had his VIP laminate scanned by five different off-duty cops before he made it into the bowels of the arena, where Grover was sitting in a mint-green cinderblock dressing room. Upstairs, Hess was getting only derision from the audience, thousands who had shown up to see Grover and his puppets. The amplified lute music snaked down the stairwells, as did the dull roar of uninterested conversation, punctuated by an occasional scream, the age-old "Get off the stage!"

Grover was drawing on the chalkboard. His road manager, whose name was either Carlin or Carlton, sat in a rocking chair next to the untouched catering table. The table had the usual cheese tray, meat tray, drinks on ice. It also had a row of boxes of Grover's favorite breakfast cereals, unopened. Grover put the chalk down, dusted his hands off on his coveralls, and then shook hands with Hanes.

"Hi. How are you?" he said blankly. Then, before Hanes could respond, he blurted, "Just a second." He backed away around the divider to the bathroom.

"Howdy," the road manager said, oblivious to Grover's hasty retreat. Hanes nodded and sat down on top of a cooler and waited. The road manager went back to flicking his fingers around on the computer screen in his lap.

Minutes passed, with no noise coming from behind the divider. Hanes helped himself to a wet bottle of Evian from the gray plastic trough filled with slush; it was something to occupy his hands and his mouth, so he didn't have to feel bad about not talking to the road manager.

Grover reappeared and shook Hanes's hand again. Then he gestured at the chalkboard.

"I want to do a new show, one with robots," he said. "Can I get the Omnibot 2000? Do you know where I can get a bunch of them?"

"It's pretty rare to find working ones—"

"Okay, well, just ship the one you've got down to the next show. I want to get right on this. Carlton can give you the address."

Carlton started pushing things around on his little computer's desktop.

"Just a second," Grover said, holding up his hand. They were the last words he would ever say to Hanes. He scuttled off to the bathroom again.

Hanes set the water down and left without speaking to Carlton. He sat through the show, hugged Lexene good-bye, and got on a northbound train.

After Lexene left with the hip-hop band, Hanes made arrangements for another trip to Australia via Edmonton, where he had a line on a roomful of Logical Davids, early-eighties desktop computers that you could supposedly program in twenty-one different natural languages, if all you wanted to do was add and subtract numbers. He would meet up with Lexene in Sydney, where she had a day off.

The weekend before he left, he drove down to the Englishtown market. It was quiet. He glided through, nothing piquing his interest until he found the Greek at the far end of the cluttered field. The Greek had a video poster tacked up on a warped sheet of plywood leaning against the station wagon. The poster flickered out a little ten-second clip, hazy in the glare of the high sun. Then the clip started over again. Looping.

"Is busted. Play button is stuck. I give you deal," the Greek said.

On the poster, a thin silhouette, backlit from the waist up, manipulated two little puppets. The puppets were the bipedal horses, sneaking out of Dog City after they'd planted the bombs. Sneak sneak sneak. Then, at the end of the clip, one of Lexene's lights would go pop and that meant Dog City had blown up. The frame jerked for a second, then the clip started again.

"I'll take it," Hanes said. He paid the Greek, rolled up the poster, and walked back to the van.

Workshop Comments

Karen Fowler: "This is a very muted story with curiously disconnected characters. Within this dampened setting the difficulties, but also the possibilities, for moving us are enormous. We don't have to solve the mystery of Grover's death, but we do need to solve the mystery of his absence. What does it mean to the rest of Hanes' life that Grover is gone? *Good* ending."

John Kessel: "It's perfect. Don't change a thing. I *mean* it. This is a great story. Loved the lute player. Loved the fan in the clown suit. The street person. The Omnibot. The backstage scene. The names of Grover's performances. Maybe a little more—*but not much.*"

Carol Emshwiller: "Stay muted. Don't add a lot of emotion. I'm almost in agreement with John. So stay affectless."

Nancy Kress: "The writing here is a pleasure, smooth and detailed. You need more dramatization of scenes involving Grover, and a more definite stance from Hanes. Without either of those, we're just too distant from everyone's emotions."

Robert Frazier: "This needs a child. The true power of the story lies in the aftermath, in those left behind in a suicide. Seeing the child and a struggling Lexene would set the stage with the most powerful situation."

Bruce Sterling: "Any story with popstars, media, junk, bricolage, détournement, capitalist exploitation, hacking, retrofitted apartments, Russian fan kids, and uprooted urban artists with postmodern sensibilities has got to command my attention. Now I want you to really rub our noses in it."

James Patrick Kelly: "Although the writing is wonderful, the characterization is too enigmatic. Grover's death means little to us, everything to Hanes. Your story must be telling us why."

Maureen McHugh: "Illuminate the mystery at the heart of this story."

Alexander Jablokov: "There's a story here, but you haven't yet written it. The story is the rise and eventual destruction of an artist, a childlike artist. You have trouble focusing on it, and keep distracting yourself. Still, somehow, some of that tragic emotion comes through. Grab it and pull it through the story."

Gregory Frost: "The problem throughout for me is specificity—that's what is lacking and what will fix it."

Mark Van Name: "I had no trouble reading this story, and I generally enjoyed the experience. Unfortunately, at the end I just didn't care as much as I should have about the characters."

Jonathan Lethem: "A Jonathan Carroll story minus the intense emotions. Cute geniuses had better be suffering hard or they're insufferable."

Michaela Roessner: "A numbered-dot puzzle without the lines filled."

Afterword to "Horses Blow Up Dog City"

It is not at all a bad gig, blowing off most responsibilities for a week and just being a writer in the company of writers. One gets the urge to don the old velvet suit, take up smoking a pipe, that kind of thing. Even the Sycamore Hillians who write professionally for the other 358 days a year will tell you that it's a cool deal. So for a semi-unknown (uh, that's me, in case you were wondering) to join in with Mark and John as one of the Secret Masters of Sycamore Hill, to be treated as a peer by some of the bright lights of the literary SF community—what more could I ask for? How, indeed, would I have *known* to ask for such extracurricular activities?: a late-night dance contest starring a frantically gyrating Alex; the endless quest that Bob, Greg, and I undertook for the perfect spiral notebook; the discovery of a cache of fifties pulp magazines that featured Carol as the cover model. An exceptionally medicated game of "I've Never" comes to mind, as do the three extra hours of conversation with Karen while we waited for her plane to emerge from the maelstrom in Dallas and take her home.

The payback for all the good times and writerliness is your critique session. In many cases, a loose consensus will develop—you'll get thirteen hammers, or thirteen puzzled looks, or maybe thirteen paeans of praise. The folks at the tail end of the circle (the ones who don't have some prized Freudian or deconstructionist reading to trot out) usually hack away at the opinions already expressed: "I agree with Carol about the tone, and Jim's idea for a slight tweak on the ending is good." That kind of thing. Even the heavyweights pay some attention when a consensus develops. But what do you do when you get a few hammers, some puzzled looks, and some praise? Is that worse than a sound drubbing? No, it's not, but it does make you wonder about whom to listen to when you're doing the rewrite.

Well, I took the advice of John, and Carol, and Karen, so I didn't change a whole hell of a lot. If nothing else, I am quite proud of the fact that my story caused Bruce, who normally yowls about things like "the spearhead of cognition" and "burning the motherhood statement," to scream at me during the critique for making my characters seem criminally unemotional. Some folks wanted more puppetry, and it's not there, probably because I find most descriptions of new art forms in SF pretty tedious. Thanks are due to Bruce and Greg for pointing out a potentially embarrassing error in the tech of the story, and that's a good thing, since my day job *is* computer journalism.

Is the story too muted? I guess it depends on how sensitive your ears are. . . .

Richard Butner

The First Law
of Thermodynamics

JAMES PATRICK KELLY

HE HAD DROPPED acid maybe a dozen times, but had never forgotten his name before. He remembered the others—Cassie, Lance, Van—even though he'd left them waiting in the parking lot—when? A couple, ten minutes ago? An hour? Up until then, the farthest out he'd ever been was in high school, when he stared through the white on a sixty-watt bulb and saw the filament vibrating to a solo on Cream's "Sitting on Top of the World." It called to him in guitarese and he shrieked back. The filament said all life vibrated with a common energy, that we would exist only as long as our hearts beat to that indestructible rhythm. *Brang-brangeddy-brong, brang-brangeddy-brong!* Or something like. Actually, he might have been on mescaline the time the light bulb had played him the secret of the universe, or maybe it was Clapton, who was wailing back then like the patron saint of hallucinogens. But tonight his mind was well and truly blown by the blotter acid his new friends had called blue magic.

He wasn't particularly worried that he couldn't remember his straight name. He didn't feel at all attached to that chump at the moment, or to his dreary future. A name was nothing but a fence, closing him in. He was much happier now that the blue magic had transformed him into the wizard Space Cowboy, whose power was to leap all fences and zigzag through Day-Glo infinities at the speed of methamphetamine. Remembering the name on his student ID card was about as important as remembering the first law of thermodynamics. His secret identity was flunking physics and probably freshman comp, too, which meant he wasn't going to last much longer at Notre Dame. And since his number in the draft lottery was fourteen, he was northbound just as soon as they booted him out of college—no way Nixon was sending *him* to Cambodia! So long, Amerika, hello Toronto. Or maybe Vancouver. New episodes in the *Adventures of Space Cowboy,* although he wasn't all that excited about picking snot icicles from his mustache. Lance said Canada would be a more happening country if it had beachfront on the Gulf of Mexico.

He realized he had forgotten something else. Why had he come back to his room? Nineteen years old and his mind was already Swiss fucking cheese! He laughed at himself and then admired all the twisty little holes that were busy drilling themselves into the floor. The dull reality of the dorm emptied into them like soapy water swirling down a drain. The room reeked of Aqua Velva and Brylcreem, Balsinger's familiar weekend stink. *That's it.* Something to do with Balls, he thought. But his roommate was long since gone, no doubt sucking down quarts of Stroh's while he told some Barbie doll his dream of becoming the world's most polyester dentist. Balls was the enemy; their room was divided territory, the North and South Vietnam of Walsh Hall. Even when they were out, their stuff remained on alert. His pointy-toed boots were aimed at Balls's chukkas. Pete Townshend swung a guitar at Glen Campbell's head and *Zap Comix* blew cartoon smoke through the steamy windows of *Penthouse.* Now he remembered, sort of. He was supposed to borrow something—except the paint was melting off the walls. He picked the black cowboy hat off a pile of his dirty clothes, uncrumpled it and plunked it on. Sometimes the hat helped him think.

There was a knock. "Space?" Cassie peeked in and saw him idling at the desk. "Space, we're leaving."

It was Lance who had abridged his freak name—Lance, the wizard of words. Space didn't care; if someone he didn't like called him Space, he just played a few bars of Steve Miller's "Space Cowboy" in his head. Cassie he liked; she could call him whatever she wanted. In his opinion, Cassandra Demaras was the coolest chick who had ever gotten high. She stood almost six foxy feet tall and was wearing a man's pin-striped vest from Goodwill over a green T-shirt. Her hair was black as sin. Space lusted to see it spread across his pillow, only he knew it would never happen. She was a senior and artsy and Lance's. Not his future.

"Did you find it?" she asked.

"Ah . . . not yet," said Space cautiously. At least *someone* knew why he was here.

She stepped into the room. "Lance is going to split without you, man." Space had only joined the tribe last month and had already been left behind twice for stoned incompetence. "What's the problem?"

Her question was an itch behind his ear, so he scratched. She stared at him as if his skull were made of glass and he felt the familiar tingle of acid telepathy. She used her wizardly powers to read his mind—what there was of it—and sighed. "The key, Space. You're supposed to be looking for what's-his-face's key."

"Balls." Suddenly he was buried in a memory landslide. They had been sitting around waiting for the first rush and Lance had been laying down this rap about how they should do something about Cambodia and how some yippies at Butler had liberated the ROTC building with balloons and duct tape, and then Space had started in about how Balsinger was at school on a work-study grant and had to put in twelve hours a week pushing a broom through O'Shaughnessy Hall, the liberal-arts building, *for which he had the key,* and then everybody had gotten psyched, so to impress them all Space had volunteered to lift the key, except in the stairwell he had been blown away by a rush so powerful that he'd forgotten who he was and what the hell he was supposed to be doing, despite which his body had continued on to the room anyway and had been waiting here patiently for his mind to show up.

Space giggled and said, "He keeps it in the top drawer."

Cassie went to Balls's desk, opened it and then froze as if she was peering over the edge of reality.

"What's he got in there now?" he asked. "Squid?"

As he came up behind her, he caught a telepathic burst that was like chewing aluminum foil. She was freaking out and he knew exactly why. This was where Balls kept his school supplies: a stack of blank three-by-five file cards held together with a red rubber band, scotch tape, a box of paper clips, six number 2 pencils with pristine erasers, six Bic ballpoints, a slide rule, an unopened bottle of Liquid Paper, and behind, looseleaf, graph, and onionskin paper in perfect stacks. But it wasn't just Balls's stuff that had disturbed her. It was the way he had arranged everything, fitted it together with jigsaw-puzzle precision. In a world burning with love and napalm, this pinhead had taken the time to align pencils and pens, neaten stacks of paper—Space wouldn't have been surprised if he had reorganized the paper clips in their box. All this brutal order was proof that aliens from Planet Middle America had landed and were trying to pass for human! Space was used to Balsinger, but imagining the straightitude of his roommate's mind had filled Cassie with psychedelic dread.

"Space, are you as wasted as I think I am?" Her eyes had gone flat as tattoos.

"I don't know. What's the date?"

She frowned. "May 2, 1970."

"Who's president of the United States?"

"That's the problem."

He held up a fist. "How many fingers?"

She shook her head and was recaptured by the drawer.

The key to O'Shaughnessy Hall was next to the slide rule. Space picked it up and juggled it from one hand to another. It flickered through the air like a goldfish. This time when she glanced up, he bumped the drawer shut with his thigh. "Hey, remember what the dormouse said."

"No, I'm serious." She shook her head and her hair danced. "It's like time is breaking down. You know what I mean? One second doesn't connect to the next."

"Right on!" He caught the key and closed his fist around it.

"Listen! I've got to know where the peak is, or else I can't maintain. What if I just keep going up and up and up?"

"You'll have a hell of a view."

Maybe it was the wrong time for jokes. Space could see panic wisping off her like smoke. When he breathed it in, he got even higher. "Okay," he said. "So the first wave is a mother. But I'm here and you're with me, so we'll just ride it together, okay?" He surfed an open hand toward her. "Then we groove."

"You don't understand." She licked her lower lip with a strawberry tongue. "Lance has decided he wants to score again, so we can trip all weekend. He's weirding me out, Space. My brains are already oozing from my fucking ears and he's looking for the next hit."

The blue magic was giving him a squirrelly vibe; he thought he could feel a bad moon rising over this trip. Space had seen a bummer just once, back in high school, when a kid claimed he had a tiny Hitler stuck in his throat and thrashed around and drank twenty-seven glasses of water until he puked. Space had been paranoid that whatever monsters were chewing on the kid's brain would have him for dessert. But this kid—Space remembered him now—Lester Something, Lester was a pinched nobody who couldn't even tie his shoes when he was buzzed, not a wizard like Cassie or Lance or Space, with powers and abilities far beyond those of mortal men.

"Am I okay, Space?" She had never asked him for help before, put herself in his power. "What's going to happen to us?"

"We're going to have an adventure." Although he was worried about her, he was also turned on. He wanted to kiss his way through her hair to the pale skin on her neck. Instead he tugged at the brim of his hat. He was Space Cowboy. His power was that nothing could stop him, nothing could touch him. And so what if things were spinning out of control? That was the fun in doing drugs, wasn't it?

"Ready to cruise?" He beamed at her and was relieved to see his smile reflected palely on her face.

Somewhere in the future, a van honked.

"Say 'wonderful.' " Lance was giving Cassie orders.

The spooky moonlight spilled across the cornfields. Space glanced up from the floor of the van occasionally to see if the psychic ambience had improved any, but the lunar seas still looked like mold on a slice of electric bread.

"Wonderful," she said absently.

"No, mean it."

"Won . . . der . . . ful." Cassie's voice was a chickadee fluttering against her chest. Space knew this because she was wedged between him and Lance and they had their arms around her, crossing behind her back and over her chest, protecting her from lysergic acid diethylamide demons. He could feel her blood booming; her shallow breathing fondled his ribs. The Econoline's tires drummed over seams in the pavement as its headlights unzipped the highway at sixty-five miles an hour. He found himself listening to the world with his shoulders and toes.

"Full of wonder." Lance was smooth as an apple as he talked her down; his wizard power was making words dance. "I know, that can be scary, because you don't know where you're going or what you're going to find. Strangeness probably, but so what? Life is strange, people are strange. Don't fight it, groove on it." He squeezed her and Space took his cue to do the same. "Say you're a little girl at the circus at night and a clown comes up in the dark, and it's like, *holy shit,* where's mommy? But throw some light on him and you're laughing." He reached to flick on the overhead light. "See?"

It was the right thing to say because she blinked in the light and smiled, sending them flashes of pink cotton candy and dancing elephants and an acrobat hanging from a trapeze by his teeth. Space could feel her come spinning down towards them like a leaf. "Wonderful," she said, focusing. "I'll try."

Space was suddenly aware that his elbow was flattening her left breast and he was clutching Lance's shoulder. He shivered, let his arm slip down and wiped his sweaty palm on his jeans.

"Heavy, man," said Van. "You want to turn the light off before I miss the turn?" Van was at the wheel of his 1962 Ford Econoline van. It had a 144-cubic-inch, six-cylinder engine and a three-speed manual shift on the steering column and its name was Bozo. Van had lifted all Bozo's seats except his and replaced them with orange shag carpeting and a mattress fitted with a tie-dyed sheet. He had the Jefferson Airplane on the eight-track; Grace Slick wondered if he needed somebody to love. The answer was yes, thought Space. Yes, damn it! Lance was holding Cassie's hand. Van checked the rearview mirror, then braked, pulled off the highway and drove along the shoulder, craning his head to the right. Finally he spotted an unmarked dirt track that divided a vast and unpromising nothingness in two.

"Where the fuck are we?" said Space.

"We're either making a brief incursion into Cambodia," said Van, "or we're at the ass end of Mishawaka, Indiana." Van had the power of mobility. He and Bozo were one, a machine with a human brain. No matter how stoned the world turned, Van could navigate through it. No one demanded poetry or cosmic truths from Van; all they expected of him was to deliver.

"Looks like nowhere to me."

"To the unenlightened eye, yes," said Lance. "But check it out and you'll see another frontier of human knowledge. Tripping is like doing science, Space. You can't just lounge around your room anymore listening to Joni Mitchell and dreaming up laws of nature. You have to go out into the field and gather data in order to grok the universe. Study the stars and ponds, turn rocks over, taste the mushrooms, smoke some foliage."

"Would someone take my boots off?" said Cassie.

"It's freezing, man," said Van. "Your feet will get cold." As Bozo bumped down the track, the steering wheel kept squirming in his hands like a snake.

"I've got cold feet already."

"Science is bullshit!" said Space. "Nothing but a government conspiracy to bring us down." He slid across the shag carpet and rolled the right leg of Cassie's jeans over an ankle-length black boot. "Like, if they hadn't passed the law of gravity, we could all fly."

Van laughed. "Maybe we could get Dicky Trick to repeal it."

"Somebody should repeal that asshole," said Cassie.

"Science is napalm," said Space. "Science is plastic. It's Tang." He eased her boot off. She was wearing cotton socks, soft and nubbly.

"It's the bomb," said Lance.

"Are we going to the farm?" Cassie wiggled her toes in Space's hand. "This is the way to the farm, isn't it?"

Her foot reminded him of the baby rabbit that Katie McCauley had brought for show-and-tell in the sixth grade; he hadn't wanted to put it down, either. He pressed his thumb gently against her instep.

"You've never been to the farm, have you, Space?" said Lance. The road spat stones at Bozo's undercarriage.

"He's home," said Van. "I can see lights, man."

"Who?" Space said.

"Do you follow baseball?" Lance started to laugh.

The farm buildings sprawled across the land like a moonbathing giant. The barrel-chested body was a Quonset hut; a red silo arm saluted the stars. The weather-bitten face of the house was turned toward them; its narrow porch pouted. There were lights in the eyes, and much more light streaming from the open slider of the Quonset. Van parked next to a '59 Studebaker Lark that had been driven to Mars and back. He opened his door, took a deep breath of the night and disappeared.

"Oh, wow!" They could hear him scrabbling on the ground. "I forget how to walk," he said.

Space was the first to reach him. Van was doing a slow backstroke across the lawn toward the house. "For a moment there, man," he said, "I could've sworn I had wheels."

"Come on, you." Lance motioned Space to grab Van's shoulders and together they tried to lift him. "Get up." It was like stacking Jell-O.

"No, no, *no.*" Van giggled. "I'm too wasted."

"I'm so glad you waited until now to tell us," said Lance. "How the hell do we get back to campus?"

"Oh, I'm cool to drive, man. I just can't stand up."

They managed to fold him back into the driver's seat and Cassie slapped Big Brother into the eight-track. Space glanced over to the Quonset and saw a silhouette on the canvas of light framed by the huge open doorway. For a moment a man watched—no, *sensed* him. When he sniffed the air, something feathered against Space's cheek. Then the man ghosted back into the barn.

"Old Rog doesn't seem very glad to see us," said Lance.

The barn was fiercely lit—north of supermarket-bright, just south of noon at the beach. The wildly colored equipment seemed to shimmer in the hard light. A golden reaper, a pink cultivator, and a lobster-red baler were lined up beside a John Deere that looked like it had been painted in a tornado. The man had poked his head under its hood.

"Evening, Rog," said Lance. "Space, this is Roger Maris."

The man turned toward them; Space blinked. Roger Maris was wearing a pair of black jeans with a hole in the left knee and a greasy Yankees jersey over a gray sweatshirt. He stood maybe six feet tall and weighed a paunchy two hundred and change. He had that flattop crewcut, all right, and the nose like a thumb, but Space wasn't buying that he was Roger Maris. At least not *the* Roger Maris.

He'd been ten years old when Maris hit sixty-one home runs to break Babe Ruth's record, but in 1961 Space and his parents had been National League fans. They lived in Sheboygan and followed the Milwaukee Braves. Space's imagination had been more than filled by the heroics of Hank Aaron and Eddie Matthews; there was no room for damn Yankees. But then the Braves moved south in 1966 and Space had to accept the harsh reality that not only was God dead, but Warren Spahn was pitching in Atlanta. After that, he'd lost interest in baseball. He had no clue what had become of *the* Roger Maris since.

"Space?" Maris waved a socket wrench at him. "What the hell kind of name is Space?"

"Short for Space Cowboy," said Cassie.

Maris considered this, then put the wrench down, wiped his left hand on the pinstriped jersey and offered it to Space. "A hat don't make no cowboy," he said.

They shook. "A shirt don't make no ballplayer," said Space.

Maris's smile bandaged irritation. "What can I do you folks out of?" He gave Space a parting grip strong enough to crush stone.

"You got any more blue magic in your bag of tricks?" said Lance. "We're thinking of going away for the weekend."

"To where, Oz?" Maris shut his eyes; his lids were the color of the last olive in the jar. "Cowboy here ever done magic before?"

Now Space was annoyed; he was proud of his dope résumé. "I've dropped Owsley, wedding bells, and some two-way brown dot."

"Practically Ken Kesey." Cassie laughed. "And only a freshman."

"That shit's just acid," said Maris. "Magic goes deeper."

"He handled the first rush all right," said Lance. "We all did."

"You driving around with a head full of blue magic?" Maris frowned.

"Actually," said Lance, "Van's driving."

But Maris wasn't listening. He had closed his eyes again and kept them closed, his head cocked to one side as he received secret instructions from outer space. "It's your funeral," he said abruptly, and strode from the barn as if he'd just remembered he'd left the bathwater running.

"I guess we scored." Lance shrugged. "Hey Rog, wait up!" He paused at the door of the Quonset, glanced uncertainly at Cassie and Space and then plunged after Maris.

"What does he mean, our funeral?" Cassie had turned the color of a saltine.

"Don't ask me; I'm the rookie. Can't you see these training wheels on my head?"

"Deeper? Deeper than what?"

Space put his arm around her shoulder and led her from the Quonset into the baleful night.

Pacing Roger Maris's front parlor, Space remembered what Cassie had said about things getting disconnected. How could anyone deal acid and live in a place as square as a doctor's waiting room? The wallpaper was Midwestern Hideous: Golden, flag-bearing eagles flapped between Civil War cannons on a cream field. If he stared long enough, the blue magic animated the pattern for him. Madness, *madness*—and Norman Mailer wondered why we were in Vietnam! Lance and Cassie waited for Maris on a long, low brown couch in front of an oval rug braided in harvest colors. Cassie watched the brick fireplace in which four dusty birch logs were stacked. Nearby, a television the size of a Shetland pony was tethered to the wall socket.

Space couldn't stand still. "Where did you dig this loon up?"

"He found us." Lance shot a quizzical look at Cassie. "After the Santana concert?"

She bit her lip and said, "Don't talk to me. I'm not here."

"Okay." Lance was teeth-grindingly patient. "That's cool."

By the door, a heavy brass pot was filled by a man's black umbrella and three baseball bats. "I mean, check this room," said Space.

Lance laughed. "I keep expecting Wally Cleaver to materialize and ask if I want to sniff some glue."

On waist-high shelves beside a rocking chair were stacked a

build-it-yourself Heathkit tuner, amp, and turntable. Next to them was a rack of LPs. Space worried through them; they contradicted everything in the room. Maris had the rare nude version of John and Yoko's *Two Virgins*, *Weasels Ripped My Flesh* by the Mothers of Invention, Moby Grape, everything by Quicksilver Messenger Service, Dylan's *Blonde on Blonde*, the Airplane's *Surrealistic Pillow*.

"Look at this!" Space waved a copy of *Workingman's Dead* at Lance. "This is *not* Roger Maris—he's not anyone. His pieces don't fit together."

Lance pointed silently at a framed Western Union telegram that hung beside a painting of Guernseys.

My heartiest congratulations to you on hitting your 61st home run. The American people will always admire a man who overcomes great pressure to achieve an outstanding goal.

John F. Kennedy

"So?" Space didn't know why it had become so important to him that this clyde wasn't the famous ballplayer. "He could've got this anywhere—could've sent it to himself." Everything seemed so slippery all of a sudden; he felt a familiar twinge of dread. Just when he'd finally figured the world out, he was afraid he might have to stop believing in something. Again. This was exactly how it had felt when he had given up on baseball, Catholicism, America, love, "Star Trek," college. What was it this time? The only illusions he had left were that nothing mattered, that acid was wisdom, and that he was a wizard.

He heard Maris on the stairs and skittered back to the couch next to Cassie, who was still elsewhere.

"A dozen hits of magic." Maris offered them a plastic baggie with a scatter of confetti clinging to the inside. Space took it. Each blotter was the size of a fingernail and was labeled with a blue ∞. "Sixty," said Maris.

Lance pulled two twenties and a joint from his T-shirt pocket. "Want to smoke?" He liked to close deals with some ceremonial pot. He said it was the Indian way, and also helped detect narcs.

While he lit up, Space counted out a ten, a five, and five ones and put an empty wallet back in his jeans.

Lance passed the joint to Maris, who took an impatient toke.

"You said this is deeper than acid." Space jiggled the baggie. "What's that supposed to mean, anyway?"

Cassie twitched and returned from the dark side of the moon.

"You take a trip, you come back, nothing really changes." The smoky words curled out of his mouth. "This shit makes you become yourself faster, kind of hurries things along."

"Something wrong with that?" said Cassie.

"Depends on who you're supposed to be." Maris tucked the wad of money into his jeans. "But if I was you kids, I'd take the long way to the future." He offered Cassie the joint; she waved it over to Space.

"Sounds like Timothy Leary bullshit to me." Space took a deep, disgusted pull and immediately regretted it. Lance's pot tasted like electrical fire; it was probably laced with Mr. Clean.

" 'Timothy Leary's dead,' " sang Lance. "So if I'm not myself, who am I? Marshall McLuhan? Abbie Hoffman?"

"You're faking it, that's what being young is all about. When you're young, there ain't all that much of you, so you pretend there's more."

"Hell, you're the one preten—" Space couldn't hold it in anymore; he was racked by a fit of coughing.

"Space," said Cassie.

"You never hit sixty-one homers." Space gasped; his head felt like it was filling with helium. "I bet you've never even been to Yankee Stadium."

Maris's face was hard as the Bible. "You want to see my license, Cowboy?" In the uneasy silence, he fetched an ashtray from the hi-fi shelf. "Me, I stayed young a long time, mostly because I never did nothing but play ball. Growing up ain't something they really encourage in the bigs. When I got traded to the Yankees, I was just the kid who was going to play right field next to Mantle. I was MVP that season. 'Sixty." Talking about baseball seemed to calm him. He took another drag, ashed the joint and then offered it again to Cassie.

"Mantle?" This time she puffed politely.

"Mickey Mantle played center field," said Lance. "Tell them

about the home run." Space wasn't sure whether Lance really believed or was egging Maris on for a goof.

"That was the next year, when me and Mick hit all the homers. Only he got sick and I still didn't have the record on the last day of the season. We were playing the Red Sox at the Stadium. By then a lot of people had given up, probably thought I didn't have sixty-one in me. I remember it was a cool day but real bright, the sun beating down on all the empty seats. The fans who showed were jammed into the right-field stands, just in case. The Sox started Tracy Stallard, a righty, fastball pitcher. I flied out to Yaz in the first but when I came up in the fourth . . ."

The contours of his body changed, as if the weight of the last nine years had fallen away.

"He started me with two balls away. Then the third pitch, he made a mistake, got too much of the plate. I was always a mistake hitter. I got a real good cut at it and then . . . I just stood and watched. It landed near the bullpen, about ten rows into the stands, people scrambling after it. There was a fog of noise; it was like I couldn't find my way around the bases. When I got back to the dugout, Blanchard and Skowron and Lopez wouldn't let me in, they were blocking the top step, making me go back out into the noise. That was the problem, I couldn't never find my way out of that goddamned noise."

"Is that why you left baseball?" asked Cassie

"Nah." Maris closed his eyes again; he was definitely listening to *something*. "Nah, it's 'cause I ain't a kid anymore." Suddenly he looked spent; Space could see a looseness under the chin. "I'm thirty-six years old."

"That's still pretty young," said Cassie.

"Well then, there's this." He rolled up the gray sweatshirt, uncovering his left forearm. A scar, smooth and white as the belly of a snake, sliced from the ball of his thumb up toward the elbow. "The VC likes to rig these homemade mines, see. Couple of fragmentation grenades with the spoons attached to a tripwire. Me and Luther Nesson were walking point outside of Da Lat and the poor bastard stepped into one. Died in a splatter and left me a souvenir. A chunk of shrapnel chewed on my *palmaris longus* muscle and severed a couple of tendons."

Space contemplated the wound with vast relief; for a moment

back there, Maris had almost convinced him. Now he felt a grudging admiration for Maris's creativity, his devotion to detail, the weight of his portrayal—the man had elevated lunacy to an art. And of course the 'Nam angle made it all the more poignant. Space imagined that, if he had seen what Maris had seen, he might well be strumming a ukulele and warbling like Tiny Tim.

"Bummer." Lance stubbed the roach out and took the baggie. "Hey, we better go check on Van, make sure he didn't float away." He stood. "So anyway, thanks, man." He reached for Cassie's hand.

"What's happening?" Cassie scooted away from him and bumped into Space. "We're going already? What about the rest of the story?"

Maris waved at the parlor. "Sister, you're looking at it."

Outside, Van was amusing himself by flashing a light show against the side of the farmhouse while he sang along to *Sgt. Pepper*. High beam–low beam–right blinker–off–low beam–left blinker . . . "—the *girl* with ka*lei*doscope *eyes.*" He had a voice like a loose fan belt.

Maris followed them onto the porch and watched, flickering in the headlights. As Cassie ducked into Bozo, Maris called out. "Cowboy! How much you want for the hat?"

"Huh?"

"Pay no attention," Lance hissed. "Just get in."

"It's not for sale." Space stepped away from Bozo.

"Sixty bucks says it is."

Space tugged at the brim; he had almost forgotten he was wearing it. He started back toward Maris. It wasn't much of a hat—Space had stepped on it many times, spilled Boone's Farm apple wine on it, watched as one of Lenny Kemmer's Winstons had burned a hole in the black felt crown. "Is this some kind of joke?"

Van killed the lights and Beatles. Lance and Cassie deployed on either side of Bozo.

Maris came to the top of the porch steps. "You got doubts," he said. "You think I've been shitting you all night."

When Space tried to deny it, his tongue turned to peanut butter.

"Hell, Cowboy, you don't believe in nothing."

"So?"

"So I want to buy the hat." Maris came down the first step. "For a experiment." Second step. "And you gotta help." Bottom step. "Sixty." He unfolded the wad of bills and thrust them at Space.

"Hey, Rog," said Lance. "He's just a kid. Leave him alone."

Abraham Lincoln gazed up at Space, appraising the quality of his courage.

"What kind of experiment?" said Cassie.

"Scientific. Cowboy and me are going to measure something."

Space nipped the money without speaking and offered Maris the hat.

Maris clapped him on the shoulder. "You just hold on to that for now." He turned Space toward the Quonset. "See that barn? How far would you say it is?"

As Space peered into night, the Quonset receded and then flowed back toward him. "I don't know. Fifty, sixty feet?"

"More like a hundred, but that's okay. Now you're gonna stand in that doorway and get a good tight grip on the brim." He raised Space's arm. "Hold it to one side, just like that. Arm's length."

"Space." Cassie slipped between them. "Give him back his money and let's get out of here."

Maris brushed past her and surveyed the shrubbery along the porch. He poked by a couple of crew-cut yews, a rhododendron in bud, a forsythia already gone by.

Cassie kept insisting. "Time to *go*, man." Like she was his mother.

The edge of the garden was defined by a row of smooth beach-stones, painted white. Maris knelt with a grunt and hefted one the size of a peach, only flatter and more egg-shaped.

"Everyone remembers me for the homers, but I could play the field too." He brushed dirt off the stone. "Won a Gold Glove, you know. Didn't nobody stretch a single on Roger Maris."

"Jesus God," said Cassie, "what are you morons trying to prove? That your balls are bigger than your brains?"

That summed it up nicely, thought Space. Maris was playing a

testosterone game with his head. Space was at once a creature of
the game and a spectator. A poor nervous physics major sat in the
stands, watching in horror, while Space Cowboy was grooving
on a Grade A adrenaline high. And why not? He was a nineteen-
year-old wizard whose power was that nothing could touch him,
nothing could stop him. He looked over at Lance, who was pale
as the moon. "Right *on!*" Space said.

He counted the paces off: thirty-nine, forty, forty-one.
Forty-two to the Quonset's open doorway—figure three feet to
a pace, so let's see, three times two was six and three times four
was twelve—was that right? He had won his high school's Math
Medal back in the Pleistocene. A hundred and twenty-six feet
was just about the distance from third base to first. He bowed,
flourished the hat to Cassie and then held it up in his moist, outstretched hand.

Maris turned at a right angle to the Quonset; he held the stone
behind him, just off the hip. He scowled at the hat over his front
shoulder and then paused. He shut his eyes and listened to the
howl of the Dog Star long enough for a bead of sweat to dribble
from Space's armpit. Then Maris nodded, reared back and strode
quickly forward—*Open your eyes, goddamnit!* His arm snapped
past his ear and the stone came screaming at Space like the head-
lamp of God's own Harley—or maybe it was Space who
screamed, he couldn't tell, he couldn't move, his entire future had
collapsed into an egg-shaped stone and time stopped and for an
eternity he thought, *What a fucking waste,* and then time
resumed with a sneeze and the hat spun him halfway around but
he held on to it and something *thwocked* against the concrete
floor of the Quonset and again, *thwocka-thwocka-thwok!* For a
moment there was utter silence, which drummed in his ears like
the finale of the *1812* Overture. Space whispered, "Out of sight,"
and giggled. Then he shouted so the others could hear. "OUT
OF SIGHT!"

Space was surprised that the stone hadn't ripped off the top of
the hat but instead had come through the pinch on the front side,
leaving a hole big enough for Lance to put his fist through. Lance
handed it to Van who offered it to Cassie who wanted no part of
it. "Are you boys about through?" Her voice was a fistful of
nails.

"Yeah," said Lance. "Time to cruise."

Van brought the hat to Maris, who was kneading his biceps. Maris stared right through him. "See what magic can do, Cowboy?" His smile had no teeth in it. "You can make yourself into a star, if that's who you're supposed to be."

"Mr. Maris," said Space, opening his wallet. "How much for that hat?"

Van, Space and Lance staggered out of Kresge's and across the parking lot, laughing. The cashier had rung up the eight cans of Rust-Oleum—two each of red, yellow, green, and black—the one-pound bag of Fritos, the four Almond Joys, the six packages of Fun Tyme Balloons, the dozen rolls of crepe ribbon, the two packs of Teaberry gum, and then, as the register stuck out its paper tongue at her, she had asked them who the party was for. When Lance had said, "President Nixon, ma'am," she was so transparently croggled that it was all Space could do to keep from dropping to his belly and barking like a seal.

Cassie, who had been waiting for them in Bozo, didn't see what was so funny, but then she hadn't eaten that second blotter of blue magic, either. Ken Kesey and the Merry Pranksters had a saying: You were either on the bus or off. Space was no telepath, but it occurred to him that Cassie might be about to stand up and pull the signal cord for her stop.

"She's probably calling the cops on us right now," Cassie said.

"For what, indecent composure?" said Lance. "Chortling in a No Humor Zone?"

"How about possession? You've got Space here mooning around in a cowboy hat with a frontal lobotomy and you two are so wasted you're tripping over gum spots on the parking lot." She shook her head. "You guys are dangerous, you know that?"

"Only to ourselves." Van swerved Bozo around an oncoming Vega and roared onto the highway, headed back toward campus. "Break out the chips."

They crunched to themselves for a few moments. Space was glad that Cassie was no longer freaking out, only now she had turned so fucking sensible that she was stretching his nerves. They were tripping, *ferchrissakes;* this was no time to be responsible. "How about some tunes?" he said.

Van turned on the radio.

"*—of student protests continued today in the wake of President Nixon's decision to send troops into Cambodia. In Maryland, Governor Marvin Mandel has put the National Guard on alert after two days of unrest on the campus . . .*"

"I said tunes!" Space leaned forward to punch a selector button.

"Ssh, listen." Lance yanked him back.

"*And at Kent State University in Ohio, a fire of undetermined origin swept through the ROTC building this evening. Firemen responding to the blaze were hampered by students throwing rocks and cutting hoses.*"

"Hey, man," said Van. "Maybe we should go after ROTC too."

"*Earlier today, a group of two thousand students marched through downtown Kent, prompting local officials to order a dawn-to-dusk . . .*"

"No," Lance said. "That's where they'll be expecting trouble. Besides, we've got the key to O'Shag."

"This whole gig is bogus." Cassie nudged the paper Kresge's sack with her boot. "It's not going to accomplish anything, except maybe get us arrested."

"Hey, we're going to wake up this fucking campus," Space said.

"Fucking A!" said Van.

"Shake the jocks out of their beds."

"Right on, man, right on!" Van pumped his fist.

"Light a fire under old Hesburgh."

"Tell it, brother!" Van leaned on the horn.

"Lay off, you guys," said Lance. "Cassie, you heard the radio. People all over the country are protesting. We've got a chance to make a statement here."

"With balloons and spray paint?"

"Better than guns and bombs." Lance rested his hand on her knee. "You thought it was cool before."

"That wasn't me, that was the acid."

"*Turning to sports, Dust Commander has won the Kentucky Derby. A fifteen-to-one shot . . .*"

She rested her cheek against the window. "Look, I'm going to graduate in a couple of weeks. I'm too old to be playing Wendy to your Lost Boys. Maybe I should just go back to the dorm and crash."

"And in the American League, the Angels beat the Red Sox, eight–four, it was the Yankees seven, the Brewers six . . ."

Space fingered the hole in his hat and wondered if he had it in him to be a star.

Van sauntered toward the main entrance to O'Shaughnessy Hall. The liberal-arts building was one of the largest and ugliest on campus, a stack of four Gothic Revival ice cube trays with a yellow brick veneer. Cassie, Space, and Lance watched from the chill shadows as Van waltzed innocently up to the door, tried it as if he'd expected O'Shag to be open at eleven thirty-four on a Saturday night, shrugged and cruised on.

"Of course, if it wasn't locked, we wouldn't be breaking and entering." Cassie made no effort to keep her voice down. "Jerry Rubin would have to take points off."

Lance had used his wizard power to talk Cassie into sticking with them, but Space wasn't sure it had been his swiftest move of the evening. Doubt was contagious, especially when your feet were wet. They had left Bozo in student parking and stolen across the tidy greens of the campus, weighting their shoes with spring dew. The night was getting colder; Space could see his breath plume. He ground his teeth to keep them from chattering. It took Van forever to circle back to them.

They slunk around to O'Shag's smaller north entrance, checking for any signs of activity inside. The classrooms were all dark but that didn't mean some English professor might not be late-nighting in one of the windowless offices, slugging Jim Beam and writing poems about English professors for the *Dead Tree Review*. This time the others stayed behind while Space approached the door, clutching Balls's key. It wasn't until he was fitting it into the lock that he realized there might be an alarm. He looked back at the others in a panic but they were no help. Neither were the stars, some of which were flashing blue like the cherry on a cop car. He could almost hear the Pleiades shrilling at him as he tried to turn the key to the right. It wouldn't budge. He thought the moon's alarm would sound deeper and more reproachful, like a foghorn. He turned the key left and the deadbolt clicked. *Moon, spoon, you fucking loon.* He pushed against the door and it swung open, dumping him into O'Shaughnessy Hall.

He went through a dimly lit stairwell to the long, dark hall of the first floor. The block walls on either side were pierced by wooden doors. Space could not make out the far end. Although he had passed this way every Monday, Wednesday, and Friday for eight months, Space felt lost. The place he knew and hated teemed with sound and light and bodies. This one was empty, silent as a dream and all the doors were closed, creating an odd pressure in the hall, as if the building were holding its breath.

He heard a door tick open, a squeak of sneakers against the rubber mat in the stairwell, the whisper of corduroy pants. Lance said that the reason Van always wore corduroys was that he needed more texture in his life.

"In here," said Space.

"No lights?" Van peered.

"No."

They joined Lance and Cassie in the stairwell. Lance knelt in a corner of the stairwell and handed out supplies from the Kresge's bag. "We'll each take a floor," he said. "Fifteen minutes and out."

"But what should we say, man?" asked Van.

"Like I said, just make a statement," said Lance. "It's your life and their war."

Cassie waved off a package of balloons. "Keep the party favors." She went up the stairs with a can of Rust-Oleum in each hand.

"Bring the empties back, and no fingerprints, okay?" said Lance. "Fifteen minutes—let's do it!" He and Van took the stairs two at a time.

Space sprayed a blue peace sign on the door to room 160 but was strangely unconvinced by it. Then what kind of statement did he have in him? He immediately regretted the *Fuck Nixon;* it was obvious as air. *Hell No, We Won't Go* sprawled the entire length of room 149 and came to a disappointing conclusion on 147. Room 141 read *Out Now.* He took a balloon from his pocket, blew it up, and almost fainted but managed to hold it pinched between thumb and forefinger. Out of where? Cambodia? Vietnam? Notre Dame? Instead of tying the balloon,

Space let it go and it leapt, hissing, from his hand. He wrote *Revolution* on the east wall, *Make Love Not War* on the west, then left them to futile debate. He was now deep into the hall; the visibility was less than a classroom in either direction. He could feel the future watching as he wrote *Acid Test* on room 133. Pale secondhand moonlight glimmered through the tall wire-reinforced glass slits in each door. One twenty-five said, *God Is Dead.* Long red runs dribbled from the *O* in *God*, like blood from the crown of thorns. Was proclaiming the demise of the deity a political statement? *Maris 61/61* on 117. That would leave the campus fuzz scratching their balls even though Old Rog had proved that it was cool to *talk the talk*, man, just as long as you can *walk the walk.* But Space still couldn't see the end of the fucking hall.

At that moment, something splatted on his cheek. Space swiped at it, thinking it might be his own sweat. The finger came away dry; he could feel his skin tighten in fear. *Pa-chuk.*

"Hey!"

Pa-chuk, pa-chuk. The two drops hit his left arm like marbles on a snare drum and he spun wildly away. *Pa-chuk.* Space moaned and started to run. A phantom storm in the middle of O'Shaugnessey Hall was hairy enough, but these weren't just polite raindrops. They were big and cold and rude as eggs. *Pa-chuk.*

And this was it, he realized: the bummer he had helped Cassie dodge was seething all around him and he knew he had to get out—get *out*—that he had been wandering blindly and without purpose down this hallway ever since he had come to Notre Dame *papa-chuk* but he could no longer go back to his parents and Sheboygan and Cathy, that lying bitch *pa-chuk*, but there was no sense in going any farther because the hallway stretched on to some distant and unknowable infinity and besides, he had to get the hell out, which was when the doors began to vibrate and the light of insight came knifing through the long, thin windows and he saw the hall with the same acid clarity with which he had heard the filament of a sixty-watt bulb riffing about the mysterious energy that abided in all life, only now he could sense a new secret *papa-chuk*: that there was no future in wandering down an empty hall, that in order to find his life he would have to choose where to expend his energy. Pick a door, *damn it.* Room 110 was right in front of him but it was even and Space knew he had to be odd. He about-faced; nothing could stop him. The doorknob of 109 was warm as a kiss.

Space put a hand to his forehead to shield his eyes. Sunlight poured through windows which framed snow-covered mountains. The sky was the blue of heaven; the snow on the ground glistened. He had entered a classroom all right, but it obviously wasn't in the same corner of reality as South Bend, Indiana.

A balding man stood behind the head desk and typed with two fingers—the teacher, Space assumed. He was wearing suede cowboy boots, black pants, a denim workshirt buttoned to the neck and—*holy shit*, the dude had a gold earring!

He did not seem to notice Space.

Neither did the students now filing in behind him. They seemed too young to be in college; they had that stunned glaze of high-school seniors—except that some of them had tattoos. The sides of one girl's head had been shaved to a gunmetal shadow. A boy in a flannel shirt had on the flimsiest headphones Space had ever seen; they were attached to a transistor radio hooked to the kid's belt. *Walkman*—the word sprang unbidden to his mind. *Walk the walk*, man.

Space's first instinct was to bolt from the room, or at least slouch like a student behind a desk in the back, but instead he approached the teacher. As he got closer he saw that the squashed typewriter had no paper in it, that it wasn't any kind of machine Space had ever seen before, but then there was another strange word melting on his tongue like a lifesaver—*laptop*. It was a funny word and he might have laughed, except that he had by now come too close to the teacher, close enough so that he could wiggle his toes inside the man's boots, so close that he could jingle the keys to an '88 Dodge Caravan in his front pants pocket and, in the back pocket, feel the bulk of a wallet not quite filled with thirty-eight dollars and a NatWest Visa card with an unpaid balance of $3,734.80 on which he was paying a 9.9% APR and a California driver's license and a picture of a pretty little blonde girl named Kaitlin, so impossibly close that he could feel the weight of a single gold band around the fourth finger of his left hand and remember Judy's breath feathering against his neck after she kissed him good-bye that morning.

The bell rang and the class came to what passed for attention at Memorial High.

"Good morning, people." He turned to the board and scrawled, *1st law of thermodynamics* in handwriting which was almost as legible as an EKG scan. He faced the class again. "Can anyone tell me what this is?"

He was astonished to see Ben Strock with his hand up. Most days the kid sat looking as if he had just been hit in the head with a shovel, even though he *was* pulling down a B-plus. "Yes, Ben?"

"Uh . . . bathroom pass, Mr. Casten."

Jack Casten waved him from the room. "Anyone else?"

Of course, Feodor Papachuk raised his hand. *Fucking suck-up,* thought the part of Jack Casten that was still Space Cowboy and always would be. "Go ahead, Feodor."

"The first law of thermodynamics," said Feodor Papachuk, "is that energy can neither be created or destroyed, but may be changed from one form to another."

Workshop Comments

Carol Emshwiller: "I love this. I wouldn't change anything except about three places where I thought your wonderful language stretched a tiny bit too far."

Greg Frost: "Killer story, dude. Really enjoyed it and its aesthetic. Perhaps it will stand as the anti–*Forrest Gump.*"

Karen Joy Fowler: "A stupendous story. The Maris scene carries the emotional weight—without it, or with it in a truncated form, I'm not sure the ending would wring us as it now does."

Nancy Kress: "I like this a whole lot. It's funny, poignant and stylish. I think, though, you could shorten the Roger Maris section a bit: it's sticking out in relation to its overall importance in the story."

Bruce Sterling: "This is pretty much swell. Needs more of a sense of the toll acid takes on your body. He should grind his teeth. His palms don't sweat anywhere near enough. A final objection is the obligatory genre tie-in. The first law of thermodynamics seems like the tiny hinge to the genre which enables you to sell this to *Asimov's.* It is irritating because it feels like a tactical, market-driven decision."

Michaela Roessner: "Kelly! This is a little scary. It is so immediate that I'm worried you never left. Do we need to go back and get you?"

Alexander Jablokov: "Superb story, although Drug-Addled Tales of the Sixties is not my favorite genre, particularly in this gentle and unparanoid form."

John Kessel: "The first part is hard to read because you've captured the awful self-indulgence of so many of us so well. Picks up a great deal when Roger Maris shows up. I love the way the ending happens so fast. *Don't* slow it down."

Richard Butner: "Fire up the lava lamp, Maude, it's 1970. Staggeringly accurate details bridge the gaps between Roger Maris, dope-addled hippies, and nineties yuppiedom. You just need to smooth over the seams."

Jonathan Lethem: "I adored this from start to finish. Omit topical references on the radio—this story doesn't need to appropriate Kent State. Maris accomplishes all that and more. Bravo."

Maureen McHugh: "The first read-through was delightful but for me it is too long, mostly because I don't have any emotional connection and resonance in the Roger Maris section. I think I'm not your reader. But I love the first section."

Mark Van Name: "I liked this story a great deal and encourage you not to change it much. I would consider dropping the Kent State background on the radio because I think it distracts more than it enriches, but that's a close call."

Robert Frazier: "Dope will get you through times of no plot better than plot will get you through times of no dope."

Afterword to "The First Law of Thermodynamics"

"The First Law of Thermodynamics" is a story I've known I wanted to write since college, but which eluded me for more than two decades. Even after I began work on it, the damn thing squirmed and wriggled out from beneath my fingers and almost escaped. Originally I chose a first-person point of view, but revisiting this all-too-familiar material in first person tempted me to impose Jim Kelly on Space, instead of treating him as a character. You see, I was neither as boneheaded nor as alienated nor as brave as Space when I was at Notre Dame. Eventually the story stalled and I set it aside.

It took more than a year before I was able to jump-start it. I used a trick John Kessel taught me. Almost always when I lose momentum in first draft, it's because I've got one of the fundamentals wrong. So I might consider a sex change for the main character, or else I'll switch tenses or try a new point of view. When I rewrote what I'd done from first to third person, the story started to roll again. To keep some of the spirit of my earlier effort, I chose a "hot" narrative style. I use adjectives like "hot" and "cool" to measure the psychic distance between reader and character. In hot narration you are one with the viewpoint character; the story feels like it's happening to you. As narration cools off, you are subtly led to make distinctions between yourself and the character. In the coolest narration I might actually step on-stage to analyze the character for you. Since I was attempting to show what happens through the distorted lens of a nineteen-year-old hippie wannabe on acid, I also wanted to re-create the swirling, mindblown diction of the time. To help re-psychedelicize myself, I went to my bookshelf and pulled down Tom Wolfe's *The Electric Kool-Aid Acid Test* and Hunter S. Thompson's *Fear and Loathing in Las Vegas*, personal faves which I think of as the literary equivalents of Woodstock and Altamont.

"The First Law of Thermodynamics" is *not* a typical James Patrick Kelly story, and I wasn't sure what Sycamore Hill would make of it. The risk, of course, in bringing any story to workshop is the confusion that results from conflicting advice and alternate readings. As it turned out, the Roger Maris section and the radio reports drew the most critical attention, not surprising since on the surface they serve similar functions in establishing the context for Space's trip. Okay, Nancy and Maureen, I knew the baseball stuff was going to bore some readers; in the final draft I went through the Maris section and trimmed it word by word. More I could not do—after Space, Maris is my favorite character. The most surprising critique of the workshop came when John mentioned that he thought my Maris never went to Vietnam. I believe he did go, but John's reading is not contradicted by the text. Could Maris have been lying to *me?* The possibility is at once delicious and disturbing. And yes, Jonathan and Mark: the Kent State report may well be a misstep, but it's one I felt I *had* to make for personal reasons having to do with why I wrote this story. I take Bruce's point about false genrification; it is a real and ultimately corrupting phenomenon. I leave it for the reader to decide whether "The First Law of Thermodynamics" is an example of this or not.

James Patrick Kelly

The Turkey City Lexicon: A Primer for SF Workshops

EDITED BY LEWIS SHINER

INTRODUCTION

This uncopyrighted lexicon focuses on the special needs of the science fiction workshop. Having an accurate and descriptive critical term for a common SF problem makes it easier to recognize and discuss that problem. This guide should help workshop participants avoid having to "reinvent the wheel" (see section 3) at every session. Over a period of years many workshops developed these terms. We acknowledge in parentheses at the end of each entry those terms identified with a particular writer. Bruce Sterling and the other regulars of the Turkey City Workshop in Austin, Texas, provided particular help for this project.

1. Words

"SAID" BOOKISM

Artificial, literary verb you use to avoid the perfectly good word "said." "Said" is one of the few invisible words in the language; it is almost impossible to overuse. Infinitely less distracting than "he retorted," "she inquired," or the all-time favorite, "he ejaculated."

TOM SWIFTY

Similar compulsion to follow the word "said" (or "said" bookism) with an adverb. As in, " 'We'd better hurry,' said Tom swiftly." Remember that the adverb is a leech sucking the strength from a verb. Ninety-nine percent of the time it is clear from context how something was said.

"BURLY DETECTIVE" SYNDROME

Fear of proper names. Found in most of the same pulp magazines that abound with "said" bookisms and Tom Swifties. This is where you can't call Mike Shayne "Shayne," but substitute "the burly detective" or "the redheaded sleuth." Like the "said" bookism it comes from the entirely wrongheaded conviction that you can't use the same word twice in the same sentence, paragraph, or even page. This is only true of particularly strong and highly visible words, like, say, "vertiginous." It's always better to reuse an ordinary, simple noun or verb than to contrive a cumbersome method of avoiding it.

EYEBALL KICK

That perfect, telling detail that creates an instant visual image. The ideal of certain postmodern schools of SF is to achieve a "crammed prose" full of "eyeball kicks." (Rudy Rucker)

PUSHBUTTON WORDS

Words you use to evoke an emotional response without engaging the intellect or critical faculties. Words like "song" or "poet" or "tears" or "dreams." These words are supposed to make us misty-eyed without us quite knowing why. Most often found in story titles.

BATHOS

Sudden change in level of diction. "The massive hound barked in a stentorian voice, then made wee-wee on the carpet."

BRAND-NAME FEVER

Use of a brand name alone, without accompanying visual detail, to create false verisimilitude. You can stock a future with Hondas and Sonys and IBMs and still have no idea what it looks like.

2. Sentences and Paragraphs

COUNTERSINKING

Expositional redundancy. Making explicit the actions a conversation implies, e.g., " 'Let's get out of here,' he said, urging her to leave."

TELLING, NOT SHOWING

Violates the cardinal rule of good writing. You should allow readers to react, not instruct them in how to react. Carefully observed details render authorial value judgments unnecessary. For instance, instead of telling us "she had a bad childhood, an unhappy childhood," show us specific incidents—involving, say, a locked closet and two jars of honey.

LAUGH TRACK

Characters give cues to the reader as to how to react. They laugh at their own jokes, cry at their own pain, and (unintentionally) feel everything so the reader doesn't have to.

SQUID IN THE MOUTH

Inappropriate humor in front of strangers. Basically the failure of an author to realize that the world at large does not share certain assumptions or jokes. In fact, the world at large will look upon such writers as if they had squids in their mouths. (Jim Blaylock)

HAND WAVING

Distracting the readers with dazzling prose or other fireworks to keep them from noticing a severe logical flaw. (Stuart Brand)

"YOU CAN'T FIRE ME, I QUIT"

Attempt to diffuse lack of credibility with hand waving. "I would never have believed it if I hadn't seen it myself." As if by anticipating the reader's objections the author had somehow answered them. (John Kessel)

•

FUZZ

Element of motivation the author was too lazy to supply. The word "somehow" is an automatic tipoff to fuzzy areas of a story. "Somehow she forgot to bring her gun."

DISCH-ISM

Intrusion of the author's physical surrounding (or mental state) into the narrative. Like characters who always light cigarettes when the author does, or who think about how they wished they hadn't quit smoking. In more subtle forms the characters complain that they're confused and don't know what to do—when this is actually the author's condition. (Tom Disch)

BOGUS ALTERNATIVES

List of actions a character could have taken, but didn't. Frequently includes all the reasons why. A type of Disch-ism in which the author works out complicated plot problems at the reader's expense. "If I'd gone along with the cops they would have found the gun in my purse. And anyway, I didn't want to spend the night in jail. I suppose I could have just run instead of stealing the car, but then . . ." etc. Best dispense with this material entirely.

FALSE INTERIORIZATION

Another Disch-ism, in which the author, too lazy to describe the surroundings, inflicts the viewpoint character with space sickness, a blindfold, etc.

WHITE-ROOM SYNDROME

Author's imagination fails to provide details. Most common in the beginning of a story. "She awoke in a white room." The white room is obviously the white piece of paper confronting the author. The character has just awakened to be starting fresh, like the author. Often exists to make characters ponder their circumstances and provide an excuse for Info Dump (see below).

3. Background

INFO DUMP

Large chunk of indigestible expository matter the author uses to explain the background situation. This can be overt, as in fake newspaper or "Encyclopedia Galactica" articles in the text, or covert, in which all action stops as the author assumes center stage and lectures.

STAPLEDON

The name of the voice that takes center stage to lecture. Actually a common noun, as: "You have a stapledon come on to answer this problem instead of showing the characters resolving it."

"AS YOU KNOW, BOB . . ."

The most pernicious form of Info Dump, in which the characters tell each other things they already know, for the sake of getting the reader up to speed.

"I'VE SUFFERED FOR MY ART"

(And now it's your turn.) Research dump. A form of Info Dump in which the author inflicts upon the reader irrelevant but hard-won bits of data acquired while researching the story.

REINVENTING THE WHEEL

In which the novice author goes to enormous lengths to create a situation already familiar to an experienced reader. You most often see this when a highly regarded mainstream writer tries to write an SF novel without actually reading any of the existing stuff first. Thus, you get endless explanations of, say, how an atomic war might start by accident. Thank you, but we've all read that already. Also, you get tedious explanations by physicists of how their interstellar drive works. Unless it affects the plot, we don't care.

USED FURNITURE

Use of a background out of central casting. Rather than invent a background and have to explain it, or risk reinventing the wheel, let's just steal one. We'll set it in the Star Trek Universe, only we'll call it the Empire instead of the Federation.

SPACE WESTERN

The most pernicious suite of used furniture. The grizzled space captain swaggering into the spacer bar and slugging down a Jovian brandy, then laying down a few credits for a space hooker to give him a Galactic Rim Job.

THE EDGES OF IDEAS

The solution to the Info Dump problem (how to fill in the background). The theory is that, as above, the mechanics of an interstellar drive (the center of the idea) is not important. All that matters is the effect on your characters: They can get to other planets in a few months, and, oh yeah, it gives them hallucinations about past lives. Or, more radically: The physics of TV transmission is the center of an idea; on the edges of it we find people turning into couch potatoes because they no longer have to leave home for entertainment. Or, more bluntly: We don't need Info Dump at all. We just need a clear picture of how the background has affected people's lives. This is also known as "carrying extrapolation into the fabric of daily life."

THE GRUBBY-APARTMENT STORY

Writing too much about what you know. The kind of story where the starving writer living in the grubby apartment writes a story about a starving writer in a grubby apartment. Stars all his friends.

4. Plots

CARD TRICKS IN THE DARK

Authorial tricks to no visible purpose. The author has contrived an elaborate plot to arrive at the punchline of a joke no one else will get, or some bit of historical trivia. In other words, if the point of your story is that this kid is going to grow up to be Joseph of Arimathea, there should be sufficient internal evidence for us to figure this out.

THE JAR OF TANG

"For you see, we are all living in a jar of Tang!" or "For you see, I am a dog!" Mainstay of the old "Twilight Zone" TV show. An entire pointless story contrived so the author can cry, "Fooled you!" This is a classic case of the difference between a conceit and an idea. "What if we all lived in a jar of Tang?" is an example of the former; "What if the revolutionaries from the sixties had set up their own society?" is an example of the latter. Good SF requires ideas, not conceits.

ABBESS PHONE HOME

Takes its name from a mainstream story about a medieval cloister which the author sold as SF because of the serendipitous arrival of a UFO at the end. By extension, any mainstream story with a gratuitous SF or fantasy element tacked on so the author could sell it.

DEUS EX MACHINA, OR GOD-IN-THE-BOX

Miraculous solution to an otherwise insoluble problem. Look, the Martians all caught colds and died!

PLOT COUPONS

The true structure of the quest-type fantasy novel. The "hero" collects sufficient plot coupons (magic sword, magic book, magic cat) to send off to the author for the ending. Note that you can substitute "the author" for "the gods" in such a work: "The gods decreed he would pursue this quest." Right, mate. The author decreed he or she would pursue this quest until sufficient pages were full to procure an advance. (Alex Stewart)

Sycamore Hill Attendees

This list shows everyone, in alphabetical order by last name, who has attended Sycamore Hill since its inception:

Michael Bishop
Michael Blumlein
Richard Butner
Orson Scott Card
Steve Carper
Wendy Counsil
Bradley Denton
Harlan Ellison
Carol Emshwiller
Karen Joy Fowler
Robert Frazier
Gregory Frost
Lisa Goldstein
Alexander Jablokov
Richard Kadrey
Gregg Keizer
James Patrick Kelly
John Kessel

Nancy Kress
Jonathan Lethem
Shariann Lewitt
Jack Massa
Bruce McAllister
Jack McDevitt
Maureen F. McHugh
James Morrow
Pat Murphy
Rebecca Ore
Susan Palwick
Michaela Roessner
Richard Paul Russo
Scott Russell Sanders
Lewis Shiner
Martha Soukup
Bruce Sterling
Timothy Sullivan
Mark L. Van Name
Connie Willis
Allen L. Wold